C000092245

Stepping Up to the Plate

A Sports Romance

Nashville Songbirds
Book 2

Kat Summers

This book is a work of fiction from the author's imagination. Though inspired by the world around us, all of the characters, places, and events are fictional and not based on any one source. Any resemblance is entirely coincidental.

Stepping Up to the Plate (Nashville Songbirds, Book 2)

Edited by Emma Jane of EJL Editing

Cover Illustration by Booked Forever

Copyright © <2023> <Kat Summers>

All rights reserved.

ISBN-13: 979-8-218-31610-5

No portion of this book may be reproduced in any form without written permission from the publisher or author, except as permitted by U.S. copyright law.

To all the women who fought to publish their stories so I can write smutty sports romcoms today.

Playlist

1. Heartbroken - Diplo, Jessie Murph, Polo G
2. Figure You Out - VOILÁ
3. Leave Me Again - Kelsea Ballerini
4. Unwritten - Natasha Bedingfield
5. Love Myself - Hailee Steinfeld
6. Good Girls Go Bad - Cobra Starship ft. Leighton Meester
7. Doin' What She Likes - Blake Shelton
8. If He Wanted To He Would - Kylie Morgan
9. Miss Me More - Kelsea Ballerini
10. Fight Song - Rachel Platten
11. QUARTER LIFE CRISIS - Taylor Bickett
12. The 1 - Taylor Swift
13. Naked - Avril Lavigne
14. Dancing With Our Hands Tied - Taylor Swift
15. Out of the Woods- Taylor Swift
16. Fancy - Reba McEntire
17. Dear John - Taylor Swift

18. Breath (2 AM) - Anna Malick
19. Miss Americana & The Heartbreak Prince - Taylor Swift

Listen to it on Spotify.

Dick-tionary

For those of you who want to find or avoid the spice in this book, take note of the following chapters:

- Prologue (spicy elements, no smut)
- Chapter 5 (spicy elements, no smut)
- Chapter 16
- Chapter 17
- Chapter 19
- Chapter 25
- Chapter 30
- Chapter 34
- Chapter 37
- Chapter 38

Prologue

February

"I cannot believe I let that pint-sized Barbie knock off talk me into this," I mutter under my breath as I readjust my mask. The blonde in question saunters in front of me as we make our way down the dimly lit hallway. While I admire the swanky wallpaper and luxurious carpet, she turns back to glance at me over her shoulder. She shoots me a smirk that says 'I know you want to back out, but it's too late now without looking like a little bitch.' Encouraging, right?

In a moment of weakness, I let my best friend, Tiffany, convince me that the best way to get over my gaslighting, cheating ex is to get under someone else. I should have known when I agreed it wouldn't be as simple as going to a bar and finding a decent-looking guy to take me home. No. Nothing with Tiffany is simple.

Forgetting that is how I found myself heading to a room in Club Hedone, Nashville's premier kink and sex club. A room where some

1

stranger is going "rail me into forgetting all about that small-dicked son of a bitch." You can't say Tiff isn't descriptive.

The champagne I drank on the way over here is slowly wearing off as we get closer to our rooms. The club has a two-drink policy which I can respect since consent is paramount in this type of situation. But also, I could go for about three shots of tequila to settle the tension radiating through my body right now.

I am beyond nervous. I haven't been this nervous about sex since losing my virginity after homecoming with my high school boyfriend. Which is surprising since this should be the lowest-stakes first time sexual encounter I've ever had. There is no guesswork here. Whoever they matched me with is not only DTF, but they were also given a list of my limits and preferences beforehand. There shouldn't be that awkward dance of figuring out what the other wants. Not that it is too complicated for me. I am about as vanilla as my taste in lattes.

Our guide, a raven-haired woman with nose piercings and wearing a corset, stops in front of a set of doors. Pointing to the one on the left, she tells Tiffany to make herself comfortable and that her match will be there shortly. My vivacious friend turns to me and says, "Good luck, Bunny. Enjoy the first manmade Os you've gotten in years," before shutting the door behind her. I try not to die of mortification when I see our guide hold back a laugh, pointing to my door on the right.

"Enjoy your evening, miss." Before leaving, she shyly adds, "If you ever need any help with woman made Os, I assist with the toy demonstrations on Thursdays and always need volunteers."

"I'll keep that in mind," I squeak out before hustling into my room and closing the door.

Taking a few beats to collect myself, I am shocked when I open my eyes and survey the space. I know this is an expensive club, but a part of me still expected the room to be a little cliché. But no, it's similar to a suite in a five-star hotel, if five-star hotels had sex swings in the corner. I am sure there are more kink-focused rooms, but as a novice, I am glad they gave me a 'normal' one.

The staff gave me a general spiel on what to expect tonight, but they didn't explain how unbearable the waiting is. I don't have my phone on me, but it feels as if I have been standing here for at least fifteen minutes. Is it supposed to heighten the experience? All it is doing is making me wonder if my match backed out. That couldn't happen, right? He didn't see me walk in and decide I didn't meet his standards? Or read my file and think I'm too boring and ask for someone else?

That's what my ex, Phil, did. Technically, he wanted to keep me. It was a have his cake and eat it, too, situation. Aka do dirty, kinky things, just not to me, his *wife,* because he "respected me too much" and I was the "future mother of his children."

I'm sure he assumed I wouldn't be any good at them. Which is probably what this guy is thinking, too. He read my file and figured I would never be good enough. A man who is a member of a sex club has to be good in bed. Why would he want to have sex with someone who hasn't had sex for months and before that usually had missionary once a week with the lights off? There are surely way more skilled partners he could have. I saw the women in the bar when we arrived. I don't hold a candle to all that leather and fishnets.

As I fall deeper into my spiraling mind, there is a knock on the door and the handle turns. Oh God, what am I supposed to do? Should I already be in bed? Naked? Should I have been by the door to greet him? Before I can move from where I'm rooted in the middle of the space, a behemoth of a man steps inside. My jaw drops.

This may be the sexiest man I have ever seen. Where Phil was all slender limbs, this guy is buff with a capital B. His broad shoulders are almost as impressive as the scruff-covered chiseled jaw. It would have taken Phil a week to grow what I suspect this guy considers a five o'clock shadow. He has on a mask over half his face, but it doesn't distract from the piercing, pale blue eyes that are locked in on me.

As he makes his way further into the room, I am hit by how big he is. Sure, those shoulders were hard to miss, but he's also crazy tall. The man has over a foot on me. I am pretty short at 5'1" but if I had

3

to guess, I'd say he is 6'4" on a bad day. How is this going to work logistically with that much of a size difference? I start to run through scenarios in my head, but I am interrupted by his deep, smooth voice.

"Are you going to stand there staring at me all night, you dirty little slut? As much as I enjoy your eyes devouring me, I have plans to fuck them into the back of your head," he booms. All responses fall out of my head as I stare at him, stunned. That is not exactly the opener I was expecting. Realizing I'm frozen in place, he continues.

"Not used to a man calling it like he sees it? Not used to a man ready to use your body for his pleasure? Don't worry, if you're a good little whore, I'll make sure you're so exhausted you sleep for a week," he croons. "Come here."

Slut? Whore? Why is this guy talking to me this way? I didn't specifically list names I did and did not want to be called, but the vibe he's got going does not match what I filled out. Maybe he has a thing for dirty talk? Although in most of the books I read, dirty talk usually involves being called a "good girl." I'm not sure why I got "dirty little slut" guy. Probably the stupid dress Tiffany forced me to wear.

Not knowing what else to do, I slowly move towards him until I'm a foot away. Any closer and I'd have to crane my neck to see his face.

"She does know how to obey. That's good, pet," he taunts. "Turn around."

I spin around tentatively until my back is to him. We're facing a floor-length mirror and I can see him behind me. His eyes travel up and down my body appraisingly until they meet mine in the reflection.

"Do you remember everything they went over in your paper-work?" he asks. When I nod, his jaw ticks before he utters, "Words."

"Yes," I reply softly, even though at this precise moment I don't think I could even remember my own name. I recall learning about limits and consent and colors. But I am thrown so far off-kilter by his behavior and how hot he is that I can't seem to remember any of those details.

"Normally, I'd tell a slut like you to get on your knees, but I don't think you'd be able to reach my cock from there," he murmurs almost to himself. "Take off your dress and kneel on the bed."

When I hesitate, he lands a sharp slap on my ass. "Move!"

I scurry over to the bed at his command. I haven't said more than one word the entire time he's been here. Internally, I am panicking. Spanking was a soft limit for me. I am a little freaked out that he went there already. I mean it wasn't a *spanking* spanking, but still. If this is where we are starting the night, I am nervous to see where we end up.

I didn't expect hearts and flowers when finding a hook up at a sex club, but this guy doesn't appear all that interested in me. My bar isn't that high. I am mostly hoping for an assisted orgasm from someone who makes me feel more desirable than I did with my ex-husband. It's been a long time since someone wanted me and this encounter has yet to change my assumption that no one could.

Instead of coming over to me, he walks over to the dresser and disrobes while staring at me. I'm on my knees at the edge of the bed in only my lace thong. My boobs are small enough that I didn't need a bra. Plus, the spaghetti straps and deep cut of the velvet dress I have on don't leave a lot of room to wear one covertly.

The man, whose name I realize I don't know, drapes his suit jacket over the edge of an armchair before removing his shirt and revealing abs that would make a washboard jealous. This guy is cut. When I peek back up at his face, his smirk tells me he caught me checking him out.

"Look at you on your knees waiting for me. You're needy, aren't you? Pathetic and desperate for my cock? Your greedy pussy is going to have to wait until I'm ready. I want you begging for it before I give it to you," he mocks.

I rear back at the insults. Pathetic? Desperate? What is happening here? He catalogs the movement and tilts his head to the side as he assesses me. He appears confused and even apprehensive as he goes to speak again.

5

"What's wrong, pet? You don't want me to call you desperate? But you are, aren't you? You came here tonight to be my fuck doll. Desperate for me to make a mess of you. That's what you want, isn't it? To be my pathetic little whore?"

I must finally reach my breaking point from everything he is saying and months of pent-up emotional damage because instead of answering him, I burst into tears.

His eyes widen and he stares at me in shock before moving towards me. I flinch and scoot back to the far end of the bed, which halts his efforts to get closer.

"Why are you being mean to me?" I cry, unable to stop the words from slipping out.

"Mean?" he questions, bemused. I nod. He takes a second to consider his next words before he grits out, "Color?"

"What?" I ask between sobs. If I thought what he was saying to me was humiliating, crying in front of him is worse. I wrap my arms around my stomach as I curl into myself.

"What color are you?"

"White," I breathe out. "Although I'm Italian... Maybe olive?"

His voice is much softer than it was earlier, almost cajoling when he clarifies, "No, baby, what stoplight color are you? Green, yellow, or red? Do you need to safe word?"

"Safe word? We aren't having sex yet."

"That's not—" he starts to reply, but there is a loud knock on the door. He assesses me with a bewildered expression before going to open it. I don't hear everything he says over my weeping, but I do hear the words, "mistake," and, "Craig," before he tells me he'll be right back and to wait there.

Yeah, fuck that. I don't want another encounter with that guy. I take a few deep breaths to compose myself, throw on my dress, and hightail it the hell out of dodge. Tiffany can get an Uber in the morning. I'm going home to wash this night off me and drown my sorrows in a pint of ice cream.

Chapter One

July, Seven Months Earlier

I press the end call button a little harder than necessary as I throw my phone across the couch. I love my cousin, I truly do, but she is being such a drama queen right now. What a first world problem: the hot man who is completely devoted to me has to go back to his job where he makes millions of dollars. Get real.

I would never say Carina has had it easy, but her life is pretty cushy. Her early years may have been rough, but even then her life was filled with love. She doesn't have a frame of reference for dealing with conflict. Robby is her only "adult" relationship, and the dude bailed when things got tough. Neither of them has ever had to stick through the tough times. Being committed is hard work. It isn't all rainbows and sunshine. I should know, I'm living in one.

I've been married to my college boyfriend, Phil, for four years. Once the honeymoon phase is over, you realize you are two people who are trying to make it on this earth as one unit, and that is hard

7

work. Sometimes you get snappy with one another. Sometimes you fight. Sometimes you work through your anniversary and your wife is asleep by the time you get home. Again.

Ugh. I shouldn't have been that harsh with Carina. Being long distance is a legitimate worry for her. I'm honestly jealous. I know how much Robby loves her. I saw the way he snuck glances at her when I video called them over the weekend. He is smitten with his Kitten. When was the last time Phil looked at me like I was his world? Or with even the smallest hint of adoration?

I want to chalk it up to us being in an established, mature relationship, but I'm not sure. Does the fact that we've been together since I was nineteen mean that he's never going to gaze at me adoringly again? Does that go away with time? They say women stop giving head once they get married, but do men stop giving affection? That's been my experience. Our honeymoon phase has been over for a long while. And physical affection? Non-existent.

When we first got together, we couldn't keep our hands off each other. Even in our first year of marriage, Phil was constantly touching me. He was never the most considerate guy with his actions or words, but his love language is touch. He showed his love that way, but ever since he was given more responsibility at work, things have changed.

He's not the same affectionate guy he used to be. He's snappy and distant. He's uninterested in the things we used to do together. All he does is train for his marathon, work, and attempt to make a permanent butt indentation on the couch.

I can't put all the blame on him, though. Maybe I've changed, too. His lack of physical affection has certainly caused me to pull back from him. Perhaps it's a self-fulfilling prophecy, and he is taking his lead from my distance. Intimacy isn't the only change in our relationship, though.

Phil used to talk constantly about our future and the family we would build together. Unlike most college guys, he was vocal about wanting kids. I always wanted to be part of a tight-knit family, but it wasn't in the cards for me growing up. His closeness with his parents and brother were one of the things that initially attracted me to him. He is still close to them, working with them every day, but he put the brakes on starting our own family until he is more established in his career.

I desperately want to get back to where we used to be – and on track to building a family together. I can't wait around for him to notice our issues. He is either oblivious to them or doesn't know how to fix them. If I want a change in our dynamic, I am going to have to make the first move. But my father always told me that no one is going to fight your battles for you. If you want something, you have to make it happen on your own.

I resolve to do exactly that. I told Carina it was hard work to be in a long-lasting relationship and here I am coasting in discontent. Living at a tolerable level of unhappiness. When was the last time I tried? Am I particularly interested in Phil right now? No, his lack of attention has me feeling unwanted. But maybe he is in the same boat and I need to be the bigger person and reach out first. I don't love being the aggressor but if that's what it takes, I'll do it.

With that in mind, I head off to my bedroom. Phil and I ate dinner together on the couch a little while ago. I know he will be there for the duration of the baseball game he has on. Hopefully once he sees what I have planned he won't be, but at least he will be distracted long enough for me to set the mood.

I hustle around our room, tidying up. I spot the candle Carina got me for my birthday last year and think about lighting it. I know it smells amazing. I've been saving it for a special occasion, though. I want to savor that candle; enjoy it. I don't think Phil will appreciate the scent and I would hate to waste it. I pull out some Target candles instead. They'll offer the same ambiance without the anxiety of wasting the gift.

After sneaking into the kitchen to grab a bottle of wine, I change into a silk nightie I know Phil loves. I wanted to get it in pink, but Phil said pink is for 'sugar babies and college girls, not grown women.' Black it is. Pouring the wine, I take a sip and call

Phil into the bedroom, "Honey, can you come in here for a second?"

"One sec. The bases are loaded and the Huskers are down by two!" he shouts from the den. I twiddle my thumbs and wait for what feels like an eternity for him to come find me.

"What's up?" he asks, barely surveying the room. I'm splayed out on the bed in a skimpy nightie and all he says is "what's up?" not exactly the reaction I was hoping for. I guess I need to up my game.

I sit up on my knees and reach out to him, giving my best come hither stare as I run my hand down his arm. "I thought we could turn in early tonight... together."

"I'm not that tired, and it's only the fourth inning. I'll probably be up for a while. I might game with the boys for a bit, too. You don't need to wait on me," he says with an expression that I can only describe as disinterest. He bids me goodnight before returning to his precious sectional.

I kneel there a minute, stupefied at his retreat. I glance around the room and down at myself. Is it not clear what I was asking for? Was I too subtle? Unsure of myself, I take a mirror selfie that includes the room and send it to the one person I know will give me honest feedback.

8:36 PM

TIFF

Hot damn, Bunny. Phil is in for a treat tonight ;)

ME

Not too subtle?

TIFF

Sweetie, you couldn't be more obvious if you had a neon sign that said, Pound Town Population: You.

ME

Is that a real sign?

TIFF

I may have seen it in a guy's bedroom a couple of weeks ago.

ME

Of course, you did

TIFF

😌

Enjoy your night, I can't wait to see you in Miami next month!

ME

Thanks, girl. I can't wait, either.

Tiffany's confirmation that my intent was clear makes me deflate even more. Now, I can't pretend Phil didn't know what I was hinting at. Men are known to be oblivious, but not when it comes to sex. I used to have him pawing at me every night. Now it's been over a month and he was completely unfazed by my proposition.

Downing the rest of the wine, I blow out the candles and change into my normal, worn pajamas. As I lay in bed and think about everything that happened, I can't help but remunerate in the sting of rejection. When was the last time I truly felt wanted? The rejection is all too familiar and dredges up childhood baggage I thought I'd put behind me. All of a sudden, I'm the little girl whose mommy chose substances over her. Thankfully, before my wine-induced spiral can take me too far down the rabbit hole, sleep pulls me in.

The next morning, I decide I don't have the energy to confront Phil about all this. I don't really want to hear his excuses or platitudes.

Even worse, I don't need him to confirm my deepest fear: that I am unwanted.

August

Trudging to my car, I fully understand why TGIF is a thing. I am thanking both grown up and baby Jesus that it is Friday. I don't think I could have taken even another hour of work this week. It's not that I hate my job, but I hate my job. It could not be less fulfilling.

I went into journalism because I wanted to help people understand the world around them. I wanted to share stories and personal experiences that spoke to people and made their lives better. Instead, I work for the Clayton Chronicle and write about PTA meetings and who had the best yard this month. It is droll to say the least. I want to find a better job, but the market is not great right now, despite having a master's degree from Mizzou. Honestly, I don't even know what type of job I would want, anyway. But after this week I'd take anything to get away from the Real Housewives of the St. Louis suburbs that fill my articles' comment sections.

On the drive home, I consider what I want for dinner. I am too tired to cook. Hopefully, I can convince Phil to order toasted ravioli from that place we love on The Hill. When I pull up to an empty driveway, I am surprised he's not here yet. He's been working a lot of late nights, but he usually gets home early on Fridays. I decide to call, hoping he can grab takeout.

"Hey, where are you?" I ask cheerily when he picks up.

"I'm in Baltimore."

"What? Why are you in Baltimore?"

He responds with a sigh. "I told you I had a client meeting on Monday. That client is in Baltimore."

"Okay... well you forgot the part about you needing to meet in person in Baltimore. Plus, it's Friday, not Monday. Why are you there now?"

"The team wanted to get here early to make sure everything was prepared for the presentation. We have a lot riding on this meeting."

"I wish I would have known," I say quietly.

"I told you about this. You must have forgotten. You know how scatterbrained you can be," he admonishes.

"I'm not... never mind. When can I expect you back?"

"I should be back late Tuesday evening. Listen, I gotta go. We're all going out to dinner. I'll talk to you later this weekend."

"Okay, bye. Be saf—" I start before he hangs up. Isn't this hunky dory? There is no way he told me he was going out of town and I forgot. I'll add it to the list of all the other shady behavior he's done lately.

Chapter Two

Labor Day Weekend

I f I thought it was humid in St. Louis in the summer, Miami is on a whole other level. The air practically assaults me as I step out of the airport. Before I even have a second to get my bearings, a flash of blonde is running towards me. "Bunnnnnnnny," it yells.

"Ooof. Hi, Tiff. It's nice to see you, too," I wheeze in her hold.

"I'm glad you made it! I haven't seen you since Carina's birthday last year, and that is way too long. Ready to make Miami our bitch?"

I can't help but laugh at her excitement. I squeeze her a little tighter before letting go. I forgot how good it feels to be embraced by a friend. Hell, embraced by anyone. "Lead the way, Barbie girl."

I may have met Tiffany through Carina when they were in college, but it didn't take long for us to become fast friends. I was pretty quiet growing up and didn't have many friends aside from a few girls and, of course, my bestie, Georgie. I lost touch with most of them when we went our separate ways to college. At school, I met Phil during my freshman year and quickly got sucked into his friend group. They were nice, but they were always his people first. Being adopted by Tiffany showed me what a ride-or-die friend looks like.

As Tiff and I hop in the rideshare to the hotel, she tells me what she's been up to this week with her clients and all the hot gossip. I tune her out for a minute to take in the scenery but am brought back in when she says something about an after party.

"Wait, what?" I ask.

"I knew you weren't listening to me! I said Valentino – he's one of the models I've been working with – got us on the list for this amazing club that is hosting the after party."

"Tiffany, I don't have anything to wear to a club with models! I only packed swimsuits and casual clothes. You said we were being low-key," I squeal.

"Don't you worry, my little Bunny. I've got you covered," she says with a mischievous grin.

I knew I shouldn't have trusted that grin. When Tiffany said she had me covered, she meant she had me uncovered if this outfit is anything to go by. Tugging down the skirt for the millionth time, I check myself out in the mirror.

"Would you stop stressing?" she laments. "You are hot as fuck. Philly boy is going to be jealous that he isn't here to see you in that outfit. We should send him a picture."

"We don't need to do that."

"Disagree," she huffs. Grabbing my phone, Tiffany wraps her arm around my shoulder and makes a kissy face. "Smile, Lo!"

Relenting, I smile with her. Before I can stop her, she shoots the picture off to Phil and sends it to herself.

"Damn," she sighs. "It's almost a shame I look this good and no one will get to enjoy it. Maybe I can convince Valentino to have a little fun at the club."

"Tiff," I scold. "You hardly know the man."

"We can't all have found a winner on the first try. Some of us are still out here kissing frogs."

"Why do I get the sense you're doing way more than kissing and you're hoping none of these frogs turn into Prince Charming?"

Tiffany gives an innocent shrug before announcing our ride is here.

This club is packed and not my scene. Everyone here appears to be model or model-adjacent. How can there be this many beautiful people in one place? I know I am pretty, but around this crowd, I am practically a troll.

Despite that, I am having a lot of fun. I can't remember the last time I went out and enjoyed myself with friends. When Phil and I go out, it is usually to stuffy client dinners or one of the fancy restaurants downtown. We never go dancing and I am always limited to two glasses of wine because 'being sloppy' would reflect poorly on the business.

Speaking of my husband, my phone vibrated in my hand and I realize he finally responded to the picture Tiffany sent. I'm surprised he is up this late. Unless he is gaming, he is typically early to bed to be up for his morning run.

10:49 PM

PHIL

You're not seriously wearing that out, are you? It's hardly decent.

ME

Is it that bad? Tiffany said it's cute.

PHIL

Tiffany's version of cute is about the same as a hooker's in Vegas. Or Miami in this case.

ME

Are you saying I look like a prostitute?

PHIL

Don't put words in my mouth. You're too innocent for anyone to think you're a prostitute. You definitely don't look like someone's wife, though.

ME

I have my ring on.

PHIL

Like that stops men.

I don't have time to argue about this right now. I have to get up early. Behave, tonight. I know how wild Tiffany can get.

ME

Okay. Love you.

Phil's messages bring me down. I would never step out on my husband and no one is going to hit on me with all these models around. I have had a few appreciative glances that boosted my confidence, though. Confidence that is all but gone after that exchange. Now, all I feel is overexposed and out of place.

Before I get lost in those negative emotions, Tiffany reappears from wherever she and Valentino ran off to. She saunters over with a satisfied smirk on her face.

"You good?" I ask.

"I'm great. What about you, Bunny? You're a little frowny," she says, pushing on my cheeks to give me an animated smile. Valentino scoots in behind her with a friend in tow.

"*Mi cara*, there you are," he coos. "This is my friend Stefano. And you must be the ravishing Lola, I have heard about."

I hum as I finish my drink and give a small wave.

"Ya know, my Lola Bunny is Italian, too," Tiffany slurs.

"Is that so?" Stefano says, with sparkling eyes. "*Posso offrirti un'altra bevanda bellissima?*"

"*Sarebbe fantastico, verrò con te,*" I reply.

"I don't know what that was, but it was hot. Let's go dance!" Tiffany shouts, fanning herself.

"We're going to go get a drink. I'll grab you some water," I tell her as she and Valentino barrel to the dance floor.

Stefano orders when we get to the bar before turning back to me. "I mean it," he comments, "You are beautiful, *una gemma squisita.*"

"Thank you," I responded with a blush. "I don't want to be too presumptuous here, but I should tell you that I am married."

"What a shame," he tsks. "Where is this husband of yours? I would never let such a beauty out of my sight for long."

It's an obvious line, but it makes my stomach flutter, nonetheless. "He is back home. This is a girls' trip."

He stares at me appraisingly. "I see. Though, something tells me the *idiota* hasn't been giving you the attention you need. He would be blind to not appreciate the *gemma preziosa* he has. You don't comprehend how beautiful you are."

After a brief pause he asks, "Can I give you some advice?"

"Sure," I whisper, locked into his gaze as he tucks one of my long brown curls behind my ear.

"Never let a man – any man – treat you as if you aren't the world. If he's the right one, you will be his everything, *la sua luna e le sue stelle.*"

I can barely breathe at his words. I have never been anyone's world, maybe a partner, but not anything as great as what he is saying. I'm the rejected daughter, the afterthought, the suitable option. I used to feel special to Phil, but I haven't in a long time.

"Come," he says after letting his words soak in. "Let's go join our friends."

"What's wrong, Bunny?" Tiffany asks the next morning as we lay by the pool. "You've been quiet. Did Stefano try something? He seemed like a nice guy, but it wouldn't be the first time I've been fooled. Valentino can kick his ass if you want."

I can't help but laugh. Tiff is a real one. "No, no. He was great – charming without being pervy. He said some things that made me think, though."

Turning over, Tiffany scrutinizes me. "I didn't want to say anything last night, but I'm worried about you, Lo. Carina is, too."

"Worried? Why?"

"You've been off lately. Sad. Maybe a little lost? You haven't been your radiant, happy self, and we want you to know we're here for you."

I weigh my response for a few seconds. Despite being a party girl with a glamorous life, Tiffany is level-headed, kind, and loyal. She may not want commitment, but she understands relationships.

"I don't think I'm happy," I say, taking a deep breath. "With my job, with St. Louis, with... Phil. Things have been strained and I don't know what to do about it."

"I'm sorry," she commiserates. "I thought you and Phil were good. I saw that scene you set a few weeks ago. It looked like a hot night to me."

My cheeks heat, embarrassed. "Actually, nothing happened that night. Phil wanted to watch the end of the baseball game and told me I should go to sleep without him."

"What?" She shoots up, affronted on my behalf. "He saw you in that tiny nightie with all the candles and didn't jump your bones? What is wrong with him?"

"I don't know. He's been stressed and working a lot of late nights. He's been traveling to meet clients, which is new. His job is getting to him. We haven't been intimate in a while. I thought that night could rekindle some romance, but maybe I'm doing something wrong."

"Babe, I was tempted by that set up and I am firmly team peen. Phil should be worshiping at your feet. You are a goddess."

"It isn't only my relationship that is weighing on me. I don't know how my life got to where it is. I'm living the life society and other people think I *should* and not one that brings me joy. I'm not who I want to be."

"And who is that?"

"I don't know," I sigh sadly.

"Don't worry, Bunny. We'll help you figure it out."

Chapter Three

• LOLA •

December

Weeks go by, a month, two and my life is no better than it was when I was in Miami. Even worse, Phil has been acting increasingly distant and disinterested. It all came to a head at Thanksgiving. Typically, we spend the day with my Aunt Teresa and my dad joins if he can. This year though, Robby invited us to fly out to California because he was proposing to Carina.

The trip was incredible. It was nice being around my family, especially with Phil spending extra time at the office lately. He wasn't even able to make the trip because of work. I was worried he'd be alone for the holiday, but he assured me he was spending it with a colleague. His parents always take a cruise for the holiday and his brother spends it with his in-laws.

I thought I would be upset that he wasn't there, but honestly it was a relief. I didn't have this pressure to put on a show that everything was amazing between us. I didn't have to pretend to be the perfect little wife and could let loose. People asked about him but it was easy enough to deflect. Though Tiffany gave me a lot of knowing glances.

Spending time with a couple as in love as Robby and Carina warmed my heart. They deserve their happy ending after everything they've gone through. But seeing their love highlighted that I'm not in that place anymore and I don't know what to do about it. I may not have those strong feelings for Phil I used to, or that I think I used to, but what can I do about it?

I may not be *happy*, but I don't know if I'd be any happier alone. I haven't been single since I was nineteen. I wouldn't even know the first thing about dating. Everything I hear from Tiffany – and Carina before Robby came back – made me glad I was off the market. I'm not ready to dive into that. I at least need to make an effort in my relationship before I consider giving up. And that's what I've done.

I have thrown myself into Christmas prep. Our house looks like the North Pole threw up in it. I've made all of Phil's favorite treats and dishes. Tomorrow we will go see his family but tonight, Christmas Eve, is just us. It's a tradition we started when we first got married.

I'm anxiously pacing the kitchen as I wait for him to get home from work. Because of course he had to work today. For being a family business, his family certainly has no concept of work-life balance. When he isn't home by five, I send him a quick text.

5:06 PM

ME

Hey, will you be home soon? Dinner will be ready within the hour.

PHIL

I'm wrapping a few things up now. I should be there by then, but you don't have to wait on me.

ME

Of course, I'm waiting for you. It's
Christmas Eve!

PHIL

Alright, I'll try to hurry.

An hour and a half later, he makes it in the door.

"Hi, honey. I'm glad you finally made it. They're working you too hard," I greet with false cheeriness.

"Someone has to get the work done. If not the boss' son, then who?" he responds dismissively.

"Still, I can't imagine your mom is happy to know your dad has you putting in all this overtime. I think I'll remind her of that when she inevitably bugs me about grandchildren tomorrow." She is always quick to blame me for the lack of babies. Little does she know Phil is the one who put on the brakes.

Phil's face pales. "Don't bring it up to her."

"Why not?"

"The company... has been struggling and Dad doesn't want her to know. I'd hate to stress her out over nothing. We'll be closing a big deal soon and everything will go back to normal. You know what a worry wart she can be."

"Oh, I am sorry to hear that. I hope all the work you are putting in helps seal the deal."

"Won't be long now. I think this one only has a few more weeks until we're done with it," he says. "Now, how about no more work talk? I smell your Aunt Teresa's baked ziti and I am famished."

The rest of the night goes smoothly enough. We eat and share idle small talk before watching *Christmas Vacation*, Phil's favorite holiday movie and exchanging gifts. I got him tickets to the Huskers opening game and a game-worn jersey signed by his favorite player who is about to retire. It pays to have MLB connections. He got me a heart pendant and a bottle of expensive perfume.

The gifts were lovely, but I can't help but be somewhat disappointed. I know he spent a small fortune on them and I appreciate it, but they highlight how much my husband doesn't get me. The perfume is the same scent his mother wears which is a little creepy and the necklace is not my style at all. Aside from the fact it is obviously the one the mall jewelry stores have featured in their ads, it's white gold. Every piece of jewelry I own is yellow gold. Everything in our house is yellow gold. You'd think he would realize that's my preference.

Pushing that aside, I still try to make the best of the evening. But before I can suggest retiring to the bedroom, Phil is already asleep on the couch. I guess tomorrow I can show him the sexy Christmas lingerie I got.

New Year's Eve

Another holiday, another day Phil is working. I hate that he's putting pressure on himself but he said they had a lot to do before the end of the year. Since I know most of the office is off today, I decide to surprise him with lunch.

When I arrive at Robinson & Associates, there are only a few cars here. I think about calling Phil, but instead I type in the passcode and sneak in. When I make my way towards his office, a sense of impending dread overtakes me. I shake it off as I continue down the hall to his closed door. When I turn the handle and open it, my entire reality comes crashing in around me.

I stand there momentarily shocked before my brain can process what I'm seeing: Phil and his brother, Mark, both plowing into a blonde they have draped over the desk. Phil is slamming into her from behind while Mark is buried down her throat. Their heads all snap towards me as the food I was carrying goes crashing to the ground. Wide-eyed they appear as stunned as I am. For a second, no one moves but then the mystery woman smirks at me – with Mark's dick still in her mouth – and it knocks me out of my stupor. Without a backwards glance, I flee.

"Lola!" I hear Phil shout behind me. I'm in my car and peeling out of the parking lot before he has time to pull his pants up and chase after me.

I make it all the way to the house before my emotions overwhelm me. Slamming my hands on the wheel, I wonder how I could be this stupid. How could I not see that he was cheating on me? Of course, he was! The late nights, the weekend work trips, the lack of interest in sex. It's all so obvious now.

I give myself a moment to freak out before marching inside to pack a bag. I can't stay here with him, not after this. Not after beating myself up for my marriage not working. Turns out it wasn't a lack of effort on my part. It was because my husband decided to invite other people into it. The asshole in question arrives as I'm zipping up my suitcase.

He grabs my arm as I head to the door. "Honey, wait. Please, it wasn't what it looked like. This is all a big misunderstanding."

Why do they always say that? Do they think our eyes don't work? "You weren't spit roasting some bimbo with your brother? You weren't throwing our marriage away for some cheap thrill?" I ask.

"No, I mean yes we were with" – he pauses as he considers his next words – "that woman. But we were doing it for the family. She's the rep for the deal we've been working on. It's what we had to do to get the business. She's been riding us for months and we finally decided to give her what she wanted to help Dad save the business."

"Oh I'm sure she's been riding you for months," I mutter. You and I both know that is a load of shit. I've seen her before at the company picnic. She's your brother's assistant." He's either shocked I remember or for being called out, because he opens and closes his mouth several times without a rebuttal. Good. I shove him back and continue to my car. Before slamming the door, I add, "I'm going to stay with my dad for a while. Don't contact me."

Today is my birthday. I've been at my dad's house for the last few days but he left last night to go on a business trip. I almost laughed when he told me and asked if any assistants would be joining him but that is more than I need to know about my dad. Plus, he's a single man. He can do as he pleases. I'm not even a little bit surprised he won't be here for my birthday. It's not like he knew I was coming or that this is the first birthday he'll miss.

My phone is blowing up with messages and calls but I can't bring myself to return any. I haven't told anyone what happened with Phil yet. I'm beyond embarrassed. You never think it's going to happen to you. You never think you'll miss the signs, but then you do. I'm staring at all the messages Phil sent me apologizing, asking me to come home, and gaslighting me about all the reasons he went to another woman. Despite all those messages, I am the most annoyed by the fact that he hasn't acknowledged my birthday. Not that I want him to, but it is telling. I'm scrolling through his string of lies and excuses when a FaceTime from Georgie comes through. I don't want to answer, but I know I have to. Georgie will keep calling until I pick up. I put on a fake smile and hit the answer button.

"It's the birthday girl!"

"Hi, Georgie. How's Barbados?"

"Oh, you know, beautiful weather, beautiful people, delicious drinks, can't complain. Next year you have to let me fly you out to spend your birthday together."

"That would be nice," I reply distractedly.

"What's wrong, Honeybun? You don't seem happy to be turning twenty-seven. Actually, you don't seem happy at all. What gives, Lo? Who do I need to kill?"

I roll my eyes. Georgie has always been overprotective. Apparently not having any siblings of my own meant the Rivera family was adopting me. That gave me two big sisters and a big brother who were all ready to go to battle for me. I'm reluctant to tell the truth since Georgie was never fond of Phil. He was apparently slimy and had 'a face that said he was up to something,' which turned out to be true. This news is not going to go over well.

Biting the bullet, I go through the events of New Year's Eve and some of the things before that lead up to it. By the end, Georgie's voice is hard and face is red. "I am going to kill that motherfucker. No one treats you like that, Lola. No one. His days are numbered."

"Alright, calm down Rambo. You aren't going to do anything. If you go to jail, you won't get to play with those cute nieces you have or eat your mother's *pasteles* ever again."

"I'm serious. This is unacceptable. Where are you? You're not going to go back to that loser. I can fly you out to Chicago. You can move in with me. Start over without that prick. You were always too good for him."

"I'm fine, Georgie. I'm at Dad's trying to figure out my next move. I am not moving in with you. There aren't enough noise canceling headphones in the world to make that happen."

That shifts Georgie's expression from dark and stormy to a smirk. Horn dog.

"I don't know what I'm going to do next but for now, I want to lick my wounds. I haven't been happy for a while, crumpling marriage aside," I confess. "I'm considering all my options before making any life-altering decisions."

"My offer stands. You need a place to go, my guest room is always open."

"Thanks Georgie. Go enjoy your vacation! You'll be hard at work again soon."

"Bye, Lo. Call me soon."

After a few more weeks at my dad's and increasingly more hostile texts and calls from my husband. I decide that I need a fresh start and to be surrounded by friends. I pull up my group text with Tiffany and Carina and shoot off a message.

11:57 AM

ME

> I'm coming to Nashville. I'll get there next Wednesday, same as Tiffany.

Phil will be at an accounting conference all week. I'll head home Monday and pack up everything I need for a new life in Music City. Nashville, here I come...

Chapter Four

· LOLA ·

February

My first days in Nashville have been amazing. Robby hasn't left for spring training yet, but it's been a total estrogen fest at *Casa de Becker*. Considering he is about to leave his girl for several weeks, Robby has been a good sport about all the rom-coms and rosé present in his swanky condo. Tiffany and I are going to stay here with Carina until he gets back and then we'll move into the two-bedroom unit they bought a couple floors below.

A few nights before Robby leaves, he wants to make Carina a fancy dinner at home. To make ourselves scarce, Tiffany and I spend the night exploring Nashville. We stumble across a cute champagne garden that is right up Tiff's alley. As we sip our bubbles, I can tell my blonde bestie is buttering me up for something.

"So..." she probes. "You left Phil over six weeks ago. Have you made any movement in the separation front?"

"I've contacted a lawyer in Missouri, but I haven't done anything yet. He hasn't been bugging me lately and I know the second he gets served papers he's going to harass me again. I'm enjoying the peace while I can. I think he finally got the message that it's over but I don't want to tempt fate yet."

"Speaking of tempting things, are you ready to get back out there? Meet some hunk to break your two-month dry spell?"

"Two months? Try eight," I say before I can stop myself. Tiffany chokes on her drink at the announcement.

"Eight?! You haven't had sex eight months?" she whisper-shouts causing people at nearby tables to turn their heads.

"Can you shut up? People are staring!"

"I'm sorry. I just... I know you hadn't gotten physical in a while, but your husband didn't have sex with you for that long, and you didn't suspect he was cheating? Oh honey, I didn't know it was that bad. You'd think the dude would throw you a bone now and then, especially when you were offering. Who turns down a free lay?"

"Excuse me," I huff, affronted.

"I wasn't calling you easy, babe. I'm simply pointing out that it is a lot more work to go and find a mistress or a rando than it is to have sex with your wife. Wow. And you're a knockout. Phil is dumber than I thought he was."

"Can we not talk about this in public?" I ask with heated cheeks.

"Oh, no ma'am. We are talking about this. I cannot let this injustice stand. We are getting you laid ASAP."

"I am not going home with some random guy we meet at a bar tonight. I can't handle that stress or potential rejection right now."

"Fine," she sighs, then perks up. "What if I knew a way you could have sex with someone who would for sure not turn you down?"

"I'm not hiring a hooker," I deadpan.

"Not a hooker, babe. There is a club here that offers a service for finding sexually compatible people and getting them together. It's all between consenting adults and no money exchanges hands – except the membership fee."

"I don't want to have sex in some shady nightclub."

"Not a nightclub, a sex club. And it's not shady, it's super classy. You fill out a profile and they find someone who matches your preferences. Everyone who is approved has been vetted. I signed up a few weeks ago but haven't been yet."

"Tiff, you have guys hanging all over you. Why do you need to go to a club for sex?"

She shrugs. "Sometimes it's nice to have a partner who already knows what you want. That way, you don't have to go through all the pesky guesswork and pretend you don't want him to spank your ass and call you his 'naughty girl.' Plus, there are a few things I enjoy that aren't exactly one-night stand or first date material like—"

I hold my hand up to stop her. "I don't need to know all that, and I don't think this is a good idea."

"Come on, Bunny. It's perfect. It's a sure-fire way to rip off the Band-Aid with someone who won't reject you and knows exactly what your boundaries are. It's ideal for a novice!"

"A novice, really?"

"Oh, I'm sorry. Did you have a lot of sexcapades you never told me during between homecoming and freshman spring semester when you met Phil?"

"No..."

"Exactly," she exclaims. "You need someone who knows how to get you off and how to keep you comfortable. I'll help you complete your profile and make sure you get the match you need."

She's staring at me with big blue puppy dog eyes. It's hard to say no when I know she's trying to help me.

"Fine," I concede. And that's how later that night I end up huddled in bed with Tiffany answering an exceedingly thorough questionnaire about my sexual preferences.

"I don't even know what some of this stuff is," I say.

"Like what?"

"Like water spots. Do they mean jet skis?"

"They mean being peed on," she replies nonchalantly.

"Seriously?"

"Seriously."

"Why do you know that?"

She smirks at me before answering, "I've been with my share of kinky former child stars."

"Oh my God."

"Hey, don't knock it till you try it. *I* didn't get peed on."

"That is way more than I needed to know. Ugh, this is going to be the most vanilla questionnaire they've ever received. They aren't going to let me in."

"Oh please. I'm sure you've got some secret kinks in there you don't even know about. Let them worry about that. All you need to do is answer honestly."

After another hour of filling it out, Tiffany convinces me to submit an application. Later, I go to bed embarrassed but also optimistic that I'm taking steps forward even if I have no intentions of stepping foot inside that club.

"I can't believe I let you convince me to do this," I yell over the blow dryer.

"Shut up. You're going to love it," Tiffany replies with an eye roll. "You're going to meet some hunk to rail you into forgetting all about that small-dicked son of a bitch who called himself a man."

"Are we sure this is a good idea?"

Tiffany puts down the blow dryer and meets my eyes in the mirror. "This is going to be great for you, Lo. I promise."

I nod my head and she returns to helping me get ready. After she's done, I slip into the navy velvet dress she forced me to buy for the occasion. The fabric is smooth against my skin and the cinched waist gives the illusion I was gifted the curves of my Italian ancestors.

"Damn, it pays to have someone who went to beauty school as

your bestie," Tiffany comments, coming into the room. I haven't had the nerve to peek yet.

"Holy shit," I breathe at my reflection.

"Yeah babe, you look hot as hell."

"You are a magician, Tiff. I can't believe you made me look this good."

"Yeah, whatever. You're a little Aphrodite and some guy is going to cream his pants at the sight of you tonight," she says as she downs the rest of her champagne. "Alright, Bunny. Let's roll out. Don't forget to grab your mask if you want to keep up the mystery."

"Here goes nothing," I mumble as we walk out the door.

Chapter Five

"**G**ood seeing you as always," Declan Ryder says as he slaps my shoulder and makes his way out of Cole's office. Declan, Cole Viatello, and I are co-owners of Club Hedone, a sex and kink club in Nashville. The club got its name after Hedone, the goddess of pleasure and enjoyment. She was the daughter of Eros, god of love and sex, and Psyche, the goddess of the soul.

The three of us meet every couple of months to talk about the club and make big (read: expensive) decisions. Declan and I may be co-owners/investors, but we both have day jobs – if you can call being a top-selling musician and MLB first baseman 'day jobs.' Cole runs the day-to-day and is the majority owner.

As I am about to leave, Cole grabs my attention after glancing at his phone. "Fancy staying to play tonight, Miller?" he asks.

While I help in the club when I can, serving as a monitor or taking part in demonstrations, I don't play often. It's not that I don't want to or that my tastes are so *particular* that it is hard to find a playmate. It's the opposite in fact. On the BDSM-kink spectrum, I rank pretty basic.

Sure, I've done all the training and know the ins and outs of being a Dom, but it isn't really my jam. I absolutely have dominant tendencies, that is part of my personality and always will be. But I am not a Dom in the traditional sense. It can be fun to play in that dynamic sometimes to release some energy or assert control, but I don't enjoy the full power exchange that many subs are after. Nor am I into other BDSM categories like DDlg or pet play. In my everyday life especially, I don't want a relationship where I impose rules and punishments. I simply want a sweet partner I can support and care for who doesn't mind that I can be a bit of a bossy bastard.

"I wasn't planning to play tonight," I respond. "We leave for spring training next week. I've got a lot to take care of before we go."

"Think I could persuade you?" Cole questions.

"Something wrong?"

"Wrong? No. An inconvenience? Yes. One of the House Doms had an emergency and can't be here tonight. We had him matched with a woman here to play for the first time. I don't have anyone else available who would match her profile. I'd do it but I am overseeing a demonstration in the medical play room.

"She's a beginner and her questionnaire shows her interests as pretty mild. I thought you'd be a good fit since I know you don't get into the hard stuff and enjoy the sweethearts. It could be a good last hurrah before you go."

"It has been a while since I've played," I concede. "What the hell, sure. I could use some fun before spending several weeks surrounded by sweaty, whiny dudes."

"Awesome, thanks, man. Eric will have her file for you upstairs."

I head up to the second-floor reception area where I see Eric and Willa. Eric is the member relations manager and Willa is one of the attendants who help get people settled into their various rooms and assists House Dominants.

"Mr. Miller, I didn't know you'd be joining us tonight," Eric greets.

"I wasn't planning to, but Cole mentioned you had a Dom out and that I might be able to fill in with a new guest," I reply.

"Oh, I'm glad it's you," Willa gushes. Seeing my confusion, she continues, "I met the woman you're being matched with tonight. She is definitely going to need an experienced hand. She was a little nervous and unsure. Very cute, though. She's totally your type." She blushes, realizing she is rambling.

"That is good to know. I am happy to help," I remark as one of the House Doms, Craig, comes up to get his pairing. He grabs both files from Eric and hands mine over to me. He flips through his and sets it back on the desk with a dissatisfied expression

"I can lead you to the rooms," Willa comments. "They've been waiting for a little while. I bet they're getting antsy."

"We can find the way on our own. This isn't our first rodeo," Craig sneers, condescendingly. I make a mental note to have Cole talk to the Doms about how they speak to staff members. He shouldn't be giving her attitude for doing her job.

"Thank you for the offer, Willa," I say.

I review the file of the woman I'm meeting before giving it back to Eric. She has a degradation kink. I'm surprised Cole thought I would be the right match for her. Don't get me wrong, I can play any role, but the way he and Willa were talking about her led me to believe she was a good girl-type. I typically go for women who are more into praise than degradation, but since I'm playing substitute tonight, I guess I get what I get.

I make my way down the hall after Craig. When I get to the door I knock hard before turning the handle. When I open it, I am met with the sight of a beautiful creature standing in the middle of the room. Not only is she short, but she is also slender with slight curves shown off by a tight dark, velvet dress.

Her long brown hair is striking against her metallic mask, but none of that compares to the big, hazel eyes that bore into me. After I take her in for a few moments, I realize I haven't said anything, and she is frozen in place. Her file made it sound as if she has a good understanding of what she wants in bed, but Cole did say she was new. As the Dom in this scenario, it's up to me to make the first move.

"Are you going to stand there staring at me all night you dirty little slut? As much as I enjoy your eyes devouring me, I have plans to fuck them into the back of your head," I say in greeting.

She sucks in a breath but other than that, she doesn't make a move. She must need a bit more prodding.

"Not used to a man calling it like he sees it? Not used to a man ready to use your body for his pleasure? Don't worry, if you're a good little whore, I'll make sure you're so exhausted you sleep for a week," I promise. "Come here."

That kicks her into gear and she slowly makes her way closer to me. As she does, I drink her in. Everything about her is breathtaking, despite her small stature. I think my hands could span her entire rib cage.

"She does know how to obey. That's good, pet. Turn around." As she spins, I see her small curves in her dress. My hands itch to touch the soft fabric, but I need to ensure she is ready for everything about to happen first. While her back is to me now, we are standing in front of a full-length mirror. I wait for her to meet my gaze before I keep going.

"Do you remember everything they went over in your paper-work?" I ask. She nods in response. It's then I realize I haven't heard her talk yet. "Words," I grit. I need her verbal acknowledgment before this goes further.

"Yes," she breathes out quietly. Alright, then we're good to go. Examining her, it is hard to believe she is into degradation. I know you can't always tell someone's kink by their appearance, but she has this air of sweetness and vulnerability to her with those big doe eyes. I'm not here to yuck anyone's yum, though. If this pixie wants to be degraded, degraded she will be.

"Normally I'd tell a slut like you to get on your knees, but I don't think you'd be able to reach my cock from there. Take off your dress and kneel on the bed." When she remains where she is, I give her a sharp slap on the ass and tell her to get moving.

She quickly goes over to the bed and glances at me from across the room. I walk over to the dresser and start to get more comfortable. I remove my watch and take off my jacket. I take my time scanning her body without her dress. Her perfect breasts and pert, pink nipples are on display as she kneels in a pair of delicate lace panties.

I can't help but smirk as I watch her check out my abs and chest. I earned this body through hours spent at the gym and in practice. But I have never felt as proud of it as I do now with how her gaze eats me up. When her eyes snap back up to mine, I address her again.

"Look at you on your knees waiting for me. You're needy, aren't you? Pathetic and desperate for my cock? Your greedy pussy is going to have to wait until I'm ready. I want you begging for it before I give it to you," I state.

I expect to see heat flare in her eyes or watch her clench her thighs, but her body language and facial expression don't give anything away. If I was an outside observer, I would say she wasn't into this, but she is the one who filled out the profile questionnaire. She'd have no reason to lie unless she was trying to get paired with a specific Dom based on kink. There is no way for her to know who she'd match with, though. Profile matches are random and based on availability and preferences which can vary by the day. While newbies are only matched with House Doms or other approved, experienced members, regular members can match with each other.

The idea that she might have wanted to be with someone else tonight causes pain in my chest. This little doll is mine – at least for tonight, anyway. Doll is the right word for her with her big eyes and delicate features. I wish I could peer into them again, but she isn't making eye contact, it's almost as if she's staring through me which will not do. I guess I need to amp this up another level.

"What's wrong, pet? You don't want me to call you desperate? But you are, aren't you? You came here tonight to be my fuck doll. Desperate for me to make a mess of you. That's what you want, isn't it? To be my pathetic little whore?"

Just when I think she is going to respond, she bursts into sobs. For a moment, I freeze. What is happening? I've never had anyone react this way to me before. Sure, I've had partners tear up after an intense orgasm but never full body weeping. I know part of degradation is humiliation, but that should be turning her on, not making her cry.

I move toward her to try to offer a comforting touch but she flinches back and clambers to the other side of the bed. "Why are you being mean to me?" she gets out in between sobs.

Mean? That isn't the word most people would use in this context. I know she isn't experienced, but her file said degradation was her kink. She thinks I'm being mean to her? Isn't that what she wanted? Something is not right. This has gone all wrong since the second I walked into the room. I need to see where she is at ASAP. I need to turn this encounter around.

"Color?" I inquire.

I think she says, "what?" in between hiccups.

"What color are you?"

She takes a few deep breaths and manages to get an answer out. "White, although I'm Italian... Maybe olive?"

White? Olive? What the hell is she talking about?

"No, baby, what stoplight color are you? Green, yellow, or red? Do you need to safe word?"

She stares at me for a minute before responding, "Safe word? We aren't having sex yet."

Who gave this woman her safety spiel? A safe word can be used any time in any circumstance. Before I can tell her that, there is a loud, persistent knock at the door. I don't want to walk away while she is crying, but she doesn't want my comfort and the knock is insistent.

I open the door to find a flustered Eric.

"What?" I grit. "There better be an emergency if you're interrupting a session."

"What file did you read? What did it say?" he rushes out, voice sounding slightly panicked.

"The one for this room. New, probationary member into degradation and open to impact play, bondage, and a variety of toys," I repeat.

"Fuck!" he exclaims as he runs his hand though his fair. "I think the files got switched when Craig grabbed them. The one you read wasn't for her."

"What?" I grouse. If that's true, this is a huge mix up and reflects terribly on the club. We need to figure this out now to make sure it is a one time issue caused at the desk and not a systematic error.

I turn to the woman – who has thankfully stopped crying and is now only sniffling – that I will be right back. I take one last glance at her before I leave and head to meet Cole up front.

When I return to the room a few minutes later, I am disappointed but not surprised to see she is gone. She must have left through the side stairs because I would have seen her walk by the desk. I read her file when I was there. She is not into degradation at all. In fact, she might be on the entire other end of the spectrum. No wonder she reacted the way she did. I hate that she ran out and I'm not able to fix this situation. There is no telling where this encounter left her emotionally.

The idea that something I did could have hurt her sits heavy in my chest as I proceed to Cole's office to discuss what happened. I know the client relations team will try to follow up with her, but I doubt she'll respond. I could probably get into the application portal but that would be highly unethical and I would be guessing which profile was hers, anyway. Hopefully, she'll return to the club in the future and I can make it right.

Chapter Six

· LOLA ·

March

After my unfortunate night at Club Hedone, I decided to bury my head in the sand. I am mortified I sobbed in front of a complete stranger who was literally there to fuck me happy. I want to blame it on the period that came the next morning, but I can't – even if I did cry at a video of an old lady reuniting with her dog after rehabbing her hip replacement.

The whole experience showed me that I am not ready to put myself out there. No matter what the circumstances are. I need to take some time to focus inwardly, to figure out who I am and become that person before I add intimacy or another person in the mix.

Carina and Tiffany are both at work today, and Robby left for camp. I have the place to myself. Taking a break from binge-watching home organization shows, I pull out my phone and browse social media. While scrolling, I come across a quote that knocks me on my ass and jumpstarts my journey. It says, "Burn the candles, use the nice sheets, wear the fancy lingerie. Don't save it for a special occasion; today is special."

I have spent much of my life waiting for a special occasion or moment. I save things for a rainy day, but even then, I feel guilty using them. No more! Starting right now, I am a new Lola – Lola 2.0. And Lola 2.0 lives in the moment and enjoys life to the fullest.

I run into my room and tear through my closet. I grab everything I bought to wear to Phil's stuffy work parties and the city council meetings I attended for work, and toss them on the bed. Anything that doesn't bring me joy is out.

Digging through my stuff, I find the candle Carina got me for Christmas last year. The one I've yet to burn. I bring it back into the living room with me and light it. Grabbing a notepad, I map out a plan to become a new me.

Step one: Makeover. I've already started with my closet purge. I'll replace what I got rid of with new items that I love and fit my style, not the style of who I think I'm supposed to be. As soon as Tiffany gets home, I will convince her to chop off my hair. I kept it long because Phil preferred it that way, but it is a pain to take care of and fuck what he prefers.

Step two: Find a job so I can stop freeloading off Robby and Carina/the joint bank account Phil hasn't cut me off from. I scour the internet for freelance journalist positions I can do from home. I find one with the Nashville tourism board and quickly apply. I pitch myself for a column as being a new transplant to the city and exploring it. I also link to my experience writing on city matters and local interest pieces from my old position.

Step three: Deal with Phil. It's been three months since I left. It's time to finally tackle the issue. I shoot an email off to my attorney and tell her to draw up the divorce papers and file them as soon as she can. I know it's going to cause a shit storm, but I can't have this hanging over my head anymore. It's time to live for me.

Chapter Seven

I am still shaken up by the encounter a few weeks ago at Club Hedone. After Eric told me about the files getting mixed up, I went back to apologize and provide aftercare because she was rightfully upset, but I didn't get the chance. By the time I got there, she was gone. I don't blame her, but I can't help but feel like an absolute asshole.

I have protective, caretaking urges for every woman I am intimate with, but I especially had them for her. I royally fucked up that situation. I know it wasn't technically my fault, but she doesn't know that. And even if she did, it wouldn't un-hurt her feelings or absolve my responsibility. I'm annoyed I won't get the chance to make it right, but maybe it's for the best.

The whole ordeal highlighted the discontentment I have been dealing with lately. It started when my brother got married and was exacerbated by seeing our pitcher, Robby's, relationship with Carina. I've been happy with my life, but seeing two of the men closest to go ga-ga for their women makes me feel like I'm missing something.

I love taking care of people. It's part of what attracted me to the dominant side of the BDSM world. That and the fact that I am a possessive, bossy bastard. I've been fulfilled by short flings and scenes for the past decade, but now I can't help but think how amazing it would be to have that 24/7. How much better would it be if the person I was taking care of was *mine* and not a temporary partner? What would it be like to have someone to take care of every day? Someone whose life I got to be fully involved in. Sure, I do that on some level with the guys on the team, but it isn't the same.

Before I dive too deep into those thoughts, there is a knock at my door. We've had a long day, and I am exhausted, but I answer anyway. I'm the captain and someone might need me. Opening the door, I find Robby and Kent, our right fielder, with a six-pack of beer. "Hi, Papa Bear," Kent greets as he lets himself into my room.

"Sure, come on in," I deadpan.

"Thanks, man." Robby says, patting me on the shoulder and making his way inside.

"To what do I owe the pleasure of you clowns showing up?"

"Like you didn't want to see our beautiful faces," Kent teases.

"Can you ever behave?" Robby asks him before turning to me. "We came to check on you, Cap. You've been a little... high strung, and we wanted to see if everything was okay."

"Maybe he did. I came to raid your Pop-Tart stash," Kent admits. "What? Don't pretend you don't have one!" he adds when he catches my glare.

Rolling his eyes, Robby continues, "Come on, man, you're always here for us. We want to do the same for you."

"My brother's wife is pregnant," I say with a sigh.

"Kevin? That's awesome, man! Although your face says it isn't awesome?" Robby questions.

"No, it's great. They've been trying since they got married and I know they'll be incredible parents. My mom is over the moon."

"Then what's got your scowl-ier than usual?" Ken asks, handing me a beer.

"I don't know. I guess it's got me thinking about the things I'm missing out on. The things I've sacrificed. I'm not saying I want to be a dad tomorrow, but at my current pace, I don't know if it will ever happen. I thought I'd want to wait until after I retired to settle down, but that is still hopefully years away. I want to find someone who will be a forever partner, not just whoever is available when I'm ready."

"I get it, man," Robby affirms. "I thought the same thing. I thought I wouldn't want a relationship while in the game, but when I got the chance to have Carina back, I was going to miss out. You need to open yourself up to the opportunity and see what the universe sends you."

"The universe? Really, man?" I mock.

"Ugh, sorry. I've spent the last couple weeks surrounded by Carina and her best friends. One of them is into all that hippy dippy astrology shit."

"Isn't her friend single? Maybe you can set Miller up with her," Kent suggests.

Robby laughs, "Absolutely not. Tiffany and Miller would be a *terrible* match. He'd run for the hills after five minutes. Lola, on the other hand, might be a good match. She's going through some shit right now, though. Maybe after the season I can set you up."

"Thanks for the offer, but I'm good for now," I huff. "I'll see what the universe" – I add air quotes – "brings me."

"You got it. Now, let's dig into these beers and talk about which rookies we think we can get to puke tomorrow."

Chapter Eight

• BRADY •

After five weeks in Florida for spring training, I am ecstatic to get back home. I've been in the league for a decade at this point. While I love it, spending a month in a basic ass hotel with a bunch of dudes and sweating my ass off has lost its shine. Don't get me wrong, I am grateful every day to have the opportunity, but I thrive in a routine and familiar environment. Spring training throws that off.

As I lean my head back against the elevator, I hear a voice yell, "Hold it, please." I jolt my arm out to stop the door from closing. When I do, a cute little thing with short, brown hair makes her way in.

"Thank you," she exhales, catching her breath.

"No problem," I say. Giving her a quick glance. She seems familiar, but I only got a peek at her face before she turned around. "Do you live here or are you visiting?" I ask.

"I live here. I moved in last month, but I am switching units this weekend since my cousin-in-law is back. I had to run to the store to grab more moving essentials," she replies, shaking a shopping bag.

"Well, welcome to the building... again, I guess," I laugh.

"Thank you. Have you lived here long?"

"I've lived here for about five years, ever since I got traded to Nashville."

"Traded?" she questions. "Are you on the Songbirds?"

Shit. I shouldn't have said that. The last thing I need is a cleat chaser to know which floor I live on. Though in leggings and a distressed pink tee, she doesn't strike me as one.

"That is probably a crazy thing to ask randomly. I'm not a stalker, I promise. I'm Lola, Carina's cousin; Robby's fiancé. I promise I am not some creeper."

"Oh, right. Robby mentioned Carina had some friends moving into his second unit. Yes, I am on the team. I'm Brady Miller. Everyone calls me by my last name, though."

"Nice to meet you, Miller," she says, sticking out her hand. The elevator reaches my floor at about the same time, but I still slip her hand in mine and shake it.

"Nice to meet you, Lola. Let Robby know he can call me if he needs help moving anything."

"That's thoughtful, thank you," she replies with a tilt of her head, still holding my hand. When she realizes it, she drops it like a hot potato. "Have a nice night. I'm sure I'll see you around."

I'll definitely make sure I see her around. Something about her spoke to me in a way no one has in a while. She has an air of sweetness and innocence that is rare in the women I usually meet. I send Robby a text to see if he needs any help in case Lola forgets.

April

It's Opening Day and the weather could not be more perfect. It's 65°
and clear as we make our way out onto the field for the first inning. I
gave the guys a talk in the clubhouse about this being our year and
how I know we can see it through this time. It's way too early to say
that for sure, but it's the speech a captain should give.

Robby is on the mound and I'm on first. He tosses the ball to me
and we throw it around the infield to warm up. I see a determination
in his eyes, but more than that, I see a sense of calm confidence. I
can't help but think it has nothing to do with his off-season training
and everything to do with the brunette yelling his name from behind
home plate.

Apparently, Carina didn't want to spend the opening game in the
suite. She wanted a front row seat to cheer him on. It's sweet. I wish I
had someone dedicated to me in that way. Beside her, I see a blonde
who I have come to understand is her best friend, Tiffany, and the
cute brunette I ran into in the elevator, Lola. They all have on Songbirds jerseys. I wonder if they're all for Becker. The thought of her
wearing mine pops into my head, and I don't hate it.

The crowd noise rises and I realize while I was lost in thought,
they announced the lineup. The visiting team, the Sacramento
Miners, has their first batter preparing to step up to the plate. As they
approach, I shut everything else off in my mind and prepare to play
ball.

Chapter Nine

• LOLA •

"Where are you off to tonight?" I ask Tiffany as she slips into her prized Louis Vuitton red bottoms.

"I'm heading to the Bluebird to see a band whose makeup I did last week. Wanna join?" When she spies the refusal on my tongue, she amends her offer. "I'm also going to a rooftop pool party with them tomorrow if that's more your speed."

I can't help but smile at my roomie. Even though I never take her up on her offers, she still asks me. She always wants everyone to be included. "I have to finish editing a piece for work on May festivals," I respond.

"One of these days you're going to say yes to one of my adventures."

"I think we both remember what happened last time I did that," I sass.

"That is neither here nor there and you know it! You spent a long time playing house. You've got a lot to make up for."

"I wasn't 'playing house,'" I grouse. "I was living 'house.' Ya know, married and all that."

"Exactly! Now that you're single, it's time to try all the things you missed out on. Take the bulls by the horns or save the bull and ride a cowboy!"

"I don't think that is the saying."

"Well, it should be. You don't have to bar hop with D-list country bands, but there has got to be some stuff you missed out on doing being married young. Lola 2.0 is all about becoming who you want to be, right? Start doing that!"

"Okay, okay. I'll put some thought into it," I agree.

"Atta girl! I expect to see a list when I get home. Don't wait up," she says with a wink.

As much as I hate to admit it, Tiff has a point. I got the makeover, found a new job, and filed for divorce – the first three steps on the new me plan, but then I coasted. I've buried myself in the move and working. I haven't made much progress towards figuring out who I want to be.

I wish there was a blueprint on how to do this. I don't know many people who got married right after college and I know even fewer who are already divorced at my age. I know I can't be the only one, though.

Why is no one talking about this?

Maybe you should. The thought pops into my head. I want to dismiss it. That's what I'd normally do. But I stop myself. Why shouldn't I do it? No one is talking about the reality of post-divorce life in your 20s. No one is showing the journey. I'm a writer, it could be me.

I login in to social media and quickly create a new profile before buying the domain I'll need for my blog. A few hours later, the *Ex-Wife Files* is born.

I spend the next week building my website, planning content, and creating the general premise of my blog. It's not only going to be a place that discusses the realities of being divorced as a 20-something, but also where I chronicle my journey of self-discovery. I've decided to try one new thing every week and share it with readers. Whether it is a cuisine or hobby or even a new outlook.

I did research and pulled some ideas from the internet, but I am sure I'll add more as I go. I published my first post yesterday and the limited response has been positive. It will take a while to grow my audience, but I'm not worried about it. This is as much for me as it is for any subscribers.

As I put the finishing touch on tomorrow's social media post, Carina and Tiffany pull my attention up from my phone. We decided to stay home tonight and watch the Songbirds play before meeting the guys out at the bar where they have their post-game celebrations. I didn't want to go at first, but the new me goes out with her friends.

"What's up?" I ask.

"It's the top of the seventh. Time to get ready. It will take the guys about an hour after the game to get to Holler's. We need to claim seats in the VIP area before the chasers try to weasel their way in," Carina says.

Since Holler's is a casual place, we don't get too dressed up. I've chosen an off the shoulder peach cotton dress that comes in at the waist then flows down my thighs. It has an overlay of delicate flowers on it that you almost can't see. It's flirty and feminine and something I would have never worn six months ago. I love it. I pair it with strappy sandals and link arms with the girls as we make our way to the bar. Since it is only a couple of blocks away, we walk, enjoying the spring weather.

By the time we get there, the place isn't too packed but it is getting there. The game ended a few minutes ago – with the Songbirds victorious – and people are filing down Broadway from the stadium. The bouncer who insists we call him Big Ron waves us to the guys' normal table. I notice it's more crowded in the VIP than usual right as someone knocks into my shoulder.

"Sorry, didn't see you down there," the human bulldozer flirts, taking me in. A short joke, original. "You have to let me buy you a drink for my clumsiness."

I'm about to refuse him when I remember I'm supposed to be putting myself out there for new experiences. Someone other than my soon-to-be ex-husband buying me a drink qualifies. There's no harm in letting this guy pay for my pineapple seltzer.

"Cheers. I'm Mike, by the way," he says when we both have our drinks.

"Lola."

"That's a beautiful name. Does it mean anything?"

"Not that I know of," I laugh out awkwardly.

"Hmm, that's a shame. I'd have thought it meant gorgeous or stunning based on the woman who bears it."

Oh, he's smooth. Right as I'm about to respond, the crowd cheers loudly and we glimpse up to see several built bodies ambling in.

"Is that the Songbirds? I didn't know they came in here after games. How cool is this?" he shouts over to his friends before directing his next question to me. "Do you follow baseball?"

"A little."

"These guys are the best. Robby Becker is one of the greatest pitchers to ever play the game and Dela Cruz is a beast at bat."

We have a fan on our hands. Boring. Don't get me wrong, I enjoy baseball. I've been surrounded by baseball fanatics my entire life between my Dad, Georgie, and Phil. Plus, I'm related to a professional player. It isn't a topic I want to talk about to a guy at a bar, though. Before I can change the subject, I sense someone watching me. I peer up to see Miller walking my way with his eyes locked on mine.

"Holy shit, you're Brady Miller," Mike says as he approaches. "Hell of a game, man. I can't believe I saw it in person. I was just telling Layla here how incredible you guys are."

"Thanks," Miller responds before ordering a whiskey soda. "You all settled into the new place, *Lola*?" he asks, emphasizing my name and dismissing Mike, who is too enamored to notice.

"We are. Thanks for asking. How about you?" I reply nervously. "I mean, I know you didn't recently move in because you've been there for years but, um, settling into the season." Oh God, I'm rambling.

Every time I've run into Miller since meeting him in the elevator, I have made a babbling mess of myself. I don't know what is wrong with me. I'm usually articulate, but something about him throws me off. There is something familiar about him but also something that makes him seem untouchable – like I'm lucky to be in the same universe as him.

Maybe I am. He is insanely attractive. He's probably the most attractive man I have ever seen in real life. He's big and built, but he also has these piercing blue eyes that I swear can see into my soul and read all my inappropriate thoughts about him.

"I think so," he says. Shit. What did I ask? I stopped listening.

"What?"

"I think I've settled into the season. We've only been at it for a few weeks, but have only lost twice. I can't complain."

"That's, um, good."

"Yeah, it is," he says, smiling as he takes a sip of his drink. "Your friend went back to his buddies."

"My friend?" I glance around to see who he's talking about and spy Mike pointing over at us. Really? He ditched me to brag about meeting Miller to his friends? Not that he was going to get anywhere, but rude. "Mike? He's not my friend. He bought me a drink to make up for running into me."

"Then shall we go back and join your actual friends?" he asks, tilting his head to where Tiffany, Carina, and his teammates are gathered. Having his sole focus does something to me. Unable to respond with words from the weight of his attention, I nod.

His hand grazes my back as he escorts me to our group. I hate that

I lean into it a little, but I do. The touch is oddly comforting. He may be behind me, but there is no question he's leading the way. I love it. Phil used to always walk fast and would end up half a block ahead of me before he realized I wasn't there. Then he'd be annoyed he had to wait for me to catch up. God, he was a prick. It's nice to have someone walking *with* me. Geez, am I this touch and affection starved that I'm getting goosebumps from the simple gesture of *not* leaving me to walk on my own?

The rest of the night is spent orbiting our group and blushing every time Miller catches my eye, which is a lot. His presence is a beacon that draws me in. It happens every time we hang out. The man probably thinks I'm some crazy stalker with how much he catches me staring and the way I ramble every time we talk.

To be fair, he's the one who approaches me. Plus, he has to be looking at me, too, in order to catch me. Maybe it isn't only me that feels this pull between us. Not that I'd do anything about it. I'm still married for Chrissake and Miller is way out of my league.

A few hours into the night, I excuse myself to the bathroom. While I'm in there, I overhear some chasers talking about the guys.

"I can't believe Becker is off the market," one of them whines.

"I know, but it's okay. I've got my sights set on Dela Cruz tonight. I heard he's a great time. No girl leaves his bed without at least two orgasms and a limp," the other responds. "You should go for Miller."

"God, I wish. He never takes home girls he meets at bars. The man owns a sex club – why would he need to meet girls at a bar? I bet he's a beast in bed. He gives off total Christian Grey vibes with his whole silent, aloof thing. I wouldn't be surprised if he's into some super kinky shit."

I don't hear the rest of their conversation as I put the pieces together that cause me to panic. Oh my God. Miller owns a sex club. Is that how Tiffany knew about Hedone? Does he go there often? The more I think about it, the more he resembles my masked man. There is no way it was him. If he's an owner, he wouldn't be slumming it with newbies. He could get any woman he wanted.

I quickly wash my hands and run out of the bathroom. As I do, I run right into the man in question. I bounce off his chest, and he grabs my arms to steady me.

"You okay, doll? You're running into a lot of people tonight," he laughs. When I study him, it's glaringly obvious. His size, the deep voice. But, it's the eyes that seal it for me. No wonder they were familiar.

"I have to go," I blurt as I pull out of his grasp.

"Do you have a ride home? I'm not sure the others are ready to go yet."

"I-I'm fine. I just, I have to go. Right now."

With that, I leave him standing in the back of the bar and run out onto Broadway. I text my girls that I went home before burying myself under my covers and contemplating every choice that led me to a place where Brady Miller has called me his 'pathetic little whore.'

Chapter Ten

• BRADY •

I'm intrigued by my new neighbor. I've seen Lola a few times when our group gets together and caught her sneaking peeks at me almost as much as I have at her. I haven't gotten to speak to her much, but I think I make her nervous. She tends to ramble whenever we chat, which I find almost as adorable as the blush she gets every time I catch her staring.

My initial attraction to her has only grown as I've spoken to her and learned more about her. From what I've gathered, she moved here after being cheated on. How any man could not cherish that goddess is beyond me. She's precious.

I'm perplexed by my reaction to her. I don't usually get hung up on women like this. When I got to Holler's the other night and saw that preppy prick hitting on her, I couldn't stop myself from crashing their conversation. Luckily for me, he scurried away quickly when he saw the glare I was giving him over Lola's shoulder. Glad he got the message because no way in hell was I going to let some sleazy finance bro take her home.

Something about Lola calls to my protective instinct more than any woman I've ever met. Something about her that makes me want to wholly possess her, but also, I help her shine and show the world how strong she is.

The evening was going great until I ran into her outside the bathroom and she fled like her ass was on fire. I still have no idea what that was about. She gaped at me as if she was face-to-face with the villain in an eighties slasher film.

Ever since that night, she has avoided me at all costs. Instead of cute rambles, I get clipped answers and rushed responses. Instead of a pretty blush on her cheeks when I meet her eyes, they are almost never glancing my way. And when they are, she casts them down quickly. It's as if she's afraid to make eye contact with me.

I find myself missing the way things used to be and I don't know what changed. I would say it is all in my head, but she only appears to be this way with me. With everyone else, she is her happy, sweet self. It's me she can barely stand to be around.

"What'd you do to Lola, man? Shut her down?" Kent asks, saddling up to me at a party at his place down the hall.

"What do you mean?" I ask.

"She used to be all giggly school girl around you and now she can't get away from you fast enough. I figured she took her shot, and you turned her down."

"No, she didn't 'shoot her shot.' I don't know what happened. Her attitude towards me changed all of the sudden. It's really starting to piss me off."

"Interesting," he quips.

"What's interesting?"

"Seems as if she isn't the only one with a crush."

"I'm thirty-two years old. I don't have crushes."

"Whatever you say. All I know is that you watch that girl with moon eyes and when she doesn't give you the time of day, you remind me of a sad puppy."

"A puppy, seriously? No one would ever say I resembled a puppy."

"Fine," he complains. "A raging bear. Happy?"

"It's better," I snark. "Either way, I don't have a crush on her. But I hate that she isn't comfortable around me and I don't know how to fix it. She won't say more than two words to me. I'm a nice guy. I go out of my way to help people. I almost never raise my voice – at least off the field. I don't get what I did to freak her out."

"Maybe she found out you're a Daddy."

"I'm not a Daddy. I'm hardly even a Dom. I just like to take care of things... my way," I correct.

"I think you mean that you're a control freak. Maybe she found out about the club and she thinks you're a kinky freak. I get the vibe she hasn't exactly been around the block, if you know what I mean."

"Yes, I know what you mean. And don't talk about her that way, it's disrespectful."

For some reason, that makes the motherfucker smile. "What?" I ask, exasperated.

"You totally have a crush on her." He pats me on the shoulder and walks away to greet other guests, leaving me to stew in my thoughts. I glance up and seek out Lola to find her smiling at something Carina is saying. When she senses the weight of my gaze, she meets my stare but averts her eyes quickly.

Something has changed her perception of me and I intend to find out what it is. Even though I would love to get to know her more, hopefully, I can get us back to being at least friendly.

Chapter Eleven

• LOLA •

May

I've spent the last several weeks avoiding Miller. The things he said to me that night aside, knowing he's seen me practically naked is enough to make me want to never see again. Luckily, I have been plenty busy and the Songbirds are focused on their season.

As expected, Phil flipped his lid when he was served with divorce papers. I don't know what he expected considering I left six months ago, but he bombarded me with calls and texts for weeks demanding I come home and talk to him. Did he offer to come here? Of course not. I didn't want him to, but for someone who claims he wants to "make this work," Phil is making zero effort to do so. Unless blowing up my phone and complaining to our so-called friends counts. Spoiler alert: it doesn't. Thankfully, he backed off once my lawyer threatened to file harassment charges.

My new job is going amazing and pairs perfectly with my blog.

Being forced to explore Nashville for the tourism board has helped break me out of my shell and find hidden gems I'd never have known about otherwise. It's easy to try new things when they're right in front of my face. I never would have thought orange blossom lattes would be one of my favorite things, but thanks to trying one at a coffee shop opening they are. Turns out, I am obsessed with unconventional syrups.

Today, I am trying something else new: a trampoline fitness class. I saw one of my favorite actresses doing it and decided to give it a shot. I am insanely nervous, but also excited. This is so far outside of the realm of things I would normally do that I can't help but be proud of myself for signing up.

When I arrive at the studio, I check in at the front desk and get a tour. The receptionist helps me pick out my equipment and sets me up in the back. I may be excited, but I am not front-of-the-class excited. When she goes to greet another newbie, I sit down on the mat to stretch. Suddenly, a shadow falls over me and I glimpse up to see a woman clearly straight out of Themyscira. She could pass for Gal Gadot's twin.

Even though I am on the ground, I can tell she is tall. She has her hair pulled up into a ponytail and even without makeup, she is gorgeous. Not only is she stunning, but her body is wow. I don't mean she's hot. She is, but the thing I notice the most about her is how strong she is. Her body is toned and fit without being bulky, and I wonder if trampoline classes will help me get that type of strength. I wouldn't mind being able to carry all my groceries inside in one haul or moving furniture without having to call Robby.

"Hi, I'm Charlie," she says. "I'm the instructor. Is this your first class?"

"Hello," I stammer, shaking out of my trance. "I'm Lola. Yes this is my first time doing anything like this. I am usually a yoga girl."

"Welcome. We are happy to have you. What made you want to try this class if you don't mind me asking? It is quite the departure from yoga."

"I am on a journey of self-discovery and am trying things outside of my comfort zone and this... this is way outside my comfort zone."

"Don't be nervous, I'll take care of you," she responds with a sly grin. "Follow along and you'll be fine. After I show the class the exercise once, I call out modifications to make it easier or harder for people of varying skill levels."

"Oh thank God. I was worried I wouldn't be able to keep up," I sigh in relief. "I am ready to get my workout on."

"I got you," she says with a nod and walks away. I berate myself for saying 'get my workout on.' Really Lola? How lame can you be?

A few minutes later, the studio dims and colorful LED lights illuminate. The music turns up and Charlie steps on to her trampoline. "Alright ladies and gents, let's get our workout on. Remember: if you're not shaking, you're not shaping!" I pretend not to notice the wink she sends my way after repeating my phrase.

Shaking is the absolutely right word for what happened to me. Holy crap was that a hard workout. After the warm up, I pretty much did all the easier modifications and I still fear I may never walk again.

Grabbing my bag, I turn around to see Charlie. "How was it?" she asks.

"It was fun," I respond.

"And..." she prompts.

"And hard. I don't think I've ever worked out that hard in my life. My legs may be Jell-O now."

"But you're feeling good? Got that endorphin high?" When I nod she tentatively asks, "think you'll come back?"

"For sure! As soon as I can walk without crumpling to the floor, I wanna do this again. I've never enjoyed a workout this much."

"Glad to hear it. I always aim to leave the ladies with weak knees and wanting another round," Charlie laughs. "Listen, this was my last class of the day and I was going to grab coffee next door. Would you want to join me? I'd love to learn more about your journey of self-discovery."

"Do they have fun flavors?"

"I know they have lavender," she answers.

"Perfect! Fun coffee flavors are one of my favorite discoveries."

She smiles at me indulgently. "Alright then, let's go see what they have!"

The high from the trampoline workout, lavender latte, and making a new friend vanished by the time I got back to the apartment and I checked my email. Phil may not be bugging me anymore, but he and his attorney are bugging mine plenty.

I thought our divorce could be straightforward. We don't have any kids and our only major asset is the house. Apparently, taking what we came in with and splitting the house isn't enough for Phil, though. He wants to review everything of value, from our cars to our 401k accounts to the jewelry my Nonna left me, to ensure we 'equitably divide our assets.' I don't know why I thought he'd make this easy.

The most frustrating thing is that he is insisting on a gag order where neither of us can talk about the divorce until it's finalized. I don't know if he's doing it because he doesn't want me sharing what I walked in on or if he's seen my blog and wants to punish me. My audience isn't huge, but I hit 5,000 followers last week and I don't want to stop the momentum to appease his ego. I've spent enough of my life putting the wants of others before my own. My lawyer declined the gag order thank goodness.

I finish firing off a response when Tiffany stumbles out of her room.

"Good morning," she mumbles.

"You mean good afternoon?" I joke. "Aren't you a ray of sunshine? It's 1 p.m. Please tell me you aren't just now waking up."

"No, I was taking a power nap so I could rally for tonight."

"Tonight?" I question.

"Carina's bachelorette party? Tell me you didn't forget, Lola. You planned the damn thing!"

"Of course, I didn't forget." She eyes me skeptically. "I mean I did momentarily, but I am ready for tonight. I still don't think we can call it a bachelorette party when we're doing it with Robby and his friends, too. Plus, Kent did more planning than I did. That guy is oddly pumped for a party where there will absolutely, one hundred percent not be strippers."

"Maybe if we're lucky, we can get some of the guys to put their uniforms on and give us a show."

"You're incorrigible," I roll my eyes.

"What? Everyone knows baseball pants are hot. I don't make the rules, Bunny. I simply enjoy the bubble butts and bulges."

Flopping down beside me, Tiffany takes me in. "You okay?" she asks.

"I'm fine, why?"

"I don't know. You're all angsty and you forgot about the party you helped plan, Miss Maid of Honor."

"I've had a lot on my mind this morning," I defend and then tell her about the workout class and email from my lawyer.

"Your ex is such a douche canoe. I don't know how you put up with him. I have to say, I'm overjoyed you're putting yourself back out there but I did not see your journey of self-discovery going this way."

"What do you mean?"

"I know a lot of women switch teams after a shitty marriage, but I didn't think you'd be one of them."

I sputter. "Switching teams? What are you talking about?"

"Your date."

"What date?"

"With your fitness instructor," she says, as if it's the most obvious thing in the world.

"That was not a date."

"I'm pretty sure it was."

"No," I say exasperated, "she was being friendly."

"Did she pay?"

"Yes."

"Ask for your number?"

"Yes..."

"Try to make future plans?"

"Yes, but..."

"Sounds like a date to me, Bunny."

"Oh my God!" I screech. "I didn't mean for it to be a date. I mean she was lovely, but I am unfortunately attracted to men, though my taste is questionable."

"It's not your taste. It's the slim pickings. Don't worry, I'm sure she could tell. Anyone with a sense of situational awareness would know you aren't swinging that way. Speaking of swinging though, maybe tonight you'll let one of these handsome baseball boys show you his bat."

"Tiffany!"

"What?"

"You know I'm not ready for that. You remember what happened last time I tried to get with someone. I don't need to relive that disaster more than I already am."

"Don't be dramatic, that's Carina's thing. And I think you are ready for it. You're just scared. You need to sample what you've been missing. I mean, it's been over a year since you've had a man-made O, assuming Phil could get the job done before you stopped having sex."

"Meh."

"Such a douche canoe," she grumbles.

"Come on, Lo. Live a little tonight. You don't have to find Mr. Right, just Mr. Good for Tonight."

"Not happening."

"Ugh, you're no fun. At least get drunk with me. We can make a game of it. This party is going to be bananas with Kent at the helm. Let's make the most of it."

"Alright, fine. I will get drunk with you, but I am coming home alone."

"Perfect, Kevin McCallister. Let's get ready."

"It's not even 2 p.m."

"Exactly! We have tons of pampering to do in order to prepare ourselves and our livers for this epic party."

Chapter Twelve

• LOLA •

Once again, I am questioning why I listened to Tiffany. After getting ready, we decided to make bingo cards for the night that require a shot every time you check one off. Someone got bingo two hours ago but we are still playing for some reason.

And because Bach Party Bingo wasn't enough for Tiffany, she decided to add an extra layer to our game. Every time Robby and Carina lock eyes across the room we take a sip of our drink. Every time they kiss, we have to drink the entire exchange. I should have remembered that Carina is a handsy drunk when Tiff proposed the rules. But still annoyed about the Phil situation, I wanted to drown my memories.

"God, he is insanely hot," Haley, Carina's former coworker, notes as she glances over at the baseball players chatting across the room.

"He's also insanely nice. I came into the building at the same time as him and he held every door. Who does that anymore?" the redhead beside her says.

"Carina told me that when his elderly, upstairs neighbor was in the hospital, he fed her cat. He also paid for one of the usher's family to go to Disney World after his daughter finished chemo. Hashtag swoon."

"It should be illegal to be that hot and kind. Usually, the hot ones are the biggest jerks."

"I'm sure there is something wrong with him. No one is that perfect."

Realizing they're talking about Miller, I scoff. "He's far from perfect. Friend-shaped doesn't mean *friendly*."

"What?" Haley asks. Shit. I didn't mean to eavesdrop or enter into their conversation. Drunk Lola is louder than she thinks she is.

"It's a thing I heard a park ranger say once. Just because bears are friend-shaped doesn't mean they are friendly. You try to hug them and they'll rip your face off and make you cry. Same with Miller, he seems nice but get too close and he'll eat your face," I supply.

"I'd let him eat any part of me he wanted," the redhead responds. "I'd let him do almost anything to me if it meant I got to spend a night in his bed."

When I peek over at the man in question, I see him frowning at me from across the room. I give him my best glare before walking away to find Tiffany.

"How are you doing, my little Bunny?" She singsongs.

"The drinks aren't working," I grouse.

"Disagree with you there. They are working quite well on you. You are pretty wasted."

"Don't blame me. Blame him," I complain a little too loudly pointing at Robby.

"Hey, what did I do?" he asks.

"You keep kissing and I keep drinking!" I exclaim. Everyone gives us confused expressions which makes Tiffany and I burst out laughing.

"I don't even want to know," Carina mutters.

Understanding dawns on Robby and he gives us a wink as he says, "Bottom's up, ladies," before pulling her in for a long kiss. It lasts so long that I drain my drink.

"Uh oh," I say with a glimpse into my empty cup, surprised, as if I wasn't the one who finished it.

While at the bar trying to make myself a refill, I sense a warm presence at my back. I don't even need to turn around to know who it is. Miller has a magnetism that makes me acutely aware of him.

"Might be time to switch to water," his deep voice rumbles.

I whip around too fast, causing me to stumble as I snap, "You are not the boss of me, bossy man!" I snap.

"Was that supposed to be scary, doll? Because I've gotta say, you're a little too cute to be intimidating."

"There you go with the name calling again," I hiss.

He frowns. "It wasn't a name calling, sweet girl. I think it's pretty adorable. I can see why Robby calls Carina 'Kitten' now if this is how she acts towards him."

"Robby is a nice boy," I remark.

"Yeah, I guess he is," he laughs with a soft, bemused smile.

"You are not a nice boy."

"I'm not?"

"Nope," I answer, popping the p.

"Most people would say I'm pretty nice."

"Most people haven't met the real you."

"And you have?" The smile slides off his face as his irritation grows. Good, I'm irritated, too. "I have been nothing but nice since meeting you after training camp and you've barely said two words to me in weeks. If anyone isn't 'nice' here it is you."

"Yeah, *after* camp," I mutter. "And I think you've said enough for the both of us."

"Lola—" he starts to say but I interrupt.

"Listen Mr. Bossypants, I have no intention of being a dirty little slut or greedy whore for you. Bark up a different tree. That girl said you could eat her face. Maybe try your luck over there." I whisper-shout pointing at Haley and Kim. "My olive skin and I want nothing to do with you."

He and everyone else nearby are watching me with stunned expressions but I am too mad and tipsy to care. Deciding to get in the last word, I grab my drink and head off in the other direction.

Tiffany and Carina, who overheard the conversation, follow me.

"Lola!" Carina chastises. "What the hell! Why are you being rude to Miller? He's like the nicest guy in the world."

"No, he isn't," I whine. "Why does everyone take his side? He wants you to think that, but it's not true. He's nice on the outside, but on the inside he is mean. Like a reverse German Shepherd. They appear scary but they're nice. He fakes being nice, but he's actually a rude asshat!"

"That is not true."

"How would you know?" I question her. "Has he ever tried to fuck you in a club? Nooooo. Has he ever thought you were a Slutty McSlutterson? No, cause Robby would deck him. Maybe I should deck him. New policy, deck all men who are asshats." Downing my drink, I ruminate on the thought, but I'm too tired to fight a grown man tonight. "Can you do it, Tiff? I need more trampoline time to be strong enough to take him?"

"We're not going to deck him, Lola. And you'll never be strong enough to 'take him.' What has gotten into you?," Tiffany asks, trying not to laugh. "You've never been to a club with Miller before and he would never say you're a 'Slutty McSlutterson.' No one would ever say that. It's a terrible insult."

"It may not be a direct quote but it is close enough," I state, stomping my foot. "He thinks I'm a desperate whore."

"There is no way he thinks that," Carina interjects.

I can see the moment it clicks for Tiffany that Miller must be the guy from the Club Hedone. When she got back to the apartment the next morning, I told her everything.

"Oh my God," she sputters. "Lola, nooooo. Are you sure?"

"'No,' what? Sure about what?" Carina demands

"I can't do this. I told you I can't do this," I plead at Tiffany. She gives me a soft smile as her eyes shift to the door. I take that as permission to hightail it back to our apartment.

Chapter Thirteen

· BRADY ·

"Dude," Kent says beside me after Lola walks away. "What the fuck was that about?"

"Your guess is as good as mine."

"She was pretty pissed at you," he muses. "She's still fighting mad by the looks of it." He nods over to where Lola is having a heated conversation with her cousin and roommate.

If I wasn't so confused as to what the hell she was going on about, I would find the way she stomps her foot adorable. When I went over and suggested she switch to water, I was doing it out of concern. She has had a lot to drink tonight. It may have been overstepping, but no one else seemed concerned that she was glassy eyed and swaying. The last thing she needed was more alcohol. I was going to offer to grab her some food before she bit my head off. Nothing she was saying made sense.

I had no idea a simple suggestion that she drink water would evoke such a strong response. The more I think about it, the more out of pocket it is. I may not be the most congenial guy out there, but no one would call me mean. Aloof maybe, but not mean. Even on the field, I play fair and keep my composure. I am never the hot head who acts without thinking.

Even more confusing than her calling me mean is her saying she wouldn't be a 'dirty little slut or greedy whore' for me. That was way out of left field. If I spent an entire day thinking about words to describe Lola, slut and whore would never even enter my mind. She and her innocent doe eyes are begging to be coddled, not degraded.

As I watch her flee Kent's apartment, I wonder if she has someone to take care of her tonight. With how much she drank, there is no way she isn't going to be sick. And Tiffany didn't follow her out.

"Brady Miller!" a shrill voice yells beside me. I turn around to see a glaring Carina and sheepish Tiffany. "Did you call my cousin a Slutty McSlutterson?"

"What?" I rear back. "A slutty mc-what? No, I would never call anyone that."

"Did you call her any names?"

"I'm pretty sure the only 'name' I have ever called her is 'sweet girl,'" I answer indignantly. "What is happening here?"

"Lola said you tried to fuck her at a club and that you think she's a Slutty McSlutterson," the fiery Italian says.

"You know I don't go to clubs, and I would never call a woman a derogatory term like that, especially not someone as sweet as Lola. I don't think anyone would call someone a Slutty McSlutterson. That isn't even a thing. I have no idea where she got that idea from."

"I might," Tiffany pipes in.

"Care to explain?" I inquire, more annoyed by the second by the accusation.

She shifts awkwardly under the attention we've attracted. "Maybe in private?"

I nod my head and follow her into Kent's guest bedroom. "Explain." I demand once the door is closed.

She lets out a breath. "Alright, I am going to ask you some questions first to make sure I'm right and you're not going to be a jerk about it."

"Why is everyone acting as if I'm a dick tonight?" I mutter.

"I think you're a nice guy, but if I am right, then this is a massive misunderstanding that doesn't put you in the best light."

"Ask," I command.

"You're a part owner of Club Hedone, correct?" I nod. It's not exactly a secret but I don't go around advertising it.

"And sometimes you play at the club?"

"Yes, but I haven't played since right before spring training."

"And how did that go?" Tiffany inquires, hesitantly.

"I don't see what my private encounters have to do with this situation," I retort.

"Indulge me."

"Fine, it didn't go well."

"Why?"

"That is none of your business, Tiffany. And it has nothing to do with Lola."

"It could..."

"Can you get to the point please?" I bark, pinching the bridge of my nose.

"I see you aren't going to connect the dots yourself," she huffs. "Fine. When we first moved here, I may have convinced Lola that the best way to get over her jerkwad of an ex was to get dicked down by a sexy, take-control hunk. It was a good idea, except things didn't go as planned."

As the sentence comes out of her mouth, I make the connection. "No way," I stammer. "No way, that girl had long hair."

She rolls her eyes, "A haircut, really? That's what kept you from recognizing her? That is the only difference. I don't know how you didn't notice. Those masks weren't *that* effective. Though she didn't realize it at first, either."

"Fuck. FUCK!" I shout, pacing and no longer hearing her. "I never even put her and Club Hedone in the same brain wave. I'd never have thought she went there. How long have you known? How long has she known?"

"I put it together after she said the thing about you trying to have sex with her at a club. I'm not sure when she put it together. It had to be sometime between when we moved and tonight."

"Fuck. That night was a total mixup. Someone switched up the files by accident."

"They called and told us that but I'm not sure she buys it."

"I have to talk to her. I can't let her go on thinking I treated her that way on purpose or that I would ever treat a woman like that without her consent. I wanted to fix it that night, but she was gone when I got back."

"Yeah, fleeing is kind of her thing," she remarks.

"What's your apartment number?"

"You want to talk to her now?" she squeaks.

"Yes, she's upset now and she shouldn't be alone with how much she drank. I need to make sure she's okay. I won't be able to rest until I do."

"Fine. Here's my key. I'll grab the spare from Carina. Don't make it worse or I will put a curse on you and your bat."

"Thank you. You'll be okay getting back later, right? Kent can walk you."

"God," she giggles. "You really are nice. It makes this thing all the more comical."

"Nothing about this is funny," I deadpan.

"Give it a month. We'll revisit that assessment." She waves me off and I head upstairs to check on the woman who has been occupying my mind for months.

Using Tiffany's key, I let myself into the girls' apartment. The unit opens into the kitchen and living room. While the apartment is filled with Robby's old furniture, it has a distinct feminine flair. The couch has approximately three too many pillows, and the room has more throw blankets than places to sit.

There are two doors next to each other leading to what I assume are their bedrooms. Taking a gamble, I head to the door closest to me. When I approach, I hear quiet crying. Knocking lightly on the door, I call out to her. "Lola, are you okay in there?"

"Go away, you big jerk!" she yells.

"I can't do that, doll. I know you're upset, but we need to talk and clear some things up. We don't have to do that tonight, but I at least want to make sure you're okay. I'm gonna come in."

Inside, I find her burrowed under the covers in the dark. I leave the door cracked to let in some light and hopefully make her feel less trapped. It's a fairly spacious room, but I'm still a pretty big guy and don't want my presence to make her uncomfortable.

"Lola," I cajole. Seeing her curled up in her bed makes something tighten in my chest. She looks vulnerable and small, especially since I can pretty much only see her face, everything else hidden by her comforter.

"Don't, Miller. I can't do this right now," she cries.

"Do what?"

"Let you be a meanie. I gotta learn to deck. Maybe Charlie can help me," she grumbles. Who the fuck is Charlie? And what does building a deck have to do with this? I don't like the idea of some other guy teaching her how to do anything.

When I don't respond right away, she continues. "Papa Bear Miller, nice to everyone but Lola. Lola gets the grumpy, mean bear," she sniffles.

"I wasn't mean to you on purpose, sweet girl."

"No. Not 'sweet girl.' Dirty whore," she mocks petulantly in a deep voice that I think is supposed to be an imitation of mine.

"You're not a dirty whore, baby. No one is. It's just a name that some people enjoy being called. It's part of a scene, not what their partner truly thinks of them. I would never think you were a whore or

75

a slut or any of the things I said that night. If the right match had gone in, he would've realized that the information was wrong."

This declaration causes her to jolt up and face me. "What do you mean right match? My match didn't show up? They didn't want me so they sent you to barely want me instead?"

"No, no. Who wouldn't want you? The guy who was matched to you wasn't able to make it. He never even saw your information. They asked me to step in, but your file got mixed up with someone else's. Someone who enjoyed degradation and punishment. I was honestly surprised they matched me to that file since it isn't my usual type. I'm not into degradation. I am more into giving praise. I'm not a hard Dom like who should've been matched to that file."

She eyes me suspiciously. "So, you didn't want to be mean to me?"

"No, Lola, I would never be mean to you on purpose. I thought it's what you wanted until you started to cry. That's when I realized something was wrong."

Taking a risk, I sit down on the bed and slowly lift my hands to her face to wipe a lone tear off her cheek. "I hate seeing you upset, doll. I'd rather take a 100mph fastball to the gut than ever be the reason you cry again."

"I liked you," she whispers. "Before I found out you were mean."

"Accidentally mean," I correct.

"Accidentally mean," she sighs, leaning into my touch. "Miller?"

"Yeah?"

"You might have to tell me this again tomorrow, because I don't think I'm going to remember it."

"I can do that."

"Okay, good," she says before grabbing the vase beside her bed and hurling into it.

I spend the rest of the night taking care of Lola. Somewhere between cleaning up her puke and her nuzzling into my arms, I decide that she's the piece I have been missing. This girl was meant to be mine and I'm going to do whatever it takes to get her.

Chapter Fourteen

• LOLA •

I don't think my body has ever felt this weighed down. My head is pounding as if a polar bear is sitting on it. And not that skinny one we've all seen pictures of. No, this is a chunky, well fed polar bear unaffected by climate change. I think there also may be a boa constrictor around my waist. When I go to push it off in my groggy state, I realize it is, in fact, not a snake, but an arm.

Peering down, I see a muscular, veiny forearm that armporn accounts dream they were. Those thoughts are quickly replaced by panic because I have absolutely no clue who this arm belongs to. When I sense the person behind me stir, I hold my breath and dig into last nights' memories. It's a little hazy, but I remember someone following me back to my room and arguing with me.

I also think I remember them holding my hair back while I vomited what had to have been everything I have ever consumed in my life. Oh my God. I don't know what is worse, that this unknown man saw me throw up or that I don't remember what happened after that.

"Breathe," the source of my panic mumbles from behind me. "You're okay, sweet girl."

That name registers in my mind. Miller. He's the only one who calls me that even though I have no idea why. I haven't been that sweet to him since I realized he was the guy from the club. I take in a deep breath once I realize I at least know the person who has me pulled tight against his chest but it is only a small relief.

"Miller?" I whisper.

"Yeah, doll?"

"Why are you in my bed?"

"How much do you remember from last night?" he asks.

"Um, not nearly as much as I wish I did. What – did we – oh my God, did I throw up in front of you?"

The chest I'm pressed against rumbles in a laugh. "You might have gotten a little sick which isn't surprising considering you tried to out drink the entire party."

"I am so embarrassed. Please tell me I didn't make a mess everywhere."

"I could but I try not to lie."

I groan.

"Don't worry, I cleaned up after I got you back into bed. I did change you out of your dress, though. I figured you didn't want to sleep in your own vomit all night."

"Kill me now," I cry into my pillow.

"It's okay, doll. You're not the first person I've helped after they drank too much and you are way cuter than Kent after blowing your grits."

"What are you still doing here?" I question.

"For one, you asked me not to leave. You said you didn't want to be alone."

"Oh."

"Yeah, oh. Second, I figured you may not remember everything we discussed last night. I want to make sure we're on the same page so you don't go back to avoiding me. I'm guessing you don't remember, and we need to rehash the conversation?"

"Do we have to? Can't we forget all of this ever happened?"

"We could, but I don't want to."

"Why not?" I whine.

Instead of answering me right away, he rolls us so he is on top of me peering down. I shiver at the change in position. He gives me an indulgent smile as if he is thrilled by my reaction and the previous nights' event. Even barely awake he looks like a freaking God. I notice that he's still in the clothes he had on at the party and he's on top of the covers. It was thoughtful of him not to crawl into bed with me in his underwear. It makes me more confident assuming nothing happened between us.

After surveying the scene, I meet his eyes and see he is still grinning at me. Though, it now has a cocky edge, as if he could hear my thoughts.

"I don't want to forget what happened," he says, "because I want us to move forward. If we have this weird awkward situation between us, that will never happen.

"I said it last night, but I will tell you again. There was a mix up at the club and your file got switched with someone else's who was into degradation. I was surprised they matched me with you because that is not my thing but I figured they knew I could be adaptable. I should've noticed you were uncomfortable way sooner, but I didn't and that is all on me.

"I don't think you're any of the things I said to you. I didn't think them then and I don't think them now. In fact, I don't think them about any woman. Degradation is a sexual preference and there is nothing shameful or wrong about that as long as it is between two consenting parties.

"Despite the difference in preferences, I was drawn to you that night and was upset that I wasn't able to make things right once I realized what happened."

I scoff. "Of course, you were drawn to me, I was half naked and there to be fucked."

"No," he admonished. "I was drawn to you even before you took your dress off. Something about you made me want to bundle you up and whisper sweet nothings in your ear while I made you cry out in pleasure. The desire was quite at odds with the instructions I was given and the fact that I made you cry in other ways.

"I've also felt a pull to you – *Lola*, not mystery sex partner – since I met you that first day in the elevator. I thought you were adorable and sexy without even trying. You had this sweet personality that I want to bask in and these sad eyes I want to make shine again.

"I know this is a lot to process and may seem like it's coming out of nowhere, so I'll give you some time – not a lot, but some. But make no mistake, sweet girl. I have every intention of making you mine."

"Yours?" I respond, confused.

"Yeah, baby, mine. Now, how about we get some breakfast? You need food to soak up all that crap you drank last night."

"I'm not sure that's a good idea," I admit.

It is," he replies confidently. I go to argue but he puts his finger to my lips and tips my chin up to his forcing me to meet his eyes.

"Here's what is going to happen. You're going to drink the glass of water I left on your nightstand and take some Tylenol before hopping in the shower. I'm going to head to my place and do the same. In thirty minutes, I'll be back at your door to take you to get a greasy breakfast that will refresh you more than any other hangover cure can.

"While there, we can talk more about last night, what happened at the club, or simply get to know each other – whatever you need to feel comfortable moving forward. Then I'll bring you home and walk you back to your door before going to the gym. Tonight, I will text you and make plans for when we can get together again."

"Why are you telling me all this?" I ask hesitantly.

"Because I don't want you to overthink. I am a straightforward guy. When I decide I want something, I go for it. I don't do things in half measures. I'm sure of this, but I've had time to sit on it and you haven't. I don't want you worrying about me or my intentions. I plan to always make them crystal clear. I want you. I want to get to know you, to spend time with you, and to see if this, us, could be as good as I think. You got me?"

"Um, yes?"

"Not very convincing, but I'll take it for now. Can you be ready in half an hour?"

Dazed by his confession and assertiveness, I nod.

"Good girl, be back soon," he declares as he kisses my head and leaves the room.

It takes a few minutes of sitting there for me to process what the hell happened. I drink the water and take the pills before going to shower. While hot water washes away the shit show that was last night, I wonder what I have gotten myself into.

An hour later, Miller and I are sitting together eating the best chicken fried chicken I have ever had at a cute but casual restaurant on 12th South.

"Good?" he asks, watching as I pop a tater tot in my mouth.

Blushing, I nod as he smiles at me, pleased.

"I'm surprised you're eating this," I observe.

"Why is that?"

"From what I've heard you're pretty strict on your diet and don't stray much during the season."

"What you've heard, huh?" He smirks. "You're right, though. I usually eat clean but I do occasionally allow myself to eat off plan when it's worth it."

"And this greasy brunch food is worth it?"

"Meh. Don't get me wrong, the food is amazing but wouldn't necessarily be my first choice for a cheat meal."

"Then why are you eating it?"

"I know better than to make a girl eat alone. And you, my sweet girl, needed greasy food. I would've eaten McDonald's if that is what you wanted."

"That is nice of you."

"Most people would say I'm a nice guy. Although, I've heard someone is spreading a rumor that I eat people's faces off," he comments with amusement in his eyes.

"Weird," I choke.

"Yeah, weird." After quietly eating for a few minutes, he speaks again. "I think I made it pretty clear at your place this morning but in case I didn't, I'm planning to pursue you, Lola. I figure you won't make it easy on me. That's okay. I'm up for the challenge. But I need to know if you're interested because the last thing I want to do is make you uncomfortable or push you into something you don't want. It would be a waste of both our time."

Clearing my throat I reply, "I'm not *not* interested. But there are some things you should probably know about me."

"Lay it on me."

Staring down at my plate I try to figure out exactly how much I want to tell him. Before I begin, he grabs my hand in his, forcing me to peer up at his soft expression. "I know I'm putting a lot on you right now. We don't have to go through everything today. I think it would be good to lay our cards on the table now, but just know there isn't much you can say that will change my mind about you."

He says that, but I don't know if I believe him. I've got more baggage than an Amtrak. If my husband could change his mind about me, there is no reason he couldn't, too. As I consider how much I want to tell him, my mouth decides to go all in.

"I'm married," I blurt out.

"Married?"

"Well, kind of."

"How can someone be kind of married?"

"When they left their husband and filed for divorce."

"So, you're separated," he corrects. "Permanently?"

"Yes, God yes."

"Do you want to tell me what happened? It's okay if you don't."

"Yeah," I reply, "I think I do. But maybe not here."

Chapter Fifteen

• BRADY •

After paying for brunch, I lead Lola out to my truck and help her into the passenger side. She shoots me a bewildered expression as if assisting her is a crazy thing to do, but doesn't comment. I round the back to give myself a few extra seconds to think. I knew she was going through a break up, but I guess I didn't imagine it was a divorce. I have several questions swirling in my head, but I know I need to hear her out first.

After driving for a few minutes, I pull into Centennial Park. When she goes to open her door, I give my head a quick shake before walking around to open it for her. One thing she's going to learn quickly is that I'll be the one opening doors, if I'm around. I may be a little rough around the edges, but my mama raised a gentleman.

Taking her hand, I lead us over to a bench nestled into a crop of trees. It gives the illusion of being in public but offers the privacy this conversation is going to need. "This work?" I ask.

"Yes, this is nice." She smiles. Taking a deep breath, she launches into her story.

"I met Phil when I was a freshman in college. He was a junior and showered me with the attention I never received growing up. My dad worked a lot and my mom left when I was around four. Anyway, we had that classic college love story. Dated for the rest of my time in college while he went to work for his dad's company. After I graduated, he proposed, and we got married. I thought I finally had the makings of the tight-knit family I always craved.

"The past few years, we were growing further and further apart. We got stuck in this routine and our relationship became more platonic, except without the friendship part. He was suddenly uninterested and unwilling to discuss expanding our family until he reached specific goal posts which kept moving. Late last year, I caught him cheating on me with someone from work and I left. I moved here and filed for divorce a few months later.

"I should be more upset that a relationship I put almost a decade into is over, but honestly, I'm relieved. I'm now free to pursue a life that genuinely makes me happy and not only appears happy from the outside. Him being the one to mess up took away the guilt of not being content with a perfectly nice life. The kind many women dream of. I always wondered if there was something more and now I have the chance to explore that."

Taking a beat, I process the information she gave me. I'm mostly stuck on the fact that her dipshit of a husband would cheat on someone as perfect as her. I mean objectively speaking, she is stunning and I've never met a sweeter person – when she isn't avoiding me and telling people I'm a jerk, that is. Someone should kick his ass for hurting her. I'd do it myself, but I'm not exactly mad I have the opportunity to gain what he lost.

Realizing I still haven't said anything, I respond, "I can empathize with what you're saying. Though, playing ball has always been my dream and I've been working at it since I was in high school. But I went through phases of discovering who I was outside of it once I settled into my career. That's partially how I got involved with the club.

"I'm sorry your husband cheated on you. Even if you weren't in love with him anymore, I can imagine you still feel betrayed by someone who was supposed to have your back."

"Yeah," she says with a soft smile. "Walking in on your husband and his brother banging a secretary is definitely embarrassing."

"Jesus, both of them? And you walked in on it?"

"At least he couldn't pull a Shaggy and tell me it wasn't him," she laughs humorlessly. "Hard to gaslight what I can see with my own eyes."

Her expression is tighter than it was moments ago, and I can see the sadness in her eyes. I'm not about to let this guy take away any more of her light. I tuck a strand of hair behind her ear and allow my thumb to softly caress her cheek.

"Your ex is an idiot who never deserved you. I hate that he didn't see what a gift you are, but I don't hate that now I have the chance to prove it to you. You were too good for him," I say.

"You've never even met him. How can you say that?"

"Don't need to meet him. The fact that he fumbled a woman like you tells me everything I need to know about the unfaithful douche nozzle."

"Douche nozzle, that's a good one," she remarks. "I'll have to tell Georgie that one. We've been going with pencil prick. And you don't even want to hear Tiffany's terms of endearment."

I cringe. "Yeah, I don't think I do. She's got a colorful imagination and wicked mouth on her. She'd have made a good pirate."

That comment earns me the first genuine smile I've seen since we started this conversation. Before I move on to my confessions, I need to know a little bit more about Lola's technical relationship status.

"To clarify, you're legally separated, right?"

"Yes, absolutely," she rushes out. "Everything is filed, and a date is set for the divorce hearing. My attorney is handling everything. I'm hoping we can get it all straightened out and I should be able to sign the papers and put it all behind me without having to go to court."

"Anything I can help with?" I ask.

She gifts me another one of her breathtaking smiles. "That's sweet of you to offer, but no. I need to do this by myself. Close the door on that chapter of my life, you know?"

"I can understand that. But know I'm here if you change your mind or need someone to vent to."

"Why would you want that?"

"Want what?"

"To hear me talk about my ex and old relationship baggage?" she asks, bewildered.

"Lola, I know I've said this already, but I'm interested in you. I understand – given the recency of your situation – if you want to take it slow and I can absolutely do that. But I am always there for the people I care about and if that means hearing about your dickwad ex, I will. I may have to hold myself back from finding him and punching him in the face, but I will try to find that strength for you," I tease with a wink.

"As for the baggage, it makes you who you are. We all have it. I know I've got stuff that shaped me into who I am. Speaking of, there are a few things you should know about me before you decide if you want to give this thing between us a shot. My offer for help stands, regardless."

"Okay..." she wavers.

"First, you should know that the reason I was at Club Hedone isn't only because I am a member, I am also an owner."

"I may have heard that before," she replies sheepishly. "Though I am not entirely sure what that entails. Do you work there? I assume you meet women there."

"Yes and no. I am not an employee, but I do help out from time to time like the night we met. I also meet with the other owners every couple of months and occasionally play."

"You're a Dom?" she asks.

"Not exactly. At least not in the way many of the club's members are. I am dominant, especially in the bedroom. I can also be outside it. Not in a '24/7 rules/punishment dynamic' way, but in an 'I want to support and take care of my partner' way. Though, to be honest, I haven't had a steady partner in a while and I have never had one from the club.

"I've been told I'm a bossy bastard. I will make a lot of decisions without consulting you. Not because I don't value your opinion, but because I know I'm making the right choice and it doesn't occur to me to ask you. I'm used to being in control and making decisions. It's how I became one of the youngest captains in the MLB."

"What decisions will you make?" she questions.

"For example, I'll always be the one to drive us anywhere we go. You driving is an option that won't even occur to me."

"That's okay. I don't mind if you drive."

"That's one example. There are many more. Like when we're out together, I am always going to want you to be somewhere that I can see you. Some might call me possessive, but I prefer protective. If I can't see you, I don't know if you're okay or if someone is bothering you."

"So, you're the jealous type?"

"Not at all. My girl can wear whatever she wants, talk to whoever she wants, do whatever she wants as long as no one else touches what's mine. I don't want to stop her from doing what she wants. All I want is to make sure she is safe while doing it. She wants to tease me a bit and try to rile me up – that's fine. I have a long memory and will make her pay for it later."

"How will you make her pay?" she wonders out loud. The blush on her cheek tells me she didn't mean to.

Deciding to test the waters, I lean over and whisper against her ear, "I'm not sure you're ready for that, but I'll tell you, anyway. There are lots of ways I can make her pay for teasing me. I could spank her cute little ass red before fucking her hoarse. I could tie her up and edge her all night until she crying for release. Or I could give her the attention she must have been craving and eat her pussy until she's begging me to stop and then make her give me one more. There are many available payback methods, sweet girl." I kiss the spot right below her ear and smile when she shivers against my lips.

Shaking herself out of her lusty haze, she asks, "What if someone touches what's yours?"

Running a finger up and down her arm, I reply honestly, "If someone touches you, then he and I will have a problem. What happens depends on how he reacts to me letting him know that you're off limits."

I expect that to scare her a little, but her pupils dilate and breath quickens.

"We've gotten a bit off track," I admit. "After everything we've discussed, is this still something you are interested in doing? If you want me to, I will back off. But I am hoping you'll say yes and let me show you how good being mine can be."

"I'm not sure if I'm ready to belong to anyone but myself right now, but I think I want to see where this leads. We'll go slow?" she questions.

"Glacial, baby. Whatever you need, as long as you're giving me a chance."

"Okay, I want to try."

My chest constricts with her declaration and I can't stop myself from leaning in and finally tasting her lips. If I thought I wanted this girl before, this seals it. The way she melts against me into the kiss has my heart soaring. Slowly but firmly I swipe my tongue across her mouth, asking for permission to deepen the kiss. I won't always be this gentle, but I can tell right now this is what she needs. She grants me access and meets me stroke for stroke but never fights me for dominance.

When I pull away we are both breathless. "Come on, doll, let's get you home. You can nap off the rest of that hangover."

Chapter Sixteen

• LOLA •

True to his word, Miller starts pursuing me. Slowly. Glacial was definitely the right description for it. Despite that, or maybe because of it, I've found myself drawn more and more to him. He's got this quiet confidence and strength about him. He's self assured. It's almost as if I can soak up some of his confidence simply being in his presence.

Not that I've been around him much. In the two and a half weeks since our talk, I've only seen him a handful of times, thanks to a Songbirds' road trip. The distance hasn't kept him from showing up where it counts, though. Every morning I wake up to a text from him telling me to have a good day and asking what I'm up to. Most nights, he's called me to talk about our days and whatever random topics come up.

His attention to detail astounds me. Not only does he ask about the things we texted about, but he also remembers things we discussed days prior and asks about that, too. Phil didn't even ask how something was while I was doing it, let alone remember something I told him about days before.

His thoughtfulness went even further than words, though. He is a man of action. He sent me gifts to let me know he was thinking of me. The day after our conversation at the park, I received a beautiful bouquet and brand-new vase to replace the one I may or may not have puked in. When he discovered I loved unique coffee flavors, I woke up to an iced latte and a selection of mini syrups delivered to my door.

His presence in my life has provided a consistency and steadiness I didn't realize I was missing. With Phil, I was constantly wondering what version of him I would get. With Miller, it's always the same. Whether his day was good or bad, he treats me the same and that is the most unexpected gift.

Tonight is the first time I'm going to see him in almost a week. I'm rushing around town trying to get everything done for work and the blog before he gets back. As I'm leaving my workout class, the sky opens up and a summer thunderstorm rolls in.

"Lola, wait!" Charlie shouts. "Are you sure you're going to be okay driving home in this? I know you said it was a little hard to see in your car the last time it rained. You might need new windshield wipers."

"I'll be fine," I dismiss. "It's only a five-minute drive."

It ends up being much harder to see than I expected, which has me fiddling with the defroster to clear up my windshield as much as I can. By the time I pull into the parking garage, I've all but given up. I'm surprised when I see a familiar truck pulling into a spot a few down from me.

"Hi!" I say excitedly, jumping out of my car. It only takes a few strides before Miller is to me and has me wrapped up in a hug with a chaste kiss on the lips.

"Hey, sweet girl. Fancy meeting you here."

"You're home sooner than expected," I observe.

"Yeah, with the storm brewing, management decided we should

leave early to beat it. What's with your car? If I didn't know any better, I'd say two teenagers were making out in the back and steaming up the windows."

"Ha, wouldn't that be awkward?" I reply. "It was kinda hard to see on the drive over. I was playing with the defrost setting, trying to clear up the windshield."

He walks over to my car and inspects it before turning back to me. "Your wiper blades are worn down, baby. You need new ones. When was the last time you replaced them?"

"Charlie mentioned that might be the case, too." I notice his jaw tighten as I continue my answer. "Um... is that something that happens when you get your oil changed?"

"No, it's not," he says with a slight shake of his head. "I'm gonna take that as you don't know."

Avoiding his eyes, I toe the ground as I admit, "I've never handle car stuff. My dad always did that for me and then, ya know, Phil."

"Right," I hear him reply. Gentle fingers touch my chin and bring my eyes up to his. "Don't worry, baby. I'll take care of it for you."

"You don't have to do that! I'm sure I can figure it out. I'll take it to the shop next week."

"It's supposed to rain for the next several days. I can't have you driving around with bad wipers. It's not safe. Don't worry. I'll have you fixed up before our date tonight," he declares as he guides me inside.

"Wait, are you sure? I can handle it. I'm a big girl."

"You are, but you already admitted you've never handled car stuff before. I'd feel better if you'd let me do it. That way I'll know that it's done right and timely. Call it one of those protective things."

"Okay," I breathe. "If you're sure."

"I'm sure," he says with an expression so earnest I can't help but give him whatever he wants.

A few hours later, I head down to Miller's condo where he has dinner waiting. We had plans to go out, but with the storm still raging outside and his long away trip, a night in sounded like the better choice.

"Oh my God, this is delicious," I say with a mouthful of sesame chicken.

"Baby, you gotta stop making sex noises while you eat. It's incredibly distracting."

I blush hard. "I'm sorry. I didn't mean to ruin your appetite."

"Ruin my appetite? I have never been hungrier." The lust in his eyes tells me exactly what type of hunger he means.

"Your blush is so fucking cute," he comments, running a finger down my cheek. "Tell me, how was your weekend? I didn't have the chance to talk to you much today or yesterday."

"It was good. I finished a piece on Fourth of July celebrations for the magazine and wrote one with party tips for the blog."

"Sounds like you were busy. Do anything else?"

"Just my trampoline class. I need to try a different style of workout, but it's fun and Charlie is the best instructor. I've never felt that good while sweating."

He makes a disgruntled sound at my admission. "What?" I question.

"Nothing. You and Charlie seem to have hit it off. How many classes do you go to in a week?"

"Only two, but Charlie sometimes joins me when I have to go places for the magazine if Carina and Tiffany can't."

"You and Charlie spend time together outside of the gym?" he asks tightly. I'm picking up hostility from him, which I don't understand. Does he not want me to have friends outside of our group? Because I've already lived that life and that will be a problem.

"Of course, we do. We're friends. We went shopping together the other day and picked out a dress I think you're *really* going to love," I reply, trying to change the subject to a happier one.

"Jesus, you tried on clothes in front of him? Listen, I know we haven't put a hard label on this or anything, but I am not okay with you being half-dressed around people who also want you. I don't share."

"Ugh, you sound like Tiffany. Charlie is not into me. Trust me."

"You I trust," he states. "Charlie, not as much. I know how men are when they see a woman they think is vulnerable. I'm friends with Kent for Chrissake. He's never met a girl with daddy issues he hasn't tried to fill."

"What are you talking about? First off, I am not vulnerable. Second, I do not have daddy issues."

He sighs, exasperated. "I'm not saying you have daddy issues, Lola. But you have to admit you are a little vulnerable. You're in a new place on this journey of self-discovery, which has you open to new experiences and people. I don't want someone like Charlie to take advantage of that."

"Someone like *Charlie*? What the hell does that mean?" I all but shout. "I may be open to some new things, but I am not that open, Brady Miller. I have no interest in playing for the other team."

He puts down the fork he was clutching and stares at me with a confused expression. "Other team? What are you talking about?"

"Charlie! Being friends with a lesbian doesn't mean I'm going to turn into one."

"Charlie is a woman?" he questions, dumbstruck.

"Yes. Why else would I ask for her advice on dresses? If I wanted a man's opinion, I would ask you or maybe—" Before I can finish, he is bent over laughing.

"What's so funny?" I demand.

"I'm sorry, sweet girl. I thought Charlie was a man. To be honest, I was jealous of all the time he was spending with you while I was away," he says, wiping the tears that formed in his eyes from laughing."

"I thought you didn't get jealous," I tease.

"I don't usually, but something about you has me twisted up in knots. The thought of another man seeing you all sweaty in your

94

workout classes and then watching you try on dress after dress was too much for me. Forgive me?"

I should be mad at him, but I find his reaction endearing. Phil's brother used to flirt with me in front of him, and he never said anything about it. I want to play this out a little longer, but he's pulled me into his lap and is nuzzling his nose down the side of my face and neck.

"I guess I could be persuaded to forgive you," I murmur.

"Persuaded, huh? I've been known to be very, very persuasive," he says, nipping at my shoulder. As he continues to speak, his hands trail down my body, caressing the side of my breasts, giving them the barest touches. One lands on my waist, sliding up and down my curves, while the other trails down my thigh, rubbing gentle circles.

"You said something else that made me jealous, doll."

"What was that?" I ask breathily as his thumb grazes my inner thigh. His touch is so close to the edge of my panties that my mind is clouded with need.

"You said you've never felt that good while sweating. I'm a pretty competitive guy. It's hard not to take that as a challenge."

"A challenge?"

"Yup," he replies as his thumb finds my center over my shorts and swipes softly. "I think maybe it's time I demonstrate how good of a workout I can give you."

Next thing I know, my legs are wrapped around his waist and he's carrying me to the couch and laying me down. Leaning over me, he puts his hand on my waistband and flits his gaze to mine for permission to take them off. Whatever expression I give him is enough for him to slowly peel them down my legs.

With my shorts gone, his breath ghosts up my thighs, skipping over my mound. He kisses and nibbles his way up my stomach, lifting my shirt as he goes. Eventually, he makes it to my breasts and sucks my cleavage enough that I know there will be a mark tomorrow. My nipples pebble underneath the thin material of my bralette – something that doesn't go unnoticed. With a wicked gleam in his eye, he sucks one nipple into his mouth through the fabric and flicks the other with the hand not tracing up and down my torso.

"Brady," I moan.

"Fuck, baby. I love hearing you say my name," he growls before ripping my shirt over my head. With little effort, he pulls my bra off, too. I'm splayed on the couch in only my panties, panting from his ministrations. "This sight is familiar," he teases.

"Almost," I say, tugging on his shirt. He chuckles as he reaches a hand behind his head and pulls off the grey t-shirt that had been covering his ripped torso all night. I reach out and run my fingers down his chest and abs, only for him to groan and flex his muscles beneath them. His skin is hot and hard beneath my fingertips.

"If your hands get to explore, so do mine," he remarks before taking my lips into a searing kiss. It's nothing close to the kisses we've shared over the past couple of weeks. Those have been sweet and playful. This kiss is passionate and a little frantic, but still controlled. I wonder what I'd have to do for him to lose control.

He uses his nose to nudge my head back, allowing him to deepen the kiss. His tongue sweeps against mine, the taste of citrus and whiskey from our meal mix with one that is uniquely him. His hands return to my nipples now free of their cotton prison, and he rolls them between his thumb and finger.

"God, I've been dreaming about these nipples. I didn't get the chance to play with them the first time."

"Miller," I moan again. "More."

"Brady, baby. You call me Brady." His mouth begins to suck on my neck as his hand snakes between my legs. The other hand spreads me wide beneath him. He rubs a few circles on the outside of my panties before slipping below them. I should be embarrassed by how wet I am, but I can't find it in myself to feel anything but need.

"You want more? I can give you more. Shit, you're soaked. You turned on by me touching your body, Lola?"

I squirm beneath him before a soft swat hits my thigh. "Answer me."

"Yes, yes. I'm wet for you."

"Mmm, good girl. Let's find out how wet you really are." His lips slide down to one of my nipples and he flicks it with his tongue while rubbing up and down my slit, exploring my arousal. With little preamble, he sucks my nipple into his mouth as one finger slips inside me. I gasp at the intrusion, which only spurs him to add another.

Brady groans as he thrusts his fingers inside of me. "So fucking tight," he murmurs. His fingers hit something inside me that cause me to make a guttural noise that I'm not fully convinced came from me.

"You feel this spot, baby?" he asks as he pumps his fingers in and out of me, curling them to brush against my inner wall again.

"Yes," I breathe. Because I do feel it. And it feels fucking amazing.

"This is the spot I'm gonna hit over and over when I finally take you. This is the spot I'm going to rub with my cock again and again as you moan and writhe underneath me. I'm going to thrust into this spot until your body shakes and you come all over my cock. But first..."

Throughout his speech, he massages that newfound pleasure center. If this is how good he is with his hands, I can't imagine how amazing he is with his cock. His dirty words trail off, almost as if he is distracted by my reactions. Then he speeds up his movements and continues to hit that magic spot.

"Bradyyyyyyy," I mewl.

"But first, you're going to be a good girl and come all over my fingers. Come on my fingers, baby, and then maybe I'll give you my cock."

That is all the encouragement I need to shatter as his hand moves inside me. My orgasm is so powerful, I black out for a second. When I return to myself, his fingers slowly work inside me, helping me ride out my pleasure. He kisses the side of my head, telling me what a good job I did and how sexy it was to see me come.

He pulls out his fingers and slips them into his mouth. Holy hell.

"God, you taste even better than I imagined," he groans.

"You've imagined *that*?" I gasp.

"Hell yeah, I have. I thought about it when I saw you in those tiny panties at the club, when I 'met' you in the elevator, and when I tasted your lips for the first time. I want to taste every inch of your perfect body. Is that such a surprise?"

"It's just, I've never..." as I search for an explanation, realization dawns on his face.

"Has no one ever eaten this delicious pussy?" Too embarrassed to answer with words, I shake my head. He takes a steadying breath filled with equal parts annoyance and excitement.

"God, your ex is a prick. You're going to have to wait to get my cock, sweet girl."

"What? Why?" He doesn't want me now that he knows the other men I've had sex with are selfish assholes?

"I love how bad you want it," he laughs. "But there is something I need to do more than fuck you. I'm going to lick this pretty cunt until you're begging me to stop." He once again swipes his finger through my arousal and sucks it clean. If I hadn't just come, I think that sight alone would have been enough to send me over the edge.

Chapter Seventeen

• BRADY •

I want to say I'm surprised Lola's douche nozzle ex-husband never ate her out, but I'm not. I'm surprised no one has, though. I know they got together young, but I don't think he was her first. Did none of the guys she was with before want to taste her? How could they not want to eat her alive?

Peering into her eyes, I see the reservation intermingle with lust. I know she's about to tell me I don't have to do this, but what she doesn't realize is that I really, *really* do.

"Don't worry, I'm going to take care of you," I coo.

Sliding down her body, I pull her with me on the chaise of my sectional. I yank her down to the edge with her ass barely on the cushion. I sink to my knees, eye level with her delicious center and glimpse up at her before returning my focus to the meal in front of me. Since she's already come once, there is no need to tease her. I dive right in. I groan as her taste bursts onto my tongue and bring my hands down to her thighs, holding her open for me.

"You taste so fucking good," I say between laps on her clit. She's making noises that I can only describe as mewling, which makes me chuckle into her pussy. "You like that? You gonna come all over my tongue and get this pussy nice and soaked for me so my cock will slide right in?"

"Yesssss," she moans. "Brady, pleaseeee."

"Please what, baby? What do you need?"

"I don't-I don't know," she pants.

"That's okay, I do." Gripping her thighs tighter, I focus my attention on her sensitive bud. Sucking it into my mouth, I push my fingers back into her. It only takes a few seconds of suction and swirling my tongue on her clit for her to combust again. I give her a few slow licks as she comes down from her high and rub my hands up and down her legs until the shaking subsides. When she meets my gaze, her eyes are glazed over with satisfaction.

With what I know must be a feral grin, I kiss back up her body before sliding my tongue in her mouth, letting her taste herself. Pushing off my jeans, I sigh in relief that the pressure is off my cock. I reach into my wallet and pull out a condom. "Ready for this, baby?" I ask as I sheath myself.

"Yes," she replies. "Please fuck me."

"That's what I like to hear, sweet girl. But I'm not going to fuck you yet. We're going to go nice and gentle this time. Will you let me do that? Will you let me savor you this first time?" I ask, rubbing my length up and down her pussy, teasing her clit again.

She nods, but I need her words. When I pause my movement, her eyes pop open and she blinks at me before realizing what I want. "Okay," she whispers, and it is all the confirmation I need. With one languid thrust, I am seated inside her. Giving her a moment to adjust to my size, I lean down and kiss her lips, enjoying her pants. I may not be the longest guy in the locker room, but I am one of the thickest. I can't imagine her ex was packing much heat with everything I've heard about him.

"Holy shit," she mutters against my lips. "So big, Brady. Why are you so big?"

I laugh through gritted teeth. "You don't like, baby? It feels like your body fucking loves it if the way your pussy is trying to lock me inside is any indication." I punctuate my words by swiveling my hips and pulsing in and out slightly. Her body loosen around me, allowing more movement.

She doesn't answer with words but her whimper tells me that she loves it, as does the way she tightens her around me, trying to keep me from pulling away. As if I would go anywhere. Being inside her is heaven. It feels like she was made for me.

I slowly start to thrust in and out further, setting a solid rhythm. "Bradddddy," she moans.

"I know, baby, I know. Don't worry. I got you. Hold on tight." Her arms move to my shoulders and she does just that. I sense the telltale sign of her impending orgasm as her pussy flutters around me. "Fuck, you're squeezing me like a vise, baby. Are you going to come again for me, sweet girl? You gonna come on my cock and milk my cum from me?"

"Yessssssss," she screams. "Don't stop, don't stop." And I don't. I keep pumping into her with a steady rhythm. When she is about to tip over the edge, I lean down and suck on the sensitive spot on her neck I noticed early. I give it a nip and that is all it takes to have her shatter around me. The force of her orgasm pulls mine from me and we both lay there, trying to catch our breath.

She winces when I pull out, her legs flopping beside my body. I kiss her lips gently before picking her up and carrying her with me to the bathroom. Once I have us both cleaned up, I scoop her back up.

"I can walk you know," she giggles.

"Are you sure about that? Last time I checked, your legs were Jell-O."

"They might be a little wobbly," she admits with a blush. The fact that she can still be shy after what we just did is fucking precious.

I give her a smirk before sitting her down in my bed with one of my shirts in her hands and pulling on a pair of boxers.

"What are you doing?" she asks.

"Getting ready for bed. I've had a long day and we've both had a long night," I answer.

"Oh," she responds and moves to get up.

"Where do you think you're going?" I question.

"Back to my apartment?"

"I don't think so."

"You don't?" She hesitates. "Why not?"

"Because," I state, "you're staying with me."

"But I live upstairs. There is no reason for me to stay here."

"Yes, there is."

"There is? What is it?"

"Because I want you here. In my bed. With me. There is no chance in hell I'm going to make love to you and then send you on your merry way back to your place. Even if all we did was make out like teenagers on my couch, I had every intention of you spending the night in my bed."

"You did?"

"You always ask this many questions after sex?" I ask, smirking when she flushes.

"No, I just... I don't have that much experience with casual. From what I understand, men enjoy their space. Don't they usually only have women sleeping over because it would be rude to send them home?"

"One, this isn't *casual*. We're dating. You may not be ready to label it, but this is not some casual friends with benefits situation," I declare as I pull her into my lap.

"Two, I may enjoy my space, but I enjoy it even more with you in it. And three, you aren't women. You're you. We've been taking this slow, and we still can. But now that I've felt you come wrapped around my cock and tasted your sweet pussy, you're staying in my bed as much as possible. You'll be lucky if I ever let you leave.

"You recently got out of a serious relationship that ended on bad terms. I can appreciate that, but what we've got going here is *something* and I for one want to see where it goes. I plan to treat it as such.

102

That means you sleep in my bed on nights I make you scream my name and any other nights you want. Any more questions?"

"Just one," she replies. "You told me to call you Brady."

"I did. And that isn't a question."

She rolls her eyes at that before clarifying. "Should I-do you want me to do that all the time? Even in front of people? Also, why don't you want me to call you Miller?"

"That's two questions, but I'll let it slide," I say, kissing her shoulder and skating my nose up to her neck to whisper in her ear. "I want you to call me Brady all the time. Even in front of people. Preferably, even when I'm not there. Miller is who I am to the rest of the world. You're special to me and I want everyone to know it from how we treat each other to how we talk about each other. You're my sweet girl and I'm your Brady – even if you aren't ready to claim me yet. Now, get your ass into that shirt and under those covers so I can spoon you until we both pass out."

"Okay, Brady," she answers with a smile.

Chapter Eighteen

• BRADY •

July

"Papa Bear," I hear Kent singsong as I enter the locker room. "Don't you look fresh as a daisy."

"Fuck off, Dela Cruz," I respond but there is no heat to it. Even these clowns can't tamper my mood.

"I mean it, Cap. You look good this morning. Got that fresh fucked glow on ya. Get some last night?"

"Get me some? What are you, a twenty-year-old frat boy?" I admonish. He isn't wrong. Lola and I have been going strong for a few weeks now. I woke her up this morning with my face between her thighs before popping her on my lap until we both were satisfied and hungry for a real breakfast.

"Don't mind him," Robby says, joining us. "Someone gave him an energy electrolyte pack instead of a normal one. He's extra hyped up."

"Like a kid on a sugar high," I murmur.

"Accurate," Robby laughs. "But I do have to agree with him. You're looking good today. I think it is safe to assume that you and a certain Bunny are getting along?"

"Why do y'all call her Bunny?" I ask, avoiding this line of questioning.

"Lola Bunny. The hot rabbit from Space Jam." Kent states. His expression becomes indignant at my lack of immediate recognition. "Do you live under a rock?"

"I never made that connection. I figured you called her Bunny because Robby has a thing for animal nicknames."

That garners a laugh from Robby. "What?"

"Kitten, Papa Bear, Bunny, all animal names," I note.

"Huh, I never noticed that but no. The Bunny nickname long predates me. I think her friend Georgie came up with it."

"Speaking of nicknames," I say, "I nearly put my foot in my mouth the other night because Lola's workout instructor goes by one."

"What was the name?" Robby inquires.

"Charlie, short for Charlotte not Charles," I reply.

"Ah, and let me guess, Lola and Charlie were doing all kinds of stuff together?"

"Yeah, Charlie is who Lola spends time with when Carina and Tiffany are busy. I may have commented about not wanting her to do those things with another man."

"Wait, I think I've met Charlie. Isn't she a lesbian?" Kent adds to the conversation.

"Yeah."

"How is that any different?"

"Because I know for a fact that Charlie isn't packing the type of equipment Lola needs," I comment with a sly grin.

"Barf," Robby mutters.

"If you didn't end up putting your foot in your mouth, big guy, did you put something else in there?" Kent asks with a waggle of his eyebrows.

"Gross, dude! That is my cousin-in-law. Can we not talk about her sex life?" Robby groans.

"Fuck off, Becker. We've had to deal with your lovesick, sex drunk ass for the past year. But yes, we can. I'm not talking about my girl that way and none of you will either."

"Your girl, huh?" he smirks.

"Yes, my girl. Got a problem with that?" I bite.

"No problem at all Papa Bear. She deserves a guy like you – loyal, steady, and totally gone for her."

Before I can respond to his comment, team asshole, Derrick Jones, pops into the locker room. "You ladies coming? We've got a game to win."

After a solid win against Jacksonville, the whole crew decides to go out to celebrate. I wanted to pick Lola up, but she was already with the girls and they're meeting us there. Instead of Holler's, the group decide to try out one of the bigger honky-tonks on Broadway.

"Where are the girls?" I yell to Robby over the crowd.

"They're by the stage. Carina said they needed refills. Want to grab drinks before we head over?" I nod in agreement.

After a few minutes of back slaps from fans and flirty touches from admirers, we make it to the corner where the group is. The band is playing some 2000s country covers and I see Tiffany and Carina dancing together. I don't immediately see Lola, but when I do, it takes all my restraint not to crush the plastic cups in my hand.

She's standing by our friends but Derrick fucking Jones is talking her ear off and standing too close for my liking. He's lucky he isn't trying to dance with her. She meets my eye over his shoulder and gives me a relieved smile which eases the tension in my chest. Derrick's body is angled to face Lola, so he misses my approach.

When I get to them, I slide behind Lola. She pushes back, closing the distance between her back and my chest, resting her head on me. I lean down to kiss the side of her head and snake my arms around her waist, noting the way Derrick tenses at my presence. Good, fucker. If my body language doesn't get the message across, my words sure as hell will.

"Jones," I rumble. "I see you met my girl."

"Your girl?" he questions, gazing at where our bodies are joined.

"Yeah," I reply. "You didn't think a girl this gorgeous would be single, did you? She didn't mention it?"

"She may have said something about meeting someone here but since I didn't see a goalie, I figured it wouldn't hurt to take a shot," he all but sneers.

"Consider your shot blocked," I deadpan before turning my attention to Lola and ignoring my shithead teammate. "Hi, sweet girl."

"Hi," she greets. "You played great tonight."

"Thank you. I got you a vodka soda."

She takes the drink and smiles up at me. "Is that all you got me?" she asks with a pout.

"Was there something else you needed?" I wonder with a furrowed brow.

"Kiss her, dummy," Tiffany urges from beside us causing Lola to bite her lip and blush.

"Do you want a kiss, doll?" I muse.

"Yes, please."

I skate my hand up her neck until it grasps her nape and my thumb tips her head up. She rises on to her toes and I bend down to meet her for a kiss. From the gasp she gives, she was expecting a sweet peck. That isn't what she gets. I give her a kiss that lets Derrick and every other fucker in this bar know exactly who she belongs to. As my tongue explores her mouth, I pull our bodies tighter together, not stopping until I hear our friends catcalling us.

Lola peers back at me dazed and I can't help but smirk. "Is that what you were hoping for, baby?" After a beat she nods and takes a big gulp of her drink.

For the rest of the night, I keep Lola within arm's reach. The place is crowded. There isn't much room for dancing aside from the little area we've carved out for the girls. After a while, Kent disappears to find his next conquest and Robby and Carina go home. Tiffany whispers something in Lola's ear causing her to giggle while glancing over at me.

"Something you ladies want to share with the class?" I inquire.

"No thanks, big guy," Tiffany quips. "If you two lovelies will excuse me, I have a friend in town from New York to meet. Enjoy the rest of your night."

"Wait," I call out. "Are you sure you're good? I don't want to leave you out here on your own."

"Aren't you the sweetest, Papa Bear. Don't worry about me; she's right over there. But if it will ease your conscious enough to go fuck our girl silly, see for yourself," she says, pointing to someone at the bar. When she spots Tiffany, she makes a beeline for her. "Have a good night, Daddy Miller. Don't do anything I wouldn't do, Lo," she says with a wave.

Rolling my eyes, I wrap up a laughing Lola. "Think that's funny, sweet girl?"

"I mean it's a little funny. You do have some Daddy energy," she comments as we leave the bar. "Wait, is that your thing?" she asks as we walk home. The bar is only a few blocks from our condos and it for once isn't too insufferable outside.

"Is what my thing?"

"Are you a Daddy?"

"No, I'm not a Daddy. Don't you think you would've figured that out by now?"

"I don't know. You sometimes act similar to the Daddies in the books I've read."

"You've been reading Daddy Dom books?" I question, intrigued.

I didn't have Lola being a Little on my bingo card, but I could work with it. She has some Little tendencies.

"I have a well-rounded book collection, thank you very much," she sasses.

"A dirty book collection," I snort. "You let me know if you ever want to reenact any of those scenes. I've got access to pretty much anything you could want to play with."

"You do? Do you have a sex dungeon I didn't notice when I snoo—toured your apartment?"

I laugh at her slip. "You can snoop around my place all you want, Lo. I've got nothing to hide from you. But no, I don't have a sex dungeon. I don't need one, I own a sex club."

"Oh, right," she mumbles, pulling her bottom lip between her teeth.

Stopping at the entrance of our building, I lift her face to mine and remove her lip from her teeth. "What's worrying you, sweet girl?"

"Nothing."

"Lola," I warn. "Communication and honesty are the cornerstone to any relationship. You know that better than anybody."

She huffs out a breath. "Do you miss it?"

"Miss what?"

"The club. Do you miss going there?"

"I still go there," I stupidly remark.

"What?!" She shouts. But instead of letting me answer, she storms inside and towards the elevator. For having such short legs, she is speedy when she wants to be.

"Wait, Lola. Hold up." I manage to stop the doors from closing and get in with her as she punches the number for her floor. I hit mine, too.

"I am not going back to your place with you," she declares.

"Yes, you are. That came out all wrong. Hear me out."

"I don't want to hear about how you go to the club to play with other girls. Ones who are more experienced and give you what I can't."

"What are you talking about?" The elevator is fast approaching my floor and I need to convince her to come with me. "You can either come with me to my place or I can come with you to yours, but we're going to finish this conversation either way. What's it going to be?"

"Fine. Yours, that way I can leave later."

"We'll see." I have no intention of letting her sleep anywhere but in my arms tonight. No misunderstanding is going to change that fact.

With my hand on her back, I lead her into my condo where she stares at me expectantly. "Go on, tell me about all your playthings and why I should be okay with it."

"I don't have playthings, baby."

"Subs, whatever. Semantics are not the thing to discuss right now."

"I don't have subs either. Why would you think that?"

"Why else would you go to a sex club if not to get something you aren't getting from me?"

"I am getting everything I need from you, Lola. Full stop."

"No, you're not."

"Yes, I am," I grit. "What could possibly be missing?"

"I don't know! That's the problem. I am clearly not well-versed in kinky fuckery otherwise you wouldn't need to go to a sex club and I wouldn't have caught my husband mid-spit roast! You're clearly used to having out of the box experiences and everything we have done so far is vanilla."

I push her back against the door and lean down crowding her until we are eye to eye. "Let's get a few things straight right now, doll. You are and always will be enough for me. There is no kinky fuckery I am missing out on. Vanilla is A-OK with me. Are there some things I want to explore with you? Absolutely. But that is as much for you as it is me.

"If you told me you only wanted to have missionary for the rest of our lives, I would be grateful to be the one getting you to make you scream. I don't go to the club to play. I go there to meet with my partners – business partners," I correct quickly. "Nothing else."

"You were there for a meeting the night *we* met," she accuses.

"You're right. I was. And that was the last time I played at the club. I haven't touched anyone but you since that night. I didn't actually touch you that night, so it's been even longer."

"You haven't been with anyone else since you met me?" she asks, softening.

"No," I reply.

"And you don't play with anyone when you've been at the club?"

"Absolutely not."

"How many times?"

"How many times what?"

"How many times have you been to the club and not told me? If 'communication and honesty are the cornerstone of a relationship,' why is this the first I'm hearing about this?"

Shit. She's right. I should have told her. I've only been back once since she and I got together but I didn't tell her. I thought about it, but I didn't want to bring up any bad memories when things were going well.

"Once before we started dating and once after," I answer.

"And you didn't touch anyone?"

"Absolutely not."

"Did you watch anyone?"

"Watch?"

"Did you watch anyone else play?"

I rub my thumb across her cheeks. "No. I didn't watch any scenes, I didn't even go into the private areas. I went to Cole's office and left. That's it. I didn't tell you because I didn't want to upset you, but I realize now that was wrong. I won't go again without telling you. Hell, I'll take you with me if you want."

"You will?" she asks, surprised.

"Of course. You may be bored in the meeting but I'll take you if you want."

"Would you want to play when we were there?"

"Would *you*?"

She shrugs. While the idea of playing with her gets my blood flowing, I don't think she's ready to be exposed to that environment with the newness of our relationship. Clearly things aren't as settled as I thought they were if she's asking these types of questions. I make the offer nonetheless. "Baby, if you want to go play, I'll take you right now, tomorrow, next week, whenever you want."

"I don't want to go right now," she replies quickly. "I want to be enough for you. I know I don't have as much experience as you're used to, but I can try to be what you like."

"You are enough for me. You *are* what I like. Always. But if you want to explore some different sides of your sexuality you haven't before, I am happy to explore them with you. Just know, I am also equally happy with you moaning my name at home as at the club."

"If we went, would you want to share me or see me with other men?"

"Hard no. You are mine and mine alone. I don't want other men to see your body or hear your whimpers, let alone be a part of them."

She then has the nerve to giggle, "Yours, huh?"

"For all intents and purposes, yes. You are mine. Are you laughing at my claim?" I ask in mock offense. "Because I have no problem reminding you who owns your pleasure."

"No," she says, laughing harder. "I was thinking about the way you marked your territory tonight and how much more you'd need to do at a sex club."

"I don't know. I think you're making fun of me, baby. Showing the world you're mine is important. I can't let fuckers go around thinking they have a shot with you."

She giggles again.

"Laugh it up while you can, sweetheart. You're about to get a firm reminder who you belong to."

"What?" she asks, sobering quickly. I shoot her a predatory grin before throwing her over my shoulder and carrying her into my room.

Chapter Nineteen

• LOLA •

One moment, I am pressed against Brady's front door and the next, I'm landing on a soft mattress. I gaze up in time to see Brady tearing his shirt over his head and watching me with a wolfish stare. Suddenly I can relate to a zebra in the Sahara. Slowly, he strides over to my spot on the bed forcing me to lean back on my hands to be able to meet his eyes.

He runs his hands up the outsides of my thighs before meeting my gaze. "You like this dress, baby?"

"Yes, why?" I ask hesitantly.

"You've got about ten seconds to get it off then because if I do it, I can't promise it will be wearable again."

"What?" I squeak.

"Tik tok, Lola."

I grab the hem of my dress and pull it over my head tossing it across the room. "Happy?"

Brady leans his head to the side as he gives me a once over. "Not yet. I won't be happy until I've reminded you and the rest of the world exactly who you belong to."

"How are you going to do that?" My voice sounds husky even to my own ears.

"You'll see," he grins. I find myself scooting back reflexively at the threat. Promise?

"Uh, uh, uh," he tsks, grabbing my ankles to stop my backwards movement. "Don't you know never to run from a predator, baby? We love the chase."

"Brady..." I whisper cautiously as his fingers trail from my ankle to my knees.

"Shhh, I got you sweet girl. Trust me." With that request, he pounces. If I wanted to know how an out of control kiss with him felt, this is my chance. He's all teeth and tongue devouring my mouth before he moves to my neck and shoulders. He kisses my sternum, skipping over my breasts before leaving sucking kisses down my stomach. He's running his hands gently over my body in a stark contrast to the frantic energy of his mouth. The juxtaposition has me squirming beneath him.

When he reaches the top of my thong, he places little bites from hip to hip, causing a whine to slip out of my lips. I lift my pelvis trying to guide him where I want him most.

"Need something, Lola?" he asks.

"Yes, you."

"Is my girl needy? Does she want me to touch her?" he questions as his hands land on my inner thighs, grazing close but not close enough to my aching core.

"Yes, please," I breathe.

"Who do you belong to, Lola?"

"You."

"You sure about that? You were giggling earlier about me marking you as my territory. You positive you want everyone to know you're mine? That you're perfect for me? That you're everything I want and need?"

"Yes, please, Brady."

"Good answer, baby. Now that you know you belong to me, I'm going to remind everyone else. I am going to make you scream so loud there is no doubt everyone in this building will know who it is that makes you come. Who owns this pretty little pussy."

He rips the thong off my body in one quick tug and sets out to devour me. He makes quick circles around my clit, flicking it lightly with his tongue before sucking it into his mouth. He alternates between lapping circles on the pulsing nub and giving it direct contact. When he grazes it with his teeth, I come moaning his name just as he said. I expect him to let up on his ministrations, but he doesn't. After easing me through the initial wave, he doubles down.

"That's it. That's my girl. Again. Come for me again."

"Brady, fuck me. I want to come on your cock," I plead.

"You will. But for how I want to take you, I need you to be soaking wet. You're going to come on my face and fingers and then you're going to come on my cock."

He buries his face back into my pussy. Instead of filling me with his fingers as I expect, he thrusts his tongue deep into my channel. The sensation is something I have never felt before. His fingers make quick work of my clit, swiping back and forth, offering delicious friction. Just like the first time, it is mere minutes before I am shattering for him.

"Fuck, yes," he pants. As he rises, he flips me onto all fours. I hear a packet of foil ripping and startle when I feel his hands. With one hand rubbing soothing circles on my hip, the other one grips his length and runs it though my folds. He leans over me, hot breath tickling my ear and whispers, "Get ready, baby. You're in for a wild ride."

He nips at my earlobe before thrusting himself fully into me. Both hands grab onto my hips and hold me in place as he picks up a rhythm that steals my breath. Over and over, he slides into me, hitting spots only he has been able to find.

"Fuck, you're getting close again already, baby. You going to come for me? You going to come screaming my name so everyone knows who you belong to?"

"Yes," I pant. "Yes. Brady, oh God. Please don't stop."

He growls and plows into me even harder at the same steady pace. Within seconds, I am clamping down on him with an orgasm that shakes my entire body. If it wasn't for his hands on my hips, I would have collapsed onto the bed. I expect him to stop, but he doesn't he keeps going and fucks me right into another climax before reaching down and pulling me up on my knees.

My back is to his chest, and he uses both hands to toy with my nipples pinching and rolling them as he grinds and thrusts into me.

"You like this, baby? You like me showing your body how I can own it? How I can make it fall apart like no one ever has?"

"Yes, yes. I love it."

"Good girl. Give me another one. Come for me and take me with you."

"I can't," I mewl.

"You can. I want another one and I know you can give it to me."

He tilts my hips forward to a new angle, allowing him to hit a spot that has everything around me fading except the sound of our bodies slapping together and the pleasure pulsing through me.

Just when I think I won't be able to come again – even at this new, amazing angle – his hand slides between my legs. He slaps my clit one, two, three times, and I am screaming for him again. With a few more thrusts, he follows me over the edge, roaring his release.

He quickly wraps me up in his arms and rolls us on our sides. Once he catches his breath, he goes into the bathroom to dispose of the condom. I'm half asleep when he comes back but jolt when something warm swipes between my legs. Brady uses a washcloth to clean me up and kisses my forehead before tossing it into the hamper.

Crawling back into bed, he cradles me to his chest and runs his hands up and down my body. "You okay, sweet girl? I wasn't too rough, was I?"

"Shh, sleepy," I manage to mumble.

"That good, huh?" he chuckles.

"Bedtimeeeeee," I whine which earns me another laugh.

"Goodnight, mine," he whispers. Too tired to say anything, I nuzzle into his chest and drift off to sleep.

The next morning, I wake up deliciously sore, still wrapped up in Brady's arms. I try to wiggle out from under them, but he pulls me tighter.

"Too early. Stay," he mutters.

"Can't," I whisper. "I have to pee."

He lets out a grumble before releasing me. When I get done, I come back to see him face first in my pillow. Since I'm already awake, I decide to let him sleep and grab a quick shower. I consider going upstairs to use mine, but I'm not ready to go home yet and I know he won't be happy if he wakes up and I'm gone.

As the water heats, I resign myself to smelling like a forest for the rest of the day when a kiss on the top of my head startles me. "Morning, sweet girl," he rasps in his sex morning voice.

"Good morning. Are you going to shower with me?" I ask.

"Nah, I think I'm going to make us some breakfast. If I get in there with you, I'm not sure I can stop myself from touching you and I know you have to be sore."

"I'm fine," I remark dismissively. The expression on his face says he is not buying what I'm selling. "I might be a little sore," I concede. "It's not my fault you're packing a Louisville Slugger in your pants."

He snickers.

"Since you're up, do you mind if I take a shower at my place? I'll come back down when I'm done."

"Why can't you shower here?" he questions.

"As much as I love the way you smell, I'm not sure *eau de man* is the right scent for me. It's silly to not use my own stuff when it's an elevator ride away."

The man scoffs. Literally scoffs at my request.

"Hey, you may be fine using 5-in-1 to serve all your needs, but I am not. I need my girly shit."

"You don't need to go upstairs for 'girly shit,' doll. I've got everything you need down here. Did you even look in the shower?"

Peeking inside, I see one of his shelves is full of products for women. Not just women. Me. It's the exact products I use. "Did you steal my stuff?" I accuse.

"No," he laughs. "Why would I steal your toiletries?"

"I don't know. You tell me. They're all here."

He gives me an exaggerated eye roll before responding. "I bought duplicates of your products. Now you have everything you need here and don't have to go upstairs if you want to shower."

"You didn't have to do that," I mutter.

"I know I didn't," he replies. "But I wanted to. I want you to be at home here as much as upstairs and if buying froufrou smelling things does that then why wouldn't I? Now, hop in. Coffee will be ready in fifteen."

After rinsing off, I feel like a whole new woman. It probably helps that Brady has the fanciest shower I've ever seen. The rain shower head offers the perfect amount of pressure to rinse shampoo but is still luxuriously gentle.

When I walk into the kitchen, I see a shirtless Brady standing behind the island making omelets in low slung athletic shorts. He winks when he catches me checking him out.

"You gonna stand over there staring at the goods or are you going to drink your coffee before the ice melts?"

With the mention of coffee, I scurry over to the island and take a seat. He slides a glass my way and I take a sip. "Mmmmmm, this is delicious. What flavor is this?"

"Birthday cake," he replies nonchalantly.

"Brady Miller. Did you buy fancy coffee syrup?"

"Of course, I did."

"Why?"

"Because you like it," he states as if it is the most obvious thing in the world.

"Yeah, but you only drink your coffee with a splash of milk like a psychopath. This clearly has syrup AND cream in it."

"That's because it does."

"You made me special coffee?"

"I made your coffee how you take it. As any partner would do."

"Agree to disagree," I grumble.

"Any good partner," he clarifies. Plating the food, he slides a cheesy omelet in front of me before digging into his veggie monstrosity.

"Are you having any eggs with your veggies?" I tease.

He narrows his eyes. "Eat your breakfast, brat, before I forget that you're sore and decide to teach you a lesson about poking the bear."

I mime zipping my lips and dig into my food.

"What do you have planned this week?" he asks.

"With Carina and Robby's wedding days away, I have Maid of Honor errands to run. Plus, Aunt Teresa will be here tomorrow to help get everything squared away. Have you met Carina's mom before?"

"I don't think I have. You spent a lot of time with her when you were younger, right?"

"Yeah, I practically spent all my summers with her from the age of four to sixteen. Plus, most holidays were either at her house or my Nonna's. Dad wasn't exactly skilled in hosting. He left it to them to handle the most important events."

"But you and your dad are still close?"

"Yes and no," I say, pushing my food around my plate. "He raised me and put a roof over my head, but I wouldn't consider us pals. He did what he needed to do to take care of me. I don't think he knew what to do with a daughter most of the time, though."

"Sounds lonely," he remarks.

"Sometimes, but I had Carina and Teresa for anything major and my Nonna. Plus, I had friends. Georgie and I were inseparable until we went to college. We did everything together. We were even each other's prom dates."

"You went to prom with Georgie?" he questions, astonished.

"Yeah, why? You don't think a girl like me could've landed a date like that? I landed you, didn't I?"

"That you did, my sweet girl. Thank fuck for that."

"Speaking of my bestie, Georgie will be here in a couple of weeks. I can't wait for the two of you to meet."

"I'm looking forward to it," he says with a kiss to my temple. "I'm also looking forward to this wedding being over so I can have my life back. The All-Star break is supposed to be relaxing. Not full of fittings and events."

"Yeah, but I bet you'll look hot in your tux and I can't wait for you to see the dress Carina picked out for me."

"Am I going to like it?" he inquires.

"So much that I'm not giving you a peek until the wedding day."

"Now who's the mean one?" he taunts, which earns him a flick of egg to the face.

"Oh, you're in for it now!" he says with a hint of a growl. "You better run, baby. I'm taking my payback from that cute little ass."

With a yelp, I shoot off the stool and spend the rest of the day rolling around with my man.

Chapter Twenty

• LOLA •

G lancing around the room, I take a sip of my mimosa and I let the scene sink in. Carina is seated in front of a mirror while Tiffany carefully applies her eyeliner. The other bridesmaids float around the room refilling their drinks, steaming their dresses, and chatting.

A hand lands on my silk-robed back and I smile at my Aunt Teresa over my shoulder. "She's beautiful, isn't she?" she remarks.

"She is," I answer. "I can't believe this day is finally here."

"It feels like yesterday the two of you were fighting over who got to be the bride when you played with my veil as little girls," she recalls.

"Oh God, don't remind me. It's funny how the dreams of children transform. She really did get her Prince Charming, though."

"You'll get yours, too," she muses. "I am proud of you *mia fatina*."

"For what?"

"For knowing your worth. For realizing that protecting your heart is more important than appearances. For leaving that *stronzo* and starting over. You are brave, my little fairy."

"You did the same *zia*. You stayed in Memphis and raised Carina all by yourself when you could have run home to hide. Hell, you half-raised me, too."

"Perhaps, but I didn't have many other choices. You did. You could have believed his lies and turned a blind eye to remain in your comfortable life. Instead, you wanted more for yourself. Everything I did, I did for her," she says, glancing back to Carina. "I don't know if I could have done it for myself."

Wiping a tear, she quickly changes the subject. "No more sappy talk. My daughter is getting married and I can't have a raccoon face." I laugh and hug her before she runs out of the room to make last-minute preparations.

The conversation pulls my own wedding back into my memories. I was nervous while getting ready. We had a small ceremony made up of mostly his family since my dad, Carina, and Teresa were really all I had. Even though it was simple, I still had a pit in my stomach.

I remember how happy I was when we said our vows. How amazing it felt to have another person pledge themselves to me for the rest of our lives. To promise to love me no matter what, to honor, to cherish, and to always be true.

I wonder what that twenty-two-year-old girl would do if she knew then what I know now. What she would think about how Phil changed, how he betrayed us and broke all those vows. Would she still go through with it?

"Sweet Bunny, it's your turn to experience my magic brushes," Tiffany singsongs from her station, jarring me from my thoughts. When I make my way over to her, Carina has moved to the next chair where her hair is being curled into soft waves.

"You're a vision, Care Bear," I tell her.

"Thank you. I can't believe it's my wedding day. It feels like it all happened fast, but also was a long time coming."

"I'd say that is an accurate assessment."

"Speaking of things that come for a long time," Tiffany interrupts, "what's up with you and the big guy?"

"Tiffany!" I chide. She shrugs.

"I don't know what you are referring to," I say.

"Oh, please. I may have an active social life, but that doesn't mean I don't realize you rarely sleep in our apartment anymore, missy."

"Lola!" Carina gasps. "Have you been holding out on me? I saw you getting cozy at the bar last weekend, but I didn't know you were sleepover-serious."

"We're having fun and getting to know each other," I admit. "It's been nice. Brady is different from anyone I've ever been with."

"He's Brady now, is he?" Tiffany teases, causing Carina to giggle. "And of course, he's different from Pencil Prick Phil," she continues. "Miller is a man. Phil is an immature child, always trying to get the most out of every situation. Whereas Miller is always searching to see where he can give. And from the glow you've had lately, I'd guess he's quite good at giving."

"Oh my God, Tiff!" Carina admonishes.

"I call them like I see them, Meatball."

"Ignore her crassness," my cousin admonishes. "But since she brought it up, are things getting serious between you two? Are y'all a couple now?"

"We haven't put a label on it," I confess.

"Really? Miller isn't big on commitment? I didn't see that coming. Everything about him screams caveman. I was a little afraid he was gonna pee on you and hump your leg the other night," Carina states.

"Me, too," I reply. "But no. The lack of label is all me. He said he doesn't need one as long as I know I'm his, whatever that means. He's been pretty understanding that I am in the middle of a divorce and hadn't intended to jump into something this soon. We're taking it one day at a time."

"Screw that," Tiffany interjects. "That man is picking out china patterns and baby names. I can see it in his eyes. He's ready to commit. Hard. I bet you could convince him to make this a double wedding if you batted these pretty lashes at him."

"You're crazy," I dismiss.

"I don't know," Carina remarks. "I think she might be right. Not about the double wedding. From what I've heard from Robby, Miller doesn't do anything halfway. If he's pursuing a relationship with you, he's doing it with an end goal in mind."

Could that be true? He's said he is willing to take this at my pace, but he's also been clear that he wants me to be *his*. Does that mean more than I think it does? I assumed he wanted to be exclusive, but when I think about it, he's been upfront about his intentions since day one.

Is a future with him something I want? I haven't even officially ended my marriage. Surely, I'm not considering jumping into another serious relationship. It would be different with him, though. I know it. Miller shows me all the time how much he cherishes me and takes care of me in ways Phil never did. He does all those little things that add up to something huge and we aren't even officially a couple. How much would that increase if we were?

Those thoughts have no place in my mind today. Today is about marrying Carina off to the man of her dreams.

"Enough about me," I say. "We've got forty-five minutes before pictures. Then we can get you hitched to that hunk of man meat who has permanent heart eyes for you. Let's do this, ladies!"

As the other bridesmaids turn the corner to walk down the aisle, I peek behind me to see Carina. She isn't the slightest bit nervous. She is excited, a little teary, and in love.

"I know the answer, but I'd be a terrible MoH if I didn't at least ask: need me to sneak you out the back?" I whisper to her.

"I think I'm okay," she laughs.

"Yeah, you are. You got a good one. I am beyond happy for you, Care Bear. No one deserves this more than you."

"That isn't true. We all deserve this. It just takes some of us longer to get there than others. If Mom marrying Steve taught me anything, it is that love can be waiting around the corner when you least expect it. I certainly wasn't expecting Robby to come back into my life, but I'm thankful he did."

"Me, too. That's my cue," I say when I hear the music change. With a quick squeeze of her hand, I make my entrance.

I survey this gorgeous vineyard. The setting is absolutely incredible, but what stops me in my tracks is the groom. I've been to a lot of weddings, Aunt Teresa, friends from college, coworkers, distant relatives, and even my own. I have never seen a man with the expression on his face that Robby has. He appears inconsolably happy to be here; to be marrying the love of his life. He can't even see her yet and his eyes are full of moisture.

I give him a soft smile and shift my gaze over the crowd to everyone here to celebrate them. My perusal stops on Brady. He is damn handsome in his tux. It should be criminal. I blush when he smirks, catching me checking him out as always. The last time I walked down an aisle, Phil was waiting at the end. Ironically, the man who helped me heal from the neglect of my marriage is at the end this time, even if it's not to meet me.

When I get into position, the guests all stand and I watch on as Aunt Teresa walks Carina down the aisle. Tears are already falling down her face and Robby is no different. My heart clutches at how overjoyed these two people are to be joined together. As the ceremony continues, I listen to the vows they wrote each other and find myself silently crying. Carina vows to cheer Robby on no matter his endeavor and he vows to always put her first and never let her forget that she is the center of his universe.

We all cheer loudly when Robby dips Carina into a questionably appropriate kiss before they head off for a few minutes alone. Brady is paired with Tiffany and he sends me a wink over his shoulder as he leads her up the aisle. I slip my arm into Sean's, who compliments my dress as we exit together.

"You're not too shabby yourself," I remark. "Who knew the beach bum could pull off a tie."

"Hey, now," he objects. "I'll have you know I am equally comfortable wearing this tux as I am a wetsuit. How can I not be when I have all the ladies eyeing me? I am the most eligible groomsman after all."

"Is that so?"

"It most certainly is. I know you already have a date to this shindig, but if you see any interested parties, send them my way."

"Date?" I question. "I didn't come with a date."

"Oh, my mistake," he falters. "I thought you and Miller were together."

"We are. I mean, we're seeing each other. We never talked about what that meant for this wedding since we were both coming already. I guess he's my date."

"You guess?" Letting out a low whistle, he continues, "I would've thought big bad Papa Bear would have locked that down by now, not leave you second guessing what you two are."

"I'm not." Am I? I know he didn't bring a date and that he wouldn't because we are seeing each other, *exclusively*. Our friends know that. Mine do at least... Robby does, too. I'm sure we both assumed we'd see each other here and since we couldn't come together, there was no need to discuss it in detail.

"Have you two defined your relationship?"

"Not in so many words, but we know what we are to each other. It's complicated, but not Facebook 'It's Complicated.' More like we're both in interesting places in our lives and we haven't felt the need to label anything."

He shoots me a teasing grin, "Sounds like you've got it all figured out then."

"Don't you have someone to hit on? Haley is single," I sass.

"Is she now? I can tell when I'm not wanted. Time to go find someone else to dance the night away, since the glare your *complicated* beau is giving me tells me it won't be you. Later, Lola."

Confused, I peer up and see Brady beelining my way. It appears my question about whether we're here together is about to be answered.

Chapter Twenty-One

• BRADY •

"You ready, man?" I ask Robby with a pat on the back.

"I've never been more ready for anything in my life."

"Nervous?"

"Not even a little," he replies. "Honestly, I'm relieved. I have been waiting for this day 5ever. Being able to call Carina my wife feels right. I can't wait to make it official."

"I hope I'm that sure on my wedding day," I admit.

"Marry the right girl, and you will."

I chuckle in response. That is easier said than done, otherwise I would have done it by now. He is deliriously in love and he almost didn't make it here thanks to some bad choices he made as a rookie. I'm glad he did, though. He and Carina make a great couple and without them, I would've never met Lola.

The more time I spend with her, the more I can see this future for us. I get what he means about feeling relieved. I would love to have skipped the years of bullshit dating and be married. I know I would make a great husband, but you can't jump right into matrimony unless you meet in Vegas or on a reality show. The types of women that do that aren't typically the type I am interested in. I want someone a little more careful, like my sweet girl.

My sweet girl. We haven't labeled it yet, and I get why she would be apprehensive, but if she thinks we aren't already in a relationship, she hasn't been paying attention.

"Let's go get you hitched, bro," Kent exclaims, coming up with the other groomsmen.

"Don't worry," Ralphie, Robby's brother-in-law and lone NHL star of the bunch, says. "I brought plenty of tissues. We all know you're going to blubber like a baby when you see her."

"That's rich coming from the man who cried enough tears to ice a hockey rink when he married Morgan," my buddy quips.

"Exactly. I know what I'm talking about."

"Time to get into position," the officiant announces.

"Show time!" I exclaim with a smile.

Robby and Carina's wedding is taking place at an old winery that was recently updated to include an event space. We stand at the edge of the vineyard overlooking rows and rows of grapes. It's a picturesque location and has a romantic vibe to it. I'd almost say it reminds me of Tuscany, but all the Italians in attendance would be quick to correct me.

I smile as I watch the bridesmaids walk down the aisle. They're all beautiful in their silky dresses of varying shades of pinks and reds. I laugh when Tiffany mouths, "You ain't ready," to Robby before she takes her spot.

He may not be ready to see Carina, but I was equally unprepared to see Lola. She is a vision in a flowy berry dress as she floats down the aisle. She appears to be taking in the view when I sense her eyes stop on me. I smirk at the once-over she gives me, which causes her to blush and bite her lip as she hurries the rest of the way to her spot.

While everyone stands and shifts to watch the bride walk down the aisle, I can't tear my gaze away from my girl. She's breathtaking. But more than that, she radiates joy. She is so happy for her cousin and our friend that I can't help but beam. I thought today might be hard for her, considering she is in the middle of ending her marriage, but she seems elated.

Rings are exchanged and vows are read, but I barely notice. I am too busy soaking in Lola. I almost push Sean ahead of me so I can be paired with her down the aisle, but I settle for shooting her a wink as I take Tiffany's arm.

"Won't be long till we're back here," Tiffany comments.

Confused, I ask, "What? The winery?"

"No, dummy, a wedding."

"Who else is getting married?"

She gives me a sly expression, "Based on the way your eyes were glued to a certain Maid of Honor, I'd say you."

"Might be jumping the gun a little there, Tiff. Lola is skittish about anything too serious."

"Please, serious is the only thing she knows how to do. It's walking, it's talking, it's eating bread from your hand. Just because she isn't calling it a duck doesn't mean it isn't. She might be more ready than you think."

"Yeah?" I question, hopefully. I'm ready to make things official with Lola. I know her divorce is dragging. She doesn't talk much about it, but she says she has it under control. I don't know the timing of all that, and I don't really care. I want the world to know she's mine.

"You give her a safe place to be herself," Tiffany responds. "I think she spent most of her life fitting herself into a box to be what other people wanted, but you encourage her to explore what makes her, her. You never belittle the things she's excited about and you pay attention to her. You notice her shift in moods when she is a little overwhelmed by the rest of the group. You remembered she was working on a blog post about why flat matte gold fixtures are better than brass and asked her about it even though I know you couldn't care less."

"Hey, I care about the things she cares about. Talking about those things makes her happy. And how could I not notice when her mood changes? It's my job to take care of her," I state.

"Exactly. You take care of her in ways no one else ever has. It helps that your competition is a no-good-little-dicked nobody, but you'd stand out all on your own."

"He is not my competition," I grit. "He already lost the prize."

"Oh boy, you're more gone than I thought," she giggles. "If that's the case, you better go get our girl before Sean woos. I've seen him make girls swoon in board shorts with a sunburn. His powers are amplified in a tux."

I turn to see Lola laughing at something Robby's Best Man said with her arm still wrapped around his. Nope. That is enough touching. Without saying goodbye to Tiffany, I march over to where they stand. Sean separates from her and meets me a few feet away.

"You got a good one, man. Better lock it down."

"I'm working on it," I practically snap, but the fucker smiles and shakes his head, prowling the reception for a new person to talk to.

"Hi, sweet girl," I greet Lola with a peck on the cheek. "You are absolutely gorgeous in this dress. Hands down the most stunning woman here."

"Brady," she chastises. "You're supposed to say that about the bride!"

"She's got Robby to tell her she's pretty. Besides, you know I don't lie."

"Thank you," she mumbles. "You're rather dashing in your suit."

"I'm glad you like it. Shall we go find our seats?"

"Sure," she agrees. "Do you think we're sitting together?"

"Of course, we're sitting together," I scoff. "Why wouldn't they sit you with your date?"

"Oh," she mutters. "We never technically talked about it. I wasn't sure if we were here as date-dates."

"Date-dates?" I repeat.

"Yeah, I know we're seeing each other and obviously Robby and Carina do, but I didn't know how public you wanted to be since there are coaches and other players here."

"I've been calling you mine since practically the first night we got together, doll. I'm not sure where the confusion lies."

"I guess that's true," she stammers. "But that is a thing people say, ya know? I'm yours in a sexual sense." She uses air quotes around 'yours.' Clearly, she did not understand that when I claimed her, I *claimed* her. Time to rectify that.

"You are definitely mine in a sexual sense, but you are also mine in every other sense of the word. This thing between us, it's serious – at least to me, anyway. I know you're still finalizing your divorce, but I'm not the type of man to let some paperwork keep me from what I want."

She gazes at me with her wide doe eyes. "So, what? Are you, like, my boyfriend?"

I can't help but laugh at the absurdity of that term. Something feels wrong about the casualness of it and not only because I'm thirty-two.

"I think I'm a little old to be called a boyfriend, but if that's what you want to call me, have at it. Know that I am yours. Utterly and completely. And you are mine – utterly and completely. I know that may scare you, but I'm in this for the long game. You and me, we're going all the way. Do whatever it is you need to do to make that click in your pretty little head, because I'm not giving you up."

"You mean you're not giving me up easily?" she corrects.

"I said what I said." That comment earns me a shocked expression that makes me chuckle. "Come on. You look like you need a glass of wine and those hot chicken sliders are calling my name."

Chapter Twenty-Two

• LOLA •

"I think I'm going to throw up," I say.

"That's a tad over dramatic, don't you think," Tiffany states. "You've seen your man play before. What's the big deal this time?"

"The big deal is that he's playing against my best friend!"

"I thought I was your best friend," she pouts, causing me to roll my eyes.

"Don't worry, Babs, you're my bestie," Carina promises.

"Thanks, Meatball. I always knew I edged out Robby, but it's nice to have the confirmation."

"Can you ladies please focus? I am trying not to have a panic attack over here!"

"Oh my God, drink this," Carina insists, handing me a seltzer. "Why are you freaking out, Bunny? You've seen them both play before. And this is not the first time they've played each other. They're professionals. They're focused on the game, not their connection to you."

"I know, I know," I mutter. "But this is the first time they've played each other since I started dating Brady, and you know how protective Georgie can be."

"Still weird that you call him Brady," Tiffany says with a mouth full of hotdog.

"Shut up," I grumble.

"Don't talk with a weiner in your mouth, Tiff. Guys don't like that," Carina quips.

"I can guarantee you, they do. You should try it some time," she retorts.

"Y'all are too much," I sign. "I'm worried they're going to figure it out before they meet later."

"Wait. What do you mean 'figure it out'?" Tiffany questions. "Oh shit. Do they not know about each other?"

"Lola, how have you not told them about each other?" Carina chastises.

"I have!" I reply. And that's true in a technical sense. I talk about Georgie to Brady all the time. I've told him stories from growing up together and recount conversations I had with him, but I haven't told him who he is to the rest of the world. To me, he's just Georgie, the guy who helped me make it through high school. Who he is to the rest of the world doesn't matter.

As for Georgie, I told him I am seeing someone and that I want him to meet him while he's in town. I may have neglected to mention that he was also a professional baseball player. Or say his last name.

"If you have, why are you worried?" Carina asks.

"I talk about them to each other often. But I haven't *necessarily* revealed either of their last names or that they both play baseball."

"Lola, noooo," my cousin groans.

"I am elated that I decided to come to this game," Tiffany squeals gleefully. "Tonight is going to be epic."

"It won't be too bad, right? They both care about me. They'll probably find it hilarious," I mutter mostly to myself.

"I wouldn't get your hopes up, Lo," Carina responds hesitantly.

"Why?"

"They're getting a little chippy with each other on first base. Do they have a history?"

"I don't think so," I answer. "Georgie has been with the Foxes organization his entire career and Miller has been on the Songbirds for years."

Carina gives me a commiserative glance as we both watch Robby launch the ball back to Brady at first and miss tagging Georgie out by a hair. The antagonist that he is, Georgie gives him a shit-eating grin before stealing second on the next play. This may not go as smoothly as I hoped.

Sitting in the VIP section of Holler's, I fiddle with the straw in my vodka soda. I should probably have stuck to seltzer, but my nerves require hard liquor.

"You're way too pretty to be drinking alone," a deep voice says from behind me.

"Georgie!" I shout, jumping up to hug him. "I've missed you. You played amazing tonight! How are you? How is Mama? And you sisters? You look buff. Have you changed up your routine?"

"Slow down, Honeybun. You're asking more questions than the reporters at the press conference," he laughs. "I am doing great, much better now that I can see you in the flesh. All the Rivera women are good. They both send their love. And I've put on a couple pounds of muscle since I saw you last. Only you would notice such a small change. You look skinnier than last time I saw you. Mama will send you food if she finds out."

My cheeks heat at the intensity of his inspection. "You're imagining things. It's the shorter hair. I lost a little weight after the Phil debacle, but the food scene here brought it right back."

Georgie's eyes darken with what I can only describe as unbridled anger. "Don't even say his name, Lo. He doesn't deserve a single moment of recognition from you. I can still kick his ass if you want. There is no statute of limitations on punishment for fucking over my friend."

"No need for that, but I appreciate the sentiment. We're getting divorced. I've moved on. He's... I don't know what he's doing and I don't care."

"That's my girl," he praises. "Speaking of moving on, where is this new guy? I want to meet him. I already know he's not good enough, but I want to see how much."

Georgie has always been overprotective of me. It's part of the reason we went to prom together. Since he deemed no other man at our school worthy, he took me himself. Not being able to intimidate my dates when he was away for college was hard for him.

Even though he didn't like Phil, at least he knew he could scare him. And he did. They were not each other's biggest fans. It's not hard to see now that Phil was threatened by my relationship with Georgie because I had another man in my life treating me better than he did. I wonder if my marriage would have ended sooner if we lived closer.

"You can't judge him. You hardly know anything about him. He is amazing and you guys have a lot in common if you would give him a chance."

"Hmm, we'll see. Where is this guy not worthy of breathing the same air as you?"

"Be nice! He's on his way. He should have left work a few minutes ago. Listen, Georgie, I really like him. He treats me like a queen. He makes me feel things I never thought I could."

"TMI, Lola!" he interjects.

"Not like that," I gasp.

"Not *not* like that, though," a new voice says as Carina joins us.

"Carina, *hermosa*, being married agrees with you. Congratulations on the wedding. I'm sorry I couldn't make it, but some of us had to play in the All-Star game. You were a goddess among mortals in the pictures Lola sent."

"Thank you, Georgie. You were missed. You'll have to get all your flirting out now, though, before the hubby gets here."

"Possessive, is he?" Georgie jokes.

"Oh yeah. But he's got nothing on Lola's man. Have you met Brady yet? They should be here by now. You also have to meet Tiffany. She's been vying to replace you as Lola's bestie. You better step it up."

"Honeybun, how could you?!" he gasps in mock outrage.

"I didn't do anything. She's the one trying to steal your spot. She makes some good points though..." I tease.

"I'll have to up my game then," he says, pulling me into his side and kissing my hair.

Before I can respond, a voice booms over the music, "Get your fucking hands off my girl right now, Rivera, if you ever want to pitch again."

Shit. I try to scoot away from Georgie, but he tightens his grip as we turn around to see a raging Brady. This isn't off to a good start.

Chapter Twenty-Three

• BRADY •

Walking into Holler's, it is more crowded than usual. It doesn't take long to discover it's because some of the Foxes, the team we finished playing, decided to come here to lick their wounds. You'd never catch me out at a bar after losing away, but to each their own. I ignore them and search for my girl.

Her friend Georgie is in town for work and tonight, I finally get to meet her. Lola talks about her all the time, but I feel like I don't know too much about her. I don't even know what type of work brought Georgie into town.

As I approach the VIP section, I groan seeing my least favorite Fox chatting up two girls. It isn't until I get closer that I realize those girls are Lola and Carina. I watch him put his arm around Lola, kissing her on the top of the head and I see red.

"Get your fucking hands off my girl right now, Rivera, if you ever want to pitch again," I roar. As I approach, I see Lola try to shift away, but Rivera's hold tightens. He has quite the reputation with the ladies, but he is sorely mistaken if he thinks he can hit on my woman.

"Did you not hear what I said, jackass?" I ask.

"Brady, calm down," Lola interjects. Before I can respond, Rivera does.

"Wait, Brady is Brady Miller? Are you fucking with me, Lola? You didn't think to mention that at any point?" he complains.

"Hey," I say as I gently grab her arm and pull her behind me. "Don't fucking curse at her."

"You're cursing right now," he argues.

"Yeah, but not *at* her. I'm cursing at the dipshit who had the audacity to put his hands on my girl."

"Your girl. Of course, you're one of those. Sorry to burst your bubble, buddy, but I've been putting my hands on 'your girl' way longer than you've been in the picture."

"Georgie! Stop antagonizing him!" Lola yells pushing from behind me to get in between us and it all clicks. Georgie. George Rivera. Holy mother fucking shit. Lola's Georgie is George Rivera. I glare down at her in disbelief and she has the decency to appear somewhat remorseful. Before I can ask about it, Rivera beats me to it.

"Don't you remember the problems I had with him in the minors?" he reminds her.

I've been traded a few times in my career and during one of those trades, Rivera and I played on the same minor league team in Springfield. A few years younger than me, he came to the team as a rookie. He was cocky and trying to prove himself. I get it, we all were, but the dude had a bad attitude. I tried to give him some advice, but he didn't want to hear anything from anybody and decided I had it out for him. I was a little surprised when he moved up, but Chicago had some crazy injuries and issues with their pitchers. He worked his ass off once he made it and proved his worth.

Right now though, I don't care about any of that because the fucker had his hands on my girl. I don't even have the brain power to process the bomb that was dropped though because my sweet girl is sassing her friend.

139

"You have problems with a lot of people, Georgie. It's hard to keep up. You're known for your temper."

"Lola, be serious. How could you not tell me that you were dating a professional baseball player?" he demands.

"Didn't seem important," is her response. If it was anyone else, I would assume she was full of shit, but the fact that I play baseball is barely of consequence to Lola. I thought it was because she's been around Robby, but clearly her ties run deeper.

"You've got some explaining to do, baby," I state.

"Okay, I probably should have mentioned that you play baseball, but I didn't think about it at first, and then I didn't want it to become a *thing*. I wanted you to inform opinions about each other without any bias. Clearly that was the wrong move."

"Clearly," I deadpan. "Did you also maybe think you should mention Georgie was a guy?"

"What do you mean?" she questions. "Oh my God, did you think Georgie was a girl? Why would you think that?"

"I don't know. Maybe because I never heard you mention his gender when you talked about him and Georgie is a girl's name," I defend against three shocked faces.

Carina who has been silent throughout this interaction finally pipes in. "Tiffany is going to be mad she missed this. As much as I want to see how this ends, I need to find my man. Good luck, Bunny!"

Lola gives her a hug and is back to gaping at me. "I told you Georgie and I went to prom together."

"I thought you meant as friends," I say. "Honestly, would thinking *Georgie* was a girl be such a stretch?"

Instead of replying, Lola burst out laughing. Rivera's lips twitch a bit as he watches her fondly but his scowl is back full force when he meets my eye.

"You're two for two, Brady," she giggles.

"What?" I ask, confused.

"You assumed Charlie was a man, wrong. And you thought

Georgie was a woman. Double wrong. Oh man, this is great."

"Yeah, I gotta say sweet girl, I am not really seeing the humor in all this."

Tired of being ignored, Georgie shifts closer to Lola and leans down to say something into her ear. "Lola," he whispers in a low voice he must think I can't hear. "Do you know what you're getting into with this guy? Aside from being a grumpy know-it-all, he's also a kinky motherfucker if the rumors are to be believed."

"You don't know shit," I interrupt before she can respond.

"I'm a big girl. I know exactly what I'm getting into," she asserts. "I appreciate you always looking out for me Georgie, but Brady is the most respectful man I have ever been with. He would never do anything to make me uncomfortable. In fact, I'm pretty sure he makes other people uncomfortable with how far he goes to make sure I am happy and taken care of."

Gazing between the two of us, she continues, "You are the two most important men in my life. I think if you give each other a chance you might realize you have a ton in common. It's really important to me that the two of you get along. Do you think you can do that?" She's giving us both those big doe eyes.

"Fine," I concede. "What are you drinking, Rivera?"

"No way am I letting you pay for my drinks," he glowers.

"Georgie," Lola snaps with a stomp of her foot. This bratty attitude is a whole new side to her I haven't seen since the night of the bachelor/bachelorette party. I don't think I'd love it if I had to deal with it every day but I am getting a kick out of it being directed at him.

"If you don't try to be nice to my boyfriend, I swear on my Gilmore Girls' box set that I will call your mom AND your sisters."

Georgie winces at the threat. "Okay, okay. No need to pull out the big guns, Honeybun. I can play nice. I'll take a Maker's and Coke."

I glare at his term of endearment and the fucker smirks back at me. This is going to be a long night.

Chapter Twenty-Four

D espite his initial reaction, it didn't take Brady long to accept that Georgie was better known as George 'Rambo' Rivera. It helped that he never had an issue with Georgie aside from the attitude problem he has overcome since then... mostly. With a little convincing – and some time spent making *him* moan *my* name – he was able to quickly get over my omission.

On a rare day off, Brady is sitting on the sofa in my apartment watching TV while I put the finishing touches on an article for work. When I peel my eyes away from the screen, I notice he's watching a sports highlight show.

"Are you an addict, babe?"

"Excuse me?" he questions.

"It's okay if you are. This is a safe space. You can tell me. I'll support you as you get the help you need," I say solemnly.

"What are you talking about?"

I smile, pointing to the screen. "I know it can be hard, but I think it's time to admit that you have a problem. You can't go twenty-four hours without baseball. I thought you had to get your fix in person, but now I see it is much deeper if you have to resort to watching it on your day off."

He tips back his head and lets out a loud laugh. "You can be a real brat, you know that?"

"Me?" I feign innocently. "I don't know what you're talking about. I am a very good girl."

"You were last night," he responds with a wink. Despite the fact that we've been seeing each other for almost two months, he still manages to make me blush.

"What is my bratty good girl up to?" he asks.

"Now that I've finished this article for work, I need to work on a post for my blog."

"And what post might that be? A new recipe? Making your own candles? Trying meditation?"

I love that he doesn't bat an eye at all the things I try for my blog. Phil was never supportive of me taking on any side projects or hobbies which is ironic considering he didn't want to spend his free time with me. I don't know why he cared how I filled mine.

"Those are actually all good ideas," I admit.

"Of course, they are," he scoffs. "All my ideas are good ideas."

"I'm not sure mine are."

"I'll be the judge of that. What's on the docket?"

I sigh, pulling up my list. "Okay, I need to complete one of the items on my try list and write about it but I can't decide which one. Some of them strike me as daunting while others are blah. I'm having trouble choosing."

"I'm great with decisions. Let me see the list. I'll even go with you to do it."

"You will?"

"Yeah, if it's something we can get done today. I'm down. The only thing I was planning to do on my day off was spend time with you."

Even when he isn't trying, Brady can make my heart melt. Not only is he willing to spend his day off with me, but he is willing to spend it doing something solely for my benefit.

"'Lola's Try List.' Original title, baby," he teases after I pull it up on my laptop. I shoot him a glare which draws a laugh from him. I love it when he's relaxed and carefree like this. I wish he would do it more often instead of stressing over everyone else's problems.

"Let's see here: adopt a dog, volunteer with a girls-focused charity, make my own jewelry, go to a sex club?" he raises his eyebrow at me. "Haven't you already done that one?"

Oh shit. I forgot about that one. Some of those were submitted and voted on by my followers.

"Someone on social media added that," I rush out. "And while technically I have gone, I didn't do much while there. I'm not sure it counts. Is that the one you want to do?"

"Oh, I absolutely want to do it. In fact, you better not complete this one without me. But I don't think it's the right choice for today. Unless you want to?" he asks hesitantly.

"I don't think I'm up to that yet."

He nods and keeps reading. "Goat yoga, pottery class, fish pedicure." He makes a puzzled face at that suggestion but keeps reading. "Sing karaoke with a live band, make macaroons... bingo. I got it."

"You want to make macaroons?"

"Nope," he answers, peering into my eyes. "You, my sweet girl, are getting a tattoo."

"What?" I squeak. "Today?"

"Oh yeah. If you're up for it. It will probably take a few hours and I've got plenty of time to sit with you while it happens and hold your hand."

"Are you going to get one?"

"I've considered it, but never had anything worth marking myself permanently over. Besides, this is about you, not me," he states. "And lucky for you, I have the number of the guy who did Declan and Cole's tattoos. He is the most sought-after tattoo artist in the city, but I'm sure he could get us in as a favor. Do you know what you want?"

"I have a general idea. I was hoping the artist could help finish the design."

An hour later I find myself sitting in a chair at a high-end tattoo shop with Zade applying a stencil to my skin. The artist in question looks exactly how you expect him to. Almost every visible inch of his skin is covered in ink and he has an eyebrow and tongue piercing. I can't help but wonder if he has any others...

Before we left, Brady and I talked about the placement of my tattoo. I decided I wanted it on my upper ribs, that way I could hide it most of the time but still show it to other people. He insisted I wear a deep cut bralette that was only attached by a string at the bottom to keep the tattoo artist from seeing too much of my boobs. I tried to protest, but it was clear he wasn't going to budge on it.

As he finishes applying the design, Zade instructs me to lay on my side. When I do, I find Brady there sitting in a chair with a smile on his face. "You ready for this?"

"As ready as I can be," I declare with a shaky voice.

"You're going to do great," Zade reassures me. "Women sit way better for tattoos than men. Plus, you've got this big lug here to hold your hand and I bet his can take quite the squeeze." The comment makes me giggle and eases some of my nerves. "Okay, let's do this."

"Atta girl," he responds, earning him a glare from Brady that he smirks at. Brady may not appreciate Zade's flirty personality, but it puts me at ease. It is clear he knows it won't lead anywhere.

For the next two hours, Brady asks me random questions to try to distract me from the needle running over my skin. "If you were a dog, what breed do you think you would be?" he asks.

"That's a tough one. You go first," I say.

"Alright, I think I would probably be a Golden Retriever. That's what all those chick books you read talk about, right?"

I try to stifle the giggle that wants to slip out but can't. Zade doesn't even try to hide his amusement.

"What?" Brady defends. "I'm loyal, active, and nice to everyone. I've been called a Golden Retriever on more than one occasion."

We both laugh harder and then Zade speaks, "I've only been around you a handful of times, dude, but you do not have Golden Retriever energy. They're happy-go-lucky. You've got Doberman energy, if anything. You may be chill, but you're intense. You've glared at me at least a dozen times since you've been here."

"That's because she keeps wincing," Brady grits.

"He isn't a Doberman," I chide, making Brady soften. "But you aren't a Golden Retriever, either." His expression drops a bit as I contemplate. "You're a German Shepard – still cuddly and playful, but confident, protective, and always on alert."

"I can live with that," he concedes.

"Glad we got that settled," Zade remarks with the snap of his gloves, "Because we're all done here."

"Really?" I ask hopefully.

"Yep. Want to take a peek before I wrap it up and give you care instructions?"

"Yes, please!"

Zade helps me up and directs me to a mirror on the other side of his station. I stare at my ribs for a few minutes before I turn and hug him, ignoring the growl I hear behind me.

"It's incredible!," I gush. "You're an artistic wizard. I loved your idea to add the moon."

Zade designed the tattoo when I got here. I knew I wanted it to include the phrase, 'to thine own self be true' – a reminder to listen to my inner voice – and flowers to symbolize blossoming into my new self. He suggested we put the script inside a crescent moon which symbolizes rebirth in many cultures. The flowers are growing out of the inside of the moon and he added a couple stars for good measure. While it has a lot of components, it's still delicate, which is what I wanted.

Pulling me off Zade, Brady mutters, "Don't I get any credit for bringing you here and encouraging you to do this?"

"Of course, you do, babe. No one is going to believe I did this! I'll give you all the credit," I reply, giving him a chaste peck. He quickly deepens the kiss, leaving me breathless and a little dazed.

"That's better," he rumbles with a satisfied expression.

After my tattoo experience, I decide a nap is in order. Brady convinces me to take it in his bed and slides in with me, snuggling me to his side, careful to avoid my tender ribs.

"Comfortable?" he asks.

"I am," I mutter as I nuzzle into his chest, "but I don't see how you can be. You always insist on sleeping on the side by the door."

"And I always will, but that would put you on your bad side," he murmurs. "Besides, I'm not planning to sleep, anyway. I'm leaving soon."

"You are?" I pout.

"God, you're fucking adorable. Put that away," he says tapping my lip. "I'm meeting Robby and Kent at the gym downstairs for a quick workout. Then I'm going to hit up the taco truck across the street and grab us dinner. You may not even be awake by the time I get back."

"What time are you meeting them?" I ask.

"They should be getting there any minute, but I'll go down once you're asleep."

"You don't have to do that."

"I know. But I love having you fall asleep in my arms and you do, too. Close those pretty hazel eyes and go to sleep."

Butterflies erupt in my stomach as he runs his fingers up and down my back. He's right, I love falling asleep wrapped up in him. I'm clearly making up for years of being touch starved in the few months we've been together.

Before dozing off, I relay my dinner order, "I want two chicken —" but get interrupted.

"Two chicken tacos with cheese, rice, and guacamole with a medium queso. This isn't my first day, doll."

"Alright Mr. Know-It-All. What are you getting because I know nachos are not on your meal plan, even if it is an off day. See, I know what you get, too."

"She's sassy when she's tired," he chuckles. "They are not, unfortunately. But a taco salad with extra steak and black beans will help me reach my protein goal. I won't mention the guac on top if you don't. And don't act shocked that I know your order. I know what you get everywhere we go. You're a creature of habit. Plus, I couldn't take care of my girl properly if I didn't know what to feed her."

Cuddles me to sleep and knows my orders by heart? If I wasn't falling for him already, I am now. Brady takes everything he learns about me and commits it to memory. *Lola Facts* must be taking up at least 5 percent of his brain space at this point.

"Now," he croons, "close your eyes. I don't want to hear Kent complain about me pushing him into doing an hour workout in forty-five minutes."

"Yes, sir," I murmur.

"Let's put a pin in that for later," he growls as I drift off.

Chapter Twenty-Five

· LOLA ·

The next evening, I am cuddled up on Brady's couch watching the Songbirds play the Continentals. It's the top of the eighth and the guys are on the field. My phone buzzes and I grab it without checking who it is, assuming it is one of the girls calling about the impressive play Brady made.

"Yeah, I saw it," I chirp. "If that split shot doesn't move him up on the Baseball Bulges list, nothing will."

"Is that any way to greet your husband?" an unwelcome voice sneers on the other end of the line. Fuck. It's Phil. I should've peeked at the caller ID.

"What do you want?" I ask flatly. "You're supposed to go through the lawyers if you want to talk to me."

"I thought this conversation deserved discretion. There is no reason we can't speak like adults. We've known each other for almost a decade."

I can't help but laugh. "No, we thought we knew each other for almost a decade, but I don't think I ever knew you at all. I'll ask again: What. Do. You. Want?"

"I found your little blog. *Ex-Wife Files*. That's... cute."

A lump forms in my throat. I don't care that Phil found my blog, but I do put a lot of my innermost thoughts out there. It's almost as if he's read my diary. I don't know why he thinks we need to talk about it, though. He didn't care about my thoughts or feelings when we were married. Why does he care now?

"What about it?"

"Picture this. I'm sitting in my office when Mom calls to discuss how one of her tennis buddies was inspired to reevaluate her life after following this 'darling' girl on a self-discovery journey after leaving a selfish husband." The way he says 'darling' makes my skin crawl. I guess he disagrees with that assessment.

I scan my memory, wondering what could've made him angry, but I come up empty. My most recent post about how creating a gratitude practice has helped open my eyes to the good things around me. And how it allowed me to forgive myself for letting my marriage put a dark cloud over my head. I thought I'd shifted from optimist to realist due to age, but it turns out it was due to circumstance. Surely that isn't the post he's referencing, though. It's more about the ritual of gratitude than my marriage.

When I don't respond, he drones on. "Imagine Mom's surprise and mine when it turns out the woman behind the account is you. My mother read post after post about how I neglected you, made you feel undesirable, and caused you to have a quarter life crisis. Apparently, marriage to me was akin to being a prison of war or married to a narcissistic sociopath."

"So?" I question. He's making big inferences into my posts, but I don't correct him or tell him how spot on he is on that last comment. They always tell on themselves.

"So? SO?! Do you not see how embarrassing that is? What bullshit I had to spew to explain to my mother that our divorce was amicable and you were just exaggerating for clout? You need to take the posts down. I don't want it getting around that I was a bad husband. And I certainly don't want my mother to find out fidelity is one of the reasons we broke up. Do you really want to hurt her like that?"

"First of all," I practically yell, "you have absolutely zero right to make any demands over what I put on my account. Those are my personal spaces to share my experiences. Second, I don't care what you tell your mother. You've been lying to her for this long. I don't know why it bothers you to do it now.

"Not that I owe you anything, but I have at no point mentioned you by name or the scene I walked in on before I left you. And news-flash, Philip, you were a bad husband!"

I can sense him fuming through the phone. "I was not a bad husband. I provided for you, put a roof over your head, made sure we always had the luxuries you wanted. I never laid a hand on you and when I had alternative sexual desires, I had those needs met else-where instead of asking you to debase yourself."

"Oh, that's what you were doing with your brother? Meeting alternative sexual desires elsewhere for *my* benefit? I didn't exactly feel valued when catching you cheating on me. And as far as your other claims go, we both worked. You didn't single handedly provide anything that I couldn't have given myself if I were single. You can take that feather out of your cap. Also, you don't get points for *not* being abusive. The bar is low, but not that low."

"Take. Down. The posts," he snarls.

"I'm not doing that, Phil. I stopped catering to your wants when I found you tag teaming with your brother. If that's all, I was in the middle of something."

"This isn't over, Lola. You created that blog while we were still married, which makes it community property. Stop any mention of me and our marriage or I'll fight you over it in court. And I'll claim alienation of affection to let everyone know it had been months since we'd been intimate. Is that what you want?"

"You can't do that," I stammer. "No one will believe you."

"Can't I? We hadn't been intimate in months. You and I both know everyone will assume it's your fault. I had no choice but to stray," he says with a sigh.

"You really want your mom to hear that you cheated? That you and your brother were having a threesome in the office she helped decorate?"

"She doesn't have to know the details. We both know you'd never share them. They're as embarrassing to you as they are to me."

"As I said at the beginning of this wretched call, we don't know each other as well as we thought. Try me, Phil. I'm not the pathological people pleaser you married."

"Maybe not. But I doubt you want your new man to hear all the gritty details of the end of our marriage and how you weren't enough to meet my needs."

It's an empty threat, but it hits home nonetheless. I'm not worried about him telling Brady about the incident. I told him already. But I do have insecurities about being enough for him. He is much more experienced and open to new things than I am. I get the exact same dish at every restaurant we go to for Chrissake. He's clearly noticed since he knows my order everywhere.

I don't let Phil realize he hit a nerve. I know he's bluffing. He would never risk his mom hearing about the affair and I'm 99 percent sure he can't touch my blog since we were separated when I created it. The small amount of money I've made from it has barely covered the cost of my investment into it.

"This call is pointless. If you want to get a message to me again, go through my lawyer or I'll have you held in contempt for violating the no contact order."

"See you in court next week, wife," he sneers, before hanging up.

I throw my head back against the couch. That call is not how I wanted to spend my evening. Not only did it drain me emotionally, but it caused me to miss Brady hitting a home run. My mood sufficiently dampened, I decide to take a shower to wash off the grimy feeling it left me with before Brady gets home.

When I slip out of the bathroom a while later, Brady is sitting at the end of the bed, eyeing me. "Hey, sweet girl. I wondered where you were when I got home. I didn't hear from you after the game."

"Sorry," I say. "I needed a reset and the hot water helped clear my brain."

His expression shifts from playful to one of concern. "What's wrong?"

"Nothing important."

"Anything I can do?" he asks, pulling me in between his spread legs and running his thumbs across my cheek bones.

I nuzzle into his hands. "No, I've got it under control. It's something I have to handle myself. I'm glad you're home, though. I missed you, even though I could see you on TV."

"I missed you, too. I wish I could watch you on TV," he says with a mischievous twinkle in his eye. "I've been thinking about the reward I want for the bomb I hit."

"You have, have you?" I chuckle. "Am I the one giving this reward?"

"Of course, doll. You're the prize. It only makes sense you give out the rewards," he retorts as his fingers untuck my towel, letting it fall to the floor. His eyes darken as he takes me in. I put my hands on his thighs and start to lower myself, but he stops me.

"That's not what I want," he corrects.

"Then what do you want?" I question.

Instead of answering, he rips off his shirt and scoots further up the bed. "I want you to soak my face," he states, staring directly into my eyes.

"What?"

"You heard me. I want you to climb up here and let me eat that pretty pussy until you soak my face. Then I want you to ride my cock until your body milks my orgasm out of me. Get to it."

I'm speechless. I stand there naked, staring at the cocky smirk on his face. When I still don't move, he drops his voice. "Lola, I'm not asking, baby. I'm telling. Get your sweet ass over here and sit on my face. I'm not going to stop making you come until there is a sleepy smile on your face to replace that tight frown. Now!"

Since he leaves no room for argument, I do as he asks. Putting my hands and knees on the bed, I crawl up to him. He grabs the back of my head and kisses me until neither of us can breathe. His hands slide to my waist and he slides me up the rest of the way forcing my legs to part at his shoulders.

"There she is. Now, sit," he urges.

Hands on my hips, he pulls me down onto his waiting tongue. I gasp at the contact. I can feel him grin against my skin as he drags his tongue up to my clit. Usually, he loves to tease and work me up slowly. That is not what's happening tonight. He licks and sucks until I'm mewling. In a matter of minutes, he has me close to release. I rock my hips on his face as a ball of tightness and warmth forms in my stomach.

Pulling away to breathe – because despite some men's insistence they won't suffocate, they still do need to breathe a little – he bumps his nose into my throbbing nub. "Just like that, baby. Ride my face until you come in my mouth. I want you dripping down my chin," he demands. All it takes is one more deep suck of my clit and his hands on my hips, grinding me down on his face before I'm coming.

"Oh God," I shout. "Brady, oh God."

"You're not the first person to call me a God, today," he chuckles. "Although I prefer it in this context much better," he laughs.

With a shuddering breath, I shift to move off him, but he tightens his grip on my thighs.

"What do you think you're doing?"

"Getting to part two? I can't ride your dick from up here," I sass.

"Did I say I was done eating your pussy?" His deep, stern voice is back.

154

"No, but I finished..."

"You may have finished, but I didn't," he says, bringing his hand down and circling my clit with his thumb. "I said I wanted you to soak my face. It's barely wet."

"Oh, fuck," I squirm. He grins. Brady nips my thigh before soothing the sting with his tongue. There is no doubt they'll be covered in love bites tomorrow.

Another swipe of my clit, another jolt. "Aww, is someone sensitive?" he coos.

"Yes," I breathe.

"That's too bad. I'm far from done with you. You're going to come again on my face and then I'll let you ride my cock until you're coming all over it. Maybe then I'll be satisfied and let your tight little pussy milk me." He pauses to give me a long lick. "Or maybe I'll still want more. And you're going to give them all to me, right, baby? You want to be my good girl and give me all your orgasms?"

"I don't know if I can," I whimper.

"Sure, you can. I know what a good girl you are. Plus, you don't have a choice. This pussy is mine and I want it weeping for me by the time I fill it with my cum."

He gives me another swipe and lick, which makes me buck against his face.

"You can handle it, sweetheart. You know what to say if you don't."

"Red?"

"Red," he confirms.

I give him a slight nod and that's all the permission he needs to make good on his promises. With his thumb swiping, his tongue dives into my quivering channel before switching. His tongue circles my clit and two fingers slip inside. He immediately finds the spot he planted his flag the first time we were together and softly but deftly massages it.

As my legs start to shake, I slam my hands against the headboard for support before my orgasm washes over me. I didn't think it was possible to come harder than I did earlier, but as always, Brady surpassed my expectations. He quickly pushes me down until I'm straddling his hips and he runs his fingers up and down my things.

"Atta girl," he mutters, and I can't help but laugh. Only he would be proud of me for coming. In this position, I'm hyper aware of his hard cock nestled between my legs. He slowly and subtly shifts his pelvis, sliding it through my wet folds. I would have thought I was completely satisfied, but with a few glides, I'm ready to go again. As the Lola whisperer can tell.

"Is my girl needy again? Already?" he taunts. "Hop on, baby. Show me how much you want another one."

Despite his teasing tone, Brady helps lift me up, positioning himself at my opening. His eyes are glued to where we're joined as I slowly slide down his shaft.

"Fuck," he groans. "That's it, baby. You're so warm and tight. So goddamn wet from coming on my face." I clench around him as we bottom out.

"You like that, baby? You like me talking about how your perfect pussy came all over my tongue and fingers? It's going to come on my cock, too."

"Yes. So deep," I say, rocking back and forth.

"That's right, baby. I'm so deep I'm hitting every one of your sweet spots." Swiveling his hips, he lifts up and his mouth finds my nipples to suck them into hard pebbles. As I rock harder, I raise myself up and down on his rigid cock, seeing fireworks behind my eyes every time I sink down. Getting lost in the sensation, my rhythm falters and he takes over.

With one hand on my hip, he holds me still as he bucks up into me over and over again. "Fuck. You're clamping down on me, Lola. You gonna come again for me?"

"I can't," I pant, but even I know it's a lie. If Brady wants to get me there, he can.

His other hand comes to my throat. He doesn't squeeze, but he collars me, bringing my face to his and he stares into my eyes. "Yes, you can. Come for me, baby. Come hard on my cock and bring me over the edge with you."

The telltale sign of my orgasm coils around me. The sensation is everywhere. Still gazing into my eyes, he puts a small amount of pressure on my neck and, through gritted teeth, growls, "Come!" My overstimulated body is helpless to do anything but comply.

With a few more thrusts, he grunts out my name as he finds his own release and lays back, splaying me across his chest.

"How's that for a reset?" he whispers through labored breaths. All I can do is hum in response, making him chuckle and kiss the top of my head. He lets me lay on him for several minutes, whispering sweet words to me before deciding it's time to move. "I think your shower might have been in vain, doll. You got all dirty again."

"Whose fault is that?" I mumble sleepily.

"I didn't hear you complaining. Come on, you can't sleep yet. I'll clean you up and then we can drift off together."

With that, he carries me into the shower and washes my body with such tender care and adoration, I almost cry. His treatment of me is such a contrast to the attitude Phil showed me earlier. As always, he notices.

"What's wrong, baby? Sore?"

"No. I mean probably, but I was thinking how lucky I am to have a man who takes such good care of me."

He blows a raspberry before going back to washing the conditioner out of my hair. "Taking care of you is one of the easiest things I've ever done. I'm the lucky one, doll." Before I can argue, he shuts off the water and grabs a towel to dry us both off. Leaving me to handle my skincare routine, he heads into the kitchen to grab two glasses of water and check the locks on the door.

"You lock the door every time you come into the condo. Why do you check it again before bed?" I ask curiously.

Slipping in beside me, he shuts off his light and pulls me to him. "Can't be too careful. I've got my most precious things in here."

"Your not-so-secret Pop-Tart stash?" I tease.

"That," he laughs. "And my sweet girl. One of you is replaceable. The other is too special to risk."

With another fissure in my heart mended, I fall asleep that night wrapped in strong arms.

Chapter Twenty-Six

• BRADY •

August

After an amazing night with Lola, I'm forced to leave her sleeping in my bed in order to make the flight for our away series. As captain, I am usually the first one there, but it was harder than ever to pull myself out of bed.

Arriving with a few minutes to spare, I make myself a cup of tea, fully intending to sleep on the flight to Austin. As much as I love my job, it feels like a bad time to leave home. Things with Lola have been great, but I was never able to figure out what had her out of sorts last night.

When the game ended, I expected a text from her congratulating me on my home run. Not that I care, but I knew she was watching from my place. Not hearing from her was a little unsettling.

I was surprised when she wasn't waiting for me in the living room. The relief from realizing she was in the shower and not back at her place was short-lived when I saw how pink she was. She takes her showers hot, but not scalding as it must have been to show up on her skin. The night took a much better turn, but I still want to know what put her in a bad mood in the first place. I'm a fixer by nature and I can't tackle the problem if I don't know what it is.

"Papa Bear, you look tired." Kent comments from beside me. "Long night?" I answer him with a shrug. He continues on. "Someone must have gotten a nice going away present for playing well last night."

If only he knew how nice of a present it was. I swear I can still taste Lola on my tongue and I will never forget the feeling of her thighs shaking against my ears. Ever. It is permanently etched into my memory.

Plopping into the seat beside me, Robby groans. "It's too early to be this chipper, Dela Cruz."

"Agreed," I mutter.

"Geez, you wifed up guys are no fun. We're living the dream. Heading to Austin and then Vegas to dominate our competition. I know you're missing out on one of the job perks now that you have a ball and chain, Becker. But you have to admit it's a sweet gig."

Ignoring the obvious baiting, Robby answers our friend. "It's the best gig. I just wish I had a few more hours of dreams before I was living them. Why the hell did we need to be here this early? The game isn't until tomorrow. It's only a two-hour flight."

"We're doing a press thing this afternoon," I tell him. "There is a children's hospital in Austin and we're going to visit the patients."

"Ugh," he complains. "Now, I can't even be salty about it."

"Sorry, man. I'll try to make sure next time we have a press stop it's for a terrible cause."

"That's all I ask."

"Come on. Let's get in line to board so we can get seats far away from Kent," I joke.

"Hey, not cool you guys!" the man in question whines.

"Smart thinking," Robby comments as we walk out to the tarmac.

As excited as I am to take the field, I can't help thinking it's going to be a long week away from my girl and that something isn't quite right.

After arriving in Austin on Thursday, we spend several hours at the hospital talking to the kids and their families. Being around them makes my heart heavy, but also strangely warms it. Seeing families taking care of each other reminds me of growing up. It also reminds me I need to call and check on my brother. His wife is about to pop and I should be an uncle any day now.

Saturday's game was rained out. Causing us to have a double header yesterday. We didn't get to leave for Vegas until late last night. I will be glad to get back to Nashville on Wednesday and back in my bed with Lola.

We've texted a little, but with the double header, I didn't have much free time and yesterday she seemed a bit preoccupied. I figured she was working on getting her latest article ready for submission. I called her today, but she didn't pick up. I'd say she is still sleeping, but it's past noon there.

Trying to not to focus on her lack of communication, I head down to grab lunch before catching the bus to the stadium. On game days, we typically get to the clubhouse between 1:00 and 2:00 p.m. At home, we drive ourselves and as captain, I aim to be the first one there. It allows me to take stock of how everyone is when they arrive and determine if anyone needs any special attention. On the road, I settle for being first on the bus.

When I get to the conference room the team has set up for our lunch, I see Robby scarfing down a wrap. He waves me over when he spots me. "Hey man, grab a seat."

I sit down beside him and one of the team nutritionists brings over the lunch chef prepared. We could technically go out and get our own, but the team is required to provide us pregame meals as part of our contracts.

As we eat, we discuss ways to improve from the Austin series and who ended up on the injury list for Vegas. Other teammates filter in and out, but no one joins our table. Most guys enjoy down time before we are all together in the clubhouse to help get their mental game straight.

"You're surprisingly chill today, I gotta say," Robby admits.

"Of course, I'm chill. We're ahead of everyone in the standings, and Vegas isn't even in our league. Plus, we beat them two of the three times we've played them this year."

"We're obviously going to wipe the floor with them tonight with Sanchez injured and Kipner on the mound, but I mean about Lola. I figured you'd be anxious, at least until this afternoon."

"Why would I be anxious about Lola?" I ask.

"I don't know. I'd be feeling some kind of way if my girlfriend was having to face her dirtbag ex in court," he remarks.

"WHAT?" I roar. His eyes widen as everyone else in the room pretends not to be watching us. "What the fuck did you say, Becker?" I whisper-shout.

"Shit, did you not know? Lola's divorce is getting finalized today. She's in St. Louis getting everything settled. I figured you'd be up my ass all day asking if I had any updates, but now it makes sense that you weren't."

I let out a harsh breath, my blood pressure skyrocketing. "No, I did not know. She wanted to handle this herself, and I respected her decision. Last I heard, the lawyers were getting everything settled, and all she had to do was sign the papers which she could do from Nashville."

"That was the original plan before Phil started flexing his tiny dick and fighting over every little thing, forcing them to go in front of the judge. I can't believe she didn't tell you."

"Me and you both." How could Lola not tell me? I understand wanting to keep the details private. I know she's embarrassed to be

162

going through this, but to not tell me she was traveling? That's a big deal. I would have wanted to know she got there safely. I don't even know how she got there. Did she drive? Fly? Is she alone? Did one of the girls go with her? Does she have to go back to her house to get anything or be alone with her ex? My mind is reeling with questions.

"Sorry, Miller. I didn't mean to wreck your peace. Maybe she wanted to surprise you when we got back?" he suggests.

"Yeah, maybe," I say. Grabbing my plate, I toss what's left in the trash. "I'm gonna go get my stuff. Meet you on the bus."

"Alright, man. Don't stress on it too much. I'm sure everything is fine. She's a strong girl."

"Thanks."

When I get back to the room, I pull my phone out of my pocket and see a text from Lola.

12:13 PM

MY SWEET GIRL

Good luck at your game tonight. I'll be cheering you on from the couch. I can't wait until you're back home.

MY SWEET GIRL

I think I'm going to crash early tonight. It's been kind of a crazy day. Call me in the morning?

I can't wait until I am home, either. She's got a lot of explaining to do when I see her again. I told her I was a bossy and possessive bastard. It's time she learns how much.

163

Chapter Twenty-Seven

• LOLA •

It's strange being back at my dad's place. Last time I was here was right after I caught Phil cheating and decided to leave with the small amount of dignity I had left. That was only eight months ago. It's crazy how much has changed since then. I feel like a completely different person than the defeated wife hiding from the world and licking her wounds.

Thanks to my time in Nashville and largely the support from Brady, I know my worth and that I don't have to spend my life fitting into someone else's mold. I may not be 100 percent certain of who I am, but I think we all are constantly evolving and I am okay with that.

I like the woman I have become. She's more confident, independent, and unafraid to ask for what she wants. Sure, she has her weaknesses and moments of insecurity, but she is also surrounded by people who lift her up and celebrate her – something I didn't realize I was missing.

On the drive up Sunday, I listened to a podcast from one of my favorite self-development authors. After a barrage of texts from Phil belittling my blog and mocking my small following on social media, I was feeling foolish about what I was putting out there. Like maybe my dream was stupid, and no one cared what I had to say. That podcast gave me some amazing nuggets of wisdom, including: "It's not about the goal or the dream you have. It's about who you become on your way to that goal."

Who cares if I never get more followers? Who cares if no one ever reads my blog again? I didn't create it for notoriety. I created it to give myself an outlet to work through the feelings of my divorce and help other people feel less alone. If my words speak to one other person and inspire them to take back their life, then I'd call it success.

Last night, I ate dinner with Dad. It was quiet, but oddly reminiscent of growing up. Since we talk every few weeks, he has a general idea of what is happening in my life, but we don't discuss the demise of my marriage. To his credit, he never pushed me to reconsider divorce. He knows how it is to be in a relationship with someone who doesn't care about you.

I wish he and I were closer, but I understand the position he was put in when Mom left. With him being a single dad in a job that required a lot of travel, I spent much of my formative years pawned off on my grandmother. Now, it almost seems too late to have that deep father-daughter relationship I used to envy. Conversation is stilted and shallow.

"Are you all ready for tomorrow?" he asks over Italian takeout.

"Yep," I reply. "My lawyer has everything under control. She's a real shark. This should be pretty straightforward despite all the effort Phil has put into making it difficult. We each bought our cars before getting married. Our only significant asset is the house, which he can buy me out of, or we can sell and split the profit."

"Can he afford to buy you out?"

"He can't, but his parents can. They gave us the down payment as a wedding gift to begin with," I explain. "Honestly, I think he's embarrassed because no one in his family is divorced. He's punishing me for not playing the happy neglected housewife as every other Robinson woman has before."

"He should have known that no woman raised by your Nonna Leona would let someone keep her down for long. Look at your Aunt Teresa."

"Once," he begins, "when I was young, maybe nine or ten, our butcher tried to take advantage of us. Mr. Bianchi retired and his son Paulo took over. Instead of telling customers he was making changes or increasing prices, he slowly reduced the amount of meat he gave people with each order.

"Mama had a menu that she stuck to each week. She knew exactly how much meat she needed. Suddenly, she was running out on Friday nights and she couldn't figure out why. Your grandfather tried to blame it on me and say I must be eating more as a growing boy, but she wasn't having any of it.

"The next week, she marched in demanding he tell her why her meat was running out. She accused him of switching to a fatty product, causing there to be less lean meat. This was a big insult to him and he ended up confessing what he'd done and said he had no plans to stop."

"Oh no," I utter. "What did Nonna do? Find a new butcher?"

"And let him get away with taking advantage of her? Not a chance. No, she dragged me and your aunt out to the suburbs, where Mr. Bianchi had retired and knocked on his door. Complained that her son was shortchanging us on meat, and now her children were starving. Told him that he should be ashamed of himself and his son who was 'sullying his family name' by taking advantage of single-income families from the old country."

"What did he do?"

"He invited us in for dinner and called his son right then and there. Read him the riot act and demanded he give us extra lamb chops for the rest of the year!"

"Wow, go Nonna," I praise. "How did you get out to the suburbs? Nonna didn't drive."

"She didn't like to, but she knew how. I can count on one hand the number of times I saw her drive in my life and that was one of them. She didn't let fear of something stop her from demanding the treatment she deserved. I think that trait rubbed off on you."

"Thanks, Dad. I hope it has."

"You're a strong woman, Lola. Don't let that man or any other treat you as anything less than the treasure you are."

We finished the rest of dinner in comfortable silence and I went to bed early in preparation for court today.

"Your Honor, this case has gotten so far out of control it's laughable. The respondent is doing everything in his power to drag this out to spite my client who is more than ready to move on with her life. The division of assets should be as simple as determining what to do with the marital home. Mr. Robinson is using this court to assuage his ego," my lawyer states.

"Thank you for that assessment counselor. Do you have a response, Mr. Acron?" the judge asks Phil's attorney.

"Yes, your Honor. Thank you for the floor. Mrs. Robinson left the home suddenly after a disagreement and didn't allow my client to repair their relationship. He had hopes to reconcile. She denied him that recourse, and now his focus is on ensuring that all assets from the marriage – physical and intellectual – are divided equally. He wishes to leave this relationship on good terms with his wife even though she is unwilling to take any steps towards mending that relationship."

"I can understand that, but Missouri is a no-fault state, and it appears that reconciliation is not an option his wife has given him," the judge notes. "What is it he wants that wasn't able to be settled at mediation?"

"The issue at hand a campaign of slander Mrs. Robinson has started against her husband."

This makes the judge raise his eyebrows. "A campaign of slander? That is a new claim. Please continue."

Phil's attorney turns on the TV in the courtroom and pulls up a screen that has my social media on one side and blog on the other. I glance at my attorney panicking, but she gives me a quick shake of her head. Her lips curl up into a small smile before she shuts it down.

"Shortly after leaving her husband, Mrs. Robinson started a blog and social media accounts talking about her marriage and alleging misconduct by my client and defaming him. Her statements have affected his business and standing within the community."

"Mrs. Mercer, do you have anything to say before we review the inflammatory statements your opposing counsel is referring to?"

"I do, Your Honor. I would like to state on the record that nowhere on her blog or on its related social media accounts does my client ever mention Mr. Robinson by name or use defamatory language in reference to him. The focus of the account is to show my client's growth and transition as she moves into a new phase in her life.

"The further we get from this relationship, the less Mr. Robinson would appear in the content, but even if all she did was write about him and use his name, there is nothing illegal about discussing your personal experiences. Sharing her own story is her constitutional right. Any issues of slander or libel should be taken care of in a separate suit, not in these proceedings."

"I can't help but agree. This is an issue for another court. Why is it being brought up in mine?" the judge questions.

Mr. Acron interjects, "As part of the divorce decree, my client requests Mrs. Robinson cease posting about their relationship and delete the accounts entirely."

"And ordering her to do so would violate her First Amendment rights," my lawyer chimes in.

"Indeed, it would. This is a divorce hearing. I have no interest in dealing with constitutional liberties, Mr. Acron. Your client can take up his issues with his ex-wife's internet profiles in a different court.

Are there any issues relevant to this court you want to bring up before I make my decree?"

"No, Your Honor," he says sullenly. Phil is turning red as he whispers to his lawyer and gestures at me.

"Very well," the judge accepts. "Mrs. Mercer?"

"All good over here."

"Wonderful. I have the recommendation for division of assets from the mediator and as the petitioner's counsel stated it is pretty straightforward. I am ruling that the house be sold and profits be split 50/50 as well as their joint savings account. Each individual will take with the assets they brought into the marriage, retirement accounts, and sole ownership of their personal vehicles. If that's all, we can get out of here."

"One thing, Your Honor."

"Yes, Mrs. Mercer?"

"We would like included in the decree that Mr. Robinson has no vested interest or ownership of my clients' social media accounts or blogs. While they were technically created during their marriage, it was after months of separation."

"So included. I am hereby granting this divorce and I wish both parties the best as they move forward with their lives."

Chapter Twenty-Eight

• LOLA •

P hil storms out of the courtroom followed by his brother who eyefucked me the entire time. The way he leered at me makes me shiver in disgust. I guess he didn't have the same qualms as Phil did in regard to 'debasing' me. I am grateful to be done with this family.

"Is that it?" I ask my lawyer.

"That's it. You are officially a free woman," she congratulates.

"Thank you, Carolyn! I couldn't have made it through all this without you."

"Of course, honey. I'm glad you're free of that toad. I was happy to help. Your Uncle Steve was one of my close cohorts in law school. Are you driving back to Nashville today?"

"I think so. If I grab a quick bite, I can get on the road by two and make it back before sunset. There is nothing left here for me. I want to get home as soon as possible," I say.

"I don't blame you. Safe travels." With a pat on the shoulder, she says goodbye and heads out of the courthouse.

As I pull out my phone to search for a place to eat, I see Brady texted me earlier this morning.

8:57 AM

BRADY BEAR

Good morning, sweet girl. I hope you slept well. I'll be sleeping good again once I get back home to you and my bed. Call later?

12:13 PM

ME

Good luck at your game tonight. I'll be cheering you on from the couch. I can't wait until you're back home.

ME

I think I'm going to crash early tonight. It's been kind of a crazy day. Call me in the morning?

BRADY BEAR

Thanks. I'll give you a call tomorrow morning.

Brady isn't the most talkative man in the world over text, but he usually has a little more to say than that. He had a long day yesterday. He's probably tired. I feel a little guilty for not telling him about the court date today, but I wanted to do this on my own. I know if I told him he would have supported me as best he could, but I didn't want to use him as a crutch. I needed to prove to myself that I could handle this on my own.

I'm afraid he's going to be pissed when he finds out but that is future Lola's problem. Right now, I am on cloud nine and nothing is bringing me down.

The drive back from St. Louis was long but cathartic. I blasted Taylor Swift the entire way and jammed out with a lightness I haven't experienced in years. I didn't think I would be physically affected by being granted the divorce, but it's as if a weight has been lifted off my shoulders. Like the thing that has been trying to drag me down for months was suddenly cut off my ankle and I am free to float.

I go out with Tiffany, Carina, and Charlie on Tuesday to celebrate and watch the last game of the away series. We go a little too hard and I end up missing a call from Brady because I'm passed out in my bed. That's what happens when your friends encourage people to buy you "newly divorced" shots. RIP My liver. But also, worth it.

I wake up feeling how I imagine a human cannonball does the day after his stunt. I never see where those guys land, but I can't imagine it is soft. I force myself into the shower and come out somewhat less comatose. I snag a glass of water, pre-made coffee because the fancy stuff is too hard right now, and one of the emergency Pop-Tarts I keep here for Brady.

Peeking at my phone, I groan at all the missed messages from last night and this morning. The first thread I click on is my group chat with the girls.

12:03 AM

TIFF

Posting this here for posterity [video attached of Lola taking a boob shot from Carina]

CAREBEAR

Ha ha ha. I am so sending it to Robby. Do you think his jealousy will extend to my cousin?

TIFF

I doubt it, but I know you enjoy poking the bear. It doesn't hurt to try.

CAREBEAR

You are too right. This road trip has been way too long. Mama needs some attention.

1:16 AM

CAREBEAR

Bunny, where are you? There is another fine gentleman here ready to buy you a drink.

ME

I had to peeeeee! My bladder is bursting with liquor!

TIFF

Hurry back before Meatball ends up taking it instead.

1:48 AM

ME

I love you guys. And I looooove not being married.

TIFF

Yeah! Marriage is the worst! Love you, too. But where are you?

CAREBEAR

We're on the deck. Come out here. I've got a wasted Bunny on my hands and we need to get her home.

Also, being married is awesome, your husband just sucked.

TIFF

Good riddance to Pencil Prick Phil!

> Calling a ride now. I'll meet you by the
> stairs.

Oh my God. I can't believe I was that drunk last night. I appreciate them for celebrating with me but maybe we could have turned down a few of those free shots. I send a series of skull emoji before opening my thread with Georgie.

9:24 AM

> GEORGIE
>
> Congratulations on losing 175 lbs of ass,
> Honeybun. Come to Chicago and celebrate
> with me soon!

Lacking the energy to have a conversation with my bestie, I heart his message. As I do, a disheveled Tiffany appears from her bedroom.

"Food?" she croaks. I shake my head and offer her the other Pop-Tart.

"Ugh, no," she grunts and turns back into her room. "I'm going to get sustenance. If that man of yours hasn't dragged you away by the time I get back, I'll share. Otherwise, I'll leave it in the fridge."

"You are a true queen," I thank. The only other messages I have are from Brady. Knowing he should be back any minute, I open them. We didn't talk much yesterday. His mood was a bit off, but I figured it had to do with losing the night before. He struck out twice and never made it on to base.

8:45 PM

> ME
>
> Watching you guys play! Good luck! [image
> of the girls at Holler's in front of a giant TV

11:57 PM

174

BRADY BEAR

Thanks, doll. I'm glad we pulled that one
out. You home yet?

12:12 AM

BRADY BEAR

Based on the video Carina sent Robby, I'm
going to assume you are still out. Be careful
tonight. Text me when you get home,
please.

10:34 AM

BRADY BEAR

Boarding the plane. I'll be at your place
after we land. I know you got home, but I
wouldn't mind some proof of life.

2:08 PM

BRADY BEAR

En route.

That last text came half an hour ago which means he should be
here any minute. Tiffany emerges slightly more put together – hair in
a messy bun, wearing a t-shirt dress. It's an improvement over the PJs
and rat's nest she had going on earlier. She lets out a squeal as she
opens the door.

"Holy shit!"

I glance up to see Brady mid-knock attempt. "Sorry," he mutters
sheepishly.

"No problem, big guy. Since you're home now, you're in charge
of feeding the Bunny." Without any other words, she ushers him in
and takes her leave.

"Hi," I say, lamely from the couch.

"Have you eaten anything today?" he questions. I again hold up the Pop-Tart and he shakes his head. "Come on, let's get something substantial in you."

Standing up, I slip on shoes and let my man take me to get something to eat.

Chapter Twenty-Nine

I have déjà vu bringing Lola back to the diner. It's hard to believe that was only three months ago. That reminder helps calm the emotions storming through me. My feelings for her are strong, but I need to remember that we haven't known each other long and we've been in a relationship for even less time. We're bound to have missteps at this stage as much as I like to pretend we're beyond that.

I've tried not to be offended that Lola didn't tell me about the court date. I'm furious she drove – yes, I found out she drove all by herself – to St. Louis without telling me. I was amused and a little jealous last night seeing the video of her sticking her face in Carina's cleavage and pulling out a shot. If Tiffany hadn't sent me a picture of Lola passed out in her bed snuggled up in one of my shirts, I would have worried about her all night.

It's hard to remember most of those things, though, as I listen to her moan over pancakes in the same way she usually moans over my cock. "Good?" I ask.

"S'mazing," she responds with her mouth full. She's so fucking cute I can't stand it.

"Good, those pancakes have a lot of alcohol to soak up. You're in better shape than I expected."

"I drank vodka water instead of vodka soda last night. It was gross but I think it helped hydrate me."

"I'm not sure that's a thing, but I'll take your word for it."

The rest of the meal goes on relatively quietly and I drive her back to our complex with the radio on to fill the space. "Come up to my place," I say.

"Sure," she replies. I didn't technically ask her, it was more of a demand, but whatever as long as I get the same end result.

When we get to my condo, I lead us over to the couch and sit down with her facing me. I stare at her for a few seconds as she fidgets. "I'm guessing you know where I was this week and want to talk about it?" she assesses.

"Yeah, I think that would be a good idea. Why don't you start by telling me why the hell you didn't let me know you had to go to St. Louis to meet your ex-husband. He is your ex, right? The divorce was granted? I'm not sure since you never mentioned anything about this to me."

She winces before annoyance flashes across her face. I know my tone came out harsh, but I'm angry. "Yes, I am now unmarried in the eyes of the law. And I didn't tell you, because I didn't want you to have to deal with it. It was my shit, and I needed to handle it on my own."

"You know I want to help you, baby."

"I know you do and I love that. But this was something I had to do for me. My dad always taught me that no one fights your battles for you. If I let you take over this one, I don't know if I'd ever be able to face one alone again. I'd get too dependent on you."

"Do it," I state.

"Do what?"

178

"Depend on me. Lean on me. Use me to fight your battles. I'm your army to command."

"That isn't how it works," she retorts. "I can't go on the rest of my life letting you fight my battles."

"Of course, you can. You don't have to fight your battles alone, Lola. Or at all. I'm right here, waiting to be called into action. I'll take on any challenge you need me to. I know your dad told you that you have to, but it's bullshit. You're surrounded by people who would fight beside you."

She peers back at me quizzically as if this information is a revelation she doesn't know how to process.

"Honestly, you going to court and facing that douche nozzle on your own isn't even what I'm upset about. I get that," I confess.

"It's not?"

"No."

"So, we're good?" she questions, hopefully.

I laugh. "No, sweetheart, we are not good. You drove over four hours away by yourself and didn't tell me. You weren't honest with me about where you were or what you were doing for days. You know I'm overprotective. If you think I like to know where you are when I'm in town don't you think I'd want to know you went to an entirely different state? Instead, you did it behind my back."

"Behind your back is a little strong," she defends.

"Is it? I always let you know where I'm going. Sure, it's for work and you could easily find it out yourself, but I make sure you know that I arrive safely and when I intend to get back. What if something happened? I would have no idea where you were."

"Other people knew where I was," she mumbles.

"Yeah, and one of them accidentally told me. You know how that made me feel? To find out news this big from Robby? He's supposed to look up to me as his captain, not watch me freak out because my girlfriend kept something this huge from me and I haven't heard from her all day."

"I can see how that would be upsetting. I'm sorry. I just... didn't want to open that can of worms. If I told you I was going to St. Louis and you asked why I'd either have to tell you the truth or lie. By not telling you at all, I didn't have to make that choice."

I don't see why telling me the truth was such a bad option. What did she think would happen? I'd skip my game to be there? I mean, if I could have, I probably would have considered it but we both know that wasn't on the table.

I huff out a frustrated breath. "Lola, we're supposed to be part-ners. You lean on me. I lean on you. And more than that, you know how strong my need to care and protect you is. It feels like you don't trust me to do that when you hide things from me. How would you feel if I went away for days and didn't tell you?"

Her shoulders hunch as the gravity of her deception and its implications finally take root. I don't want to make her feel bad, but I need her to know I won't accept secrets between us. She can trust me with anything.

"You're right. I'm sorry. I wasn't thinking about you or how it would affect you emotionally when you found out. I'll never keep something like that from you again. I promise."

"Thank you, that's all I ask."

"Now we're good?"

We were always good, but I don't tell her that. I'm not one to hold a grudge, but this is an excellent opportunity to test her boundaries and relieve the tension from the last twenty-four hours.

"I don't know," I consider. "What you did was pretty big. I think there needs to be some sort of punishment."

Watching her reaction, I see her eyes flare with desire while also crinkling in apprehension. This is all for fun, but it is also a test of trust, something I need after what happened. She needs to know she can count on me to take care of her both physically and emotionally, even in scary or hard situations.

"Punishment? What kind of punishment?"

"Hmm, well it should fit the crime. It should be something that gives you the same discomfort I felt not knowing where you were. I was thinking I turn that sweet ass red before coming deep inside your tight little pussy. Does that sound fair to you?" I prompt.

"You want to spank me?"

"Only since the first time I ever laid eyes on you."

"But I hadn't done anything bad then!" she whines.

"Trust me, doll. You're going to enjoy this punishment much more than you hate it. What do you think? You want me to get you all messy while I pinken your smooth, full cheeks?"

Chapter Thirty

• LOLA •

Only Brady could make spanking me sound like a favor. Part of me thinks I should say no and run for the hills. I'm a grown woman; I don't need to be punished by my boyfriend like a misbehaving child.

Another part of me, though, is intrigued. The idea of him laying me across his lap and bringing his hand down on my ass has me clenching my thighs together.

Sensing my dilemma, Brady wraps his hand around the back of my neck and pulls me into his lap for an all-consuming kiss. He nips at my bottom lip until I open and allow entry to his tongue. He flicks it inside my mouth, toying with my mine until I'm squirming on his lap. With his other hand, he grabs a handful of my ass and squeezes.

His lips trail down my jaw until he scrapes his teeth across the sensitive skin below my ear and whispers, "What do you say, Lola? Want to take your punishment like a good girl so I can make you scream my name in the middle of the day? If you're loud enough we can wake Kent from his post-road trip nap."

182

The idea adds enough levity to the situation to sway my decision. "Okay," I agree.

"Yeah?" He pulls back, staring into my eyes. "You don't have to do this if you don't want to. I don't need to punish you to forgive you. I already have. But I'm not going to lie and say the idea of spanking you doesn't have my dick rock hard."

"I want to try. You'll go easy on me, right? No bruises?"

"I would never hit you hard enough to bruise, baby. Your ass might be a little pink and tender for a minute, but tomorrow it will be as if it never happened. You have your safe word if you want to stop at any point."

I nod and he gives me a salacious grin. "Let's start by getting you naked. Strip. Now."

I'm jarred at the abrupt change in his tone. He went from concerned to bossy in two seconds flat. I shiver at his sternness and it sets me into action. Quickly as I can, I pull off my shirt and shove my shorts and panties off, leaving me completely bare in front of him.

His gaze travels down my body before meeting my eyes. "Lay across my lap," he instructs, patting his thigh. I carefully drape myself over him and his hand comes to the small of my back, rubbing circles. Sliding across my skin, he runs his hands over one ass cheek, then the other.

"It's a count of six. That's how many days it's been since I've gotten to see this sexy body. Put your hands on the armrest and don't move them. I don't want to risk hitting them. Got it?"

I nod. "Words," he insists with a quick slap to one cheek.

"Yes, sir," I utter.

"Good girl," he coos.

With no other preamble, he brings his palm down. I'm more shocked by the noise than the sensation. His hand leaves my ass and smacks the other cheek.

"Green?" he questions.

"Green," I confirm. His hand comes down on each cheek again with quick succession and I moan when he rubs the sting. I try to push my thighs together to seek out friction, but he stops the motion, keeping them apart.

"I think someone is enjoying this. Do you like laying on my lap, Lola? Does me leaving handprints on your juicy ass turn you on?" Before I can answer, he trails his fingers between my legs and rubs my slit. "You don't even have to use your words, doll. Your body is telling me for you." He rubs faster, working me up before removing his fingers.

He laughs at the keening sound I make. "You've still got two more," he reminds me before delivering two smacks harder than the others. I jolt forward a bit but braced against the armrest, I don't move too far. He again rubs away the sting before toying with my swollen, arousal covered lips.

"God, I missed this pussy. I thought about it every night while I was away. Thought about how wet it gets for me. How tightly it grips my cock when I hit that spot you love," he taunts, slipping his fingers inside to rub against my walls. I buck into this hand and he laughs. Laughs at my effort for more friction!

"Oh no, baby. This is a punishment. You get what I give you," he says, sliding his finger back out and making slow circles around my clit. He keeps alternating between fingering me and rubbing light circles until I am positive I'm going to explode with need.

"Pleaseeeee, Brady," I beg.

"Please what? You know you have to use your words. Tell me what you want. What you need."

I moan as he applies marginally more pressure to my clit. "Fuck me, please."

"Gladly," he replies before sliding me off his lap and positioning me on my knees, chest pressed into the couch.

"This is going to be fast, baby," he announces, rubbing his cock against my folds. "It's been too long since I've been inside you. I know I won't last long."

"I don't care, Brady. Fuck me. Please. Now!"

His chuckle at my desperation turns into a groan as he pushes inside me. With slow shallow thrusts, he lets me get used to his size before he withdraws further and slams back in.

"Fuck," he shouts. "You feel incredible. Nothing has ever felt as right as being in your pussy. It's perfect. You're perfect."

"Yes," I scream. "More, please more!"

"That's it, baby. You getting close for me? Going to come with my cock deep inside your sweet pussy?"

"Yes, yes, yes," I chant as he tilts my hips up further, angling him even deeper inside me. "God, right there. Don't stop!"

He pumps faster and reaches a hand around until his fingertips land on my clit. He's rubbing in circles again, but this time he's adding a delicious amount of friction.

"Brady, Bradyyyyy!"

"I know, baby. I sense it, too. You're so close. Let go. Come for me, Lola. Come!" he barks.

I feel him start to empty inside me as my own release is triggered. He continues to rub my clit with his dick seated inside me as my orgasm racks through my body. When my body stops shuddering, he wraps both arms around my middle and kisses my shoulder. "That's my girl. Let's get cleaned up and you can tell me everything I missed this week."

Chapter Thirty-One

• BRADY •

A fter our explosive afternoon together, things are better than ever between Lola and I. She's been in my bed every night and hangs out with me in the mornings before I go to the stadium. We eat lunch together and then she goes back to her place to work. Sometimes she and the girls come to the games and sometimes they don't. Tonight, though, they're here because Robby's sister, Morgan, is in town.

I'm sitting in the clubhouse at my locker, scrolling through my phone as the guys filter in. I spend a few minutes chatting with a new outfielder who was recently called up when Kent makes his way over. "Getting a tongue-lashing from Cap already, Crews? I thought he saved that for Lola."

"Fuck off, man," I admonish. "If you need me to give you tips on how to please a lady, all you have to do is ask."

Crews lets out a snort as he walks away. "Listen, if they're in my bed, they aren't exactly *ladies*, but none of them leave unsatisfied," Kent retorts with a wink.

"Stop being a perv, Dela Cruz, or Carina won't let you come to her charity event this weekend," Robby says.

"What is it, 'pick on Kent day'? I am nothing but nice to you guys. I haven't even mentioned the fact that my midday nap was interrupted earlier this week by some loud lovemaking, because that would be uncouth," Kent states with a teasing tone.

"I don't know what you're referring to," I insist, but the smirk on my face gives me away.

"I take it midday lovemaking means things are picking up between the two of you? I'm seeing a lot more of Tiffany lately, which leads me to believe her roomie is otherwise occupied," Robby surmises.

"Yeah, things are going great. Really great. We've hit a couple bumps in the road, but considering what she's been through the last year, that's to be expected."

"I gotta say, I was a little surprised how fast she moved on, especially after how that douche canoe treated her. I always got a bad vibe from the guy," Robby grouses.

"You and me both," I respond. "She was apprehensive at first, but their marriage was over emotionally for a while. She was more concerned about the optics than needing time to get over the relationship."

"If those noises were anything to go by, our boy is keeping her more than satisfied. He treats her way better than he treats me, that's for sure," Kent adds. I definitely do. I don't want Lola to go another day where she doesn't realize how fucking precious is. Where she isn't treasured and cherished. Not on my watch.

"Should I mark off some time in the off season for a wedding?" Kent teases.

I shrug and Robby smiles.

"Wait, seriously? I was joking!" The right fielder claims. "You guys have only been together for a few months and she's been divorced for a week!"

"Relax, playboy. His being smitten by a woman doesn't mean you

187

will be, too. It's not contagious. But when you know, you know," Robby says. "Besides, being married is awesome. 10/10 recommend locking down your dream girl. That's what she is, right?"

"She's better than anything I could have ever dreamed, man," I confess. "I never thought I'd find a woman who fit with my personality so well. I know it's soon and I'm not planning to propose tomorrow or anything, but I can see it heading in that direction. I know we both want the same things. I'm trying not to scare her off with too much, too soon, to be honest."

"I'm happy for you. It couldn't have happened to two better people. You know, once we're semi-related, we can *really* start excluding Kent from things by calling it a family outing," Robby says with a wag of his eyebrow.

"Why must you hurt me? You're lucky your moms are happily married, otherwise you might find yourself calling me Daddy," Kent threatens.

"Hard pass on that one. Linda would see through your charms."

"Marilyn would, too," I note. "My brother Jimmy is single, though. Shoot your shot." With that statement lingering in the air, I stand up to go chat with a few more players before it's game time.

Chapter Thirty-Two

• LOLA •

I t's the end of August and I've found my groove with work at the magazine and my blog. I've gotten to not only explore my new city but also myself thanks to all the writing I am doing. I am getting a much better handle on who the real Lola is, not the woman who tried to make everyone else's life easier.

A huge part of that has been my relationship with Brady. He is more supportive than I ever knew a partner could be. I never had a great example of what a relationship was. The closest thing I had to role models for healthy relationships were Teresa and Steve, and they got together during my teen years. Plus I only saw them in the summer and sporadically during the year.

Brady's support is major yet subtle. He just *does* things. He noticed one of the lights was out in my bathroom and the next day it was magically replaced. I said I wanted to drink more water and a cute, emerald water bottle appeared on the island. I mentioned – in passing – that I missed the toasted ravioli from my favorite place in

St. Louis and the next night I found myself at a hole-in-the-wall Italian bistro stuffing my face with cheesy, marinara goodness.

He never calls attention to these actions, simply does them as if they're no big deal. Competency kink unlocked. It shines a stark light on how much crap I was putting up with in my last relationship.

When we first moved into our house, the porch light went off after a few weeks. I nagged Phil about it for months because I hated coming home to a dark house. After three months, I changed it myself and he had the audacity to complain that he preferred cool toned lights over warm toned ones.

Today is another example of Brady selflessly doing things for me and how much he gets me. It's his only day off this week and he decided he wanted to use it to help me check another thing off my bucket list. I've been putting a lot of work into my blog lately. Thanks to a post about finalizing my divorce going semi-viral and Morgan tagging me in a few photos during her visit, I hit over 50k followers.

A man who loves surprises – giving not receiving – Brady won't tell me what we're doing. He won't even tell me what to wear. He said to start off in workout clothes and he'll have Tiffany pack the rest.

Normally surprises make me nervous since I am a type A person. But with Brady, I don't worry about that. He is the most competent person I know. Whatever he has planned, he has thought through and made proper preparations for. It's refreshing to be able to go with the flow. This must be how Tiffany feels all the time with Carina and my perfectionist asses constantly playing cruise director.

Being with Brady allows me to relax in a way I never could with Phil. Anytime my ex did anything 'sweet' or 'considerate' for me, they were way off base from what I truly wanted or secretly for him. I didn't want fancy or showy. I wanted real. Booking a helicopter tour may seem romantic, but it isn't for a girl who is afraid of heights. One Christmas I asked for a cheap espresso machine or French press. Instead, Phil got me an outrageously expensive tea kettle that was never once used. I could have been enjoying delightful lattes years sooner if he had given me what I wanted instead of what *he* wanted me to have.

As I slide on my sneakers, I hear a familiar knock. I grab my new water bottle and bound to the door. When I open it, Brady is there looking like a snack. It should be illegal to be as sexy in athletic shorts as he is. He kills me with those damn five-inch inseams.

He eyes me hungrily as his teeth roll over his bottom lip. "Good morning, sweet girl. That workout set is really doing it for me."

"Thank you," I reply. "You are quite delicious yourself this morning." Standing on my toes, I give him a quick peck which, per usual, he deepens into a heart-stopping kiss.

"Ready to go? We have a tight schedule to keep," he says as he pulls away.

"Are you going to tell me where we're going yet? Please don't say you're making me go for a jog. I'm not like you people. I don't have the stamina."

"You people? You mean athletes?" He questions.

"No, lunatics who think running is fun."

He laughs. "It's not that we think running is fun. We think it is beneficial, especially considering I have to do it as part of my job. It helps with stamina, which you don't need since I am more than happy to hold you up when your legs give out."

"Brady!" I admonish.

"What? I'm just saying. Is that the bag Tiffany packed for you?" he asks, pointing to the tote beside the door.

"Yep. She wouldn't even let me peek at it."

"Aww, poor baby," he coos with a fake pout. "You'll see what's inside soon enough. Let's get moving."

Grabbing the bag – because God forbid, I carry it – Brady leads me to his truck. When he opens the passenger door, I am pleasantly surprised to be greeted by an iced latte and breakfast tacos.

"Yum! You're the best," I exclaim.

"You're an easy woman to please," he remarks as he slides into his seat. "The first stop is about forty-five minutes away. I figured you would need something to keep hangry Lola at bay." Handing me the aux cord, he throws his car in reverse and we head to our first destination.

Brady and I enjoy a comfortable silence as he navigates us through the hills outside Nashville. When I am starting to seriously wonder where he is taking us, he pulls into Lavigne Vineyards.

"Little early for wine, don't you think?" I ask. "I'm down for a breakfast drink, but if this is how the day begins, you might actually have to hold me up by the end of the day."

"Cheeky thing this morning," he retorts. "What I have planned is better than wine. Come see for yourself."

We walk for a few minutes, passing the main building and side yard where Carina had her ceremony. As we approach a pavilion with a makeshift fence around it, I finally notice mats laid on the ground and people stretching.

"A yoga class?"

"Not any yoga class," he states. "What item on your bucket list is yoga-related?"

I ponder for a moment until it dawns on me. "We're doing goat yoga?!" I ask excitedly. Whipping my head around, I search for the animals as Brady chuckles beside me.

"We're doing goat yoga," he confirms.

"How did you find out about this?"

"Somehow, through my groomsmen duties, I subscribed to their newsletter. I received an email last week that talked about goat yoga and I remembered it being on your list. Ten minutes and $38 later, we were all signed up.

"Now that they have a few months' experience under their belts, the owners are introducing new activities and offerings to make this a destination for more than wine tasting. Although, we do get a free glass after class."

"That is such a cool business idea! What other things are they doing?"

"One of those drink and painting classes and a charcuterie board tutorial were the other ones I saw in an email," he answers.

"Those both sound amazing," I say dreamily.

"Then we'll have to sign up for them another time. Today though, we're finding our zen with some goats."

As he finishes his statement, a woman with more fineness than I will ever possess walks through the gate at the front of the pavilion. "Good morning, all," she greets. "I'm Kristie. I will be your instructor this morning. Thank you for signing up for our beginner goat yoga experience."

Kristie goes on to explain the rules for interacting with the animals and does her best to prepare us for what we can expect out of them. When she is done with her spiel, she has us sit in lotus position – better known as criss cross applesauce to non-yogis – and brings in the goats.

Clearly not their first rodeo, they wander around the makeshift pen, going up to people to request pets. As we move through the yoga flow, they get more comfortable getting in our way. I almost fall over from laughing while in half-moon pose as one particularly mischievous goat headbutts Brady's leg. Thanks to his thick thighs, he is able to absorb the blow, but the surprised look on his face was priceless.

I'm smiling from ear to ear as we pack up to leave. Glancing down at me, Brady has a similar expression. "Everything you thought it would be, sweet girl?" he asks me with a kiss on the head.

"Yes," I beam. "Much more, in fact! Probably not the best workout of all time, but I am relaxed and centered. Plus, it was freaking cute."

"Good. Mission accomplished then."

As we're turning to leave, a young woman around twenty comes running up to us. "Mr. Miller!" she yells. When she reaches us, she takes a deep breath. "You would think trekking across campus all day would have me in better shape. Hi, I'm Emerly Lavigne. My family and I own the vineyard."

"Hi, Emerly, nice to meet you," Brady says, shaking her hand. "You can call me Miller. This is my girlfriend, Lola."

"Nice to meet you both," she responds. "I wanted to catch you before you left to see if we could get a picture of you with one of the goats? This is a new offering for us and being able to show someone as high profile as you taking part would really help get the word out. Plus, a lot of men think it's too girly, but there is nothing girly about you. You're so tall and all those muscles are—"

Brady stops her before she can ramble any further. "I'd love to. If you send the photo to me, I can share it on my channels, too. Do you mind getting us both in it?"

"Absolutely!" she beams. Emerly snaps a few pictures and I am ecstatic to be able to cuddle the goats more. Once she is done, we enjoy our free glass of wine and I change for the next location on Brady's mystery day.

"Do I get to know where we're going next, or is that still a secret?" I question.

"Not a secret," he corrects, "a surprise."

"Yeah, yeah. Take me away then, Mr. Chauffeur."

"Gladly, sweet girl."

Chapter Thirty-Three

· LOLA ·

We park in front of a small, craftsman-style home located in Music Row. When I turn to ask where we are, I notice nerves haunting his features. Crap. If he's nervous, I'm nervous. Brady is the flight attendant of this little adventure. On a flight, you don't panic unless you notice them panicking. Same deal here.

Clearing his throat, he gazes over at me. "This stop doesn't technically fulfill an item on your list, but it will help you get closer to achieving your goals by making moves in the right direction."

That's not cryptic at all... Where could we be that would help me 'make moves in the right direction' that is located inside a house in a business district? Could this be a therapist's office? That would line up with what he said, and a converted house would make a homey space to spill your guts. Talking to a therapist about all my past baggage is on my life to do list, but hadn't gotten around to it yet. Does Brady really want to open up that can of worms in the middle of our fun day together?

Instead of asking any of the semi-normal questions swirling in my mind, I blurt out, "Do you think I'm emotionally unstable?"

"What?" he rears back in surprise.

"I would get it if you did. I have had a lot going on lately, but if you thought I needed therapy, I'd rather you have talked to me about it. I know you think of yourself as Mr. Fix-It, but choosing a therapist is something I want a say in."

"I thought I was handling the divorce and the childhood trauma it evoked well. If you think I need intervention before I go full-on 2007 Britney, you could have talked to me about it first."

"2007 Britney? What does that even mean?"

"That's what we're doing here, right? Seeing a therapist?" I ask, pointing to the house.

He sits stunned for a few seconds before tipping his head back and barking out a loud laugh. It takes him a few minutes to get a hold of himself.

"You done?" I deadpan, annoyed.

"I'm sorry, baby. That was too funny," he declares, wiping tears from his eyes. "This is not a therapist's office."

"It's not?"

"No."

"Then what is it?" I huff, embarrassed by my rant.

He reaches over and tucks a loose strand of hair behind my ear. "This," he states with his head tipped to the building, "is my management team's office: Green & Kinser. The agency mainly represents athletes and musicians, but they recently began working with influencers, too. I sent my PR rep your blog, and she wanted to meet you to discuss collaborating on some upcoming projects. I thought she might also be able to give you some advice on how to take your account to the next level. You're great at the content part, but she could help you with promotion and securing more brand deals."

"You showed her my blog, and she wants to meet me?" I squeak.

"She sure does. She has been hounding me about it for weeks now and I thought today would be a good day to do it."

I glimpse down at the sundress Tiffany picked out. It's cute and decently modest, but not anywhere close to business casual. Noticing my assessment of myself, Brady interrupts my negative self-talk.

"You look beautiful, baby. As I said, they work with athletes. They're used to us rolling up in workout clothes and wet hair. Molly is about my age and from what I recall, is usually in jeans. You don't need to be dressed all fancy."

"Okay," I acquiesce.

"I'm going to walk inside with you to say 'hello,' but then I'll leave the two of you to chat. I've got to go by my agent's office down the hall to sign some paperwork, but then I'll be back to take you to the next stop. Text me if you're done before me and I'll speed it along. Sound good?"

My nod has him rounding the truck and leading me inside.

As Brady said, Molly is wearing jeans and a Ryder Brothers tour tee. From what I can see in the lobby, they must be repped by the same agency. Molly appears to be in her mid thirties with a friendly smile and the sleekest ponytail I have ever seen.

"Miller, good to see you. It's about time you brought this precious angel in to meet me," she gushes. "I am obsessed with your blog. My sister is going through a divorce and I am constantly sending her your posts. You found an underrepresented audience."

I blush at her praise. "Thank you. I realized when I was going through it how little support or information was out there. No one was talking about what it's like when your identity shifts that much right as everyone else is finding theirs. I hope I am making other women – and men – feel more seen."

"Ugh, and humble, too!" she comments. "Alright Mr. Baseball, Tyler and Macy are expecting you in his office. Go see the man before he blows up the group chat. We'll call you when we are done here."

"Alright, Molls. Take care of my girl."

"Of course," she vows.

Miller gives me a chaste kiss and promises to be here when I am done.

"Let's move this conversation to my office," Molly suggests.

I follow her into what I assume is an old bedroom. It has vibrant, abstract wallpaper on the top half of the wall and deep blue paint under the chair rail. She sits on a blue velvet chair and points to the couch beside it for me to join her.

"As I mentioned, I have already seen your blog and loved it. I think you have a unique voice and perspective that brands are aching for. Many influencers these days are cookie cutter and saturating the same audience. They lack an emotional depth that your account has in spades."

Wow. That is some high praise. I have tried hard to be as authentic as I can. I am glad it is coming across. There is no way it would work otherwise. The world didn't need another highlight reel. It needed raw takes on the realities of going through a divorce after marrying young and what the process of starting over truly looks like.

Molly continues, "Miller probably told you that I work with athletes, which is true. My counterpart Eliza handles our music industry clients, but we are planning to bring on a third partner to focus on influencers. Until then, I will be managing the vertical.

"We have a lot of businesses approach us to work with our high profile clients that aren't a good fit. We found that their campaign goals and budgets align much more strongly with influencers in niche markets. As social media has grown, the public has shifted to trusting influencers more than celebrities. Because they give people the sense that they know them.

"What we want to do here is build up a network of influencers who we can match with those brand campaigns when they pop up. We will also offer packages to help our influencers get into major publications, but they don't need the same style of representation that artists and athletes do.

"You don't need us to manage your social media or online community. You do an incredible job of that on your own. What we have found influencers need is help on the brand deals side. Companies tend to lowball micro-influencers and try to take advantage of them even though their conversions can be much higher than the bigger names. Does that sound accurate to you?

"Yes," I answer. "That lines up with what I've experienced. I've been approached by several brands of varying sizes and the bigger the company is, the more they want for less. They also don't seem to care how authentic it might be for my brand. I've had an infant product company hounding me lately to feature them. I can understand that my audience is full of moms, but I don't have any kids and neither do any of my close friends. What do they expect me to do? Try out the stroller myself? I'm small, but not that small."

This earns me a laugh from Molly. I pat myself on the back for saying anything this posh woman thinks is clever.

"Exactly," she agrees. "That is what we want to help avoid. Brands can go through us and free up your DMs for your community."

"How would this work?" I ask. "I know typically PR agencies are paid a monthly retainer or hourly fee. To be honest, I am not in a position to do that right now."

"I get that," she states. "That is why we are going to do things differently than we do with our other clients. For now, we are offering more of a commission-style arrangement. For brand deals over a certain amount, we will take 15 percent of what they pay. For brands below that amount, we will take a flat fee to ensure we are being paid fairly for the work we put in. But anything below a certain threshold isn't worth either of our time. Any deals you get on your own will be untouched by us.

"You would be getting in on the ground floor. As we grow this service, there will be some growing pains, but you'll also have the opportunity to help us create a process that works for influencers in varying niches."

I'm intrigued by what Molly has laid out. As much as I dislike the term 'influencer' I have to admit that is what I am, even if I see myself as more of a writer. The things I say do influence other people to try new things, products included. The larger I have gotten, the more brands reach out to me. It would be great to have them go through someone else rather than badgering me and filling up my inbox. Plus, it sounds like the agency has a pool of brands reaching out to them already. I could get some cool opportunities through the partnership.

As I think through the implications, Molly offers a way to test out the program. "If you're interested in a trial run, we have a local home goods company working with some of our smaller artists. I think they would be a good fit with your brand. We have a dating app, too, but based on how that man was mooning at you, I don't suppose you're in-market for that."

"No," I reply. "But I have friends who do online dating and give me feedback on it. Dating post-divorce is a topic my audience is champing at the bit for content on. Seeing as I fell into my relation-ship unconventionally, I've been nervous to share too much about it, especially with Brady in the public eye."

"As his PR rep, let me say the man could use more publicity. People think he's a recluse. Share away!" We talk for a few more minutes about my blog and experiences before we hear voices outside.

Standing, she directs me to follow her out the door. "I guess it's time I return you to Miller. He's been pacing the lobby for the last few minutes. I'll have my intern, Leah, reach out to you with all the details. Email either one of us if you have any questions. I am excited to see what you come up with for these brands."

"Thank you," I say again.

As we leave her office, Brady is waiting for me in the lobby. We walk hand-in-hand to his truck and head off to our next destination. On the drive, I can't help but be thankful for the opportunities I've been given and grateful to Brady for putting his support behind me. He went out of his way to make this happen and even if nothing comes from it, that act in itself means the world.

He hasn't said the words yet, but his actions make me feel loved and taken care of in a way I never have. I've been falling for him since the day I gave him a chance and I'm starting to think I've fallen all the way. I just hope he's there to catch me.

Chapter Thirty-Four

I was initially hesitant about introducing Lola to Molly and the rest of the PR team. Not because I didn't think they would love her, but because I didn't know if that would be overstepping. She has built her entire blog and social community by herself. I didn't want her to think I was trying to push her to make it grow or shift it in one direction or another.

Truthfully, I am proud of everything she has created. I've seen the hard work she puts into crafting her posts and all the things she is trying in the name of growth and self-discovery. I don't want her to believe I think it needs to be more successful or lucrative. She could work for free and I wouldn't care – aside from the fact that she deserves to be compensated for her hard work. I make enough that she never needs to worry about money ever again, not that she'd let me support her financially.

I should have known she wouldn't be offended by me offering help. She never is. This girl is perfect. She selflessly accepts my over-bearing tendencies. In fact, sometimes I don't even think she notices them. She's never once complained about me ordering for her or when I herd her to the non-road side of the sidewalk when we're walking. Even now she didn't make a fuss about shlepping her around town with no idea where we're going. She trusted I had it handled and has been along for the ride.

She is going to love the next stop. Tossing our smoothies in the garbage, we make our way inside the admittedly shady looking building, for our appointment. Her gaze shoots around the room as we enter the workshop.

"Welcome!" We're greeted by a middle-aged man in work clothes. "I'm Tim. You must be the Millers. We're delighted you are here, I'm a lifelong Songbirds fan."

"Thank you for having us and for your support of the team," I reply without correcting his assumption that we're married. I don't hate that we give off that vibe.

"Phoebe is in the design center getting everything ready. Let me show you back."

Grabbing Lola's hand to keep her from being left behind, I follow Tim from the workshop into what appears to be a classroom.

"Pheebs, These are the Millers. They're here for their metal working class," he tells his wife.

"Metal working?" Lola questions.

"Yes, my dear! Your beau said you wanted to create your own jewelry and we are here to make that wish come true," Phoebe states.

"Seriously?!" she exclaims, excitedly. "How many bucket list items are you planning to check off today?"

"As many as possible, baby," I smirk. "Let's get to it."

We spend the next couple hours learning how to solder and work with metal from Phoebe and Tim. They have everything we need to make a variety of items. We both choose to make a stamped item. Lola pouted when I wouldn't show her what I made and declared that I had to wait until she was ready to show me hers, too.

After we mastered that, we moved on to jewelry. Lola and Phoebe created delicate gold chain bracelets with tiny stones in them.

When I asked why she made three, Lola informed me that she made one for Tiffany and Carina as well. The bracelets all match and are permanent when put on. She called them "grown up friendship bracelets."

While they did that, Tim helped me create a bracelet for my mom. We created a design that featured two stones on each of the silver that can be adjusted to be closer or further apart based on wrist size or placement. I pat myself on the back for coming up with such a good birthday gift for her. She hates when I spend money on her, but I know she'll appreciate this, since I made it by hand.

As we're leaving, Lola asks to see my stamped creation again.

"Not yet, sweet girl. You'll see it one day, but today isn't that day."

"Ugh," she whines. "Now I don't even want to give you yours."

"Mine? You made something for me?" I question.

"Maybe," she responds shyly. "You don't have to wear it if you don't want to. I noticed several players wearing chains. I thought you might like one, but now that I think about it, if you wanted to wear something like that, you already would."

I lean in and kiss her to stop her rambling. "I absolutely want to wear whatever it is you made for me. Let me see."

She pulls a chain with a nickel-sized pendant attached. Stamped into the silver is my jersey number inside a wavy rectangle.

"Is that a Pop-Tart?" I ask. She rolls her lips to keep from giggling and nods. Shaking my head, I examine the other side. I let out a laugh when I see it says, 'Lola thinks you're hot.'

"Romantic," I tease.

"Do you like it?"

"I love it. It has all of my favorite things: baseball, Pop-Tarts, and you." I slip the chain over my head and tuck the pendant into my shirt. "I'll wear it every day," I promise.

She gives me a wide smile and moves in to kiss my lips. My hand finds the back of her neck and I pull her even closer, devouring her mouth, to let her know exactly how much I love her gift.

Driving away, she shows the pictures she's taken of today's adventures thus far, including the ones of us with the goats.

"That's a good one," I comment. "You should feature it when you write about goat yoga. My triceps look great. The trainers will be thrilled."

"Really?" she asks with a confused expression on her face.

"You don't think they look good?."

"Your arms are great, babe. That isn't what I meant. You're okay with me posting you on my account?"

"Of course," I respond. "Why wouldn't I be?"

"I don't know. I guess I thought you wouldn't want to be put out there with our relationship this new. I wasn't sure if you wanted to keep us on the DL and I didn't want you to think I was using your image to gain traction."

"Baby, if I could personally tell every person on this planet that you were mine, I would. I want everyone to know you are off the market. I'm not a man to keep things on the 'DL,' especially something as amazing as you."

"Do you want people to know you're off the market?"

"One hundred percent," I reply with no hesitation. "I only want you. Period. In fact, send me that picture, I'll post it right now."

"You don't have to do that," she whispers.

"I don't have to, but I want to. It never crossed my mind that I needed to stake my claim publicly but the more I think about it the more I'm into the idea. Besides, I told Emerly I'd post about yoga. Unless you don't want me to. This could bring you some unwanted attention."

I haven't considered that once Lola and I are *public* things might change. We haven't hidden our relationship, but we haven't flaunted it, either. I'll have to ask Robby if there is anything I need to be aware of. I haven't heard anything negative from Carina.

"I am fine with you posting me. I wanted to make sure you were sure about this. I know you're used to dating a different type of woman and don't want to disappoint you or your fans."

WTF. A different type of woman? Disappoint my fans? Pulling into our next stop, I park the car and turn to face her.

"Look at me, Lola," I demand. When she does I slide my hand to cradle the side of her face and lower my head so our eyes meet. "First of all, if they're stupid enough not to love you, I don't need them. Second of all, I don't know what you mean by 'different type of woman' but you are the exact type of woman I should be with. You are sweet, smart, and sexy as hell. I am damn lucky to have a woman like you. I don't know what I did to deserve you but I hope I keep doing it so I can have you forever."

"Forever?"

"That's the plan, baby," I declare as I bring her in for another kiss. "Don't you know my world stops and ends with you?"

"Look who finally made it," Kent shouts as we enter the music hall that serves as the final stop of the evening. Carina and Tiffany fawn over Lola when she scurries over to join them. I can't help but smile when I see her pull out the bracelets and animatedly tell them about our day.

Ever since I put that picture of us online earlier, Lola has been beaming. If I'd have realized what an impact posting us would have made on her, I would have done it weeks ago. Molly sent me a smirking emoji over text when she told me engagement was through the roof. Apparently, it is my top performing post of all time and it has only been a few hours. I'm not surprised, though. Cute goats, pretty girl, what's not to like?

"If it isn't Mr. Social Media Official," Robby teases.

"I don't care about that," Kent shuts him down. "I want to know how I can play with those goats and the certified hottie in the background of that picture."

"Of course, that's what you want to know. The goats are at the winery where Robby got married and the certified *yoga instructor* is the one who puts on the class. Clearly you didn't read the caption of my post because it talks all about it."

"Reading is for losers," he murmurs over his drink.

"You're a child," Robby chastises. "Aside from goat yoga, what else did you do? Carina was 'ooo-ing' and 'ahh-ing' over the group chat all day."

I tell the guys about metalworking, the Korean BBQ restaurant where you can cook your meat at the table, and two-step lessons. Everyone was surprised at how smooth my moves were, which was low-key offensive as a North Carolina boy. I'm a big guy. I can see why they would be shocked, but doing the splits is a part of my job.

"Damn, that's a full day," Robby remarks. "What's being checked off here?"

"This is a tricky one," I explain. "Lola said she wanted to sing with a live band. I figured music hall karaoke would fit the bill."

"Ah, it all makes sense now," he nods.

"What does?" Kent asks.

"Why the girls and I are here. Carina and Tiffany love karaoke. We used to go all the time in college."

"Exactly," I confirm. "I thought they would help ease Lola's nerves and having her own cheering section couldn't hurt."

As the band comes to the stage, the girls catch on to what is happening. Tiffany and Carina scream in delight as they head to the website to sign up and choose their songs. Lola walks over to me with a cautious expression.

"What are we doing here, Brady?"

"I think you know the answer to that, sweet girl."

"I can't go up there and sing! There are too many people," she whisper-shouts, arms flailing around as if I didn't notice the crowd.

"Yes, you can," I respond. "You can do anything you put your mind to. What's the worst that could happen?"

"I could embarrass myself and people could throw things at me?" she sasses.

"If someone throws something at you, I'll break their hand," I state more seriously than she realizes. "You got this, baby. Pretend we're in my truck and you're singing to me. It's the perfect time to knock it off your list. Your friends are here. The place isn't that crowded. And I'll get you plenty of liquid courage."

"Fine," she huffs.

"Good girl," I say, placing a vodka soda and a shot of coconut rum in front of her. "Drink up, because you're fifth on the list."

"What?!" she squeaks.

"I may have signed you up already to ensure you couldn't back out."

"I don't even know what song you chose," she complains.

"You're singing the one that inspired your tattoo," I reply, running my fingers against her ribs. I smile against her hair when she shivers in response to my touch. "You go up there and do a good job and I'll help you mark one final thing off your list tonight."

"What's that?" she questions, eyeing me with apprehension.

Making a locking motion with my lips, I slide the drinks closer to her. She rolls her eyes before throwing back the shot and chasing it with her drink.

Thirty minutes and another shot and cocktail later, Lola is bounding down from the stage with pride and relief pouring off her. She killed it. She sang that song as if it was written for her. She high-fives the crowd on her way to the corner our group is holed up in. The girls hug her before getting ready to go up for their turn. I have no idea what they're singing but they seem excited.

Lola stands between my legs and I guide her face to mine with my hand on her chin. "Great job, sweet girl. How did it feel?"

"Exhilarating! I never thought I could do that but I did."

"You did," I repeat. "We gonna make this a regular thing?"

"Oh God no," she replies. "I marked it off the list. I'm satisfied."

I nod and turn her around to face the stage and the current act. Tiffany and Carina are walking towards it as they're on deck while

Robby and Kent move to the front row to heckle them. We're left to guard the table.

With her back against my chest, I slide my hands down her arms until I reach her thighs. I rub small circles there as I kiss right below her ear and whisper, "I can think of another way to leave you satisfied."

"What do you mean?" She gasps, the sound vibrating against my lips as they trail her throat.

"I recall on the non-PG version of the list there is an entry titled 'public play.' I think this fits the bill, don't you?" I ask, moving one hand up under her dress, skating it along the edge of her panties.

"We can't do that here," she challenges.

"I beg to differ. We're back here all alone. The band will muffle any sounds you make, and the table is blocking most of our bodies from view. No one can tell that my fingers are inches away from your dripping pussy. It is dripping for me isn't it, baby?"

She lets out a whimper when my fingers drag against her clit over her thong and down towards her entrance. Slipping one finger underneath the lacy fabric I groan when my suspicions are confirmed.

"Fuck, you're soaked for me. You want this, don't you? Want me to play with your weeping cunt in this room full of people? Get you off without any of them being the wiser? I feel you getting wetter. I know you want it. Use your words. Tell me."

"Yes," she whimpers.

"Yes, what?"

"Play with me. Please, Brady."

Music to my fucking ears. I push her panties to the side and slide my fingertips up to her clit and circle it, teasing what's to come. As the current act ends, I slow my efforts much to her chagrin.

"Don't worry, baby. I'll give you what you need. We just gotta wait for the music to come back on to drown you out."

As our friends take the stage, the band cranks up again, and I thrust a finger inside her. Surprised, she grabs the table for stability as her knees buckle. I slide in another finger as I kiss her neck and shoul-

209

ders, sucking on the sensitive spot where they meet. I push my body further into hers, wedging her between me and the table.

"You've got four minutes until this song ends. You're going to come on my fingers before it's over otherwise you'll have to wait until we get home. Can you do that for me?"

"Brady," she whines.

"Tell me you can do it, Lola."

"I can do it."

"Good girl," I praise. With two fingers massaging her tight walls, the heel of my palm grinds into her clit. I can tell she's getting close as she leans harder into me and pushes herself onto my hand.

"There you go. Ride my hand, baby. Make yourself come in this dark corner with me. Make yourself come and I'll show you how proud I am of you when we get home."

I shush her when she moans a little too loud. I love seeing her like this but I'll be damned if I'm going to let anyone else. "Shhh, you gotta be quiet. The music is loud but you still have to keep it down. Can you do that?" She nods.

"They're at the bridge, baby. You've only got a minute left. You can do it. Come on my hand." I quicken the motion of my fingers and suck her earlobe into my mouth as her pussy clenches and body shakes from the force of her orgasm.

"That's it. You're doing so good. Coming on my fingers as I asked you to, Lola. That's my fucking girl." I gently stroke her through the aftershocks and right her panties as the song ends. When I slip my fingers out of her, she blinks up at me with glassy eyes. I bring my fingers to my mouth and suck them clean. The lust radiating off her is palpable. My expression offers her silent promises of much more to come when we get home.

Chapter Thirty-Five

· LOLA ·

September

W hile the boys are out of town, Carina and I grab dinner at our favorite Mexican restaurant. We'll be joined by Raven, a girl I was friends with in high school. She attended college in Nashville and stayed, making a name for herself as an interior designer. Unfortunately, she got caught in traffic. While waiting for her to arrive, we enjoy chips and queso with our margs.

"How was your first summer of programming?" I ask Carina. "I've barely seen you the last few weeks."

"I think that has more to do with a certain baseball hottie hogging all your time than me being busy, but it was awesome. With classes back in session, our after-school program is in the full swing. I am happy with how everything is running."

"That's amazing!" I praise. "And you're one to talk about baseball hotties monopolizing time. If Robby isn't on the field, he's practically glued to your side. I would have thought marriage would have mellowed him out, but it only made him worse."

She laughs. "I think he hates that we didn't get a proper honeymoon. I don't regret getting married during the All-Star break, but it would have been easier to do it after the season concluded. *Someone* didn't want to wait any longer than he had to, though."

"Who can blame him? He didn't lock you down the first time. He wasn't going to make that same mistake twice."

"Perhaps," she acknowledges. "Aside from spending time with Tiff and Miller, what have you been up to lately? I loved your post about goat yoga! I'm making Robby take me as soon as the season ends. Kent is of course tagging along."

"It was beyond fun. You're going to love it. Robby and Kent will, too. Brady said something about a DIY charcuterie class, too. We need to sign up for it."

"That sounds incredible," she gasps, immediately grabbing her phone to research it.

As I take a sip of my margarita, my phone dings. Thinking it is Raven with an update, I open up my texts. Instead of a message from my long-lost friend, it's from my mom. The chips I've eaten turn to lead in my stomach. My face must give me away because Carina is immediately alert.

"What's wrong?" she asks. "Is it Raven? Miller? Your Dad?"

"It's-it's my mom."

"Oh my God, your mom died?! I'm sorry."

"What?" I ask, confused. "No, she didn't die. She texted me."

"Oh... That's good? That she's alive, I mean. Judging by your face it's not good that she texted you, though. To be honest, I don't remember much about her. When was the last time you talked to her?"

"I wouldn't say it is good or bad, it's... weird. I haven't heard from her since I invited her to my college graduation and she didn't show," I confess.

I haven't heard from my mom in over six years. She left my dad over twenty years ago to move in with some guy she met online. She hasn't played an active role in my life since, only coming around when she was trying to convince a new boyfriend she was an upstanding citizen. The last time I saw her in person I was fifteen and she showed up high asking my dad for money. He cut her out of our lives for good after that.

Her foray into drugs was the typical story – pain meds after a surgery that spiraled out of control. Then one of her boyfriends got her hooked on heroin. She went into a downward spiral and has been jumping from guy to guy, dealer to dealer ever since. I don't even know where she lives.

Even though she missed my high school graduation, Phil convinced me to invite her to my college ceremony. I think he was embarrassed that I had such little family. To no one's shock but his, Mom didn't show or even send a response. I have no idea what she could want now, all these years later.

There was a time I was desperate for my mother's involvement in my life. Hell, even last year I would have been bursting with emotion that she wanted to connect with me again. My Nonna and Aunt Teresa were amazing role models, but no one can replace your mom – even when leaving was her choice to leave. Now, however, I am apprehensive. I don't know how she even got my number since I got a new one after my wedding.

"What does it say?" Carina wonders. I show her the message while taking a big gulp of my margarita and signaling for another.

5:44 PM

213

> Hello, my beautiful daughter. It's your mom. I know we haven't spoken in a while, but I miss you and would like to reconnect. I heard through the grapevine that you are in Tennessee with your cousin now. I would love it if you would come visit me in Florida soon. I also heard that you are dating a baseball player whose team is playing in my town next weekend. If you are tagging along, I would love to see you! We have a lot to catch up on. I miss you dearly. I am clean now and living with my boyfriend. He is a successful businessman.

> Please let me know if you are able to come. I will rearrange whatever I need to see you.

"Ugh," I groan. "Of course, she's in Miami and we'll be there over the weekend. What do you think she wants?"

"I don't know. Money, maybe? Isn't that what she was always after?"

"It used to be. I don't want to deal with it right now. Or at all. Does that make me a terrible person? I hardly have any memories of the woman and the ones I have are mostly negative."

Carina gives me a sympathetic expression. "I'm sorry, Bunny. It does not make you a bad person. I wonder how she knew you were with Miller. It's a crazy coincidence that we will be in Miami with the boys. We almost never travel for the games but after the fun you and Tiffany had last year, we had to go again."

"That is an excellent question," I comment. "How does she know about me and Miller?" I think back to his social post and the subsequent news stories about our relationship. He is in the public eye, but the country at-large isn't all that interested in who baseball players are dating unless the partner is a pop star or something.

"Only way to find out is to respond," Carina comments.

"Do you think I should?"

"I can't answer that for you," she says. "I know how important my

214

mom is to me, but I also know Tammy is nothing like her. I would have told the old you, 'no,' but you're different since the divorce – stronger. Maybe the universe is offering you an opportunity to have the relationship you never had or to close the door for good."

Carina pauses and scrunches her nose. "Oh my God. Do NOT tell Tiffany I talked about signs from the universe. She will never let me live it down!"

I laugh because she is absolutely right. Tiff is constantly talking to us about the universe and manifestation. She is also right about me being stronger and different since the divorce. With my new journey came a new philosophy. I'm on some new shit. I've been saying yes instead of no, and it has opened my life up to some amazing things. Maybe this will be one of them.

It doesn't take long to determine that meeting up with my mother is *not* an opportunity from the universe for something great. As I sit across from a woman I barely recognize, I can't help but feel sorry for her. The years and the drugs have not been kind to her. She looks at least a decade older than her fifty-three years.

Even though I told him he didn't have to come, Brady is sitting beside me in this grimy diner as we talk to my mom and her boyfriend, Rick. Mom was using the term 'businessman' liberally when describing him. He doesn't have the image of any businessman I've ever met. He's roughly her age with a beer belly and receding hairline. He gives off a George Costanza vibe if George was a giant creep and had a glandular problem. The man has been stealing lecherous glances at me when he thinks I'm not paying attention.

Brady has definitely noticed. His arm has been protectively on my leg since we sat down and I'm surprised he hasn't bent his fork with how tight his grip is. I sense him tense before I even notice Rick's eyes on me again. I am mortified that Brady is meeting my mother. I should have insisted I come alone but the glare he gave me when I suggested it told me there was a fat chance of that happening. Luckily, he has to be at the ballpark for a 3:00 p.m. game, meaning we can end this uncomfortable breakfast soon.

"You mentioned in your texts that you have taken up gardening since moving here. Do you grow anything in particular? Aunt Teresa has one and Carina brought some herbs and veggies back earlier this summer."

"Good to hear Teresa is still working on her sainthood," my mother sneers, sardonically. "I mostly grow flowers and other plants. Nothing food. Though, I guess you could put some of it in food if you wanted."

"Flowers are great in food. I have become fond of lavender in my coffee," I chirp, dumbly. The corner of Brady's lip tips up like he is in on a joke I am not. In a matter of seconds, though, I am enlightened.

"Your mom has a real green thumb," Rick remarks over his mouth full of scrambled eggs. "Her plants are going to bring us in a pretty penny when Florida legalizes weed beyond medical use."

I still when I realize the implication. She's growing Marijuana. My drug addict mother is growing Marijuana. I don't have anything against it or anyone who uses it but she made it explicitly clear to me she was on the up and up. Her illegally growing pot was not on my bingo card.

"I thought you were clean?" I ask.

She has the decency to appear sheepish before she replies. "I am. Everyone knows pot doesn't count. And I don't sample the product... much – just enough to make sure it's effective."

Seeing that I am lost for words, Brady jumps in and changes the subject. "How long have you been in Florida, Tammy?"

"I moved here about three years ago. I met Rick when he was on a business trip and it seemed like a good place to start fresh. I'd been bouncing around for a while and wanted something more permanent."

216

"So, you have been together for three years, then?" He follows up.

"Around that," she answers. "What about you two? I was surprised when I saw pictures of you together in that magazine spread of Carina's wedding. Last I heard you were married to an accountant. That sounds more your speed. It's hard to imagine the little girl who made 'grass angels' on the soccer field would date a professional athlete."

My jaw drops at her comment and Brady squeezes my leg reassuringly. "We've only been together a few months, but we are quite serious. I care about your daughter a lot. Lola is pretty active but I've yet to see any grass angels. You holding out on me?" He gazes down at me with a twinkle in his eye as he diffuses her rude implication.

"And the accountant?" She pushes.

Before he can say anything, I chime in. "Phil and I divorced. We weren't a good match."

"And a professional athlete is?" I can't name the emotion in my mother's eyes but it resembles jealousy or resentment. I don't know why she is acting as if she knows anything about who I would or would not be a good match with. She never even met Phil, and this is her first encounter with adult me.

"Tammy," Rick scolds, sensing the shift in mood.

"Miller, I did research into you. On top of your baseball career, you are quite the investor. Baseball's Ryan Reynolds they called ya. I read that you are invested in a club and several startups in Nashville. Is that true?"

"It is," Brady confirms cautiously. "I know the stereotype is that athletes blow their money and make poor financial decisions, but my parents taught me the importance of saving and making your money stretch. I want to ensure my future family and I are more than comfortable once I have to hang up my cleats."

"You're what, thirty-five? Won't be too long before that happens," Rick notes.

"I'm thirty-two, but you are right, I am on the older side for a player. However, my contract was extended last season. The team believes I have a few good years left in me before they need to put me out to pasture."

"That's nice," Rick dismisses. "I can appreciate wanting to make wise investments. And I have a great opportunity for you. You heard me mention Tammy's plants. We are getting set up to sell our product as soon as the government legalizes weed. You have the opportunity to get in on the ground floor. Maybe your girl here can even help with the marketing. She's not as blessed as her mama in the chest, but in the right outfit, she could push the product."

I am stunned at Rick's proposition. I glance to my mother and see her staring between Brady and Rick with eager eyes. My gut instinct was right. This is about money. If I thought I was embarrassed before, my humiliation grows tenfold. Of course, she isn't interested in a relationship with me. She saw the pictures of me and Brady together and saw dollar signs. She is using me to get to him.

I don't even want to begin to process Rick's comments on me marketing their product in the 'right outfit.' I have a master's degree in journalism. The articles I've written have gotten hundreds of thousands of hits and my blog is steadily increasing in popularity yet here is he regulating me to weed model? Is that even a thing?

I freeze, having no idea how to react in this situation. Thankfully, as always, Brady takes control.

Chapter Thirty-Six

I got the vibe last night that Lola didn't want me to go with her to meet up with her mom and her boyfriend. But there was not a world in which I was letting my girl meet people she doesn't know in a place she isn't familiar with. This entire breakfast reaffirmed that decision.

Despite his opinion about Lola not being as blessed as her mother 'in the chest,' he hasn't stopped leering at her the entire time we've been in this dingy restaurant. It has taken all my self-control not to snap at him to keep his eyes to himself.

If that wasn't bad enough, Lola's mom has been a grade A bitch to her the whole meal. She has constantly talked down to Lola and made snide remarks about her family. The comment about her Aunt Teresa did not go unnoticed. I felt her tense beneath my hand. I can tell she is embarrassed by her mother's behavior – not that I would ever hold it against her.

I was counting down the minutes until we could excuse ourselves. I have to be at the stadium early today since we have an afternoon game. With Rick's proposition, I invest in his Marijuana business, it appears the time to leave has come blessedly sooner.

As he finishes his spiel, I recite my canned response. You'd be surprised how often I am approached to 'get in on the ground floor' of some scheme or another. "Sounds interesting. I'm not looking for any new investments at the moment but if you want to send your business proposal over to my financial advisors, I can have them review it for consideration."

"Oh, we don't need all that," the balding man retorts. "We're family. Right, honey? I'm practically your dad!"

Lola cringes at that and shifts her gaze back to her mother. This man isn't seriously trying to pretend he has any type of bond with her, is he? This is the first time they've ever met and my understanding is she hasn't seen her mom in over a decade.

"Absolutely," Tammy chimes in. "Any man who is generous enough to take on Lola is family in my book."

What the fuck does that even mean? 'Take on Lola?' As if she isn't the most incredible woman in the world. Did decades of drugs mess up her eyes as well as her brain? Lola is drop dead gorgeous and Tammy's boyfriend clearly agrees. On top of that, she's kind, smart, funny, and loyal. What more could she ask for in a daughter?

When I peek over at Lola, I can tell everything is starting to get to her. I need to get her out of here while I still have some time to remind her how amazing she is. Standing and reaching into my pocket, I grab cash from my wallet that will more than cover this shabby breakfast and lay it on the table.

"Thank you both for meeting us today. We are going to head back to the hotel. I have to get ready for the game this afternoon. Tammy, I want you to know how grateful I am that you brought this beautiful, intelligent, perfect woman into the world."

I gaze into Lola's eyes even as I address her mother and run my hand down her hair before offering it to her. She takes it like a lifeline and slides out of the booth behind me.

"Wait, you can't leave yet. We haven't finished discussing your investment. I know you want to get one in before the game, but the ass will be there afterwards," Rick stammers. That has me turning back to face him.

"What did you call her?" I grit out.

"Don't be so sensitive," Tammy sneers. "We all know there is only one reason a guy like you would be with a girl like her and it ain't her cooking."

Reading the anger vibrating off me despite my quiet demeanor, Lola jumps in. Ignoring Rick, she addresses her mother, "Brady is not now, nor will he ever invest in your 'business.' Your current operation is illegal and even if it wasn't we have no intention of enabling you. I shouldn't be surprised that you reached out to me to get to him and not to apologize for all the shit you've done but I am.

"A small part of me thought you might have turned your life around and wanted a genuine relationship with your daughter. I won't make that mistake twice. Never contact me again, Mom. You should've run out of chances years ago and today I have finally run out of fucks to give. Have a nice life. Keep me out of it."

With that declaration, she turns on her heel leaving a slack-jawed Tammy and red-faced Rick in her wake as she pulls me behind. We make it all the way back to the car before she lets out a shuddering breath. Lola peers up at me, pretty doe eyes filled with unshed tears. I know despite her strong words, that confrontation cost her.

I pull her into my chest, and run my hand soothingly down her back. "It's okay," I coo. "You did so good, baby. I'm so proud of you."

The sob she lets out all but wrecks me. "That was awful," she cries.

"I know, sweet girl. But it is over. You closed the door and we never have to open it again." I continue to hold her and whisper reassuring words until her breath evens out and crying subsides. "Are you okay to go back to the hotel? I want to hold you properly before I have to report to the clubhouse."

She nods in response and lets me guide her into the car. She is silent on the ride home, clearly drained from the entire experience, but the way she clings to my hand in her lap makes me feel ten feet tall. I love being her lifeline. I will be her rock in every situation from now until the end of time if she lets me.

After securing a win against the Sharks, the group is getting ready to go to a party thrown by a friend of Tiffany's. Apparently, the girls went to the same party last year. We rarely get a night out with everyone, but since it's Labor Day Weekend, we have the night off thanks to the early afternoon game.

I'm sitting in the lobby waiting for girls and Robby to come down. Tiffany insisted they all had to get ready together. She said something about a special dress she got for Lola. When it comes to the blonde mastermind, I've learned not to ask too many questions.

Kent takes a seat beside me as we wait. "You ready to get wild, Papa Bear?" he asks.

"You know we have a game tomorrow, right?" I remind him.

"Yes," he retorts. "I know we have another game tomorrow but we're leading the series. I'm not worried about it. Did you see me at the plate today? I can't be stopped."

I roll my eyes. I love Kent like a brother, but the guy can be a lot, especially on a night out. "Try to keep it manageable tonight. I want to have a chill evening. I don't have the energy to wrangle you."

Kent chuckles. "I think any chance you had of it being chill tonight is out the window, buddy."

"Why do you say that?" I question, glancing up from my phone.

In answer, he tips his head towards the elevators where the rest of our group is walking our way. My breath catches as I take in Lola. She is a vision in a sparkly, rose gold dress. It dips low in the front to show off her collarbones and cleavage. "Holy shit," I mutter, then elbow him in the side when he makes a grunt of agreement. "Stop staring at my girl."

Kent gives me a knowing grin when I glare at him.

Lola appears nervous as she approaches me, twisting her hands together. I stand to greet her when she gets within a few feet.

"You look like a fucking goddess, baby," I compliment.

"You think?"

"Absolutely. Where did you get this dress and can we get it in every color?" She blushes, but I am only half kidding.

"You can thank me for the outfit, big guy," Tiffany interjects. "I take gratitude in the form of Veuve."

"Done," I promise.

"Do you really like it?" Lola asks with a turn. As she spins around, I see the low dip of the back. I can see the indentations above her ass. "You don't think it's too much? Too revealing?"

"It is fucking hot. If I didn't know how much you were looking forward to tonight, I would be hauling you upstairs."

Instead of reveling in the praise, she pales a little.

"What's wrong?" I question.

"You want me to go upstairs and change?"

"What? No. That's not what we'd do upstairs. Why would I want you to change?"

She peeks up at me through her lashes, worrying her red painted lip. "You don't care that it's slutty?" she whispers the last word so quietly I almost don't hear it.

"Slutty? Why would you think that?" She glances around avoiding my gaze. "Lola," I warn. I hope this doesn't have anything to do with what her mom's creepy boyfriend said.

"Last year, I sent a picture of my outfit – which covered more than this one – to Phil. He said it was slutty, and I 'didn't look like someone's wife,'" she admits.

The douche canoe strikes again. Phil's shittiness never ceases to amaze me. How he could talk to his partner that way is beyond me. When he should have been instilling her with confidence, he brought her down.

"Look at me, sweet girl," I say, tipping her chin up with my fingers, forcing her eyes to meet mine. "Nothing you could wear is 'slutty.' Nothing you could wear makes a statement about your relationship status. I don't care what you wear as long as you feel beautiful. I may have to break a few hands tonight if they try to touch you, but that is a sacrifice I am willing to make." I finish my statement with a wink and she offers me a shy but genuine smile.

"Okay," she breathes. "Let's go."

A few hours later, the girls are coming back from their latest stint on the dance floor to get more champagne. I slide a glass of water to Lola and she smiles at me gratefully. When I am about to ask her if she is enjoying herself, Tiffany lets out a squeal as two men approach the table, "Valentino! Stefano!"

I am firmly team-female, but even I can admit these guys are exceedingly attractive. I am confident in my own appearance, but that doesn't mean I want them near my girlfriend. While one of the men stays to chat with Tiffany, the other comes up to Lola and embraces her. "*Gemma preziosa,*" the mystery man states. "*Come stai, bella?*"

"I am good, Stefano," she answers in English as she steps out of the hug, not a moment too soon. The possessive caveman inside me was clawing to get out. I want this dude away from my girl pronto. Before I can pull her away, Lola introduces us.

"Stefano, this is Brady. Brady, this is Stefano. I met him last year at this same party."

Stefano gives me a firm handshake as he appraises me. I scowl back at him. Turning to Lola, he speaks in Italian again. "*È questo il marito?*"

Rolling her lip, Lola shakes her head. "*No, Brady è nuovo. il marito non c'è più.*"

With a pleased expression, he counters, "*Ti tratta come la sua luna e le sue stelle?*" What the hell is this guy so happy about? I have no idea what she said to him, but I don't like that it has him grinning at her.

Lola unabashedly returns his smile and replies, "*SÌ.*"

Stefano's grin grows even wider and before I can ask what the fuck they're talking about, he shifts to address me. "It is wonderful to meet you! When I met this *bellezza* last year, her eyes were sad. Now they are filled with light. She deserves the light."

"I couldn't agree more," I say.

"We must celebrate. A bottle on me!" he exclaims, causing Tiffany to cheer in Valentino's arms. Lola laughs. When I glance down at her, she is beaming up at me.

"What?" I question.

"Seeing Stefano reminds me of how far I have come in the last year. A large part of that is because of you."

"I haven't done anything but treat you the way you should have always been treated," I remark.

"*Come la tua luna e le tue stelle,*" she whispers with awe in her eyes. I don't know if it's wishful thinking, but I see love in there, too. We haven't said the words yet, but I feel them pulsing between us. Moments later, Stefano returns with a round of drinks and we spend the rest of the night together like old friends. I get the sense we may be. That he may have planted the seed that led Lola to me.

Chapter Thirty-Seven

• BRADY •

Pulling into the parking garage, I glance over at Lola, who is asleep in the passenger seat. The girls made the most of their getaway, and are now paying for the lack of sleep and overexposure to the sun. She and Carina may have gone on and on about how they're Italian and "the sun loves us," but all three women – Carina, Tiffany, and Lola – were incredibly sleepy when Robby and I met them at the airport.

They didn't have the luxury of riding on the team jet, but we swung around from the private terminal to take them home. Robby slides out of the car and tells me he will return for their bags after he gets Carina upstairs. I make a similar plan as I don't want to wake up my girl when she is sleeping peacefully.

When I asked Tiffany if she needs help, she mumbled something about being an 'independent woman who don't need no man,' and wandered to the elevator with a salute. I manage to get Lola out of the car and all the way to my doorstep while she snoozes.

It takes some maneuvering to unlock the door with her in my

arms, but I am able to without waking her. That is, until a familiar woman yells, "Surprise!"

The second I open the door, I hear the greeting. Lola jolts and I almost drop her in my startled state. It takes a moment to register that my parents are standing in the living room of my condo, greeting me as if it's a birthday party. My mom has the decency to appear embarrassed, but not as much as Lola as I lower her onto her feet.

"That's one way to welcome them, Marilyn," my dad laughs.

"I guess we should have called first," she responds. "Hi, honey. We came to surprise you with a visit."

"I can see that, Mom." I chuckle. Walking over to her, I pull her in for a hug. After a few squeezes, I turn to my dad and give him one, too. "I'm happy to see you both."

Having shaken her shock, Lola appears anything but comfortable as she shifts from foot to foot by the door. That won't do. My parents are the most easy-going, kindest people I know. Given the chance, they will love her as much as I do, and I want her to be comfortable around them.

"Come over here, doll," I encourage. When she steps close to me, I pull her in front of me to face my parents.

"Lola, these intruders are my parents, Marilyn and Ray. Mom and Dad, this is my girlfriend, Lola."

"Hi," she greets nervously, reaching out her hand.

"Oh honey, it is nice to meet you!" My mother exclaims before pulling her from my arms and into hers. "I'm a hugger."

Lola is stiff for a second before her body relaxes into the hug.

"Mare, let the girl breathe," my dad comments, amused. "It is nice to meet you, Lola. We've heard some wonderful things about you."

"You have?" she questions.

"Of course!" Mom answers. "This one doesn't talk much, but when he does, it is mostly about baseball and you. Sit, sit. You two are probably tired from traveling. Why don't you take a seat? I'll make us something to eat."

"Mom, you don't need to come to my house and cook for me. I can do it, or we can order out."

"Nonsense," she replies. "You hardly ever come to see us. When else am I going to get to feed you?"

I try to disagree, but my father stops me. "It's a losing battle, son. She made me stop at the grocery on the way here to get all the ingredients she needed to make Grandma's meatloaf."

"Do you need any help?" Lola asks.

"No, honey. You go sit and relax. Beware, Ray may chat your ear off, though."

Dad rolls his eyes with a scoff. "Everyone knows you're the chatty one, dear."

A while later, the four of us are sitting around my kitchen table enjoying meatloaf, mashed potatoes, and butter beans. It's definitely not a trainer-approved meal, but no way am I turning down my mom's home cooking. I watch my girl laugh as Mom animatedly tells the story of when Kevin, Jimmy, and I thought we could build a raft to float across the pond near our house. Plot twist: random branches aren't airtight, and we all fell in.

Dad catches my eye and gives me a knowing smile. I can tell both he and Mom are as enamored by my sweet girl as I am. Lola is mesmerizing right now, her head tossed back, cheeks pink from laughing.

"Alright, it wasn't that funny," I mirthfully say.

"It absolutely was. I've never seen the three of you as dirty as when you trudged up to the back door covered in mud. I wouldn't let them inside until Ray sprayed them off with the hose."

"Speaking of being covered in things, how are Kevin and the poop monster?" I ask. My niece, Chloe, may be cute as a button, but according to Kevin, she has had quite a few blowouts.

"She is wonderful," Mom beams, pulling out her phone and showing it to Lola. "Have you seen her? You have to see the pictures from when they went to the beach!"

"I have seen a few pictures, but not those. Oh my gosh! That is the cutest thing I have ever seen," Lola gushes.

"Isn't it? I'm trying to convince them to get her something similar for Halloween. She is the cutest mermaid. Megan wants her to dress as a pumpkin, but I think they can be more original than that!"

"I told Kev to dress her as a baseball player. She's got a Songbirds onesie already," I interject.

"We are not dressing this cute little baby as a baseball player, Brady," Mom tuts. "She needs something frilly and fun!"

"I don't know," Lola comments. "I think a little baseball player would be adorable, especially with the cap."

The moment the words come out of her mouth, I can picture it. Lola holding a baby girl with her big, hazel eyes and a shock of my brown hair, and me playing catch with a blue-eyed little boy who has his mom's coloring. The two of us could build the most extraordinary life and family together. That's where I want this to go. I think she does, too.

We haven't explicitly discussed it, but the way her eyes light up at pictures of Chloe tells me she wants a baby of her own. I'm going to be the man to give that to her. I'll give her everything she's ever wanted if she lets me.

My parents blessedly booked a hotel to stay in. They didn't want to 'cramp my style.' Normally, I would fight them on that since I have a perfectly good guest room, but not tonight. Tonight, I've got plans for Lola and I do not need my parents within earshot of them.

As I walk them to the door, my mother leans in conspiratorially and says, "Hold on to this one. She's good for you."

"That's the plan," I whisper back.

Once they're gone, I swing around and watch Lola for a moment.

She's digging through the suitcase I ran downstairs to get earlier. When she senses my eyes on her, she glances up and smiles. The intensity of my stare has her lips drop a bit in confusion. Before she can say anything, I am across the apartment and sealing my mouth to hers.

I kiss her as if it's the only thing keeping me alive; like she's my oxygen. I finally pull away when both our chests are heaving. A grin creeps on my face at the flush creeping down her skin. She rolls her eyes and pushes against me, but I grip her hips tighter, immovable.

"Everything okay?" she asks.

"Everything is amazing. *You're* amazing. Thank you."

"For spending time with your parents? They were nice. And the stories they had about you as a kid were delightful. I need more of those."

Her saying 'kid' has my wheels turning back to her having mine. Simply thinking about her pregnant with my child has unlocked some primal part of my brain. I'm always a little feral when it comes to my need for her, but I feel even more so right now.

I graze my hands down the side of her thighs and back up to grab her ass. I lift her, forcing her to wrap her legs around me. Without a word, I walk us towards the bedroom.

"Babe, I need to shower the airport off me," she complains.

"Later. I need you. Now. Seeing you with my family. It did some-thing to me. I realize it's everything I want. I want you and my mom sitting around the table laughing. I want you telling my dad about our travels. I want to see you doting on my niece. Playing with a baby. Our baby. I know this is going to sound crazy, but fuck, I want to put a baby in you."

I divulged more than I intended and when Lola tenses I'm afraid I went too far, but it's out there now.

"You-you want to have kids with me?" she questions.

I could try to backtrack, but I don't want to make the mistake of this woman not knowing how I feel about her. "I'm not saying I want to have kids right now, but one day? Soon? Abso-fucking-lutely. The thought of seeing you swell with my child has my dick hard enough to chop wood."

She barks out a disbelieving laugh. "You really think I'd be a good mom? Did you forget about the breakfast from hell we had this weekend?"

Sliding her down my body, I place Lola on the mattress and then cage her in with my arms. "Listen to me carefully, sweet girl. Your mother's inability to be the parent you needed in no way reflects how you'll be as a mom. In fact, I bet it will make you an even better one. I would be honored to know my kids shared half their DNA with someone who is as kind. Smart. Beautiful as you." I punctuate each compliment with a kiss on her face before tipping her head back to recapture her lips.

"Let me show you exactly how much I want you and our future together. Consider this a practice run," I purr, kissing up her neck to her ear.

When she licks her lips in anticipation, I lean forward until her body is flat on the bed and I am hovering over her. My fingers trail down her torso until I reach the bottom of her shirt and I slowly lift it over her head. Once it's removed, I kiss down her chest, swirling and sucking everywhere but where she wants me. I have such an uncontrollable need for her, I want to drive her crazy with me. When I get to her ribs, I let my tongue trace the outline of her tattoo, making her shiver beneath me.

She pulls on my shirt and I pull it off before going back to teasing her with my tongue. I run my fingers lightly up and down her body, occasionally grazing her nipples. When she arches her chest in the air and makes a mewling sound, I know I've got her where I want her: needy and desperate for me.

I kiss up to her breasts and suck a nipple into my mouth while my fingers tweak the other. I go back and forth between the two, letting my free hand drift between her legs. She's so wet, I can feel her warm heat through her leggings.

"Fuck, baby. You're soaked, aren't you? Are you getting messy for me? Are you so turned on by the idea of me putting a baby in you that your pussy is practically weeping?"

She squirms, trying to force my hand to give her more friction, but I keep steady. "Needy, baby," I coo. "Don't worry, I'll give you what you want... eventually. I want you desperate for it – desperate for my cock."

"I am," she huffs.

"Not yet. But you will be."

Chapter Thirty-Eight

• LOLA •

When Brady told me he wanted to make me needy, he wasn't kidding. He spends what feels like an eternity teasing me. He's not edging me per se because he won't give me enough of anything to let me even get close.

That's how I find myself shaking with desire as he laps small licks on my clit. He's holding my legs open in his large palms. I am completely at his mercy. The heat from them sears into my skin like a brand as I plead for relief.

"Brady, please," I beg. "I need you."

"Do you Lola? What do you need? Tell me and I'll give it to you."

"I've been telling you for half an hour!" I shout. My frustration only makes him chuckle. He smiles against my thigh.

"You've been begging, but you haven't told me what you want. What you *really* want. Tell me, Lola. Do you want me to suck on your clit?" He does long enough to elicit a moan and then a groan when he stops.

"Want me to finger fuck you into an orgasm?" He thrusts his fingers in and strokes my G-Spot.

"Or," he says, continuing his ministrations, "Do you want me to shove my cock in your pussy until you combust around me? Fuck you nice and deep, just how you like it until I can't take it anymore and fill your tight little cunt with my cum. Tell me you want me to breed you. I'll give you whatever you ask for."

Holy hell, is that hot. Why is it so hot? We both know I'm on birth control. I've had an IUD for years since Phil wasn't ready to have kids yet, but didn't like wearing condoms. Even though I know I won't get pregnant, a small thrill goes through me at the idea he wouldn't mind. In fact, I don't think he'd be upset at all if it happened.

Out of my mind with need, I finally tell him what he wants to hear. "Please fuck me, Brady. Breed me. Mark me as yours."

Without responding, he stands up from where he was kneeling with my legs on his shoulders. I whimper at the distance, but he quickly lets my legs slide down until my ankles rest beside his head instead of my thighs. In one movement, he seats himself fully inside me. We both groan as we adjust.

"Fuck, baby. I'll never get tired of how tight you are. You're choking my cock like such a good girl." I clench at his words, making him hiss. "You keep doing that and this isn't going to last long."

He pulls all the way out to the tip before sliding back in. After a few agonizingly slow thrusts, he picks up the pace. The force of his thrusts increases with his speed until he has a steady rhythm. When he leans down to kiss me, it gives him an even deeper angle to hit spots that cause sparks to fill my vision.

"Brady, oh my God!" I cry.

"Yes. That's it, Lola. You're gripping my cock so good. Come for me, baby. Come for me and take me with you. Milk my cock until it fills your hot little pussy."

I can feel every inch of him sliding in and out of me. With each thrust, his pelvis grinds into my clit. When he fucks my mouth with his tongue in the same rhythm as his cock, I follow his command. As promised, he comes right along with me and I feel his cock twitching inside me. It's the most erotic thing that has ever happened to me.

Brady slides my legs off his shoulder and brings his hands beside my head to support his weight. His kisses grow softer and less frantic as he catches his breath. "Holy shit. That was incredible," he remarks.

Dazed, I lay there, sucking in air. He brushes the hair out of my eyes and smiles down at me. As he slowly pulls out, I see the satisfied glint in his eyes as he examines the mess he made. After a few moments of watching his cum slide out of me, he scoops me up into his arms.

"Where are we going?" I rasp out.

"While I could watch me leak out of you all night, my sweet girl needs a shower and a goodnight's sleep," he answers.

Ever since that day a few weeks ago, Brady has made it a habit to wash me when we shower together. I've told him he doesn't have to, and he told me he 'doesn't do anything he doesn't want to.' He shampoos my hair until I'm making little kitten noises and then conditions my ends. After quickly washing himself, he wraps me in a towel and sets me on the counter.

He then, step-by-step, goes through my skincare routine. He cleanses, tones, applies eye cream, rubs in my serum, and moisturizes. I didn't even have to tell him what order to use the products in. He knew. Tiffany would be proud. Everything that has happened tonight is making my heart want to leap out of my chest and into his capable hands.

One day, someone will ask me when I fell in love with Brady Miller. I suspect my mind will return to the night he fucked my brains to mush and applied $87 night cream before I blissfully drifted off in his arms.

When I wake up the following day, Brady has already left for his morning workout at the stadium. Stumbling into the kitchen, I find a hibiscus latte waiting for me in the fridge along with a sticky note that reads, 'I hope I made it sweet enough, though nothing tastes as sweet as you.'

God, this man, he is thoughtful and cheeky. As I sip my drink and add hibiscus to the 'approved flavors' list in my mind, I can't help but reflect on everything that went down yesterday.

The Millers were incredible. Marilyn and Ray were both welcoming and down to earth. It's no wonder Brady is such an amazing guy, being raised by those two. It put into perspective how much I got shafted in the parent department. Don't get me wrong, my dad loves me and worked hard to take care of me, but he isn't Mr. Warm and Fuzzy. And my mom... hopefully, I won't hear from her for a long time, if ever again.

The things Brady said last night about wanting me to have his babies should scare me. I haven't been divorced long, and even when I was with Phil, a family wasn't on the radar. At first it was because we were too young. Then it was because he wanted to progress further in his career and 'enjoy our time together,' which was more often than not spent apart. Eventually, I was trying to survive on the crumbs of affection I could get. There was no room for a child in that world, even if I have always craved being a mother.

With Brady, I can imagine having a child. And not only the end result, the entire process. I can see him reading all the baby books and rubbing my tired feet. I can envision him cradling our newborn and cooing at them during late-night feedings. I can picture him chasing a toddler around and play wrestling. He would make a fantastic dad.

Love. I realize that's what this is. I love Brady Miller. It is wild to think that after everything that has happened in the past year, but I know in my heart it is right. No one has ever treated me better and put me first the way he does. He seems to not only enjoy spending time with me, but he also gets pleasure from my pleasure and from taking care of me. He is everything I've ever needed in a partner and didn't know I wanted.

I can't even begin to process what it means that everything he said last night was a major turn-on. I didn't think I had a breeding kink, but he certainly brings out new cravings in me.

As I arrange my thoughts, my phone buzzes. It's a video call from George. I answer as I take another sip of my coffee, smiling at my bestie.

"Hi, Georgie," I greet.

"Good morning, Honeybun. I was worried you would answer from bed with your caveman. I'm glad I don't have to see his naked ass this early in the morning."

That garners an eye roll. "As opposed to other times of day? You two are going to have to get past this grudge. You are both important to me and in my life for the long run. Don't make me call Mama."

George gasps. "You would never!"

"Try me," I sass.

"Wow, I don't know what happened to my timid little Bunny, but I can't say I hate this confident side. You're back to your old self."

"No, I'm an entirely new self. The old Lola would die seeing my life today. This version of me is full of gratitude and happiness, and I want to stay that way."

"I'm proud of you," he praises.

"Me too."

"I guess this means things are good between you and Miller? Are you sure you aren't jumping into something too soon? You're welcome to stay with me if you need to slow things down."

"Don't be dramatic," I chide. "You should be glad I'm with a guy who treats me the way I deserve. We are both deliriously happy and on the same page for what we want in the future."

237

"Which is?"

"Which is to be together; to have a family. I think this could be it. And I know that is a weird thing to say as someone who recently ended a marriage that she at one point thought would last a lifetime, but things with Brady are much more real and solid."

"It's a little sus for a guy to be that enthusiastic about being tied down, especially one with the options he has."

Georgie's words feel like a punch in the gut. I'm not ashamed to admit I have moments where I wonder why Brady is with me. He could have any woman he wants – ones who are curvy, kinkier, and with way less baggage. As much as I've tried to push it out, my mother's voice still sneaks into my head. But hearing those same sentiments from my best friend both stings and makes me defensive.

"First of all," I grit out, "not everyone wants to jump from person to person. When you find the right one, wanting them is as natural as breathing. Just because you're incapable of caring about women who haven't known you since you were eight doesn't make it weird.

"Second, it sounds as if you're saying I'm not good enough for a guy like Brady to commit to, which is a shitty thing to say to a friend. I may not be as hot as the models you hook up with, but that isn't the only factor that matters in a relationship. I bring a lot to the table."

At this point, I am fuming. I realize my reaction is a bit oversized, but he hit me right in the soft spot of my insecurities. I may be strong in many ways, but the dissolution of my marriage still left me a little fragile and feeling inadequate.

"Whoa, slow your roll," he urges. "None of that is what I meant. Of course, you're good enough to be with him. In my opinion, you're way too good for him. He'd be a fool not to want you, but most men are foolish. You are far and away better than all the women I date, Lo. Don't even put yourself in the same category."

Seeing my still firm features, he continues, "And you're right. I'm putting my baggage of dealing with clout-hungry users onto your relationship, and that isn't fair. Although, I'll have you know I didn't know Lucia when I was eight, and she's my favorite person in the world."

"She's your niece, and she's four," I deadpan. "She wasn't even alive when you were eight."

"Semantics," he jokes. "But seriously, Lo, I'm sorry. What I said was insensitive. You are the most special woman in the world whose last name is not Rivera. Men should worship the ground you walk on for the chance to be with you. If you are saying Miller does that, then I am happy for you. I'll be on standby to cave in his face should he deserve it in the future, though."

"You know there are over two million Riveras in the world, right? That puts me pretty far back."

"Lola," he says, exasperated. "Are you accepting my apology, or do I need to send you some Garrett Popcorn?"

I snort at his question. "You always need to send me Garrett Popcorn, but yes, I forgive you."

"Good. Let me know if I need to kick his ass."

"If there is anything left after Tiffany gets a hold of him, you'll be next in line," I quip.

He mutters something under his breath, but I don't catch it. "The offer still stands to come visit me. You haven't come to see me in ages and I miss you. It would be nice to have a female presence around here that isn't after my money."

"Who says I'm not after your money?" I sass. "I'll think about it. I can work remotely, but with how insane the MLB travel schedule can be, I don't know if you'll be in Chicago when Brady isn't in Nashville. The Songbirds play in Chicago next week. Maybe I'll come up then."

"Oh goodie, I'll get to see you and lover boy. My door is always open, Honeybun. Come visit whenever you want. My doorman has your name."

"Thanks, Georgie. You're the best."

"I know."

Once our call ends, I spend the rest of the day working on an article about fall events in Nashville and exchanging emails about a potential brand partnership. Before I know it, Tiffany comes home and asks if I want to have a girls' night in.

I don't have any plans with Brady, and he tells me to 'have fun' when I text him about it. Tiff and I spend the evening binge-watching an early 2000s high school drama before bed. I dream peacefully of Garrett Popcorn with no idea of the shitshow tomorrow will bring.

Chapter Thirty-Nine

I soak in the familiar atmosphere as I stroll into Club Hedone for an impromptu owners' meeting. The low murmuring of voices and soft music, the dim lighting and cozy decor, and the unique scent blend of ylang ylang, orange, and frankincense combine to put my mind and body at ease.

The club's main room features a bar and a relaxed yet elegantly sexy vibe. Even though I didn't play often, I still came in a few times a month for a drink and to check in with the staff. Cole does a great job running the place, but I think the employees appreciated knowing there was someone else they could go to if they had any issues. Plus, I can always get a drink without being bothered by fans or paps. While I occasionally got hit on, the extensive membership application process weeded out most opportunists.

Since dating Lola, I have hardly shown my face here. If I am not with the team, I am with her. I'd love to bring her back, even if only to grab a drink. She's not ready for that yet, though. She may have enjoyed our playtime at the music hall, but exhibition isn't her thing. She won't even have sex with me if Tiffany is in the next room.

That is fine by me, though. I relish having her all to myself. We have plenty of fun without all the extras the club has. I'll be waiting when she is ready to explore her sexuality further, but I am enjoying what we have in the meantime.

I told her I was going to a meeting tonight, but I didn't mention it was at the club. I know I should have, but she's been a little on edge lately after everything that went down with her mom. I don't want to stress her out more by having her worry about me being here. I can tell her after the meeting to save her the anxiety. I don't feel great about it, but it is what it is.

Despite how incredible sex is between us, she still carries some insecurities about our mismatched sexual experiences. Part of it is how we met and how much experimentation I've done. No matter how many times I reassure her that I am more than content with what we have, I can tell she still has reservations.

The other factor that plays into her self-consciousness is her fucking ex. Instead of exploring his desires with his incredible, gorgeous, responsive as hell partner, he went to other sources to meet those needs. Granted, I doubt Lola would have been interested in bringing his brother into the mix, but communication and openness are the foundation of any relationship.

Wanting to purge the douche nozzle from my thoughts, I grab a drink and chat with the bartender, Travis, until it's time to head into my meeting. When I get there, Cole and Declan are engaged in a conversation about the recent Ryder Brothers tour.

"What are your plans next?" Cole asks.

Declan takes a sip of his water before he responds. "I've got a solo EP coming out early next year. I'll be heading back on the road for a mini-tour to promote it."

"Are you guys breaking up?" I ask.

"No, we're taking a bit of a break, though. Jack has a girl now he wants to spend time with. Grayson is in talks to judge a reality show.

And I've had a few songs collecting dust in my notebook that don't fit the group's sound. With the others preoccupied, now is as good of a time as any to share them with the world."

"Congrats, man," I say. "I can't wait to hear them."

"Thanks, Miller. I'll be sure to save you tickets for the Nashville show."

As the conversation concludes, Cole shifts the conversation to the club. He goes over the memberships, financials, and other details about the business side of things. He tells us some of the improvements made to the rooms and goes over the proposal to upgrade some of the equipment. The three of us agree on adding a playroom to attract more people in the DDlg community and to test out a new lube provider.

"All said and done, I think that was one hell of a productive meeting," Cole notes.

"Agreed," Declan confirms. "Let us know if you need anything else. I'll be in town until early spring." As he swaggers out of the room, I shake Cole's hand and do the same.

After leaving the meeting, I head on to the main floor to say 'hello' to a few people I saw on my way in. When I get there, I see Willa lingering near the exhibitionist hall. My Spidey-Sense starts tingling and I walk over to her.

"Everything okay?" I ask.

She peers up at me, biting her nails as her eyes dance. "I'm not sure..." she mumbles.

I raise my eyebrows, urging her to keep going. "I was walking by the shibari area and something felt off. I'm sure it's fine, though. I've never worked in that area. I'm sure Craig knows what he's doing." Despite her reassurances, she does not appear convinced.

"I'll go check it out," I state.

"Really?" She rushes out, relieved.

"Of course. There is no harm in getting a second set of eyes on things. There is a fine line between risky play and actual risky situations. Trust your gut."

She gives me a nod and I make my way down the hall. Craig is an experienced Dom. I'm sure he has the situation in hand, but as I told Willa, it never hurts to take a peek. It's an exhibition area, they expect spectators.

When I come across the scene in question, I'm glad I decided to check. Not only does Craig have a sub suspended, he has her hands bound and a gag in her mouth as he delivers blows with a crop to her flesh.

In this state, I cannot conceive a scenario where she would be able to safe word. She needs at least one way to signal him. I know there are some subs who say they don't need a safe word, but that is not a practice of Club Hedone. The ability for any party to end a scene at any time is a standard here.

It isn't typical for a scene to be interrupted, but in this case, I would rather have a sexually frustrated member than a hurt one. Craig clocks me as I approach and frowns.

"Red!" I call out. We typically have monitors who walk the public areas that should have stopped this, but I don't see one.

"What are you doing?" Craig asks, annoyed.

"Ending this scene. This arrangement breaks protocol. We can discuss it once we've checked on your sub."

Thankfully, she is in a cocoon suspension and I am able to easily lower her onto her side. Why her hands are also bound, I have no idea. I pull the gag out first and search for injuries as I make quick work of the ropes.

"Color?" I question.

"Red," she exhales. Her voice is husky as if she had been making noises for a while. The second her arms are free she wraps them around herself, visibly trembling.

"It's okay. You're okay," I croon, trying to comfort her. What I want to do is rage at Craig for putting her in this position, but right now helping her is my priority. I scoop her up and turn to the soon-to-be banned Dom. "Send a monitor over here and wait for me in Cole's office."

"But I need to give Mandi aftercare," he grouses.

Mandi tenses and shakes her head against me. She clearly doesn't want him anywhere near her and I can't blame her. "Don't leave me," she rasps.

"I've got this," I bark at him. "Monitor. Office. Now." I can't even say complete sentences anymore with the amount of anger coursing through my body. Craig reluctantly shuffles away but not without a lot of muttering under his breath. I carry Mandi to the seating area we have in the exhibition hall for aftercare.

There are only two other groups in here tonight. By the stocks gather half a dozen men and women watching a Domme tease her sub. The only other people are a couple engaged in pet play being watched by a lone woman who peeks in our direction a few times.

Cheryl, one of the monitors, rushes over to me. "Craig said you needed me," she states.

"Yes. Mandi needs a bottle of water, aloe, and a washcloth, ASAP. She came out of an unsafe suspension."

"Do you need anything else?" I direct at Mandi.

"A robe, please."

"And a robe," I repeat to Cheryl. "Please bring those items to me and inform Cole I want to speak with him and Craig once Mandi is settled. I don't know how long I will be. I expect an explanation on why there was no monitor in the area when I am done."

"Yes, sir," she answers sheepishly and leaves to complete my requests. I make several attempts to release Mandi, but it takes a while for her to stop clutching me and let Cheryl take over.

Four hours later, I finally leave the club. It took Mandi two hours to calm down and feel safe enough to change and head home. I asked Willa and the member relations team to follow up with her tomorrow to ensure she is still doing okay and not experiencing sub-drop.

Despite excuses and whining, Craig was relieved of House Dom duties and banned from the premises. Cole assured me he would contact other clubs nearby to give them a heads up about this incident. Any reputable club has a zero-tolerance policy for what went down and that combined with his haughty attitude will not make him any friends.

After sending Craig packing, we call Declan and catch him up on the situation as well as our legal and PR teams. I don't expect anything to come from this since we made sure to let Mandi know our course of action with Craig. We also offered her several support options should she need them and refunded her membership with the bonus of a free year if she wants to remain a member.

She was in good spirits when she left and as an experienced sub, she acted as if she understood the situation. She thanked me for how I handled everything. I hate that I ever needed to, but am glad I was there.

It's past midnight when I get home. Since I have an early morning workout with the team trainer tomorrow, I crash as soon as my head hits the pillow.

Chapter Forty

Willa emailed me earlier today to let me know Mandi was okay, but not expecting anything to come from the incident was wishful thinking. As I leave the stadium, I check my phone to see a shocking number of missed calls and texts.

I make a note to return the texts and calls from my parents and brother later after I get something to eat and maybe nap. I don't have any messages from Lola since she told me goodnight. We didn't have our usual before-bed chat, so I don't know what she is up to today. It was weird sleeping without her, but I crashed before I had the chance to tell her I was home and invite her to join me.

The group chat with Kent and Robby has blown up, which isn't atypical. What is out of the ordinary is a 9-1-1 message from Molly to meet her at her office ASAP. I'm not sure if this is about what happened last night, but I have a sinking feeling it is.

When I get to Green & Kinser, the receptionist rushes me into Molly's office, where I am met by her, my agent, Tyler, and his junior agent, Macy. The latter gives me a sympathetic smile while Tyler looks annoyed and Molly appears angry.

"Okay, I'm here. I'm tired. Let's get this emergency meeting over with," I state.

With a roll of her eyes and no context, Molly displays pictures on her wall monitor. Due to the dim lighting, it takes me a minute to understand what they are. When I realize what I'm seeing, my stomach drops.

Four images dance across my vision – all from last night. One has me standing behind Mandi while she is rigged up. The second is me kneeling beside her on the ground when I untied her. The third is me holding her in my lap in the aftercare section. The last – and potentially most damning – shows me with my hands on her shoulder, peering down at her in what appears to be a loving way.

"Fuck," I curse under my breath. "Where did you get these?"

"They were sent to me by a media contact," Molly replies, irritated. "They hit the press this morning."

"What?" I shout. "These are out?! Why didn't you stop them?"

"Excuse me? I didn't receive them until *after* they were already out, and reporters wanted a comment. Why didn't you not cheat on your girlfriend in a sex club?" Molly grouses.

I recoil back at her accusation. "Cheat? I didn't cheat on Lola. I would never cheat on Lola. Ever."

Before Molly can shout at me again, Tyler jumps in. "Listen, we aren't here to judge. We understand the life of an athlete of your caliber."

"I. Did. Not. Cheat," I roar.

Tyler holds his hands up in surrender. Everyone is silent for a moment. With Molly angry and Tyler afraid to piss me off more, Macy takes over.

"We believe you, Miller," she says, giving Molly a pointed glare when she scoffs. "Why don't you tell us what is going on in these pictures?"

I give my team a high-level overview of what happened. I can't go into much detail for confidentiality reasons, but they get the gist. Molly seems relieved that I didn't cheat on her new favorite client, while Tyler appears disappointed the story isn't juicier.

"Shit, I need to talk to Cole. Someone needs to tell Ma—the member. She's been through enough, and now naked pictures of her are circulating," I say.

"You can't see her face in any of them. The focus of the images is you," Molly assures me, not that it is much of a consolation.

At the same time, Tyler comments, "You can barely see any good stuff, anyway." That earns him a scowl from everyone in the room. I text Cole and Declan, who are livid both over the club's security breach as well as on behalf of Mandi and me. A full investigation has been launched. I have a sneaking suspicion that the arrogant asshole, Craig, was involved somehow.

Once I know my co-owners are on the case, I turn to my team, and we discuss the plan to tame the media circus. I spend over an hour listening and strategizing with Molly, and Macy provides good insight, specifically related to my endorsement deals. The Songbird's PR manager is conferenced in, and we all agree I should spend the next few days if not weeks lying low. People didn't care much about me before but finding out I own a sex club is going to increase their interest.

The team and Molly are putting out a joint statement that what happens in the private life of players is no one's business. It isn't my favorite wording, but my personal statement also includes my commitment to my sport and partner. I am hopeful that will quell any infidelity rumors, but I doubt it will help much. Club Hedone has already emailed our members about the breach of the rules and released a statement regarding the investigation, which calls for privacy for affected members.

When I am finally able to leave, it is long past lunch and I am famished. As I wait for a to-go order from a nearby food truck, I finally sift through my messages. They are all about the incident.

9:40 AM

KENT

Good boy Miller finally made a headline.
Have you seen this? [link to article]

ROBBY

I'm going to reserve judgment until I talk to
you, but just know if Carina asks me to, I
will kick your ass. I can't imagine you would
do this to Lola after everything that went
down with her ex, but if you did...

He's damn right I wouldn't. Even if she hadn't been cheated on, there is no world in which I would touch someone other than Lola. Since the day those pretty doe eyes peered into mine, I haven't even thought about another woman. She's it for me.

2:16 PM

ME

This is all a misunderstanding. I was
handling a situation at the club. I wasn't
involved with that woman except to ensure
she was okay after an incident.

KENT

We believe you, Papa Bear. You've been
glued to Lola since the day she let you into
her honey pot.

I exit the group chat and send Robby a separate message. As much as I love Kent, he tends not to take things seriously enough. I think it's a mask for his own feelings of inadequacy, but regardless, I need frank answers right now.

2:20 PM

Has she seen it?

ROBBY

I don't know. I was at the Becker
Foundation office when I found out. Tiffany
sent the article to Carina, along with several
colorful threats. I'd avoid her if I were you.

ROBBY

If Tiff knows, I bet Lola does, too. Have you
heard from her today?

ME

No, I haven't heard from her since last
night. She texted me while I was in the
middle of the whole mess that she was
going to bed. I crashed as soon as I got
home. I sent her a message this morning,
but nothing yet.

ROBBY

What are you going to do?

ME

Just left G & K. I'm heading to her place
now. I need to see her in person. She
knows how I feel about her and that I would
never cheat.

ROBBY

Maybe. But she thought the same thing
about Phil...

ME

I am NOTHING like that asshole.

ROBBY

I know, man. I'm simply pointing out that
she may be experiencing similar feelings of
betrayal you'll have to deal with. Don't take
it personally if she doubts you. Getting
cheated on can give you relationship PTSD.

You're right. In person, she'll see the truth. We've been talking about forever. I wouldn't throw that away for anything.

ROBBY

Good luck. Let us know if you need anything.

I toss my phone in the cupholder as I run a hand down my face. The last twenty-four hours have been a shitshow. I need to know where Lola's head is at and reassure her that she is my everything and absolutely nothing happened despite how it may appear. I can only hope she doesn't let her experience with Phil color this situation. It's different. I'm different. All I need to do is prove it to her.

Chapter Forty-One

• LOLA •

I wake up alone in my bed. Part of me hoped Brady would sneak in. It's rare we sleep apart anymore. Since the other night, our connection has become even stronger. Neither of us have dropped the L-bomb yet, but we are both dancing around it.

I see a good morning text waiting for me, but I need coffee first. Tiffany and I indulged in a little too much wine last night and my head hurts. I down a glass of water while the coffee brews and go through feedback from the editor on my latest piece for the magazine.

I smirk when Tiffany makes her way into the kitchen appearing as rough as I feel. "I'm glad I'm not the only one hurting this morning. You look hot, Tiff."

"Shove it, Bunny. I blame you."

"Me?! You're the one who opened the second bottle. I was perfectly content stopping after two glasses."

"But you gave me non-bubbly wine. My body needs the bubbles, Lo. It needs them," she whines.

"There are more things to drink in the world than champagne," I comment.

"Yeah, prosecco... And coffee. Gimme," she demands, making grabby hands at my latte. I sigh, handing it over as I turn the machine on again.

Tiffany is lost scrolling on her phone as I catalog what I need to do today. I glance up when I hear her gasp. "You okay?"

"Yeah. I'm fine," she squeaks in a small voice.

"You don't sound fine." When I study her, she's gone pale and is frantically scanning her phone. She is obviously reading something that is upsetting her. After a minute, her gaze flits up, and she wears a concerned expression.

"What is going on, Tiffany? Did Taylor Swift get canceled?" I joke. When she doesn't laugh, a knot forms in my stomach. "What is going on? Tell me," I implore.

"Okay, don't freak out."

"Not off to a great start," I mutter.

"How are things with you and Miller?"

"They're great, why?" I ask.

She gulps, peering at her phone and then back at me. "Where was he last night?"

"He said he had a meeting and then I assume he went home. *Why?*"

I can see her war with herself before she slides her phone across the island. I don't understand what she is showing me at first. There are four pictures of a man and a woman. In two, she's tied up. In the third she is cradled in his lap. The images are too grainy to make out either person until you see the fourth image.

The fourth image shows Miller staring down at a woman in a robe. He is staring into her eyes with his hands on her shoulders. It clicks in my brain that the man in the other images has on the same outfit as Miller does in the fourth. What the hell?

"I don't understand," I say. "Where is this? Who is she? Why is he with her?"

"I don't have those answers, babe. But Miller will. I'm sure he has an explanation. He isn't the type to cheat. He's obsessed with you."

My brain can't process what I'm seeing or what Tiffany is saying. I am having serious déjà vu. This experience is all too familiar.

"Sweetie, you're buffering. Sit down," she cajoles and I plop down on a stool, still staring at her phone. "I think it's safe to assume the pictures are from Club Hedone. He didn't tell you he was going there last night?"

"No," I force out.

"Is it possible that's where his meeting was?"

"Meeting?" I question. My conscious mind is officially offline. It is in a tailspin. I focus on trying to remember if Brady mentioned he was going to the club. If he was, why didn't he ask me to go with him? Is it because he wanted to play in a way he didn't think I'd be game? Things have been good lately. We've been trying more things. Why would he do that?

"You said he had a meeting last night. Could he have been meeting with someone at the club?"

"He has owner's meetings at the club. But those are only once every couple of months," I answer.

"Has he had one lately?"

"Not that I know of. Why wouldn't he take me with him? I told him I was fine if he wanted to go back. He promised to tell me when he went."

"If it was for a meeting, he probably didn't think it made sense to have you sit around. Maybe this was part of a demonstration or something."

"I-maybe. Oh God, Tiffany. I can't do this again. I can't be with another man who needs someone else to fulfill his fantasies. Leaving Phil hurt, but being betrayed by Brady..." I can't even finish my thought because pain seizes me.

"Lola!" Tiffany yells. I glance up and see her standing right in front of me. "You're spiraling. Take a deep breath. There's got to be an explanation. I'm sure he was planning to tell you. It's okay. In and out, babe. Breathe for me."

Following her instructions, my chest loosens as my lungs fill with air. Everything she is saying sounds right. Everything I know about Brady points to him being loyal. The man won't even stray from his favorite Pop-Tart flavor. There has to be an explanation.

"Are you going to be alright on your own? I have to get ready for work, but I can call in sick if you need me," Tiffany offers.

"I-I'm fine. Go. Don't worry about me."

She doesn't appear convinced, but she heeds my wishes, anyway. "You're one of my besties. I'll always worry about you. Text me if you need anything, including beating Miller's ass. I don't care how big and bossy he is. I'm scrappy."

I think she's trying to lighten the mood with that last comment but it doesn't work. Patting me on the shoulder, she goes to get ready. I remain at the island until she leaves for work. That's when I make the self-destructive decision to dive deeper into this. I sit on the couch, scouring the Internet for articles about Brady and this mystery woman. Then I stare at the ceiling and wonder how I ended up in the same position twice in less than a year.

I didn't think I was sitting there for long, but it must have been hours. I'm jarred from my disoriented state by a loud knock at the door. When I check the clock, it's almost three p.m.

"Lola," I hear someone shout from the other side of the door as the knocks get louder. I realize it's Brady. I peel myself off the couch and wander over to the door.

"What do you want?" I ask.

"Baby, can you open the door? I need to talk to you."

"Maybe I don't want to talk to you."

"Lola," he pleads. He says my name with such gentle sincerity it compels me to let him in. When the door opens, he scans me as if he expects to find me injured. When he gets to my face, his eyes soften. He lets out a sigh of relief as he enters the apartment.

He walks through to the living area and paces across the floor. I stand several feet away and wrap my arms around my waist as I wait for him to tell me what he came to say.

"You wanted to talk," I prompt. He eyes me wearily and I can tell he is stopping himself from reaching out and comforting me. He can sense how guarded and uncomfortable I am.

"Shit. I don't even know where to begin," he utters. I don't know either, so I remain silent.

"You've seen the pictures," he states. It's not a question. We both know I've seen them. "It isn't what you think."

I can't hold back my scoff.

"It isn't. I would never, under any circumstances, cheat on you. Deep down, you know that is true. Aside from the fact I'd never intentionally hurt you, my reputation means too much to me to squander it on some short-sighted physical release."

What he's saying makes sense. He values how his friends and the community see him as someone with character, someone they can count on. But Phil valued his reputation, too. That didn't stop him from doing what he wanted. It just made him sneaky.

Like with Phil, I have proof right in front of my eyes. I can't imagine another scenario that explains these images or why he didn't tell me he was going to be at the club. Going to a sex club is a thing you mention to your partner, especially since I have straight up asked him to in the past.

I decide to come right out and ask what I need to know. "Did you have sex with her?"

"No," he responds with no hesitation. His eyes bleed hurt at the accusation.

"Did you play with her?"

"No," he repeats. "I didn't touch her."

"You're touching her in the pictures," I point out.

"I touched her, but I didn't *touch* her," he bargains. "I didn't touch her sexually. I haven't looked at a woman in that way since we got together. Hell, since the night we met at the club. You know you're the only one for me."

Does he expect to get out of this through semantics? He didn't *touch* her, he just touched her? How dumb does he think I am? He clearly has his hands on a naked woman – naked woman in the midst of a scene.

As if he can't stand the distance anymore, he closes the gap between us and grabs my hands in his. "You are everything to me, sweet girl. Other women barely exist."

"Then how do you explain those pictures? What am I seeing here?" I ask, pulling away. I don't miss the pain in his eyes, but I can't have him touching me right now.

"I can't go into much detail for privacy's sake, but something happened at the club and a sub needed to get out of the situation. I was there and helped her."

"You untied her?"

"Yes."

"Did you tie her up initially?"

"No. Someone else did," he answers.

"Why couldn't they help her down?"

He pushes out a breath as he contemplates his next words. "He wasn't performing his duties in a satisfactory way. I had to step in."

I recoil at this. "In a satisfactory way? Did you satisfy her instead?!" I demand.

"That isn't what I meant by satisfactory. This is where I can't say much. It's confidential and her privacy has already been compromised enough. The Dom wasn't following the proper safety procedures."

"So, you made her safe?"

"Yes," he says as if relieved that I am finally understanding him, but I am not. I grab my phone and pull up the images of her in his lap and wave my phone in his face.

"She doesn't look endangered here. Why are you cuddling her?" I practically shout. Brady's jaw tightens showing his frustration. Welcome to the club, buddy.

"I was providing aftercare. A sub needs care after a scene to help regulate their emotional response, especially after a scene that goes beyond their limits. You're not in the lifestyle. You wouldn't understand."

He might as well have slapped me with how hard his words hit. 'I wouldn't understand.' Because I'm not 'in the lifestyle.' Because I'm not a sub. Because I don't do the things he's used to. These thoughts cut deep and reopen the old wound Brady helped heal.

"How could I have been this stupid?" I mutter mostly to myself. "I knew this would happen. Everyone knew this would happen. I knew you'd get bored and want things you used to have. You fooled me for a while with all your talk about wanting a family and wanting me to depend on you. But we were always going to end up here."

"We were not 'always going to end up here,'" he asserts. "We aren't 'here' now. I swear to you, baby, this is all a big misunderstanding."

I can't help but bark out a laugh. His words are practically an exact mirror of Phil's. Do I attract bad men or am I truly not enough? Are other women offering their partners something special to keep them faithful and I wasn't copied on the memo?

"You sound like Phil," I finally say. His jaw ticks and he clenches his fist. That comment struck a nerve. Good. I'm done tailoring my words to pacify men. I let one man silence me. I won't let another.

"I am nothing like him," Brady seethes.

"You sure? Because from where I'm sitting, you're almost exactly the same."

"I did not cheat on you, Lola."

"Prove it," I demand.

"Prove it?"

"Yes, if you weren't cheating, prove it. Give me security footage,

259

witness accounts, a fucking statement from that woman that says you didn't sleep with her. Prove it to me."

"I can't do that. It breaks the confidentiality agreement of the club. Our members pay a premium for discretion." Is he serious? He is really putting his business over me? Over proving that he isn't exactly like my scumbag ex that he hates? When I can think about this rationally, I will probably see his point, but right now, all I see is a man covering his ass.

"Not doing anything breaks *us!*" I yell. "What were you even doing there? You told me you had a meeting. You never mentioned it was at the club. That's an important detail to conveniently hide from me, especially considering you *promised* to tell me before you went. This is not the first time we've talked about this."

"I didn't hide it from you, I just didn't tell you outright. I know the club is a sore subject for you. I didn't want to nudge at your inse-curities, especially since we've been in such a good place this last week. I was going to tell you after the meeting but then all that shit went down and I had to deal with it."

My frustration with this conversation is ratcheting higher by the minute. I can't believe the audacity. "That's rich coming from the man who freaked out when I didn't tell him I was going to St. Louis. I went to leave someone, not pick them up!"

"I didn't pick anyone up. Nothing. Happened," he grits.

"Prove. It," I counter.

"I can't do that," he says somewhat chagrin. "I have to protect the other parties involved."

"If your business' privacy is more important than my certainty of your fidelity, then this relationship isn't as serious as I thought it was."

"It is. It is serious. It couldn't be more serious," he pleads. "Baby, I love you. You have to know that."

He did not. He did not tell me he loves me for the first time while trying to prove to me he isn't a lying, cheating sack of shit.

"Don't you dare say that to me right now. You've had weeks,

months to tell me you love me and you choose to do it when I've caught you being unfaithful?"

"I wasn't. I swear on my life."

"I need time to think," I reply. "You need to leave. I don't have anything else to say and I don't want to be near you right now."

His expression flashes with panic. He didn't think I'd ask him to leave. He must have assumed he could convince me that my eyes were playing tricks on me. That isn't going to happen. But the longer he stares at me, the more my resolve weakens.

"Lola," he pleads.

"Please go," I mutter, voice cracking. I squeeze my eyes closed, but don't miss the sigh he exhales. My body goes stiff when he wraps his arms around me and kisses the top of my head.

"I'll leave. For now. But this isn't over. When you've had some time to cool off, you'll see. You know me, sweet girl. Better than anyone."

When I don't respond, he lets me go and walks to the door. I don't open my eyes until I hear it shut behind him. Only then do I crumple onto the floor. When I manage to put myself back together, I know what I need to do. Or at least what I want to do. I grab my phone and send off a text.

ME

Changed my mind. Be there tomorrow.

Chapter Forty-Two

Leaving Lola's apartment last night was one of the hardest things I've ever done. I wanted nothing more than to fix the shattered expression I saw in her eyes but I know I'm the one who put it there. I have been trying to think of how I could have prevented this, but aside from telling her I would be at the club, I come up empty. Even if she knew beforehand, I don't think we could have avoided the doubts she's having.

I could convince Cole to give me the footage she wants to see, but the way her mind is spiraling, I don't think it would help. All I can do is give her time to process and show up to reiterate my devotion. Damn, is it tough, though.

Waiting on my draft call was less anxiety-inducing than sitting on my hands waiting for Lola to reach out. This is torture. I'd hoped to hear from her this morning, but she must need more time. We head out of town in a few days for an away series and I can't imagine going with this hanging over us. The idea that my sweet girl is suffering cuts me beyond words.

It hurts me even more than the shit people are saying about me. Once the pictures were out, online trolls did some digging and blasted my affiliation with the club. Thankfully the sex-positivity movement has kept me from losing any endorsement deals. Shaming someone for being sexually expressive would be a bad move for the few brands I work with.

I hate that some of my fans are disappointed in me but that is their issue, not mine. I am not ashamed of my investment in the club or my involvement in the community. The only thing I'm ashamed of is not pushing for Craig to be kicked out after the initial room mix. How much destruction did he cause between that night and the incident with Mandi?

The investigation discovered that he was behind leaking the photos. Apparently, the woman lingering in the exhibition hall is a sometimes partner of his and was taking pictures to blackmail him into rekindling their relationship. He decided to use them to get back at the club. Our lawyers have slapped them with a fat lawsuit. Play stupid games, win stupid prizes.

Walking into the clubhouse, I can see whispers and stolen glances from the staff. Some of them appear uncomfortable or guilty for knowing my never-was-a-secret 'secret.' Others regard me with disgust. The worst reaction is the women eyeing me with lust. The idea of being with anyone aside from Lola genuinely makes my stomach roil. Not that my stomach wasn't in knots already. I don't think I am going to be eating much of my pre-game meal.

When I make it to the locker room, everyone gives me a wide berth. I don't know if they're being respectful or if my expression screams 'don't fuck with me' but I appreciate the space. Even Robby and Kent mostly leave me alone aside from a quick greeting.

When we get out to the field, I try to keep my focus on the game, but my mind keeps going back to Lola. I should have checked on her this morning or at least before the game. I'll go see her once we're done and offer her more reassurance. I hate that all the shit Phil pulled means that she can't give me the benefit of the doubt. I get it, but it sucks.

In the dugout, I scan the stadium. I see fans holding up signs directed at me. That is fairly common, but they don't normally say, 'Miller can tie me up anytime' or 'Let me be your good girl.' They never say 'Spit ball in my mouth' and include a phone number. I'm shocked the stadium would allow a sign that crude with all the kids present.

When Crew's pop fly is caught by the shortstop, the inning turns over and we go back onto the field. I can only hope the game goes by quickly. I need to get to my girl.

We lost 2-3 to New England. Even though baseball is a team sport, I can't shake the sense of responsibility I take on as captain. Especially when I made an error that allowed a runner on base and hit average at best. It wasn't my worst game, but I can absolutely play better. The only thing keeping me from dwelling on my performance is planning out what I am going to say to Lola.

Exiting the shower, I spot Kent and Robby changing into their street clothes after talking with the media. The team decided it was best I avoid interviews for now.

"Hey, man," Kent greets. "How ya holding up?"

"I'm doing okay. It's surreal to have this much attention on me. I'm not used to it like you clowns." They both smile but sympathy is radiating off them.

"Wanna grab a beer?" he asks.

"Nah, I'm going to try to talk to Lola again. With a day to process everything, I hope she will be more receptive." Kent and Robby trade loaded expressions.

"You're going to talk to Lola like on the phone?" Robby questions.

"This is more of an in-person conversation," I reply.

His features scrunch in confusion. Kent searches around nervously as if he's hiding something.

"Miller, Lola isn't here," Robby finally says.

"Obviously. I didn't think she would come to the game. I'm going to her place."

"No," he hedges. "She isn't *here*. She isn't in Nashville. She left this morning."

"WHAT?!" I roar.

"You didn't know?" Kent questions.

"Do I look like I knew? Where the fuck did she go? Back to Missouri?" I can't believe Lola left without telling me. We've had that fight before. To be fair, I don't have a leg to stand on at the moment in terms of full disclosures and repeat disagreements, but still. I can't believe she would leave without telling me. She is clearly running away.

"She went to Chicago. I overheard Carina and Tiffany talking about George's guest room. I would avoid Tiff, by the way. She isn't your biggest fan right now," Robby notes.

"She is the least of my concerns. I've got to go get my girl."

"Whoa, let's slow your roll there," Kent interjects. "You can't get to her tonight, dude. We have another game tomorrow."

"I don't care about that," I rasp, reeling. Lola is gone, and I had no idea.

"As much as I hate to say it, Kent is right," Robby says. "You can't run off to Chicago guns blazing. What are you even going to say?"

"I don't know. I'll figure it out on the flight."

"Don't be careless, man. Lola deserves better than some half-cocked attempt to force her home," he reasons. "We'll be in Chicago in a few days for the away series. Take the time to get your head on straight and figure out what you can do to get your girl back and convince her this is all an unfortunate mistake."

"You guys believe I didn't cheat?" I ask. I hadn't put much thought into what anyone aside from Lola thought happened.

However, I am relieved to know my friends don't think I would stoop this low.

"Of course not," Kent replies. "You're the most stand-up guy I know. You'd never betray someone, especially Lola." Robby nods in agreement.

"I love her," I state.

"I know, buddy," my best friend affirms. "It will all work out."

I hope he's right. I don't know what I'll do if I can't convince Lola to come back with me. She quickly became my entire world and without her, everything is empty.

Chapter Forty-Three

· LOLA ·

I arrived in Chicago yesterday afternoon and have done my best impression of an ostrich during my stay. I have remained completely off the grid with my head buried in the metaphorical sand. I shut my phone off to get on the plane and never turned it back on. George let Carina know I got here and had a driver waiting for me when I landed.

He hasn't asked a lot of questions, but I know he knows about the photos. He has been letting me hide out in his guest room and giving me space to process my emotions. While the silence is nice, it also means I have had plenty of time to ruminate on my situation.

My gut tells me that Brady wouldn't cheat on me. My heart, though, is broken that he let us end up in a situation where I could doubt him. My mind is telling me not to be the fool twice. I've ignored the signs before and shouldn't risk doing it again.

I'm completely torn. On the one hand, I love him and desperately want the life we could have together. On the other hand, I don't know if I can ever get over the fear that he will need more than I can give him. Even if he doesn't go outside our relationship, there is no guarantee he wouldn't resent me or leave to find someone who can meet all his needs. The worst part is *he* is the person I turn to when I have doubts or insecurities. I'm floundering without that support and I hate that.

Deciding I can't completely cut myself off from the world anymore, I turn on my phone. I initially avoid my texts, and for the first time since I first learned of Brady's indiscretion, I log into social media. My account is flooded with messages. Most of them are followers asking if I am okay, what is going on, or sharing their solidarity. A small subset – mostly men, surprise, surprise – comment that I should have expected some infidelity when being with a professional athlete. My history aside, this is such a bad take and my audience is quick to point that out.

Since I've been radio silent, I hop up off the couch and go to George's balcony., I take a picture of the view and post it on my story with Taylor Swift's *Dancing with Our Hands Tied* playing over it. The song isn't a perfect analogy, but it mostly encapsulates my thoughts on the predicament. My love had been frozen when I met Brady but he painted me golden. He showed me what love *should* be.

I spend the afternoon soaking up the sun on the balcony and listening to podcasts I missed while I hid. After I'm caught up, I decide to channel the emotions I'm experiencing. I grab my computer and open a blank blog post. While people might expect an exposé on everything that went down with Brady and I, I take a different approach.

The post I write is about being your own inner peace. It is about how easy it can be to lean on others and lose yourself in them. I realize I did that with Brady. I write that while a support system is important, at the end of the day you have to be comfortable being alone and finding strength from within.

The past several days have made me realize how ill-equipped I am to do that. I was in Nashville for all of a few months before I allowed Brady's strong and protective nature to suck me in. If it wasn't him, it was Tiffany and Carina. I overcorrected my isolation in my marriage to surround myself with others who lifted me up. It was amazing, but I can see now how I used it as a crutch to not deal with all my emotions. I need to take more ownership of my mental well-being. I vow to do exactly that, and it may be the biggest 'try' of all.

Two days later, George announces he is over my hermit routine. He knocks on my bedroom door at nine a.m. and sits against the head-board as I rouse.

"Good morning, Honeybun," he coos.

"Morning, Georgie," I yawn.

"How are we doing?" he asks.

I blow out a raspberry and genuinely take stock before I answer. "We're doing okay. I'm still confused and have countless unanswered questions, but I realize much of my hurt was that I escaped into my relationship instead of dealing with my trauma. And then it felt like that relationship was pulled out from under me."

"So, we've decided he isn't a cheating bastard?"

"Yeah," I reply. "With the grueling schedule you guys are on during the season and how most of his free moments were spent with me, I don't think he had time to cheat. Plus, he didn't exhibit any other red flags. He was always open with his phone, leaving it face up and giving me the passcode to search things for him. He never disappeared to take calls, and he was reachable virtually any time he wasn't on the field."

"Hmm," Georgie hums in response. "I still find his story a little too convincing."

"You don't believe him because his story makes too much sense?" I question.

"Yeah, it's fishy."

"Or maybe it's that you don't like him and want to think the worst?"

"It could be that," he surmises. "If you believe him, does that mean you forgive him and plan to take him back?"

That is the question of the hour. In all my thinking and reexamining of the situation, I realize how weak his response was. Not only did he purposefully not tell me information, he never apologized for what occurred. He focused on trying to convince me he hadn't been unfaithful; he never apologized for the position he put me in.

Helping that woman may have been the right thing to do, but it has repercussions on my life. It affected my sense of self and played into my insecurities. He should have spent less time covering his ass and more time dealing with the repercussions of his actions.

"I'm not sure yet. I think I need a little time to be by myself. Everything with Brady developed so quickly I didn't have much time to root my strength in myself. Then when I realized he could be gone, everything fell apart. I don't want that to happen again."

"Are you going to talk to him while he is here?"

"I don't know," I say. "He texted me about it, but I haven't responded yet. I haven't replied to anyone except to offer proof of life to Tiff and Care."

"I'll let you get to it, then. There is a ticket with your name on it at will call for tonight and tomorrow if you decide to come to the game. No pressure," he says ruffling my hair as he takes his leave.

Knowing I need to talk to more than only Georgie, I grab my phone and scroll through my unread messages.

Wednesday, 2:31 PM

CHARLIE

Missed you the last few days at the gym.
Let me know when you're back in town. If
you need me to spread rumors about Miller
having a small peen, I know the guy who
runs the Baseball Bulges site.

270

I have no idea how she knows the person who makes that list, but it is good to know for future reference. I miss working out with Charlie. I love Carina and Tiffany but having a friend not connected with them or the team is a nice change of pace. I realize I need more of that. People who know me as me and not in relation to other people.

Friday 9:42 AM

ME

I think I'm good for now, but thanks for the offer.

I close out of that thread and move on to my other non-baseball friend, Raven. She sent me a picture of a house she recently finished redecorating.

Thursday 10:17 AM

RAVEN

As soon as you get back, we are getting pampered. The homeowner's gifted me a day at their spa as a 'thank you.' When I told them about your work with the magazine and your blog, they were VERY interested in you coming with me.

Friday 9:44 AM

ME

That sounds incredible. I could use a massage.

She texts back immediately.

Raven

I could use a mani-pedi like you wouldn't believe. How are you doing, babe? Need anything?

ME

I'm doing okay all things considered. Trying to decide whether I want to go to the game tonight.

RAVEN

Oh yikes. Do you? Would you have to see Miller?

ME

I always loved watching Georgie play. And the guys. I could always go and not see Brady, but that would be a coward's way out. I owe it to him and more importantly myself to finish hearing him out and give him the opportunity to say his piece.

RAVEN

You're a better woman than I, Lo.

ME

I'll text you when I plan to come back. I think I need a few more days hiding out.

RAVEN

Of course! I'm here if you need me.

Aside from my thread with Brady which I checked yesterday, I only have one more unread text. It is from the last person I ever want to hear from: my ex-husband. Our divorce has been final for months. He shouldn't need to talk to me about anything as it is all settled and dealt with.

Thursday 6:32 PM

272

PHIL

PHIL

WTF Lola. Why would you do this? Cassie already told my mother everything when we wouldn't give her a raise. Is that not penance enough?

Seeing as I have no idea what he is talking about, I tell him as much and ask him to leave me alone. His texts right back.

Friday 9:56 AM

PHIL

Don't play dumb with me, Lola. This is low even for you. I didn't peg you as vindictive. You aren't the woman I used to know.

ME

Thank God for that.

I can assure you, I did nothing to seek revenge against you, Phil. Maybe you have more enemies than you think. If you contact me again, I will file a restraining order for harassment.

While I know I didn't do anything to Phil, I have a sneaking suspicion someone I know might have. To confirm my theory, I pull up the group chat with Carina and Tiffany.

Friday 10:02 AM

ME

Would either of you happen to know why Phil is texting me about some revenge ploy?

CARE BEAR

I certainly don't. Babs?

273

TIFF

What did he say…

ME

He asked me why I would do "this?" And
said he didn't know I was "vindictive."

TIFF

I smell bitch TikTok

ME

Tiffany! What did you do?

TIFF

I don't know if I'll ever get out of her what she did and I'm sure as hell not going to ask Phil. I'll have to chalk it up to one of life's big mysteries. Even though I decided I need to rely a little less on my support system, it is nice to know they have my back.

Chapter Forty-Four

The last several days without Lola have been brutal. Besides a single text asking if she can talk while I am in Chicago, I haven't reached out. She clearly wants space and I have no choice but to give it to her. If I want a chance to make things right between us, bombarding her is not going to do me any favors.

I've yet to hear back from her and I'm wound tight with anxiety. I had the team set aside a ticket for her in case she decided to come, but last night's went unused. We play tonight and again tomorrow before heading back to Nashville, and I am hopeful she will attend at least once.

I need to keep my head in the game since this is our last away series. Winning one more of the two games left here will clinch us as the division lead guaranteeing we make it into the divisional championships. After losing their last season, we want that title.

As I study my teammates, I think we have a good chance of taking it all the way this season. Aside from a few tough losses, including the one earlier this week, we have been on a hot-streak during the back half of the season. As long as we keep our eye on the prize, I have faith we can do it. Easier said than done in my situation.

"Master Miller," a familiar voice jeers from behind me. I take a deep breath in order to find the patience I need to deal with Derrick.

"What can I do for you, Jones?" I ask dryly.

"Just checking in. Wanted to see how you were doing now that you've fallen off your pedestal. How is slumming it with the rest of us?"

This guy has been a problem since he was traded to the team. Hell, before that even. He's the one who caused Robby's injury last season. Granted, that worked out in the end since it brought him back to Carina, but Derrick never misses a chance to stir the pot.

"Never thought I was better than anybody else. That must be your own inferiority complex. Everyone on this team is at the same level."

"If that were true, we'd all be paid the same," he says with an eye roll. Talking about salary is crass. There are a variety of reasons for different levels of pay, some of which, such as agent quality or cash flow, have nothing to do with a player's skill. Derrick is not even one of the top five in terms of salary, so I don't know why he's talking about this.

When I don't take the bait, he tries a different tactic. "I haven't seen your cute, little plaything around lately. Toss her to the side for a new model?"

Button. Pressed. That comment has me rising to my feet, but a few of my teammates get there before I have the chance to do anything.

"Take a walk, Jones," Robby growls as Kent and Crews hold me back.

"No one on this damn team can take a joke!" Derrick yells, throwing his hands up in the air. One peek at my thunderous expression, though, and he heeds Robby's warning.

"You good?" Robby asks.

"I'm fine," I shrug as Kent and Crews drop their hands from my shoulders. "I wasn't going to fuck him up too badly."

"Don't worry, Cap. Karma is going to come back and bite him on the ass one day for all of us."

"I can't fucking wait," Robby mutters.

"I'd ask how you're holding up, but from how easy it was for him to rile you up, I'm gonna guess not great," Kent observes.

"I don't know, man. Nothing feels right. Waking up alone, only making one coffee, not hearing the sound of her typing bounce across my condo, it's all wrong. I didn't realize how dull my life was before she was in it. It's as if the rest of the world was black and white and she was screaming color. I can't stand the distance between us. I need to see her."

"You know who can make that happen, right?" Robby prods.

Fuck. I was hoping to do this without having to make nice and ask for help from the one guy I want to talk to even less than Derrick. I guess I'll have to bite the bullet after the game and grovel to yet another one of Lola's friends for info. Hopefully, he'll be more receptive than Tiffany.

The atmosphere in the Foxes' stadium is tense. They need to win all of their remaining series to make it to the wildcard game. Based on their performance tonight, that isn't a likely scenario and their fans are feral.

Rivera has been scowling at me the entire game and if looks could kill, I'd be long dead by now. Thankfully, he struck out and had a flyout to right field during his at bats, keeping him from ending up on my base.

It's my turn in the batter's box and he has been throwing wild to me all night. I don't think there is any strategy behind his throws except to piss me off. He is getting increasingly agitated since he has been unable to rattle me. I singled in the first to bring in a run and he walked me in the third. His anger at me is palpable. I know part of it is how much this game means to the team, but I can't help but think it has more to do with Lola.

His first throw to me is a ball, high and inside. The second is a curveball strike. I'm expecting a fastball for his next throw, but what I don't expect is for it to peg me in the stomach, knocking the air out of me. As I hit the ground, I hear my teammates and coaches yelling loudly as a mixture of cheers and grunts come from the fans.

I wave off the trainer as he was coming over to me and stand. Rivera has a smug air that makes me want to charge the mound, but I inhale deeply and take my base. As much as I want to retaliate, I know that's exactly what he wants. I also know Lola wouldn't want us to fight.

I manage to score, bringing the tally to 4-1, before the inning is over. Rivera is second at bat in the fifth. Thanks to a hit landing in an alley in the outfield, he ends up on first. Coach decides at that moment to put in the relief pitcher, leaving the two of us to awkwardly wait together while the new pitcher warms up. At least, I thought it would be awkward, but Rivera is ready to goad me the second the first base umpire steps away.

"How ya feeling, Miller? Didn't bruise your abs too much did I?" He taunts.

"Laugh it up, Rivera. Payback will be coming," I reply.

"Nah, that was payback. My conscience is clear," he retorts. "If anything, you should thank me for helping you fulfill at least one of your promises."

Is he serious? I should thank him for pegging me? Curious, I ask, "What promise?"

"You'd rather take a 100mph fastball to the gut than ever be the reason Lola cries, right? I made that happen. Consider it a lesson to keep it in your pants. I can aim lower next time."

"What the fuck, man?" I say, stepping towards him.

"What the fuck to you!" he shouts back. "You hurt one of the most important women in my life. You didn't think that could go unpunished, did you? She deserves better than your sorry ass."

"You don't know what you're talking about. I treat Lola like a queen. She is *the* most important woman in my life."

Rivera's eyes narrow as we stand nose to nose, umpires and coaches hurrying towards us. "You have a funny way of showing it. She's been holed up in my apartment all week. She's strong, but this almost broke her. You need to get your shit together and grovel your ass off or give her the closure she needs to move on."

Move on? Is that what she wants? To move on from me? Before I can say anything in response, we've been pulled apart. Chicago sends over a pinch runner to take Rivera's place and the game continues. We pull out the win, but it's a hollow victory.

Chapter Forty-Five

• BRADY •

After the drama of today's game, there is no getting out of the post-game press conference. Norris called down from the box and all but demanded I make an appearance and be on my best behavior. Reluctantly, I attend no matter how much I want to tell everyone to fuck off.

"Miller, what was going on with you and Rivera? What got the two of you riled up?," one reporter asks.

"This was an important game for both teams and we got overly passionate in the moment. I respect a player who wants to help his team succeed even if it means ruffling a few feathers," I say, giving my practiced answer. Molly should be proud.

"That peg seemed personal," another reporter calls out. "You two were teammates in Triple-A. Any lingering issues from back then?"

"I enjoyed my time as part of the Foxes organization in Springfield. Rivera and I overlapped briefly during his rookie season. We haven't had any issues in any previous matchups. As I said, we both got a little carried away with the playoff implications at stake."

"Is it true that Rivera went to high school with your rumored girl-friend? Ex-girlfriend?" A third voice shouts out, causing me to clench my fists.

"I don't answer questions about my personal life," I state as flatly as possible. "If there are no questions about the team or the game itself, I think we can call this."

Without listening to any of their responses, I storm out of the press conference. Stomping towards the locker room, I almost plow into someone lingering in the hallway. As I go to apologize, I realize who it is.

"Lola," I whisper.

"Hi," she replies meekly.

"What are you doing here?"

"You said you wanted to talk. This is where you were. Let's talk."

"Here?" I question.

She shrugs. "It's as good as anywhere else."

Not really, it's dark, stuffy and not at all private, but I sense I shouldn't push her on this. If it is the best I'm going to get, I'll take it.

"How are you?" I ask. From what Rivera said, I'm worried. I run my gaze up and down her body to take her in for a moment. I don't know what I expected, but she appears okay. She has dark circles from lack of sleep and her eyes are missing the sparkle they normally have. I can't blame her, I have the same circles and my beard is unkempt.

I have to hold back my scowl when I see she's wearing a Rivera jersey. I know I don't have the right to demand she wear mine right now, but seeing another man's name on her annoys me beyond measure.

"I'm..." She pauses as if to consider how open she wants to be with me, and that stings. "I'm alright. I've spent time reflecting and have a better grasp on how I'm feeling about everything you told me last week."

"And how is that?"

"Disappointed. Hurt. Enlightened," she shares.

I suck in a breath. I expected the first two, but they still suck to hear. It's the last one that scares me, though. I have no idea what that means. What could she be enlightened by?

"I didn't cheat on you," I say for what may be the thousandth time. But I will tell her a million times if that is what it takes for it to sink in.

"I know," she states.

"You do?"

"I mean, I don't know for sure, but I believe you if you say you didn't. You're not a liar and frankly, I don't think you had the time or emotional capacity to cheat."

Filled with relief, I pull her into my chest. It takes a moment to realize she isn't returning my embrace. I lean back to peer down at her. She's stiff as a board, worrying her lip. "You say you believe me, but it doesn't feel like we're okay."

"Are you sorry?" she asks.

"For what?"

Her neutral expression shifts to one of annoyance and sadness. "For purposefully misleading me, for betraying my trust, for putting us in the situation to begin with."

"I didn't betray you, I swear. I could have been more forthcoming, but I was trying to save you from unnecessary anxiety. I did what I thought was best based on how the night should have gone. I won't apologize for trying to protect you, but I am sorry you were hurt. The situation spiraled beyond my control."

She lets out a disappointed sigh. "I'm not saying it was your fault, but it was your responsibility. While you've focused on defending your need to protect me, you haven't considered how I was affected in the aftermath. You're not the only one caught up in this. Your reputation is linked to mine. You never addressed the pictures more than to ask for privacy. You didn't deny cheating allegations."

"Because I didn't care what people thought!" I snap.

"Did you ever think that I might? That while people may think you were a cheater, they would think of me as the poor woman who wasn't enough? Or that the brand I'm building has its foundation set in boundaries and openness and people might think I wasn't being true to that? Not to mention how embarrassing it is to have people assume you've been cheated on, *again*."

Shit. I didn't think about that. I have never put much stock into people's opinion of me. I have thick skin and my livelihood is largely unaffected by the fickle court of public opinion. I forgot others don't have that luxury. I knew I would be cast as the villain, but I didn't consider how Lola would be judged or pitied the way a woman usually is when publicly scorned. Stay, go. It's a lose-lose proposition for them. With her career focused on social media and how active she is within her community, of course she is forced to face the opinions of others.

When I don't respond right away, Lola launches into a further tirade. "You should have told me what happened at the club as soon as it was over. It would have saved me the shock of sitting with those images for hours – days, really – questioning their validity. You were too busy trying to manage my perceived insecurities that you set us up for failure. I'm not fragile, Brady."

"You're right. I didn't think about how any of this was affecting you outside of the scope of our relationship. I'm so sorry, Lola. No matter how unintended, my actions had consequences that affected you in ways I couldn't anticipate. Had I been more forthcoming from the get-go, a good deal of this hurt could have been avoided. I truly apologize.

"And I know you aren't fragile, baby. You're one of the strongest people I've ever met. But I wanted to protect you anyway. I didn't think any good would come from you knowing I was at the club. It would have stressed you out, and I wanted to keep the peaceful bubble we were in as long as I could. At the end of the day, it was about my own selfishness.

"It's my job to manage situations that could negatively impact you. To try to stop hurt before it can get you. I failed this time."

"That right there is our true problem."

Her statement confuses me. "Our problem is that I don't want to hurt you?"

"No. Our problem is that you are constantly trying to manage my emotional responses and I've let you. By letting you take on the bulk of my emotional baggage, I've neglected to process it and truly move forward from it. I let myself hide in your strength and care for me, as well as that of my friends, to avoid being alone with my emotions.

"I had been emotionally checked out of my marriage for months, if not years. But that doesn't mean I was unaffected by it, as we can clearly see by the big emotions I had when I thought you'd been unfaithful. I let you take care of me so much that I forgot I could also take care of myself."

"I love taking care of you," I remark.

"You can still take care of me and not be the sole source of my inner peace. I spent a lot of time trying a lot of things. Over the past few days, I realized most of them were only skin deep. If I am going to be the best version of myself, I need to heal the wounds lurking under the surface. I can't let you or Carina or throwing myself into work do that for me. I have to do the work on my own.

"Someday you might need me to shoulder more of the load. There will undoubtedly come a time when you need me to take care of you, no matter how much you try to avoid it. I need to be able to do that for you. I think I need some time to be on my own.

"I was on my own initially after leaving Phil, but I was still reeling from the betrayal. As a more whole and healed person, I need to prove to myself that I can stand on my own."

I know there is a lot to unpack there, but I'm laser-focused on her saying 'someday.' To me, that means she is still in this, that there is still a chance. If that is true, then I can deal with anything she throws my way. As long as it is us together in the end, I can endure anything.

"What do you need, Lola?" I ask her, finally.

"Time," she responds. "Alone."

"You want to break up?" I know I said I could endure anything, but a breakup would be tough to come back from. Not being able to say she is mine will be next to impossible. We are meant to be. Can't she see that?

"Not a breakup," she asserts. "At least not permanently. I need to be on my own to show myself that I can. The same way I faced my divorce alone, I need to know I can thrive alone. I can't test that if you are always there for me to lean on. I think this is the perfect time. You're about to be in the playoffs. You don't need the distraction of a tumultuous relationship."

"You are never a distraction. Everything else is a distraction from you," I say, causing her to smile softly. "I don't want to break up."

"Not a break up, a break."

"Robby made me watch FRIENDS with him a few spring trainings ago. I know they're the same thing," I refute.

"Not this one. We're two people taking time the same way we would if one of us traveled somewhere with no cell service."

"What is your proposal, exactly? Lay it out for me," I request.

"We stop seeing each other, temporarily. We limit communication. We both focus on our goals and then, after a predetermined amount of time, we come back and evaluate if we still want to be together."

"I will always want you," I declare. "How long?"

"Until after the World Series?" she suggests.

"That could be over six weeks, Lo." I don't know if I can go six weeks without talking to her. Six weeks without knowing if she is safe and okay? That would be the ultimate distraction.

"It's a long time," she agrees. "But I don't think it's fair to do anything less when you will need your focus on the game. Having it end in the middle would steal that focus. If the team doesn't advance, we can potentially end the break sooner."

"Are you going to be dating during this break?" I ask. Lola pales at the question.

"No. I will be concentrating on myself. This is a break, not a break up. I would prefer we remain exclusive. If you don't want that, I understand but—"

I don't let her finish before I'm slamming my lips into hers. "I don't want anyone else," I whisper as I pull away from her lips and rest my forehead against hers. Like an addict, my body lights up at the taste of her. I was going through withdrawals after this long without her.

"You need this?" I question. She nods.

"Okay," I acquiesce. "But I can't go without contact. I'll go out of my mind if I don't know you're alright."

"That's fair. How about we meet once a week for a twenty-minute coffee date to catch up?"

I think about her suggestion. It's way less than I want, but I sense I won't get more. That doesn't stop me from countering, "And one text exchange per day. I won't reach out more than that, but I need to hear from you daily, even if only to say 'good night' or share a meme."

She ponders my offer before agreeing. "Deal."

When she reaches her hand out to shake, I grasp the back of her neck and pull her into a searing kiss. It's slower than the one we shared earlier. I'm savoring it. I don't know when the next time I'll be able to kiss her will be. Unlike when I embraced her earlier, she sinks into me.

"I know you need to take this journey for yourself, but if you need anything, don't hesitate to reach out. I meant it when I said I loved you. It was the wrong time to tell you and now isn't any better, but I need you to know. I'll be waiting for you, my sweet girl. Hurry back." With all my cards on the table, I leave for the locker room. I can't say I feel any better about the situation, but I take comfort in knowing she still wants me, even if she needs time first.

Chapter Forty-Six

A fter my talk with Brady, I returned to Georgie's and promptly passed out. It's the best night of sleep I've had since this entire ordeal began. The Songbirds and Foxes have one more game left in the series. Since it is a two p.m. first pitch and I managed to sleep past ten, I know Brady is already at the stadium. Following the terms of our deal, I sent him a text wishing him luck.

11:43 AM

BRADY BEAR

Luck isn't needed, but thank you. 😊 When is our first coffee date?

ME

Thursday morning?

Brady 'likes' my reply to avoid breaking our one text rule on the first day. While it's comical, I appreciate that he is respecting my boundaries.

Around eight that evening, Georgie comes home with dinner. "Are those Italian Beef sandwiches I smell?" I squeal.

"I should've known the Italian would be able to sniff it out. I hope you're hungry because I over ordered," he replies. When he glances around the room, he can tell I've started packing up my things.

"You don't have to go, Lo. I know I leave for an away series Tuesday, but you're welcome to stay as long as you want. Hell, ditch Tennessee and stay forever." His eyebrows raise as he makes his suggestion.

"I think one move for a fresh start is enough. Besides, I like Nashville. You'd like it, too, if you gave it a chance," I remark. He gives me a disbelieving glance.

"And I'm not leaving because you have an away series. It's time. I can't hide from my life anymore. I have work commitments and plans with friends I don't want to back out on. I talked to Brady last night, and we came to an understanding."

"Which is?" he prompts.

"We're going to take a break," I say.

"Oh God, Lola. Was that his idea? Everyone knows breaks are drawn out break ups."

"It was mine. And they don't have to be," I argue. "I need time to learn how to be on my own and rely on myself. He needs to focus on the playoffs. It makes sense for both of us to table our relationship issues instead of splitting our focus. In six weeks, we're going to decide whether we break permanently or stay together as better versions of ourselves."

Georgie's mood dampens a bit at the mention of the playoffs. Back-to-back losses to the Songbirds mean that his team isn't in contention for the Wild Card game.

"I'm sorry about your season," I tell him.

"Thanks, Honeybun. It's okay. The team wasn't as competitive this year as they could have been. Management made some dumb trades that messed with our mojo. I think it may be time to consider a trade myself."

"Really? But you've been here your entire career."

"I know, but I want the chance to win, and I don't see that happening here. Maybe I can get on to the Huskers and be closer to my family."

"Maybe you get traded to Nashville and be closer to me!" I suggest enthusiastically.

"Don't get your hopes up," he deadpans.

"No matter where you go, I'll always root for you, Georgie."

He gives me a genuine smile. "Thank you. And no matter where I go, there will always be a room for you to hide in."

On Tuesday, Georgie and I ride to the airport together. He promises to come visit once the season is over, and I promise to keep him updated on everything with me. He says he can throw harder next time if I need him to.

One of the things that hit me most when I returned to Nashville last night was how at home I felt. This may have been the place I escaped to after my marriage fell apart, but coming back is right. I belong here more than I ever did in St. Louis. Does it help that my cousin and bestie are here? Probably.

Tiffany ambushed me the second I walked in the door and all but took me to the ground. She immediately called Carina, and we spent the evening with the world's most loyal men – Ben & Jerry – eating our weight in pizza and watching 2000s rom-coms. It was exactly the reset I needed.

Waking up this morning, I feel refreshed. Even though I miss Brady and it's weird not sleeping in his arms, I know I made the right decision. I let myself slip into his world too seamlessly. I need to shore up the footings of my own. It also helps that I woke up to a text from the man in question. I breathe a sigh of relief that he hasn't changed his mind about us.

9:06 AM

Brady
Almost managed to get a row by myself on the plane. Then Kent sat down. Did you know he talks in his sleep? He's dreaming about the Pillsbury Dough Boy and it does not seem platonic.

Me
Wow. There is a lot to unpack there.

As much as I would love to spend all day in the comfort of my bed, I came back to Nashville to stop hiding and get on with my life. I pull myself out of my bed and head into the kitchen to make myself coffee. When I go to pull out my syrup, I notice it's getting low. I'll need to order more soon. I only have a small amount of lavender left. Maybe I should see what fall flavors there are now that we are almost into October.

While sipping my coffee, I open up my handy dandy notebook. This moment is reminiscent of my first days here. Reading over my old list, I see I only added a few more steps after my initial night of planning.

Step 1: Makeover
Step 2: Find a Job
Step 3: Deal with Phil
Step 4: Create Blog
Step 5: Try List
Step 6: Secure Brand Deal

I am happy to say I have completed all six steps listed. But now it is time to refocus on moving forward. I have been doing good on the job/blog front, but on my personal growth, not as much. As I review my list, a few ideas come to my mind right away and I jot them down.

Step 7: Find a Therapist
Step 8: Start Meditating/Daily Affirmations
Step 9: Attend Self-Development Event
Step 10: Make a Five-Year Plan

It isn't the best list ever created, but it is a start and that gives me a sense of purpose. Completing step seven – finding a therapist – is the most important. Hopefully, they can help me improve on the other steps.

I had toyed with the idea of therapy in the past, especially after I cut all contact with my mom. Phil discouraged it, though. He acted as if getting professional help was a weakness or blemish on my character. Maybe he was afraid a therapist would point out all the ways our relationship was flawed. I shouldn't have listened to him then and I certainly am not going to now. I can hear Brady's voice competing with his in my head, telling me to do whatever I need to be whole and happy.

That's the crux of the entire matter, though. I hope therapy will replace the voices I hear inside myself with my own. I want to be the one I rely on for inner guidance. I've spent too much time questioning my gut – with both good and bad outcomes. It is time to let my intuition run things.

As I stand outside the coffee shop I'm meeting Brady at, I peek inside and see him sitting at a table near the door. He positioned himself in such a way he will notice as soon arrive. Judging by the two drinks I see at his table, he has already ordered. I should be annoyed at him assuming my order, but I know that's how he is. If he was meeting Kent, he'd have gotten his order for him, too. Plus, he knows what I like.

Taking a deep breath, I will myself to enter. When I do, those omniscient, pale blue eyes lock into mine. I stutter step before regaining my composure and approach his table. His gaze doesn't shift away from mine. He stands to greet me and his fingers flex as if he is having to stop himself from reaching out to touch me. Despite that, a fraction of tension leaves his shoulders. It's as if seeing me again in person is giving him some measure of relief.

It's the same for me. I wasn't initially excited about these meetings, but the sense of calm I get being in his presence is something I hadn't accounted for. Seeing each other weekly will help me focus on my journey, not detract from it. If I don't have to worry about the status of our relationship, I can truly put all my energy into myself.

"Hi," I greet. It's a bit stilted and awkward, but at least it got the ball rolling.

"Hey," he replies. "I got you the apple pie latte. I hope that's okay."

"That is great, thank you. I haven't tried that yet."

Brady's chest puffs out at that. "Good," he states. "I figured if we only had twenty minutes, we shouldn't waste any of them in line. How are you?"

"I'm good. How are you? Feeling good about the end of the season?"

"I'm okay. I think the season is wrapping up nicely. Austin can't catch us in the standings, so we are already locked into the playoffs. As long as we all stay healthy, we will be in good shape."

"That's great," I reply, searching for something else to say. It's awkward again. I see him hesitate before reaching his hand out to grab mine.

"This doesn't have to be weird. You know me, Lo. I know you. This temporary pause doesn't change any of that. Tell me what you've got planned this week."

I exhale, glad he called out the elephant in the room. I'm both relieved and envious of how self-assured he is in this situation. That is exactly what I am hoping to gain from this break.

Brady listens to me talk about the commitments for the magazine and an influencer event I'm attending before I drop the therapy bomb. I know inner Brady was all for it, but a small part of me is anxious IRL Brady won't be. Not that it would stop me, but the people pleaser I am trying to rein in still wants his approval.

He nods his head as he takes the last sip of his chai. This time, his smile reaches his eyes. "That's great, Lola. That will be a good resource to help you deal with everything that has happened in the last year."

"I think it will. I've heard nothing but amazing things about her. I am excited to have her help processing everything and getting help to move forward."

"I'm sure she'll be great. And if not, the team's psychologist would have recommendations I can ask for." He glances down at his watch and frowns. "Our time is up. I'll walk out with you."

As we stand beside my car in front of the coffee shop, he pushes a stray curl behind my ear. "I already know the answers but I'm going to ask, anyway. Are we still good?"

"Yes."

"And you'll call me if you need anything? Anything, Lola."

"Yes."

He searches my face for signs of deception as indecision haunts him. I see the moment whatever was warring in his mind is settled before he curls that hand around the back of my neck and kisses me. *Kiss* might not be a strong enough word for what this is. Brady is devouring me on this sidewalk. He is both taking my breath away and breathing it back into me. He is putting into this kiss all the words he wants to say but knows he shouldn't. He is telling me with his lips how he feels about me and about us. It's a mix of frustration, desperation, and total devotion. It's humbling and uplifting at the same time.

By the time he pulls away, I am gasping. I think he's going to say something else, but with a nod of his head and a smirk, he turns and walks towards his truck. I don't miss the way he waits for me to pull out before doing the same. I drive half in a daze to my next errand of the day.

Chapter Forty-Seven

• LOLA •

October

It's been three weeks since I returned from Chicago. The Songbirds managed to clinch the division championship and are now on to the League Championship series. Despite his apprehension to the break, Brady has been diligently following my boundaries. We've texted once a day and have gone out for coffee three times.

I tried insisting we split the bill, but Brady has shown up early each time and ordered ahead. Conversation flowed more easily after our initial meeting, though it is mostly me telling him what I have been doing. Normally, I would push for him to share more, but I know right now he is living and breathing baseball. I think he is grateful to talk about anything else. At the end of each date, he has given me a kiss that can only be described as indecent and walked away with a smug smirk on his face.

Today is my fifth appointment with my therapist, Lynn. We've been meeting twice a week since she knows about the six-week time frame I've imposed for this break. She applauded us both on our adherence to the rules. In fact, my text-of-the-day informed Brady of that praise.

Lynn and I have been diving into my childhood issues in order to help me understand my anxious attachment style. While I was thrilled to learn I wasn't co-dependent as Dr. Google diagnosed, I had a lot more baggage to unpack than I thought.

The abandonment by my mother and emotional absence of my father did a real number on me, apparently. It's part of why I settled for a partner like Phil. He was a safe option, especially with the way he loved bombed me in the early years. It wasn't until after we were married and he pulled away that I began compartmentalizing my life in order to endure it.

Lynn thinks it's why I believe Brady will seek a more sexually adventurous partner despite his reassurances of the contrary and no evidence that he has needs I am not meeting. Once our break is over, she thinks it would be a good idea for him to come with me for a session or two and shockingly he agreed. I didn't think he'd want to open himself up to a stranger, but he told me that he would do anything I needed to be secure in our relationship, including therapy.

As I sit on the cushy sofa in Lynn's office, I am struck by the nugget of wisdom she dropped on me. "I'm going to need you to repeat that," I say.

She smiles at me, her warm brown eyes shining in understanding. "You are defined by the next decision you make, not the last one." After a pause, she asks, "What do you think that means?"

I take a few moments to process before I respond. "That I should be focused forward and not worrying about the mistakes I made in the past?"

"In a sense," she replies. "There is a lot we can learn from the past. It can inform why we see the world and ourselves the way we do. It can explain why we have certain attachment styles, coping mechanisms, and things of that nature. But spending too much time overanalyzing our past can be harmful. At a certain point we need to take what we've learned and apply it to how we move forward. We can't change what happened or how we reacted to it. All we can do is try to make different, better choices in the future.

"You often refer to yourself as Lola 2.0. I take that to mean that you are doing that: making different, better choices. Would you agree with that assessment?"

"Yes," I confirm.

"What has been your motivation?"

I answer instantly, parroting her phrasing back to her. "To prove that I am different and better."

"Prove to who?"

"What?"

"Who are you trying to show that you are different and better? And why?"

"I-"

She's throwing me for a loop with this question. Who am I trying to prove that I am different and better? My mom? Phil? Myself? I don't have a firm answer.

"I'll let you mull that over for yourself. The answer doesn't change my take on it or the meaning behind my statement about being defined by your next decision and not your last.

"What that phrase illustrates to me is that in a world that is constantly changing and moving, so are we as people. Who we are and what decisions we made last year, last month, and even last week are insignificant to our self-perception. We aren't making different, better choices to *show* we've grown. We're making different, better choices *because* we've grown.

"Right now, you're in the middle of the tunnel. There is a light at both ends. You have to make the choices that will get you to the other side and not take you back. At this exact moment in time, I think you're paralyzed in the middle. You're so stuck 'overcoming' your past, it's hampering your future.

"Focus on making moves for the life and achievements you want rather than proving to whoever it is that you are a better version of yourself. If they can't see the growth and changes you've made, then they aren't worth your time. Make decisions that take you where you want to go and leave behind anything that doesn't serve you."

Lynn lets her words sink in before giving me homework for the next session. First, I must determine who I am trying to prove myself to. Then I have to consider all the ways I don't need to prove myself and how it wouldn't matter to them, anyway. Doubters will alway doubt. Haters will alway hate.

Second, I am supposed to write down my decisions in a day and determine which ones move me forward, hold me back, or keep me stagnant. From there we will determine my next steps.

The next morning starts off rough. I wake up later than I want and am running around trying to get ready for an interview. The outfit I wanted to wear was wrinkled, and I burned my hand on my curling wand.

I'm meeting with the Lavignes at their winery. Which is a ways out of town. The new classes they offer caught the eye of my editor and she was thrilled to learn I have a personal connection to the owners. She wants me to do a profile on the fall/holiday activities they have in addition to their formal event capabilities.

With a long drive ahead, I know I won't get there in a happy mood if I don't have caffeine. My mind shifts to the last time I went there with Brady but I quickly shut that down. I rush into the kitchen to make my latte. When I go to grab my syrup, it is empty. Tiffany enters the kitchen at the perfect moment to witness my breakdown.

"You okay, Bunny?" she asks.

"No," I lament on the verge of tears. "I'm out of my syrups. I checked the website last week but I couldn't figure out how to buy more. I think they stopped selling them."

I am not proud how close to crying I am right now, but it is happening nonetheless. I have been extra sensitive and raw lately as I am processing everything with Lynn. I also am probably about to start my period but regardless of those facts, this feels like at least a DEFCON-3 situation.

"It's okay, Lo," Tiffany coos, trying to comfort me. "Leave the bottle on the counter and I will take care of it. I'm sure I can call someone and get it sorted out."

"Are you sure?"

"Positive," she replies. "I'll place an online order for you at Starbucks before you hop on the interstate. I know it's not ideal but at least you can get some caffeine in your veins. Doesn't a PSL sound good?"

"I guess," I grumble.

"Good! Now get out of here so you can make it to your interview."

Following Tiffany's instructions, I pick up my latte and make it to the winery with two minutes to spare. I listened to my favorite playlist on the way which helps center me after the chaotic morning. As soon as I step out, I meet who I assume is one of the owners. This guy is extremely attractive. I'm not usually into blonds, but I can see the appeal. His dark blond hair is cropped short and his golden skin glimmers in the mid-morning sun.

"Hey, I'm Marc. Are you Lola?" he asks.

"Hi. Yes, I am Lola. It is nice to meet you, though I thought I was supposed to meet Josh?"

"You were," he supplies. "He's my brother. He had to put out a fire in our bottling facility."

"Oh my God! Should we wait for the fire department?"

"What?" He questions confused before understanding crosses his face. "Sorry, that was hyperbole. Figurative fire, not literal. He will join us a little later. I handle all the sales and business development for the winery, so he asked me to take over while he deals with the mess. You're in good hands. My tour will be more interesting, anyway. You'll get more story and fewer nuts and bolts. Shall we start in the main tasting room?"

"Sounds great," I reply.

"You said Josh is your brother. Does that make Emerly your sister?"

"It does," he says with a smile. "I didn't realize you'd met our little Bubbles."

"Bubbles? Yes, I met her when I came to goat yoga a few months ago and my cousin worked with her to plan her wedding here."

"Oof, don't tell her I told you that nickname. I'd never hear the end of it. It's something we've called her since she was young. She was always bubbly and personable. She's five and six years younger than Josh and I, respectively. It's hard to view her as anything other than our baby sister."

"I get that. The three of you run the winery together?" I ask.

"Along with our cousins. The three of us are more on the business side while they do the actual winemaking since they grew up with our grandparents. As I mentioned, I handle the sales while Josh manages the day-to-day operations. Emerly, as you know, handles our marketing and events. Penny tends to the grapes and the grounds. Payton is our Vigneron and oversees every batch of wine we make. He trained in France with some of the top winemakers in the world."

Marc goes on to tell the heart-wrenching story of how he, his siblings, and cousins found themselves managing the winery after the death of their grandparents. After answering some of my questions, he gives me a tour and as promised, Josh joins us. They show me the process from start to finish and even let me take home wine I bottle myself.

Emerly takes over after the tour and fills me in on all the upcoming events and offerings they have for the rest of the year. I end up signing Carina, Tiffany, and myself for a Pinot and Pilates class in a few weeks. I spend most of the morning at the winery before meeting with Molly to go over brand opportunities and then working out with Charlie.

By the time I make it back to my apartment, I am wiped. All I want to do is enjoy some carbs and comfort TV. When I open the fridge to pull out Aunt Teresa's homemade pasta sauce, I see fresh bottles of syrup in the fridge. Not only are my beloved lavender and orange blossom back, but there is also a bottle of toffee flavor. A sticky note is stuck to the top of one of the bottles. It reads, "These came today. Auto-ship?"

If I wasn't tired, I might question the timing. Instead, I am grateful. I spend the rest of the night lulled by Sandra Bullock and Hugh Grant, ignoring all my responsibilities.

Chapter Forty-Eight

I t's been three and a half weeks since Lola and I embarked on this break. As much as I hate it, I understand this is something she needs to do. I can see now how we let our emotions overwhelm us and got ahead of ourselves. Everything was so perfect, it was too hard to hold back. But when you know it is forever, what's a few more weeks?

I wish things could be different, but I have to trust that our bond is strong enough to withstand this break, and it will ultimately make us better. Today we are meeting for coffee again. I scroll through our texts as I wait for her. Only messaging her once per day is killing me, but it would be much worse if we weren't communicating at all.

A part of me was afraid she would cancel since we play our first game in the League Championship tonight, but she didn't mention it. To be honest, I am as grateful for the distraction as I am to see her.

I don't know if it is because I haven't seen her in a week, but I am mesmerized when she walks in. In the months since we started dating, she's allowed her hair to grow below her collar bones. It's halfway between the long locks she had when we first met and the bob she had when I returned from camp. Something about the length highlights for me how much she's grown from both those women. She radiates a new sense of self-confidence and assuredness that looks good on her.

"I'd scold you for ordering for me, but I don't think it would do any good," she chides, taking her seat.

I offer her a knowing smirk. "But then you may not have gotten a s'more latte and chocolate chip scone."

She takes a sip before giving me an approving moan. Fuck, I missed hearing that sound. She must read something carnal in my expression because her cheeks pinken.

"Ready for tonight?" she asks.

"As ready as I can be. We know what we have to do, it's simply a matter of doing it. This is the furthest we've gotten in the past decade. We can make it all the way if we put our mind to it."

I love that she is interested in my career, but the last thing I want to talk about is me. I know how I'm doing. I want to hear about her. "I read your post about that spa," I say. "Sounds like you had a good time. I'd never heard of a salt cave before."

"You read my spa article?" she questions.

"Of course."

"Why?"

"Because you wrote it? I read all your articles."

"Even if they don't interest you?"

"Why wouldn't they interest me? You wrote them." Tenderness flashes in her eyes. She sips her drink to cover it up. I don't know why this surprises her. I'm her biggest supporter and number one fan. I'd read a vacuum manual if she wrote it.

Embarrassed by my admission, it's her turn to change the subject. "How is your family? Have they made it to any games?"

We spend the next ten minutes talking about my family and the matching grandma-granddaughter outfits my mom had made for her and Chloe to watch the games in. I wish I could've recorded the melodic giggle Lola let out when I showed her the pictures. I would listen to it on repeat every day. I sigh when I see our time is up again and take a risk placing my hand on her back as I lead her out to her car.

When we get there, I get lost in her hazel eyes. After a minute, she widens them at me expectantly.

"What?" I inquire.

"Aren't you going to ask?"

"Ask what?"

"The questions you ask every time. 'Are we still good?' and 'Will I reach out to you if I need anything?' *Anything*," she mocks in a deep voice I think is supposed to be me.

"Are we?"

"Yes."

"And will you?"

"Yes," she sighs. I smile, running my knuckles down her cheek. When she leans into my touch, I pull her closer and softly kiss her. I deepen the kiss, but nowhere near as much as I usually do. I don't feel the same need to claim her today. Something about her reaction to my reading her articles settling me.

I give her another kiss on the forehead before walking to my truck. As I watch her pull out, I head in the other direction to the stadium. It's earlier than I normally get there, but I could use the extra time to get my mind game-ready.

When I get to the locker room, I am surprised to see I am not the first one there. Kent is sitting at his cubby, hair wet, playing on his phone.

"Hey, man," I greet. "You good?"

"Hey, Papa Bear. Fan-fucking-tastic."

"You sure? You seem a little... on edge."

He meets my gaze then before pocketing his phone. "I ended things with Kristie."

"Ending things? Since when did things begin?"

"That's what I said," he exclaims, throwing his hands in the air. "I went home with her after the division championship win the other night. When I refused to stay over, she got on me to 'define our relationship.' She hasn't stopped harping on it since."

"Why didn't you spend the night?"

"It's against the rules."

"The rules? What rules?" I question.

"My rules. Spending the night sets up expectations I am not interested in meeting. She's known what this is from day one. I am not a commitment guy."

In the years I've played with him, Kent hasn't been in a single relationship. Kristie would be the closest thing he's had to one. She's the longest lasting situationship he's been in to my knowledge. I have no doubt that she knew the score before she slept with him. He makes what he wants abundantly clear to the women he gets involved with and ensures they are on the same page. But she's a bit of a cleat chaser, and he isn't the only player she's tried this on.

Despite his avoidance of one, Kent would be great in a relationship with the right person. He's loyal and a great friend even if he can't take anything seriously. Which leads me to prod. "Would committing be such a bad thing?"

"Uh, yeah," he answers. "Nothing good comes from having a ball and chain in your life."

"A ball and chain? That's a little harsh man."

"That's what relationships are. Don't get me wrong. I'm happy that you're happy, but you've got to admit being with Lola changed your life. You used to go to the club all the time and sample whatever kinky shit it had to offer. Now, you're locked down with just one woman. I don't see the appeal. She is a nice girl, but most of the ones circling us are only interested in what we can offer them, which is fine. They know what to expect from me – a few orgasms and a night they won't forget. And I know to expect they'll brag about it to all their friends."

"First of all, if you ever talk about Lola as anything other than a blessing in my life, you'll regret it. We don't disrespect women in my locker room and we sure as hell don't disrespect mine."

"I meant no dis—"

"I'm not done," I interrupt. "Second, when you're with the right person, a relationship lifts you up, not holds you back. I'm fucking glad my life changed when I met Lola. I wanted it to. She gave me a reason to live the life I wanted, the same way Carina did with Robby. Not all of us enjoy that playboy lifestyle. Some of us want love and emotional bonds and someone to come home to every night. You deserve that as much as we do, even if you aren't ready for it yet.

"As long as you surround yourself with snakes, that's what you're going to get. When you're setting these types of expectations, you're only going to get women who are okay with a certain type of relationship. A woman who will be a true partner, support you and your goals won't be down for that shit. She wants and deserves more than being a name on your roster."

He sucks in a breath and holds it for a minute before letting it out. I think he's going to argue, but his shoulders sink and he agrees. "You're right, Cap. I've got a fucked-up view of commitment. I know you guys are happy and I love Lola and Carina. It's hard to remember there are other women out there who want more from me than clout and don't see me as dollar signs when Kristies constantly surround me."

"I know what you mean," I concede. "But if you're only meeting women who are in it for a night of fun, you aren't going to find any who want the long haul, man."

"I don't think I'm built for the long haul."

"I don't know, Kenny Boy. I think someday soon, the right woman is going to knock you on your ass and have you breaking all your rules."

His only answer is a look of skepticism. He may not believe me now, but his time is coming, and it is going to be a rude awakening. Kent is a good guy behind his playboy facade. I'm not sure why he is afraid to open up. Even with me and Robby, he keeps things light. He rarely goes deep into his emotions or thoughts. It makes me wonder if he has some past baggage I don't know about.

Before I can dive into that further, he asks about me. "How's that going for you? You're more at peace today than you've been in a few weeks. Get things sorted out with Lola?"

"Not yet," I say. "She is still taking time to work on herself. We've made progress, but I don't think she's ready to be full-on again."

"She'll get there," he states.

"I know," I reply, blowing out a breath and reaching for my warm-ups. "Until then, let's focus on bringing the Commissioner's Trophy home."

Chapter Forty-Nine

• LOLA •

While on this break with Brady, I have been making major progress on my blog. Turns out you can get a lot done when you're resisting the urge to text someone or show up at their apartment unannounced. At least it has paid off. Several brands have contacted me through Molly, but I need that one big deal to transform my blog from a hobby to a full-time gig.

For that reason, Tiffany might say I manifested this call with an opportunity that is a huge step forward in my career.

"Hi, Molly," I greet.

"Lola, sweetie. How are you?"

Molly has been incredible throughout the entire process. Aside from asking if she needed to find Brady the most embarrassing endorsement deal imaginable when I first got back, she hasn't brought him up. I was nervous things would be awkward since he is an actual, paying client, but she has been nothing but professional and supportive.

"I'm doing well considering my friends and I tried out the mixers from that organic cocktail company last night."

"Now that sounds like a good time. Any favorites?"

"Carina and Tiffany are obsessed with the peach bellini but the watermelon mint marg was my favorite."

"Awesome, I can't wait to see your content using them. I'm glad to see you are enjoying the brand partnerships we've been able to bring you. I was approached about another opportunity that I think is going to be of great interest to you. Are you sitting down?"

"Yes... I am sitting. What is it?"

Molly takes in a deep inhale as if she is struggling to hold back her own excitement. "I received a call yesterday from the producer of Cami Graham's show. Cami discovered your blog while navigating her divorce and loved it. With all the lifestyle and mental health content you've been doing the past few weeks, they wanted to see if you would be interested in a weekly self-care segment."

My heart stops. I heard the words Molly said but I cannot comprehend them. Cami freaking Graham, winner of Singing Sensation season one, wants me to do a segment on her daily talk show.

"The woman was too stunned to speak," Molly says, amused. "You okay, Lo? Need a minute?"

"Wha-ho-why, Cami Graham?!" is all I manage to get out.

"Cami Graham," Molly repeats. "The segment can be whatever you want. Some ideas the producer offered were DIY spa treatments, everyday workout or meditation routines, comforting girl dinners, etc. The only parameters are that they be geared towards women 21-45 and accessible to the everyday American, which is already your brand."

"Oh my God!" I stammer.

"I can see we aren't going to get much business discussed until you have time to process this," she laughs. "The show said if you were interested, they could have an offer drawn up and sent over by Thursday. I'm going to let them know you are interested."

"Yes!" I blurt out.

"Can you come in Friday morning to review the details?"

"Yes. For sure. I will be there. I can't believe this," I utter.

"You deserve this, girl. You've worked your ass off and bared your soul these last few months. You make it easy for everyone to relate to you and you care deeply about your audience. I can't wait to see what you make of this opportunity."

"Thank you for everything, Molly."

"You know it, girl," she states before hanging up.

My first instinct is to text Brady, but we've already messaged today. The team has the first game of the Championship series tonight and I don't want to split his focus. Instead of reaching out to him, I open the group chat and tell the girls to clear their schedules for a sleepover Friday night. I also mention that I have pee-your-pants big news.

As we sit around the living room in our pajamas, Tiffany, Carina, and Raven all congratulate me on the talk show segment. They are as over the moon as I am. We spent the last forty-five minutes brainstorming ideas. We only stopped when our Thai food arrived.

"Why is Asian food the best?" Raven moans over her stir fry.

"If you think this is good, you need to have Kent's silog. It is hands down the best breakfast I have ever had," Tiffany mouths over her Pad Thai.

"Kent's been making you breakfast?" I ask, eyebrows shooting up to my hairline.

"Not like that," she snorts. "We occasionally stumble back to the building at the same time and when we do, he plies me with food so he doesn't have to eat alone. He is surprisingly needy for female attention of the non-sexual variety."

"He gets plenty of the sexual variety," Carina mutters under her breath. "Sorry," she apologizes sheepishly when she notices we're all holding back laughter at her outburst.

"Don't mind her. She's just bitter," Tiffany laughs. "Robby was about to make breakfast out of her earlier this week when Kent called him for a ride."

"He's on my list," my cousin grouses. The laugh I was holding back finally escapes. I have no doubt Robby made up for the interruption tenfold.

"One of these days, you ladies are going to have to introduce me to these baseball boys. I hear all about them, but the only time I see them is on TV and social media. And neither of those places give the impression Kent Dela Cruz is a man who cooks a woman breakfast platonically. Or at all."

"He's a smooth-talking playboy, alright. I think of him as a slightly less dumb Joey Tribiani. Out in the world he's sowing his wild oats, but with us he is a stand-up guy," Tiffany states.

"'*Slightly* less dumb' being the operative phrase," Carina jokes. "But he is loyal and there when you need him, even if he requires a bit of handholding."

As they converse, I get lost in my thoughts. I still haven't told Brady about the Cami Graham news and I don't know why. I am desperate to, but it is an in-person conversation. I want to see his face light up when I tell him. A small – okay, large – part of me also wants to *hear* him say he's proud of me and not read it over text. I've missed his praise.

Aside from when he kisses me goodbye at our coffee dates, he hasn't been flirty or affectionate at all. I know it's because he is respecting my boundaries, but I can't help but wonder if he is losing interest. Or if this break showed him we were both dickmitized – or whatever the male equivalent is – and his life is better without me.

"Earth to Lola," I hear as a pillow hits me in the head.

"Hey!" I yell.

"Sorry, babe. But we said your name three times already. What are you over there thinking about so hard? If it's the show, you don't have to submit your first segments until December. You have plenty of time."

"It's not that," I sigh. "I miss Brady." All three women offer me sympathetic smiles.

"How many weeks has it been?" asks Raven.

"A little over four," I answer. Four weeks and two days to be exact, but who's counting?

"Why don't you just go to him?" Carina suggests.

"I don't want to distract him during the series."

"If they lose tomorrow in LA, they're out of the series, anyway. Based on what I've heard from Robby, it isn't looking too good," she states.

Being a distraction is only part of the reason I haven't seen him outside of our agreement. I realized a week ago that I was ready to dive back in with him. Even Lynn agreed that she thought I was in a place to trust both him and myself.

"He still wants you," Tiffany declares.

"I didn't—" I start to argue before she waves me off.

"You didn't have to. I've known you for years and I can see it in your eyes. You think that he's lost interest but I guarantee he hasn't."

"How do you know?" I ask.

She searches my face for a moment while warring with herself on how to respond. With the roll of her lip, she explains. "You know how Brady texts you every day?"

"Yes."

"He texts me, too." When I tilt my head in confusion, she continues. "He texts me to *really* check on you. To get my assessment on how you are doing and if you need anything you're too stubborn to ask for."

"I am not stubborn!" I defend, half-heartedly. "What have you told him?"

"The truth," she answers. "Some days you were better than others. Some days you struggled. Some days you were PMS-ing and cried when you ran out of lavender coffee syrup and couldn't figure out how to buy it."

311

"I did not cr—OMG. There is no auto-ship, is there?!" Tiffany shakes her head.

I scoured that coffee shop website the day after the syrups arrived to see what other flavors they had but I couldn't find any mention of them for sale. They must have been bottling them just for him.

"He sent the syrup. What else?" I ask narrowing my eyes at her.

"Did you ever wonder why your car magically stopped telling you that it needed wiper fluid? Or why the doorman stopped being rough with your packages? Daddy Miller was on the case."

"Why would he do all that?" I wonder out loud.

"Maybe Lola is a slightly dumber Phoebe," I hear Raven whisper, earning her a glare.

"Bunny," Carina says, patting my hand, "he did it because he loves you and wants to take care of you."

"But I made him give me space," I reply.

"You did. And he did. As much as he is capable, anyway. He took care of things behind the scenes while you took care of you," she shares.

I don't know what to say to this information. I can't believe that even when I was pushing him away, Brady was holding me close. He did things to make my life easier while for all he knew, I was off deciding not to be with him anymore. God, how selfless is this man?

"I love him," I say.

"We know," they all confirm in unison.

"I need to tell him."

"You will," Carina assures me. "But it's going to have to wait until the team gets home."

She's right. There is nothing I can do about it now. They guys have another game in LA. If they win, they come back here for a final game to determine who is going to the World Series. It's a lot of pressure and the last thing Brady needs is me adding to it. I'll bide my time and continue our routine until I can talk to him face-to-face again.

Chapter Fifty

T he team squeaked by with a win in LA over the weekend, but lost last night at home, knocking us out of the World Series. We made it further than last year, but it sucks to be this close and not reach your goal.

Adding to my frustration, I haven't heard from Lola today. I wanted to text her first thing this morning, but I waited in case she wanted to say something about the loss. Now, I feel like an idiot because she might be wary to reach out if she thinks I'm upset.

Instead of stewing at home and waiting for her to reach out, I decided to let my frustrations out at the batting cages. Considering our season is over, the stadium is pretty much vacant aside from office staff and essential personnel.

Getting into a good rhythm, I don't hear the door open until a loud squeal reverberates, jerking me out of the zone. I rush to the wall and hit the shut off button when I see someone hit the deck. Peeking up at me from her spot on the floor is none other than the woman I was trying to block out of my mind. Before I can say anything, security comes running in. They skid to a stop when they see me.

"Mr. Miller. We're sorry to interrupt your workout," one of the men stammers. "You didn't happen to see a woman come through here, did you?"

"Hello, gentlemen," I greet rolling my lips to try to stop from laughing as I lean against the side of the cage. Lola stares up at me wide-eyed. There is netting blocking her from their view as she puts her finger to her lips, signaling my discretion. "I can't say I've seen anyone here who doesn't belong." The men nod and survey the room a final time before moving on.

When they leave, I turn back to my girl. "Hey there, rule breaker," I say with a smirk, pushing off the chain link to offer her hand up. She takes it and dusts herself off, whipping her head around the room. "The coast is clear," I chuckle. "You wanna tell me what's going on?"

"Tiffany told me she could get me into the stadium. She did *not* mention her methods were less than legal," she huffs.

"Why did you need to sneak into the stadium?"

"Because Kent said that's where you were."

"You could've called, ya know? Or at least texted. I would have let you in. Properly. Or met you at home."

I almost laugh at the term 'home.' My house has felt anything but with her gone. The smell of her on my sheets faded weeks ago. I kept everything where she left it, but it still wasn't the same. I even used her ridiculously sweet syrups in my coffee to give me some sense of her.

"I couldn't wait," she responds. "I needed to see you now."

"Is everything okay?" I ask.

"Yes-no. I don't know."

"Whatever it is you can tell me, sweet girl."

She gazes at me with eyes full of mixed emotions. "I don't want to be on a break anymore."

My heart squeezes in my chest. Fuck. I thought I had more time to show her why we should stay together. The series has eaten up all my time but now that it's over, I had plans. I need those days. She promised me six weeks and I want them all.

"I don't want that," I state.

Hurt and shock shadow her features before her expression steels. "You don't?"

"No. We said six weeks, and it hasn't even been five yet."

"Oh," she whispers. The pain is evident in her voice and cracking through the facade she erected. She's upset I'm putting off her breaking up with me? That's a weird response. "Okay. I'm sorry I bothered you. If you point me to the exit, I'll let you get back to your workout."

She risked breaking into the stadium to dump me and now she's going to leave that easily? Something isn't adding up here. Scrutinizing her more closely, I realize she has her face turned away from me. Movement catches my eye and I watch a lone tear trail down her cheek. That's all it takes for me to forget our boundaries and pull her to me.

"Baby, what's the matter?" I question wiping the tear away with my thumb. Another falls.

"Nothing." She shakes her head. "I just thought this conversation would go differently, I guess. But I'm the one who asked for this break. You're allowed to want to stick to the terms of it," she mutters sadly.

I'm baffled by this reaction. "I need more time, sweet girl. I'm not ready to let you go."

Her eyes shoot to mine. "Let me go?"

"Yeah. I've been preoccupied for the last four weeks, I wanted to spend the last two reminding you why we're perfect for each other," I admit.

"You want to stay on a break to show me why we shouldn't break up?" She inquires, scrunching up her nose, voice laced in confusion.

"Is that so wrong?"

A slow smile graces her lips and her arms drift to my forearms.

My palms are still cupping her face. I can't bring myself to let go. It feels like forever since I've touched her and I need the contact.

"What did you think I meant, when I said I wanted the break to be over?"

I roll my shoulders to attempt to loosen some tension before answering. "That you were done."

"I am. Done being on a break."

"Done with me," I reiterate. She shakes her head as much as my hands allow.

"No," she states. "Done being without you."

My heart skips a beat. She wasn't breaking up with me?

"If that's what you want," she adds, quickly.

"Yes!" I all but shout and she laughs as more tears spill down her rosy cheeks. "Of course, it is, baby. I never wanted to be on a break to begin with. I know you think we needed time to let our brains catch up with our hearts, but I didn't. I've known what I wanted since the first time I kissed you: you."

"I love you," she says.

Now it's my turn to smile. I pull her face into mine and seal our lips together. It's not a sweet kiss, but it isn't frantic, either. It's full of all the words I haven't been able to say the past few months. It's full of love and devotion and promises of forever. When my lungs are seizing, I pull away to breathe and smirk in satisfaction at how her chest heaves, and the way she clutches my shirt.

"I love you, too," I remind her. "Does this mean we can go back to normal?"

"No," she replies.

"No?"

"I don't want normal. I want extraordinary," she declares, smiling.

"One extraordinary life coming up." I kiss her a final time before gathering my things. "Let's get out of here. We've got several weeks of orgasms to catch up on."

She giggles and slides into my side as I wrap my arms around her.

She lays her head on my shoulder and confirms, "So you're good with ending the break?"

"You bet your sweet ass I am. Although I'm a little bummed I won't get to finish my secret message."

"Secret message?" she questions, intrigued. I grab my phone and pull up our text thread.

"Every text I've sent you on this break has started with a letter that after thirty-nine days would spell out a special message for you. Since it's only been thirty-three days, it wasn't done yet, but see for yourself."

"L-A-M-I-A-L-U-N-A-L-E-M-I-E-S-T-E-L-L-E-I-L-M-I-O-I-N-T-E-R-O-U-N," she spells.

"*La mia luna, le mie stelle, il mio intero universo,*" I translate. "It's what you said talking to Stefano. You, Lola, are my moon, my stars, and my entire universe. You're my whole fucking world. Now let's go so I can prove it to you."

The Texts

September 20 11:42 AM

LOLA

Good luck today.

BRADY

Luck isn't needed, but thank you. 😉 When is our first coffee date?

LOLA

Thursday morning?

September 21 9:06 AM

BRADY

Almost managed to get a row by myself on the plane. Then Kent sat down. Did you know he talks in his sleep? He's dreaming about the Pillsbury Dough Boy and it does not seem platonic.

LOLA

Wow. There is a lot to unpack there.

September 22 8:57 AM

LOLA

Where do you want to meet tomorrow?

BRADY

Molly told me about a new coffee shop in the Gulch. Meet there at 10?

September 23 2:15 PM

BRADY

I saw a billboard for the new Reese Witherspoon show. Have you watched it?

LOLA

Yes, it is amazing.

September 24 9:32 PM

LOLA

Great game tonight!

BRADY

Always good to pull out a win.

September 25 1:14 PM

BRADY

Look at you: [link magazine feature: Nashville's own discusses finding yourself in your late 20s]. Can I get your autograph before you forget about all the little people?

LOLA

😊 Can't exactly autograph a webpage, but I'll see what I can arrange.

September 26 12:29 PM

LOLA

Unagi has a new roll named after the team! Have you tried it?

BRADY

Uh huh. They sent us some over the other day. It was pretty good.

September 27 7:20 PM

LOLA

[selfie wearing a face mask] Think I'll scare the food delivery guy like this?

BRADY

Nah, you pull it off. Might want to add a sweatshirt though if you don't want him to get a free show.

September 28 9:16 AM

BRADY

Already over this flight. [image of Kent drooling on his shoulder]

LOLA

Sometimes I think he's more dog than man.

September 30 11:56 PM

BRADY

Late-night thought: New York is suspiciously beautiful in the fall.

LOLA

I wouldn't know. I've never been. Though I'm not sure how a city can be suspicious.

October 1 3:22 PM

BRADY

Ever seen two grown men giggle like
schoolgirls? [video of Robby and Kent
laughing]. I'll take you one day.

LOLA

What was so funny?

October 2 8:52 AM

BRADY

My coffee may have spilled on Derrick. 🙀

LOLA

I'm sure it was a total accident.

October 3 11:23 AM

BRADY

I have a new appreciation for Carina. Robby
is needy AF. I wonder if she can qualify as
his support human and travel with us?

LOLA

Haha. Yeah, he can be clingy.

October 4 1:44 PM

LOLA

I did a Taylor Swift themed spin class today!
[sweaty selfie]

BRADY

Everything about that sounds terrible but I
am glad you had fun.

October 5 2:37 PM

BRADY

Saw your latest blog. I'm not sure
acupuncture is for me.

If you like cupping, you can handle a few needles. Aren't you the same guy who took me to get a tattoo?

October 6 10:18 AM

Lynn is proud of how well you are honoring my boundaries.

BRADY

Tell Lynn I would do anything for you. Also, who is Lynn?

My therapist

Even going to therapy with me?

October 7 8:03 AM

BRADY

Even going to therapy with you. I will do anything you need to feel safe and comfortable.

October 8 12:38 PM

BRADY

Lesson of the day: Don't let Kent pick the restaurant. [image of guys at Chuck E. Cheese]

Wow. I have no words.

October 9 9:01 PM

Sorry about the game. It was a close one!

BRADY

Losses are harder when they're close.
Thank you, though.

October 10 10:47 AM

LOLA

[Phoebe singing 'Good Luck' TikTok]

BRADY

Every occasion has a FRIENDS clip, huh?

October 11 12:01 AM

LOLA

🐝🐞

9:13 AM

BRADY

I am exhausted, but last night was amazing.
Division champs!

October 12 3:52 PM

LOLA

[link to Baseball Bulges latest ranking]

BRADY

Lola, everything about that is wrong.

LOLA

Are you jealous Robby is still ahead of you
or embarrassed you moved up?

October 13 10:38 AM

BRADY

Maybe both. I hope you are having a
good day.

LOLA

I discovered a new coffee flavor: Crème
brûlée. What better sign that it's going to be
a great day?

October 14 6:24 PM

LOLA

Robby said to ask why you had to walk
home from the stadium today.

BRADY

I plead the fifth.

October 15 11:22 AM

LOLA

[picture of me cuddling with a puppy] 😍

BRADY

Oh, the lucky bastard.

October 16 2:57 PM

BRADY

I shouldn't be shocked that of all the
Halloween costumes you could have done a
post about you chose the bunny costume
from Legally Blonde. A little on the nose
don't you think?

LOLA

If the shoe fits...

October 17 11:13 PM

LOLA

Do you like watermelon mint margaritas?

BRADY

Nope, but I bet you are having a few right now if you're texting this late.

LOLA

[Hair Flip GIF]

October 18 11:26 AM

LOLA

The beard is looking really fresh [Songbirds IG post]

BRADY

Thank you

October 19 4:48 PM

BRADY

Everything good with you?

LOLA

Of course, a little rain can't keep me down! It helps when I don't need to leave the house for anything.

October 20 7:12 AM

LOLA

Way to go! You guys killed it!

BRADY

Really weren't sure we were going to do it but it is nice to pull out the W.

October 21 1:55 PM

BRADY

Universe manifestation, yea or nay?

LOLA

Since I live with Tiffany, I don't think I can say anything other than yea.

October 22 10:11 AM

LOLA

Did you have your pre-game Pop-Tart?

BRADY

Never doubt my commitment to Pop-Tarts.

Epilogue

December

It's a little after three p.m. when I slink into Brady's condo. I was hoping to avoid him until tomorrow but he would suspect something if I didn't at least pop by. As I pull my coat off, I see him come out of his bedroom.

"Hi, sweet girl," he greets.

"Hey, babe," I reply. He walks over and gives me a quick kiss on the lips, grabbing my coat to hang up in the closet. He sticks his hand out at me expectantly for the scarf I technically didn't need. Even though it's December now, the weather is still pretty mild. It was a balmy fifty-five degrees today.

"You planning to wear that scarf all day?" he jokes.

"Maybe," I quip. My voice sounds shakier than intended and he narrows his eyes at me.

"Hand it over, Lola," he says.

"No, thank you."

328

"No, thank you?"

"Yep, I am good keeping it on."

He scrutinizes me further examining my neck as if he has x-ray vision and can see through the scarf. I'm sure his mind is spinning but there is no way he will guess the reason I don't want to take it off. It all started with a pitcher of margaritas...

The night before...

"I love you two so, so much," Carina mumbles.

"We love you, too, Meatball," Tiffany laughs.

"We should do something to commemorate our love," my cousin asserts.

"You're already married, sweetie," I inform her. "As much as I love a 'why choose' I don't think Robby or Brady would be happy having to share or be shared."

She snorts. "No, we should get tattoos!"

"You want to get a tattoo?" I question, surprised.

"Yes! Friendship tattoos."

I glance at Tiffany who has a grin on her face that rivals Tim Curry's when he discovers Kevin was using a stolen credit card in *Home Alone 2*.

"Oh no. I know that look, Babs. Whatever you're thinking, don't. We already have friendship bracelets. We're good."

"Too late," Tiffany singsongs, whipping out her phone. "I've been studying up on Greek gods and goddesses lately and decided which one we each are."

"Of course, you did," I mutter.

"Anyway," she glares at me pointedly before continuing. "I was considering getting a small tattoo to symbolize my goddess. It would be the perfect way for us to get friendship tattoos without being cheesy or matchy-matchy."

"Oh, fun! What goddesses did you come up with?" Carina asks as if this isn't a harebrained idea.

"You, my beautiful bestie, are Demeter, the goddess of harvest since you ensure people are fed."

"I love that!" Carina exclaims.

"You, my adorable little Bunny, are Eos, the goddess of the dawn. You bring light to our lives every day."

That hits me in the feels. I was fully prepared to shut this idea down, but she put real thought into it and I'm a sucker for praise.

"And who is yours? Aphrodite?"

"That would be too obvious," she retorts, tossing her hair. "I identify with Eris, the goddess of chaos."

Carina chokes on her margarita and I can't hold back my laugh. "I think the boys would definitely agree with you there," I say. "What do the goddesses have to do with the tattoos?"

"We could get symbols that represent them. That way, we all have the same theme tattoo. We should also get them in the same spot. I was thinking behind our ears. We'd get them small enough to be dainty and hidden by our hair when it is down."

"That actually isn't a bad idea," I hedge. Tiffany's eyes twinkle with mischief and satisfaction that I am seemingly on board.

"Now, if only we knew someone who had the number of Nashville's premier tattoo artist..."

Rolling my eyes, I pull out my phone. "I'll text Zade and see if we can get appointments soon."

"I was thinking right now," Tiffany responds.

"You want to go now?!"

"If we don't go tonight, I'll probably chicken out," Carina states. "Or I'll tell Robby and he'll want to come, which will ruin our bonding time."

"Ugh, fine," I grouse. Surprisingly, when I explain the situation to Zade, he says we can come by his shop in an hour. We call Raven on the way so she can join in as Hestia – goddess of the hearth and home. By nine p.m. we are finished with strict care instructions and permanent symbols of our friendship.

Present day...

"Lola," Brady cajoles in a silky voice, closing in on me. "If you don't take that scarf off right now, I am going to use it to tie you up later."

"Is that supposed to be a threat?" I tease.

"It is when I'll edge you all night long," he counters.

With a squeak, I unwrap the scarf and hand it over. He smirks at me victoriously until he spots the wrap on my neck.

"What happened?" He questions. "Are you hurt? Who did this to you?" He grabs my chin and gingerly tilts my neck to the side to get a better look.

Leveling me with his glare, he asks, "Is that what I think it is?"

"That depends. If you think it is a hickey from a sexy Brazilian tennis player I met at the grocery store, then no. If you think it is a tattoo, then yes."

His lips tip at my joke but his eyes remain locked on my neck, studying the sunburst that decorates my skin under the plastic.

"Did Zade do this?"

"He did." Something akin to jealousy flashes in his eyes.

"Did you go alone? When did you get this done? It wasn't there yesterday when we woke up. I know I spent more time between your legs than by your ear, but I would have noticed it."

My mind travels back to waking up yesterday to a wet tongue licking me. Brady stayed down there until I orgasmed twice and then made me come on his cock while he 'cleaned me up' in the shower. It was a fantastic morning.

"Stand down, caveman. I went with the girls. We got friendship tattoos."

"Friendship tattoos? You know what, we can dive into that later. Dinner is in the oven and then I have a surprise for you."

My eyes widen. Brady loves to surprise me with little and big things. The last one was when he rented out a movie theater and invited all our friends to watch *Legally Blonde* to celebrate me hitting 100k followers.

"A surprise? What is it?" I ask.

"If I told you, it wouldn't be a surprise," he says with a boop to my nose. "There is a glass of wine poured for you on the island. Dinner will be ready in ten."

After a delicious dinner of salmon and balsamic glazed Brussel sprouts, Brady pours me another glass of wine and leads me into the living area.

"Ready for your surprise?"

"Yes," I respond, gleefully.

"Okay, I'm going to go get it. Close your eyes."

"Really?"

"Yes, really. Do you want it or not?"

"I want it," I mumble.

"Then be a good girl and behave. It will be worth it."

I let out an exaggerated sigh, but comply. A minute later, I hear a jingly noise. I squeal when something cold and wet touches my hand. My eyes fly open and licking my fingers is a puppy.

I glance up to see Brady staring at me. "Who-whe-how? What?" I exclaim, puzzled.

He laughs as I snuggle the puppy into my chest and comes to sit beside me.

"This," he says, "is Dolly. A friend of mine mentioned his dog had puppies and when I saw her, I knew she would be perfect for us. She's a German Shepherd-Golden Retriever mix."

"She's ours?"

"She's ours," he repeats.

"This is the best surprise ever!" I whisper-shout as to not startle the fluff ball in my lap.

"You haven't seen the best part yet," he remarks. "Check around her neck."

I run my hands over Dolly's collar and grab her tag. On one side, it lists her name and Brady's number. When I flip it over, it is embossed with the words, 'Say Yes.'

"That's cute," I comment. When I peer up from the tag, Brady isn't sitting on the couch anymore. He is kneeling in front of me. On one knee. He smiles when he takes in my shocked expression.

"Since the first time I saw you, I have been entranced by you. Every second I have spent with you has only solidified further that you're the woman I want to spend the rest of my life with; to start a family with.

"I know it's soon, but there is no doubt in my mind that you and I are meant to be. I am ready to get on with the rest of our lives. Starting with you being Dolly's dog mom, and my wife. Lola, will you marry me?"

I stare, stunned as he pulls out the most beautiful ring I have ever seen. It's an oval stone with a cluster of three round stones on each site set on a yellow gold band. I glance from the ring to his face and back again several times as tears form in my eyes, grinning like a maniac.

"I love that you're smiling, sweet girl, but I am going to need an answer."

Placing Dolly on the couch beside me, I launch myself into Brady's arms. Thankfully, he maintains his balance and catches me. "Yes," I finally reply. "There is nothing I want more than to be yours."

His hand glides to the back of my neck as he brings my lips to his. The kiss is slow and steady but filled with emotions. When he pulls away, he slips the ring on my finger.

"It's gorgeous," I murmur.

"I'm glad you like it. Phoebe and Tim designed it."

"The metalsmiths?" I question as I admire my new bling.

"Uh huh," he replies. "They were more than happy to help me create something as beautiful as you."

"Hey! You never showed me the stamped pendant you made that day!" I recall.

Brady smirks at me. "Yes, I did."

"When?"

"Right now," he says, pointing to Dolly's tag.

"You made Dolly's tag? You didn't even know you were going to get a dog."

He laughs. "This may have been in the works for a little longer than I let on. Getting a puppy was on your try list. I may not have marked it off on 'try day' but I got the wheels in motion."

"But we had only been together for a couple of months," I point out. Brady shifts up, seating himself on the couch while I straddle him. He uses one hand to tuck my hair behind my ears and the other to rub gentle circles on my lower back.

"I told you, doll. You've had me from the first moment I locked into these hazel eyes. I was a goner from day one even if I didn't know it yet. It only took me a couple of weeks to realize I was going to spend the rest of my life loving you. I held on to hope that you'd be beside me, loving me back."

"Always," I reply.

March

"Stop pacing," Tiffany grouses beside me in the kitchen.

"I can't help it," I complain. "I'm freaking out. How much longer?"

"127 seconds. Relax, Bunny. It's going to be fine either way."

"I know. I just can't believe this is happening," I remark. "What are the chances?"

"With how much sex the two of you have? I'd say pretty high. I thought you had an IUD, though," Raven comments.

"I did," I reply. "But I had it removed when it expired and switched to the shot since it didn't have as long of a time commitment."

"Were you and Miller planning to try soon?" she questions. "When do you think you conceived?"

"It is clearly a honeymoon baby," Tiffany answers for me. "Did you see those two at their wedding? I'm surprised we didn't all leave pregnant."

She's not wrong. Brady and I planned a trip to Vegas for my birthday and convinced all our friends to come along. Halfway through the trip, he asked if I wanted to tie the knot while we were there. I'd already had the traditional wedding with Phil and did not want a repeat of that.

Brady had never wanted a fancy ceremony and said all he cared about was legally making me his. We arranged to fly out my dad, aunt and uncle, and his family the next day. Even Georgie was able to make it on short notice. In true Vegas fashion we got married at the Little White Chapel a few days later.

After the stress of my first wedding, eloping was amazing. Tiffany did my hair and makeup and Raven had a friend that was a photographer who took the pictures. We extended our trip to have an impromptu honeymoon on Catalina Island before coming back to Nashville to get ready for spring training. While there is no way to know yet, Tiffany's assumption of a honeymoon baby probably isn't far off.

"To answer your first question," I say to Raven while glaring at Tiffany. "We were planning to start trying after spring training to time the due date with the off season. Now, I'm probably going to have a baby in the middle of the World Series! Oh my God, I'm going to be pushing out a Miller-sized baby all alone. Chloe was ten pounds! My body can't handle a baby that big!"

"Lola, get a grip!" Tiffany shouts. "It will be fine. First of all, we don't even know if you're pregnant. Second, there is no way in hell Miller would leave you alone. Third, even if he couldn't be there for some reason, you have plenty of people who can step in, us included." Raven nods in confirmation.

"You're right, I'm sorry, I'm spiraling. I've been having a lot of big feelings lately. I thought they were because I missed Brady but now, I'm wondering—" My statement is cut off by the sound of the timer and I stare wide-eyed at Tiffany.

At that same moment, Carina barrels in the door. "Did I miss it?" she asks.

"Made it in the nick of time, Care Bear," Tiffany remarks.

"I can't look!" I stammer. "Can one of you do it?"

Carina glances at me and after a silent conversation with Tiffany, she walks over to the other side of the island where the test sits. After peering down at it, she meets my gaze as a smile creeps on her face. "I'm going to be an Auntie!"

My hands immediately go to my belly and mouth as I burst into tears. "I'm having a baby," I cry. My girls surround me and murmur congratulations in my ear. After several minutes of celebrating, we sit down in the living room.

"When are you going to tell Miller?" Raven asks.

"I hadn't even thought about it. He's still in Florida for another ten days. Should I go down there? I can't tell him over the phone."

"I don't think that's a good idea," Carina says.

"I'm with Meatball," Tiffany agrees. "You aren't going to get to enjoy the moment as much in that setting. Wait for him to come home. Plus, that gives us time to plan out a fun way to drop the news. He is going to be ecstatic."

"You think?" I muse.

"Oh yeah," Carina interjects. "That man has had baby fever since he put a ring on your finger. It wouldn't surprise me to find out he planned this."

I snort out a laugh. "You're probably right, but I can't blame this on him unless me double-booking a call with the travel agent during my OB visit is somehow his fault."

"I mean the trip was his idea..." Raven says, causing us all the giggle.

We haven't been reconnected long, but having her back in my life has been incredible. Being surrounded by people who knew me before I was married and who know the me I am now is a blessing. I lost myself during those years in St. Louis. I don't even recognize the woman I was there. The new me is full of strength and joy and supported by amazing people.

"Oh shit," Carina mutters looking at her phone.

"What is it?" I ask.

"Trade alert." When she passes me the phone, I read the headline: GEORGE 'RAMBO' RIVERA TRADED TO THE NASHVILLE SONGBIRDS

"It's a sign!" I exclaim.

"How do you figure that?"

"With Georgie in Nashville, all my people will be here to be a part of my baby's life." I am thrilled by the prospect. The only important people not living here are my father and Aunt Teresa, but it is only a matter of time before she makes the move. I bet the second Carina gets pregnant, she puts her house on the market. Maybe I can convince her to start trying soon so our babies can be besties.

Emerging from the kitchen with snacks, Tiffany asks, "What's this about George being in Nashville?"

"Chicago traded him here!"

"Just what we need, another self-righteous douche bucket around," she grumbles.

"Are you ever going to tell me what happened between you two?" The night Brady and Georgie realized they were both connected to me, he also met Tiffany. I was already home, but something clearly went down between the two. The tension between them at my wedding last month could've been cut with a knife.

"Nothing to tell," she replies flippantly. I'll let it slide for now, but I'll get it out of her, eventually. Tonight, I am going to soak up the excitement that Brady and I are growing our family."

Want to see Brady's reaction to Lola's news? Join my email list for access, bit.ly/katsummersemail.

Acknowledgments

Thank you, thank you for taking the time to read Stepping Up to the Plate. These characters are very dear to my heart and I appreciate you letting them into yours even if for a few hours.

As the dedication says, I want to thank all the female authors who came before me. It was not all that long ago that getting your work published as a woman wasn't even possible. The years of women's stories left untold is one of the things that inspired me to write today. My books may not be groundbreaking philosophy are Pulitzer-worthy works, but I have the ability to follow my dreams and not doing so would be a disservice for those who fought hard to make having your voice heard possible.

All the gratitude to my beta and ARC readers who supported this story from day one. Emma from EJL Editing does God's work helping clear up my stories and make them as good as they can be.

@BookedForeverShop knocked this cover out of the park.

I want to give a special shoutout to my Sprint Baddies authors. They helped keep me sane during this process and taught me much along the way!

I hope you enjoyed this book and stick around for more! See all my works at katsummerwrites.com.

– Kat

Also by Kat Summers

Want more Nashville Songbirds?

Sign up for my newsletter (bit.ly/katsummersemail) today for bonus scenes from your favorite Songbirds couples or read the book that started it all, Behind in the Count. It is Robby and Carina's story!

The next book in the series, Scoring Position will be out early 2024 and will follow team playboy, Kent Dela Cruz. Find out if he as lucky in love as he is at the plate. Available on Amazon for pre-order at an early bird price!

About the Author

Kat Summers is a millennial spicy, contemporary romance author living in Tennessee. Her books are filled with just enough angst to hurt your feelings, witty banter to make you laugh, and steamy, swoon-worthy men to make you blush. She creates stories with strong, sassy heroines who can hold their own but love being called a "good girl."

Kat has had a love for reading and writing her entire life. After consuming what some would call way too many romance books, she decided to take the stories she told herself to fall asleep and put them on paper.

When she isn't writing, she can be found reading (duh) and spending time with her family and furbaby or gossiping over Mexican food. Fueled by Diet Dr Pepper and a dream, Kat is excited to bring the couples that live in her mind to the rest of the world. Follow her for sneak peeks of future projects.

Find her at @katsummerswrites on all the things.

Printed in Great Britain
by Amazon

40530384R00199